Praise for
Kiss of Fire

"Paranormal fans with a soft spot for shape-shifting dragons will definitely enjoy *Kiss of Fire*, a story brimming with sexy heroes; evil villains threatening mayhem, death, and world domination; ancient prophesies; and an engaging love story. . . . An intriguing mythology and various unanswered plot threads set the stage for plenty more adventure to come in future Dragonfire stories." —BookLoons

"Deborah Cooke has definitely made me a fan. I am now lying in wait for the second book in this extremely exciting series." —Romance Junkies

"Wow, what an innovative and dazzling world Ms. Cooke has built with this new Dragonfire series. Her smooth and precise writing quickly draws the reader in and has you believing it could almost be real. . . . I can't wait for the next two books." —Fresh Fiction

ALSO BY DEBORAH COOKE

Kiss of Fire
Kiss of Fury

KISS
OF FATE

A DRAGONFIRE NOVEL

DEBORAH COOKE

A SIGNET ECLIPSE BOOK

SIGNET ECLIPSE
Published by New American Library, a division of
Penguin Group (USA) Inc., 375 Hudson Street,
New York, New York 10014, USA
Penguin Group (Canada), 90 Eglinton Avenue East, Suite 700, Toronto,
Ontario M4P 2Y3, Canada (a division of Pearson Penguin Canada Inc.)
Penguin Books Ltd., 80 Strand, London WC2R 0RL, England
Penguin Ireland, 25 St. Stephen's Green, Dublin 2,
Ireland (a division of Penguin Books, Ltd.)
Penguin Group (Australia), 250 Camberwell Road, Camberwell, Victoria 3124,
Australia (a division of Pearson Australia Group Pty. Ltd.)
Penguin Books India Pvt. Ltd., 11 Community Centre, Panchsheel Park,
New Delhi - 110 017, India
Penguin Group (NZ), 67 Apollo Drive, Rosedale, North Shore 0632,
New Zealand (a division of Pearson New Zealand Ltd.)
Penguin Books (South Africa) (Pty.) Ltd., 24 Sturdee Avenue,
Rosebank, Johannesburg 2196, South Africa

Penguin Books Ltd., Registered Offices:
80 Strand, London WC2R 0RL, England

First published by Signet Eclipse, an imprint of New American Library,
a division of Penguin Group (USA) Inc.

First Printing, February 2009
10 9 8 7 6 5 4 3 2 1

PUBLISHER'S NOTE
This is a work of fiction. Names, characters, places, and incidents either are the prod-
uct of the author's imagination or are used fictitiously, and any resemblance to actual
persons, living or dead, business establishments, events, or locales is entirely coinci-
dental.

The publisher does not have any control over and does not assume any responsibility for author or third-party Web sites or their content.

KISS
OF FATE

Prologue

The *Pyr* gathered at Erik's lair for the eclipse.

Erik's lair was in a warehouse that had been partly converted to lofts. It was large and industrial and in a lousy part of town. Rafferty wondered who would see the high circle of dragons on the roof of the building and what they would make of the scene. The idea made him smile.

As usual, Rafferty was hopeful that, this time, the firestorm would be his. He was older and he had waited longer, though even his legendary patience was thinning. The Great Wyvern had a plan for each of them; Rafferty believed that with all his heart.

So he would wait his turn as well as he could.

The company stood on the roof, watching the moon slip into the earth's shadow. It took on the hue of blood, casting the earth in surreal light.

"Quickly," Erik said with more than his usual impatience. "The full eclipse will last less than half an hour this time."

Rafferty understood Erik's concern: This was the third of the full eclipses, three in a row before the final battle between *Pyr* and *Slayer*. After this eclipse, the die would be cast and the battle for ascendancy over the planet's fate would begin in earnest.

Rafferty wasn't precisely sure how that would manifest, but he wasn't looking forward to it. He knew enough about old prophecies to respect them, even when they were ominous and enigmatic.

Especially when they were ominous and enigmatic.

Once on the roof, the *Pyr* shifted shape in unison. At this eclipse they were joined by the two most recent human mates, both of whom were pregnant. Quinn, the Smith, was scaled in sapphire and steel in dragon form; his mate, Sara, the Seer, stood petite and fair at his side. Donovan, the Warrior, took his lapis lazuli and gold dragon form, while his tall and dark-haired mate, Alex, the Wizard, looked on with pride. There were two strong partnerships made at this vortex of change.

This would be the third, if the *Pyr* could make it work.

Rafferty intended to do what he could to help.

Erik turned to an onyx and pewter dragon, while Rafferty became an opal and gold dragon. Sloane had brought Delaney and kept him between himself and Niall, although Rafferty suspected that it was Delaney who was most worried about what might happen.

After all, the spark in Delaney's eyes was much brighter. Rafferty believed that Sloane's treatment was working, and that the darkness inflicted upon Delaney was steadily diminishing.

Sloane changed form, his tourmaline scales shading from green to purple and back again, each one edged in gold. Niall, meanwhile, became a dragon of amethyst and platinum, glittering in the light. Delaney changed to an emerald and copper dragon. Nikolas of Thebes, new to this ceremony, shifted to a dragon of anthracite and iron, then quietly observed. Unlike the other *Pyr* and *Slayers*, Nikolas had no scent by which he could be discerned, but his presence was formidable.

Erik murmured the ancient blessing once they were all in dragon form. Rafferty watched Erik spin the Dragon's Egg, saw the moon's light touch the round dark stone. Gold lines appeared upon its surface almost immediately, prompting a startled gasp from both Alex and Nikolas, who had never seen its abilities before. Rafferty watched hungrily as the gold lines triangulated a location.

Would this be his chance? The Dragon's Egg glistened as Erik leaned closer to read its portent.

"London," a woman's voice said from behind them all. Rafferty pivoted to find the Wyvern lounging against the fire escape, still in her human form.

He doubted that he was the only one surprised to find her there. Sophie was wearing a white skirt that floated around her ankles. Her long blond hair was loose and flowed down her back. She looked as much like a graceful swan—one made of glass or moonlight—as she did in dragon form.

How did she keep herself from shifting shape under the eclipse's light?

She smiled as she regarded them, smiled so knowingly that Rafferty wondered whether she had heard his thoughts.

She strode closer and crouched down beside the Dragon's Egg. "Why don't we ask it to tell us something we don't know?" It wasn't like her to be so direct, and Rafferty was concerned. If Sophie felt urgency, matters were worse than he had believed.

"I do not have your skill, especially as you choose not to share it," Erik said in old-speak. His irritation was clear.

"Listen," Sophie bade him in old-speak, the single word resonating in Rafferty's chest. She murmured a chant. It was short and wordless, either a string of sounds or a language forgotten. It sounded old to Rafferty. Potent.

She repeated it and Erik echoed the sound. She nodded

approval and beckoned to him. Erik leaned over the Dragon's Egg at her urging and the two of them chanted in unison, Erik's voice gaining strength as he learned the chant.

Then Sophie blew on the dark globe of stone. The golden lines disappeared immediately, like ripples blown from the sand, and a woman's face came into view. She could have been swimming to the surface of a lake, her hair streaming back and her eyes closed.

Then she opened her eyes and looked directly at Erik. Even from his position, Rafferty could see that her eyes were a glorious blue. The hair that flowed around her face was wavy and chestnut brown. It billowed, as if she were underwater and it moved with the current.

Erik recoiled in shock. "Louisa!"

"Yes," the woman murmured, as if remembering something she had half forgotten. "Yes, I was called that, once."

Erik stared at the Dragon's Egg.

"This time my name is Eileen Grosvenor," the woman said, her words clearly enunciated. She raised a hand and, moving as if he couldn't do otherwise, Erik extended a talon toward her. When there was only a handspan between them, a spark leapt from the water to Erik's claw.

Erik swore and took a step back. The woman smiled so brilliantly that the Dragon's Egg was lit from within. Then she took a deep breath, closed her eyes, and sank out of sight. Her hair flowed around and over her; then the ends disappeared with a flick. She might have been a mermaid or a siren.

Erik gave a cry and seized the Dragon's Egg just as the eclipse ended. The stone turned black again, reverting to the smooth orb of obsidian stone it usually was, but a crackle of sparks lurked beneath Erik's talons.

"How can this be?" he demanded of the Wyvern.

Sophie straightened and smiled as the *Pyr* around her shifted back to human form. She gave Delaney a hard look, then nodded once at Sloane. "You are half-done," she said. "Do not falter without banishing the shadow completely."

By the time Sloane had nodded agreement, Sophie had turned and walked to the lip of the roof. She lifted her arms over her head, laughed as the wind teased her skirts, and leapt.

Rafferty was the first to reach the edge. Even having guessed what he would see, he was still surprised.

Below them a white dragon soared, long white plumes streaming behind her. She glinted in the changing light, reflecting and refracting the hue cast by the moon, like a dragon carved of crystal. She ascended and turned in a tight curve over the roof, leaving the *Pyr* staring after her with awe.

She flew straight up into the dark sky, heading directly for the moon, then abruptly disappeared. The sky was clear and there was nowhere for her to be hidden. She simply had vanished as suddenly as she had appeared.

"I hate when she does that," Donovan muttered. Rafferty didn't agree, not this time. No matter how often he saw her, Rafferty found that Sophie's appearance gladdened his heart. He realized what a gift it was to have her among them. He felt as if there was a greater force on their side, on the side of right, and he was touched by her beauty as well.

There could be only a single Wyvern, but in his many centuries, he had never known a Wyvern to be as actively engaged with the *Pyr* as Sophie was.

Rafferty found Nikolas beside him, the other *Pyr*'s dark eyes wide with astonishment. "She is real, then," he whispered. "I thought that I dreamed her presence before."

"She didn't stay long enough to be introduced. Her name is Sophie," Rafferty said. "She is the Wyvern, a prophetess who has skills far beyond our own."

"I know who she is," Nikolas murmured, avidly seeking some sign of her presence.

"Her prophecies count only if you understand them," Quinn noted, and Sara smiled.

Nikolas's wonder was undiminished. "If we do not understand, then we are not worthy of the prophecy," he said stiffly. "Praise be to the Great Wyvern that such beauty exists." He put his hand over his heart and bowed his head in an attitude of prayer.

Erik was still staring into the Dragon's Egg, his features pale. "Louisa," he whispered, raising his gaze to meet Rafferty's. "It can't be true."

Rafferty knew that it was, no matter how Erik might wish for it to be otherwise. He didn't remember all of Erik's history, but suspected that his firestorm hadn't been a success.

How lucky Erik was to have a second chance!

It was fitting, though, that the leader of the *Pyr* be proven before their greatest challenge. All the same, Rafferty knew that Erik might need his help.

"Stay with me in my lair in London," he invited. "We'll find your firestorm together."

He was relieved when Erik, ever independent, nodded agreement.

Erik's firestorm *had* ended badly, then. Rafferty hoped with all his heart that Erik and his mate could conquer their past.

Together.

The patient known as John Doe in the burn ward of a major hospital felt the tug of the eclipse as well.

He awakened stiff and groggy, his body determined to heed the ancient call. He knew what would happen instants before it did, knew that the sedative would keep him from controlling his primal urges. He tore bandages from his hands and the IV needle from his arm, flinging himself from the bed in the nick of time. No sooner had his bare feet touched the cold linoleum than he shifted shape.

Fortunately, he had arranged for a private room.

There was no question of lingering longer in treatment.

With a swing of his mighty tail, he shattered the tinted window. Before the nurses could arrive, he launched himself through the broken glass and took flight over the city. He had not recovered his full strength, but Boris Vassily had learned to make the most of whatever he had. The Elixir had saved him from death, although it had taken surgical intervention to rebuild his body.

He whispered to the wind and the sky and listened to the tales they told. He asked one question of the moon and heeded its response. Anger boiled within him as he understood with perfect clarity who would feel the firestorm this time.

There would be no happy ending if Boris had anything to say about it. Justice demanded that he ensure his father was avenged, that Boris himself got revenge.

Erik Sorensson would be cheated of his firestorm.

Just as Boris had been cheated of his beauty. The ruby red and brass dragon he became was less splendid than once he had been. His trailing red plumes were gone, his body as scarred in dragon form as in human. He could not bear to look at himself, for he had been the jewel of his kind.

He knew where to lay the blame. Erik Sorensson was the *Pyr* who had come close to killing Boris, just as Erik's father had killed Boris's father. That was a crime that couldn't be repeated. Only the Elixir had saved Boris, but now that he was healed, he would eliminate Erik forever.

First Boris sought the address he knew so well, the address where the payments had gone. He wheeled out of the sky over the luxury condominium, and his nose told him that the plastic surgeon he had retained, the same one bribed to overlook any physiological oddities in his anonymous patient, was home.

It was a perfect night for a house fire.

Boris landed on the terrace that overlooked Lake Michigan and confronted the good doctor through the sliding glass door wall. The doctor put down his glass of champagne and turned at the sound of Boris's arrival, alarm and disbelief mingling in his expression.

Boris reared up, letting the doctor see his scars, willing him to make the connection. The surgeon's eyes widened in horror; he dropped the glass and backed away with his hands held high.

That was when Dr. Stanley Berenstein understood that he would never collect the bonus payment for the successful completion of the surgery.

He would never taste the Dragon's Blood Elixir himself.

Boris laughed, kicked his way through the sliding glass door, and loosed his dragonfire.

He took great pleasure in the way the plastic surgeon's skin crackled, in the way it burned beyond the ability of any surgeon to repair. He let the doctor experience the fullness of the pain, let him see what he had become, then fried the life out of him.

Humans were such a feeble species.

Boris left the doctor dead and his apartment blazing like an inferno. The fire was his ally in destroying signs of his presence. Pesky details resolved, he then turned his attention to a matter of greater import.

The time was ripe for vengeance.

In a London hotel, Eileen Grosvenor awakened with a start. She looked around the bedroom, shocked to find it exactly as it should be.

Instead of filled with water.

She'd dreamed of swimming underwater, swimming so far underwater that she might have been a fish. It had been wonderful; she'd felt strong and agile, the muscles in her body moving in perfect concert.

That had been strange. She hated the water and had never learned to swim. In her dream, though, she had enjoyed it.

What had changed? She lay back and recalled the details

of her dream, struck again by the sense that she had forgotten something important. That sense had been growing, driving her choices, as if a forgotten experience demanded her attention.

It had brought her to England. It had taken her to Ironbridge. And now it was infiltrating her dreams, pushing her to recall a memory that lurked just out of reach.

Eileen was going to unravel it, if it was the last thing she did.

She thought of her dream, savoring the details even as they fled her thoughts. The water had been warm, turquoise, welcoming. There had been light. A warm light, like that cast by a candle. She'd moved directly to it, unable to resist its allure. She'd moved with confidence and ease.

And *he* had been there.

Her heart skipped.

Eileen closed her eyes and saw again the face of the man who had been bent over the surface of the water, looking down at her. She remembered raising a finger and seeing him reach out with one hand. She saw again the spark that had leapt between their fingers, illuminating the surface of the water.

There was something in his eyes that melted her heart. It could have been a memory of pain or of some old injury. He looked haunted and wounded. Eileen had been sure that she could heal him, even though he was beyond the water and she was beneath it. She had had a conviction that he was the elusive memory she sought.

Maybe it was a portent. Maybe she was finally going to meet a man who was worth the trouble. She'd certainly know him again if she saw him. She focused on his image, sharpening it in her thoughts. Oh, yes, she'd recognize him anywhere.

Then she felt silly for giving a dream so much credence.

Maybe the dream was just a result of the stress of being away from home, apparently for no good reason.

Maybe it meant she should take swimming lessons.

The dream made Eileen happy, though, made her feel strong and sexy and optimistic. She had a strange, irrational conviction that she was going to meet the man of her dreams.

So to speak.

That didn't sound like Eileen, ultimate pragmatist and skeptical romantic. It sounded more like her sister. She scoffed and got out of bed for a drink of water. Eileen was standing in the bathroom, drinking, when she saw in the mirror that her hair was wet.

And there was a leaf from a water plant tangled in the ends.

But Eileen didn't swim; she never had. She had a fear of the water, one she'd struggled to overcome because it was without any basis in her history.

If her hair was wet, then it couldn't have been a dream.

She met her own gaze in the mirror, recalled the man's face, and knew she wouldn't sleep any more that night.

Chapter 1

London, England
February 29, 2008

Erik and Rafferty avoided each other in Rafferty's London home, meeting only for dinner each night. Tension was high between the two *Pyr*, a situation that Erik could have done without. They waited, restlessly, for Erik's firestorm to declare itself. After one week, the air between them could have been cut with a knife. Erik missed the easy alliance he had shared with Rafferty.

It didn't help that they both wished they were waiting for Rafferty's firestorm.

Erik was in the kitchen, dicing onions, when Rafferty returned home. The older *Pyr* was smiling and looked inclined to chat. It could have been a return to old times.

"You won't believe what happened today," Rafferty said as he shrugged out of his coat.

"You felt the firestorm?" Erik teased.

"I wish!" Rafferty laughed as he got a pair of wineglasses from the cupboard. "But this is worth celebrating. I had an appointment today to assess some artifacts being auctioned off. Routine stuff. The government claims all historical finds as treasure, then often sells the less interesting pieces."

Erik returned to his chopping, thinking that Rafferty had made a find for his antiquities shop. "And you found hidden treasure?" he teased, trying to restore their former camaraderie.

"Ha!" Rafferty chortled. "These people, this Fonthill-Fergusson Foundation, actually *have* the Dragon's Teeth."

Erik dropped the knife and stared at the older *Pyr*.

"Yes! All ninety-nine of them, just as Nikolas said there would be." Rafferty opened a bottle of wine with a flourish and splashed the red wine into the glasses. He was unusually animated. "I saw them. I *touched* them. I can't believe it."

"Are you sure?"

Rafferty gave Erik a hard look. "They could hardly be anything else."

"They could be fake."

Rafferty shook his head. "No. They have the same deep vibration as the tooth that became Nikolas. No scent, just as before, but they resonate deeply of the earth. It's them."

Excited as he was, Erik doubted it would be easy to claim the Dragon's Teeth. There had to be a catch. "Where were they found? And how?"

"A hoard was unearthed during the excavation for the extension of the Jubilee tube line." Rafferty touched his glass to Erik's and took a sip. "The new stations are in Greenwich and Deptford."

"Greenwich? Where the observatory is?"

"Where the O_2 is." Rafferty held Erik's gaze. "The route passes very close to the Palace of Placentia, where Elizabeth I kept her court."

"Magnus's hoard," Erik guessed, seeing the link.

"Right. The ceiling fell in on the cavern when Donovan and I fought Magnus all those years ago. I guess he had collected all of the Dragon's Teeth, but lost most of them in the collapse."

"No wonder he hates you and Donovan."

Rafferty nodded and leaned on the counter, grinning as he seldom did. "Imagine—they plan to sell them. *Sell* them! We can buy the Dragon's Teeth and build an army of *Pyr*!" Rafferty took a swig of wine. "Things are finally going our way."

Erik felt the need to be realistic. "I doubt it'll be that easy. That's not the Great Wyvern's style."

Rafferty took a step back and surveyed Erik. "You sound bitter, even for you."

"I'm not sleeping well." That was the least of his issues. Erik's gift of foresight was gone, utterly gone, and he felt lost without its constant input. It was startling to realize how much he had come to rely upon it, and troubling to realize that once it was gone.

Gone. As surely as if he had never had it. His hand shook as he diced more onions. How could he lead the *Pyr* without his foresight?

Was that the only thing the firestorm would demand of him?

Or just the first thing?

"I noticed." Rafferty's tone was wry and Erik glanced up to find his old friend watching him closely. "You're going to pace a trough in my hardwood floors."

"Sorry to have disturbed you."

"Just stay off the Persian carpets, please. The old ones are more fragile." Rafferty refilled his wineglass, looking thoughtful, then frowned. "I could liquidate some assets," he mused.

Erik knew that wasn't what he had intended to say. He was a bit tired of not having the argument that threatened to erupt between them and was prepared to call Rafferty on it.

But the firestorm struck then, jolting Erik as surely as if he had shoved his finger into a light socket. He caught his breath and straightened, then felt the telltale heat of it slide over his skin and kindle his desire. His heart was leaping and he was sure his hair stood on end.

He chopped onions so savagely that he nearly lost a finger.

"What's wrong?" Rafferty asked.

Erik felt his lips tighten. "Guess."

There was a beat of silence between them, a tense silence. Then Rafferty braced both hands on the counter, his gaze incisive. "And you're going to cook dinner as if nothing special is happening at all?" For once Rafferty couldn't hide his resentment. "It's *wrong* to not pursue a firestorm!"

Erik understood that Rafferty's patience had finally expired. "I don't have to jump like a lapdog to the summons."

"So speaks one who doesn't appreciate the gift he's been given," Rafferty retorted. "Two firestorms in one lifetime!"

"You would have been welcome to one of them."

"You're lucky but you just take it for granted," Rafferty scoffed. "You don't make the most of opportunity."

Erik heard his voice rise. "I don't want this opportunity. . . ."

"And maybe that's the problem." Rafferty's eyes were flashing. He slammed his glass down on the counter, nearly breaking the stem. "Maybe that's why we're in such a predicament. Maybe you *did* lead the *Pyr* astray."

"No one knew this challenge from the *Slayers* would come—"

Rafferty interrupted Erik decisively. "*Everyone* who heeded the old tales knew." His gaze was cold. "But you never had time for old tales, prophecies, and myths, did you? What kind of leadership is that? And now you don't want a firestorm." He almost snarled. "Are you *Pyr* or not?"

"I would much rather this firestorm were yours," Erik retorted.

"But it isn't," Rafferty snapped. "Which leaves the question of what you're going to do about it."

"Mate and be done with it."

Rafferty scowled. "You did that before, didn't you? And it worked out so very well, didn't it?"

The *Pyr* eyed each other across the kitchen, a new and unwelcome tinge of animosity between them.

"I don't owe you an explanation."

"Maybe you do." Rafferty's eyes narrowed and he began to chant in a low voice.

> *"Third match of three demands sacrifice,*
> *A blood cost of enormous price.*
> *Then King and Consort in union complete*
> *Choose trust over ancient deceit;*
> *Shed blood alone can give the power*
> *To aid the* Pyr *in their darkest hour."*

"I've never heard that before," Erik admitted quietly. The hair was prickling on the back of his scalp, and he understood intuitively what his role in all of this would be.

He would be the sacrifice; his would be the blood shed to aid the *Pyr*. His foresight *was* only the first loss.

It made perfect sense. The firestorm beckoned him to his destruction. And Erik would go, for he cared more about the triumph of the *Pyr* than anything else.

Even his own life.

"Would you have listened if you had?" Rafferty challenged, his eyes bright.

"Probably not." Erik began to clean up the kitchen, grimly putting away the onions that he had just chopped.

Rafferty watched, his expression forbidding. Erik sensed that his friend was going to drink a lot of wine on this night.

Erik realized belatedly that his gift of foresight might have nothing to show him because he had no future. That shook him to his core, but he'd never been one to flinch from his responsibilities. He might not have always succeeded, but at least he had tried.

And he would try to consummate his firestorm before he died.

"What are you going to do?" Rafferty asked with quiet force.

"Answer the summons." Erik pulled on his leather jacket and paused on the threshold to look back at his old friend. "Whatever the price." He reached for the door handle, uncertain whether he'd ever be back or see Rafferty again. He sensed that he should make amends, but didn't know where to start. The rift between them seemed too wide.

Rafferty's hard expression didn't help. "Most *Pyr* get only one firestorm, Erik. Remember how lucky you are."

Lucky. Erik declined to comment on that.

Instead, he strode into the night to meet whatever fate awaited him.

Erik let his instincts guide him. The firestorm summoned him like a beacon, the light of a distant bonfire drawing him to warmth and heat and the object of his desire.

Downtown. He shouldn't have been surprised. Erik chose to walk, knowing it would take more time, knowing that he couldn't truly thwart the Great Wyvern's intention.

But Erik was fed up with destiny. He didn't want to have a firestorm. He didn't want to have another son, not after his first son had chosen to turn *Slayer*.

He knew, though, that the Great Wyvern wouldn't give him a choice. He'd seen how the odds could be stacked against any given *Pyr*, using his character and values to compel him to partake of the firestorm.

She'd already found his Achilles' heel in his determination to lead the *Pyr* to triumph regardless of the cost to himself. This firestorm—*his* firestorm—would be the critical third step in the *Pyr*'s preparation for the pending war with the *Slayers*. He had to follow the firestorm's call, regardless of where it led him.

He had to focus on the greater good and put his own aside.

The firestorm drew Erik steadily deeper into the city, toward the part he had known the best. The heat drew him to Fleet Street, increasing with every step he took. Erik could see the Temple Bar Memorial farther down the street, that large griffin marking the boundary between London and Westminster. It didn't take much imagination to see it as a dragon.

Erik felt the firestorm's glow become brighter, felt his body begin to respond more keenly to the proximity of his mate. She was close. He looked for her, curious despite himself.

Beyond the memorial was St. Clement Danes, a church Erik had known all too well in its earlier form. He could feel the vibration of silver in the vaults on Chancery Lane, and hear the song of old stone from the Temple.

But most important, the firestorm heated to a sizzle.

She was very close.

Erik slipped into the shadow of an alleyway and checked his watch. It was almost midnight. The street was quiet, and he wondered whether his mate was working somewhere late, wondering how he would find her, how he would introduce himself to her.

Eileen Grosvenor had been the name Louisa had given.

But what did she look like in this life? Curiosity caught and snared him.

Erik's heart changed rhythm, matching its beat to that of another heart in a way he had almost forgotten. The sensation left him dizzy, yet excited, just as it had once before. He found himself scanning the street with anticipation. A yearning he had never expected to feel again filled him with a warm glow.

It was both sensuous and bittersweet, the promise of the firestorm tainted by his own past experience, colored by the threat in Rafferty's rhyme. He felt that old rage of lust, that quickening in his body, and *wanted* with an ardor he'd forgotten.

The bells rang at St. Clement Danes and Erik frowned. Midnight. They shouldn't have rung at this hour. He knew it, but the tune of "Oranges and Lemons" echoed through the quiet street all the same. He turned to look at the church and then he saw her.

Walking alone toward him.

His heart stopped cold, then raced.

She was just passing the memorial, a feminine sway to her steps. She was tall and walked with purpose—as she should, given the hour and the location. She was slim, but athletically built. Erik was greedy for details, but it was hard to see more, given that she wore a heavy sheepskin coat.

A purple one.

If she was worried about her personal safety, she hid it well. She moved with confidence, her dark skirt swinging with her steps. She had a large knit scarf wrapped around her neck and carried a leather satchel on one shoulder. She spared an upward glance at the griffin as she strode past it. The streetlight illuminated her fleeting smile and danced in the copper curl of her hair.

Erik's chest tightened. He knew that mysterious smile. It was strange to see it on different lips, on a mouth that curved in another way, on a face of such different coloring from Louisa's.

But it was Louisa's smile, the smile that had made him forget himself. It was a smile both mischievous and secretive, a smile that hinted of mystery and promised pleasure. On this woman's lips, it seemed to be a more daring smile. Confident. Erik caught his breath and clenched his hands as he watched her.

She surveyed addresses, unsure of her destination, and Erik wondered why she was here. She couldn't be seeking him—he was following her.

To his dismay, she paused suddenly. She scanned the street, sensing something. He had a moment to realize that she could feel the firestorm; then she pivoted abruptly to face him.

Their gazes locked and Erik couldn't move.

He was in the shadows, motionless and dressed in black. She shouldn't have seen him, but she did. She didn't run. She didn't scream. She just stared back at him, as astonished as he was.

Had she had the same dream?

Did she remember it?

The heat surged through his veins as their gazes held. This firestorm wasn't content with half measures—it raged through him, setting his desire burning so hot that he couldn't think of anything other than possessing her. Erik was on fire and she was still twenty steps away. Her lips tightened and she took a purposeful step toward him, as if she'd speak to him.

She was bolder than Louisa and she moved with a determination that Erik liked more than he should have. He was aroused beyond belief, his desire raging as vehemently as his need to protect her.

All of that got worse when he caught a whiff of *Slayer*.

Two of them.

Closing fast.

It wasn't a coincidence.

Erik cursed the Great Wyvern under his breath. He spun and marched away, uncertain what his body would do and not wanting the sight of his change to be their first encounter.

Once had been enough for that scenario.

It was *him*.

Eileen had sensed someone watching her, even as she realized it was oddly warm on Fleet Street. She was not in the mood to be harassed or victimized, given how this trip had gone so far. She'd turned to challenge the looker.

But she'd seen the man from her dream.

Live and in person.

Eileen's heart leapt when their gazes met. He was taller than she'd realized, long and lean. He exuded power, even standing in the shadows of an alley across the street. His hair was as dark as ebony, touched with silver at the temples. He wore a black leather jacket and black jeans, black Blundstone boots and a dark sweater. He might have been one with the shadows, if not for the vibrant green of his eyes.

Or maybe it was the intensity of his expression. Either way, he seemed to be crackling, shooting sparks in the shadows, drawing her closer.

Like a moth to the flame.

He looked steadily back at her and waited. He might have been daring her to make the first move, testing whether she had the nerve to do anything about the crackle of attraction between them. Eileen's mouth went dry and her skin felt flushed. She was aware that her hair had worked its way loose of its braid again, that she was irritated and probably looked it.

His presence stole her annoyance away.

Maybe that was because he looked a bit irritated himself, as if he'd thump anyone who gave him any attitude. Eileen liked that they had that mood in common. His gaze softened and he surveyed her as if she were gorgeous, as if he couldn't get enough of looking at her, as if he wanted her right there and right then.

It was a tempting possibility.

Eileen basked in the heat of his gaze, tingles awakening across her skin. She felt as if a cord were pulled taut between them, knotting them together and drawing her ever closer.

She felt sexy.

She felt aroused.

And the man from her dream hadn't yet said a word.

Maybe he wasn't real, after all.

Eileen would find out. She took a step toward him and he held his ground. If anything, his eyes got brighter, his expression more intense. She reminded herself that she was sensible, that the smart choice would be to run, but she couldn't resist him.

She took another step closer.

She saw him straighten and catch a breath. Her mouth went dry and she shivered. She wanted to know how he got into her dream. She wanted to know why he was here, how he'd known where she was going, how he kissed, what his name was, where he lived. She wanted to hear his voice, his laughter, his whisper.

But he pivoted suddenly and walked away.

He moved so quickly that there was no doubt he intended to leave her behind. Eileen stared after him as he disappeared into the shadows.

Then he was gone, and she was alone again.

In dream dude's absence, Eileen felt cold again and her irritation returned. She shivered and tugged her scarf tighter. She should have been glad that he was saving her from her own foolish impulse, but instead she felt bereft.

As if she'd missed an opportunity.

Great. Now she was losing her mind on top of everything else. What better culmination to the worst trip of her life? Things had gone from bad to worse from the moment she'd set foot in Heathrow.

First, there'd been the Nigel disaster.

Then she'd had zero luck finding more about the enigmatic story that was the official reason for her sabbatical.

Then her sister had battled a household epidemic of chicken pox and forbidden Eileen to visit as planned.

Meanwhile, it had rained and rained and rained. Eileen's characteristic optimism had taken a hit, confronted by the relentless gray of an English winter. She had followed her instincts and struggled to track down that elusive memory that was driving her crazy and had come up with zilch.

Through all of this, Eileen's old roommate, Teresa Mac-

Crae, had been almost rude in her insistence that she didn't have time for a coffee together to catch up.

Not in eight weeks. Eileen didn't believe it.

This afternoon, Teresa had abruptly changed her mind and invited Eileen to meet at her place of work in the dead of the night. It had felt more like a summons.

As if Eileen might be *useful*.

Eileen's expectations were low and her bullshit tolerance had eroded to nothing. Curiosity had brought her this far, but Teresa might get more than she expected.

If there was one thing that drove Eileen bananas, it was being considered to be useful. Eileen's irritation grew as she checked the address Teresa had given her. The office in question was just across the street. She spared one last glance after the man in black, but he was gone.

It figured. Eileen jammed the specially delivered security pass into the slot beside the door. She was halfway surprised when the door unlocked. She felt watchful eyes again and glanced over her shoulder.

The street was empty. She *was* losing it. Eileen frowned and focused on the business at hand.

What *was* the business at hand? The more she thought about Teresa's call, the more convinced she was that this had to be an act of desperation. Archaeologists and antiquities dealers didn't ask comparative mythologists for their input very often—when they did, it was because there were no other options remaining.

A consultation to be done in the middle of a Friday night and a special security pass delivered by courier combined to tell Eileen that her instincts were right on the money.

What did *he* have to do with it?

It didn't matter. He was gone.

Eileen used her card again to enter the second set of locked doors at the Fonthill-Fergusson Foundation. A security guard wearing sunglasses watched her impassively from the big desk in the center of the foyer. Eileen had a feeling he would shoot to kill, just from his hard expression.

She wondered whether he knew she was coming. Before she could decide on a persuasive explanation—"I have an appointment" seemed ridiculous, given the hour—there was a staccato tapping of heels on stone.

Teresa.

Eileen would have recognized her college roommate anywhere. It wasn't just the shoes, even though Teresa had always loved her stilettos. Teresa was so petite that Eileen felt she could pick her up in one hand—she apparently hadn't gained an ounce in fifteen years. She was as tiny and elegant as ever.

Teresa had kept her dark hair long, and it was still coiled up in a knot that looked casual. Eileen remembered, though, that Teresa would fuss over her hair for hours.

Teresa had always been big on appearances. Eileen had been more interested in content. If nothing else, they'd never competed over dates—neither had had a clue what the other saw in any given man. Teresa dressed with sleek style, too, making Eileen feel sturdy and sensible. Eileen had curves, height, smarts, and acres of curly red hair.

She was good with that—most of the time.

The guy in the street had looked as if he were good with that, too. Too bad he was gone.

As Teresa came closer, Eileen saw some evidence of time's passage—there were little lines around Teresa's lips. If she hadn't held her mouth so tightly, even they would have disappeared.

"This doesn't go in the log," Teresa told the guard, her tone sharp. He nodded once, and continued to stare straight ahead.

The fact that this wasn't officially happening only fed Eileen's suspicions. Teresa claimed Eileen's security pass with a quick grab and pushed it through a shredder on the desk.

How often did they do stuff like this? Eileen was intrigued.

She was also curious about Teresa's attitude. It was true that they hadn't really kept in touch, but they hadn't parted badly. Why did Teresa resent meeting with her so much?

Or was she just irritated in general?

Eileen could relate to that.

"Good to see you," Teresa said, her tone insincere. She forced a thin smile and gave Eileen a hug that didn't quite make contact. Her fingertips merely brushed Eileen's shoulders, and air kisses were dispatched in the general direction of her cheeks.

Eileen remembered Teresa being more genuine and didn't much like the change. She saw in Teresa's body language that her friend was strung taut.

Afraid, maybe, of saying too much.

What was really going on?

"I'm delighted that you could find the time to accommodate my request," Teresa said, her tone polite. Eileen still found Teresa's English accent completely charming—very "posh," as Teresa would say.

"Well, I was curious," she said, aware that the guard might be listening.

Teresa laughed lightly. "You know what they say about curiosity killing the cat."

Eileen didn't laugh. "I didn't think the stakes were that high. You said it was a bunch of old teeth."

Teresa didn't answer, but her lips tightened even more.

Eileen understood. They weren't supposed to talk about it.

Teresa led the way across the vast empty lobby, her heels clicking on the polished marble floor. Eileen knew she'd be flat on her back in three steps if she'd chosen the same shoes.

She looked around, not hiding that she was impressed. "What exactly does the Fonthill-Fergusson Foundation do?"

They made money at it, whatever it was. Eileen was sure the paintings they passed were a pair of Renoirs.

"We verify and evaluate antiquities," Teresa said, her tone officious. "When necessary, we establish provenance."

Establish or manufacture? Teresa's choice of word caught Eileen's attention. Any antiquity or artwork with a provenance—a documented historical record of its past and age—was more valuable than a similar work without one.

Eileen wondered how much someone might pay to establish provenance for a work that didn't have one already. She had a bad feeling about this place, but she still wanted to see these teeth.

"And is that what we're doing here?" Eileen kept her tone light.

"We're just covering all of the bases, as you Americans like to say," Teresa said with a smile that didn't reach her eyes.

Eileen didn't smile. "I didn't even realize that comparative mythology was a base, at least not for archeologists and antiquities dealers."

"Don't be so sensitive, Eileen," Teresa snapped. "We acknowledge all areas of specialty. We aren't snobs at the Fonthill-Fergusson Foundation."

So they were desperate.

Teresa led Eileen to an unassuming door at the back of one gallery, unlocked it with a key card, and ushered Eileen into a stairwell. It was wide and made of poured concrete, the doors of heavy steel. There were no windows, and three more security doors to be opened as they descended. It got colder with every step.

They were going to the vault.

Eileen was surprised that there would be so much security for a few bones, but then, this might be part of their marketing plan: to treat everything as if it were exceedingly valuable. Perceptions could affect pricing, maybe even help make an established provenance more palatable.

The basement of the Fonthill-Fergusson Foundation had high ceilings and was numbingly cold. The lighting was muted and elegant. From the look of the decor, it could have been a library or gentleman's club. Eileen could almost smell the port and cigars. There were rows of bookshelves jutting into the middle of the room in opposing pairs, and chairs upholstered in oxblood leather. Persian rugs were cast across the floor. Ahead, there was a massive oak table with carved legs, presumably for the display of individual artifacts. One wall had a decent reproduction of the Mona Lisa on it that Eileen assumed could be retracted to reveal a screen.

A pair of rooms stood dark, one in each side back corner, probably for private consultations. The vault door was between them, looking for all the world as though it belonged in a bank.

Or a movie.

Teresa led Eileen to one of these private rooms. There was a desk in it, the walls lined with loaded bookcases, and a pair of those chairs. There was a antique lamp with a green shade on the desk but when Teresa turned it on, Eileen was surprised by the brightness of the light. It wasn't antique at all, but modern with a halogen bulb.

Teresa left her there and went to the vault. Eileen sat down in one of the massive chairs and ran her hands over the leather on the arms. Maybe it was fake, as well. She looked at the books and tried to pull down an edition of Herodotus.

After all, she felt like a stranger in a strange land, too.

Eileen frowned when she couldn't pull the book free, then looked more closely. She shouldn't have been surprised that old books had been glued together and sawed down so that rows of their spines could be glued to the bookshelves. They weren't books at all, not anymore. The "library" was an illusion.

Eileen heard Teresa returning and braced herself for more sleight of hand. Teresa was carrying a wooden box, which was bound with leather straps that became handles at the top.

"I should tell you a bit about these teeth before you see them," Teresa said, launching into lecture mode. "They were part of a treasure hoard discovered in the excavations for a new tube station on the extension of the Jubilee line. . . ."

"Which station?"

Teresa inhaled sharply in response to Eileen's interruption. "North Greenwich. The new station opened in 1999. There was another North Greenwich station, but it was closed in 1926." She took a breath and focused on the box, which she had put on the desk. "The site evidently had been a natural cave. . . ."

"By the river?" Eileen had gone to the Greenwich observatory just a few days before.

"It was farther to the south, toward Blackheath." Eileen's tone sharpened. "The details aren't that important. This stash was found, the government claimed it under the law as part of the country's heritage, but select parts of it are being made available for sale."

"Why?"

"There are redundancies compared to existing collections, as well as pieces that are less relevant to British history."

Eileen arched a brow at the official explanation. She wasn't much for fancy double-talk. "That's never stopped anyone from keeping valuables before."

Teresa frowned with impatience. "This isn't the Sutton Hoo, Eileen. It's not a burial site; it's not a sunken ship; it's not got any cultural or anthropological information to share with us." She flung out a hand. "It's a pile of shiny things from all over the place and all different times, jumbled up together like a magpie's hoard. Most of them just happen to be silver."

Eileen smiled that she had gotten to the root of the issue. The loot wasn't valuable. "A collection, then."

"I suppose. It's not a coherent one; that's for sure. And a lot of the pieces are unexceptional." Teresa widened her eyes. "There are buckets of silver pennies, for example, thousands of them from short periods of time. Ingots and blanks and bits of buckles and earrings." Teresa shook her head. "There's a limit to how much of this flotsam and jetsam the museums want."

Eileen was more intrigued than she had been. People who collected what was declared to be valuable by society were less interesting to her than those who followed their own obsessions. There was always a story to their rationale, and stories fascinated Eileen.

"So, this was an avid collector of shiny things," Eileen mused. "I wonder why he picked what he did."

Teresa shrugged. "Who cares?" She ran a hand across the box and frowned as she hesitated.

"Not just shiny things. He had bones, too," Eileen prompted. "If you expect me to help you, Teresa, you've got to give me some information to work with." She paused to study her roommate's discomfiture. "You've got to trust me or I might as well leave."

Teresa looked stubborn. Resigned, Eileen reached for her satchel and made to stand up.

But Teresa caught her hand. "Wait. Stay." She exhaled. "I just really hate that I'm grasping at straws here."

Eileen sat back down and waited.

Chapter 2

Teresa sat down suddenly and looked Eileen in the eye for the first time. "Okay. These teeth are weird. They're like dog teeth, but far too large. I've done DNA tests and carbon dating and nothing makes sense. No species we know matches the DNA."

Eileen leaned across the table, relieved to see her friend reappearing again. This was like old times—or would have been if they'd been drinking cheap draft beer together. "Lots of species are extinct."

Teresa shook her head. "But the carbon dating is only about four thousand years. We should at least know of the species. No one can even guess—the size of these things alone stops every biologist cold. Dinosaurs were long gone four thousand years ago and so the carbon dating stops every palaeontologist."

"So, this is about your own curiosity?"

"Not quite." Teresa bit her lip and marred her red lipstick, a telling sign of her consternation.

"Come on. Tell me."

Teresa paused, then seemed to make a decision. Her next

words came in a rush and she held Eileen's gaze as she spoke. "There's this guy, this antiquities dealer in town. His name is Rafferty Powell. He's a walking reference of the past and we deal with him a lot. He can't always give citations, but when he says something is so, it either shakes out to be the truth or it's so plausible that it might as well be. He turned up for his appointment today to see what was being auctioned from the find, and his eyes nearly fell out of his head when he saw these teeth."

"Why?"

"Well, that's just it. I don't know." Teresa sat back and drummed her fingers on the wooden chest. "This guy has such a poker face. I've never seen him surprised."

"Could he be putting you on?"

"I don't think so. I think he knows what they are, and I know he wants them. I just don't know why." Teresa slid her hands across the top of the box.

"And you're thinking that if you know what he knows, you'll be able to sell them for even more."

Teresa met Eileen's gaze and her tone turned frosty. "We are commissioned by our clients to obtain the best possible price for their artifacts."

And the foundation got a piece of the action.

Maybe Teresa was even on commission. Eileen understood. "So, why me?"

"It's a long shot, Eileen, but I was thinking of that guy in the nineteenth century who found Troy. . . ."

"Heinrich Schliemann. He used the Homeric poems as his reference."

"Right. I thought maybe there's something in old stories after all." She shrugged and Eileen caught another glimpse of her old friend. "I figured if anybody knew about some big mythical beast that could have been real—"

"Instead of the ancient variant of an urban myth . . ."

"—it'd be you."

"Thanks." Eileen smiled, happier now that they'd had an honest exchange. "You've got nothing else, do you?"

"No." Teresa exhaled. "But Rafferty Powell has undercut me for the last time." Her eyes flashed. "I want to know why he wants these, and I don't want to let him get them too cheap."

She straightened, hiding her passion with disconcerting ease, then offered Eileen a pair of gloves. "Please don't touch the artifacts with your bare hands. It will leave an oil residue on them, because they're porous."

Eileen wasn't sure she'd be able to help, even if she wanted to. There were literally hundreds of old stories of heroes vanquishing mythical beasts. Griffins, sphinxes, dragons, basilisks, the phoenix, centaurs, unicorns—who was to say what any of them really were? Who was to say whether any of them had existed? The stories often insisted that the great beast was the only one of its kind.

Maybe they were right.

She couldn't even imagine what kind of teeth they might have had, but she'd look. Eileen pulled on the gloves.

Teresa turned the box toward her; then her cell phone rang. She pulled it from the pocket of her jacket to look at the number.

"I have to take this," she said tersely, then glared at Eileen. "I'm sure I don't have to remind you that they're numbered and cataloged. You won't get out of here alive with a souvenir."

Eileen was shocked by Teresa's implication. So much for old times and camaraderie.

"I'm sure you don't," she replied coldly, and held Teresa's gaze. Eileen was insulted and didn't care if Teresa knew it. They stared at each other; then the cell phone rang again. Teresa pivoted as she answered the call. She left the room, her voice low. She left the door to the viewing room open but Eileen couldn't hear Teresa's words.

Eileen opened the box and was so shocked that she forgot about Teresa.

The teeth were huge. They each had three peaks, like the back teeth of a dog, but each was a good three inches across. The box was filled with trays, each tray divided into ten compartments, each compartment lined with blue velvet. There were ten trays, only one lacking an index number and tooth.

Ninety-nine teeth.

Whatever the beast had been, it had had a big mouth.

She picked one up and turned it in her gloved hands. Her first thought was that it couldn't be real, but she could see the hollow on the bottom where it had been attached to the gum. There was even a dark speck, a mark that could have been dried blood.

This Rafferty Powell might just want them because they were odd. But then, Teresa knew him better and she was suspicious of his motives. Eileen put the first tooth back and picked up another. It was similar but not exactly the same. It hadn't been cast from a mold. She suspected that it really was what it looked to be.

A tooth.

Ninety-nine teeth, to be precise. But from what?

Eileen got no further in her thinking before she heard the shot. It sounded as if it had come from upstairs.

"What the hell is going on?" Teresa marched toward the stairs, her cell phone already snapped shut.

Eileen reacted instinctively. She flicked off the desk lamp and shut the box, ready to run.

If there was somewhere to run.

She had no time to look for exits. The door immediately opened at the bottom of the stairs they'd descended. Two men in black stepped into the vault. They were tall and buff, sheathed in black from head to toe. Even their eyes were hidden behind sunglasses.

The first man through the door shot Teresa in the chest. She fell as Eileen choked on her gasp of terror.

Teresa didn't move again. A cloud of red spread across the carpet even as the cell phone skipped across the room.

The first man stepped closer and shot Teresa again, right in the head, from very close range.

The second crushed the cell phone under his boot heel.

Then they stepped over Teresa's body in unison, moving quickly. One was shaking open fabric bags, the other leading with his gun. They strode toward the vault.

Toward Eileen.

Eileen instinctively grabbed the box of teeth, ducked under the desk, and held her breath.

An escape plan would have been ideal, but she didn't have one.

Magnus sat in the backseat of the armored Mercedes Benz, watching the display on a cell phone. The car was black, the interior was black, and Magnus was dressed entirely in black. His *Slayer* driver and bodyguard, Balthasar, was also dressed in black. The big sedan could have been a slice of night, idling on a side street in Holborn.

It was certainly filled with darkness. The only light came from the cell phone display, which provided images from a video feed in Jorge's headset.

Magnus smiled with satisfaction as Jorge and Mallory killed the woman and destroyed her cell phone. They were into the Fonthill-Fergusson Foundation, and he could see that the vault was open.

They were getting lucky despite having made mistakes.

Jorge halted and surveyed the area, his old-speak drifting to Magnus's ears. *"There's another human here."*

"Get the hoard," Magnus commanded audibly. "You tripped an alarm in the foyer." He checked his watch and muttered. "Morons."

"Problems, sir?" Balthasar asked in old-speak.

"They've got three minutes, max." Magnus watched them enter the vault and seize the buckets of silver pennies. "The teeth!" he shouted at the cell phone, and swore. "Get the teeth!"

Jorge had an armload of jewelry pieces, making his predictable choice instead of the one he'd been instructed to make. Mallory was shoveling coins into a cloth bag. Magnus narrowed his eyes as Jorge scanned the vault, but he didn't see the box.

"The bitch must have taken it out of the vault," he told Jorge. "It hasn't left the building. It has to be there somewhere."

Jorge left the vault, moving with lightning speed. He checked the first viewing room and Magnus knew Jorge's vision was sharper than the display that came through the cell phone. Jorge kicked over the desk and chair in the room, pulled at the bookcases, and revealed that they were false fronts.

Jorge turned toward the other darkened room. *"She's here,"* he hissed in old-speak as soon as he crossed the threshold.

It made sense. Another human was examining the teeth. That must have been why the meeting had been scheduled, why the dead bitch had even been in the building. Magnus loved when the pieces of the puzzle came together.

Now all parts would be destroyed simultaneously.

Jorge moved into the viewing room with his gun pulled, targeting the desk that Magnus could just see. Jorge kicked it aside and the woman gasped. She was crouched on the floor, the box Magnus remembered so well right in front of her knees. Her eyes were wide with fear and her face was pale.

More important, she held his wooden chest.

She'd die for that.

Magnus heard Jorge chuckle, saw him aim the gun; then there was a crash. Mallory shouted a warning, Jorge turned to look, the woman scurried, and Magnus swore at the video feed.

Even bigger trouble had arrived before the police.

An onyx and pewter dragon raged through the vault, breathing dragonfire as he targeted Mallory. Mallory shifted shape, becoming a garnet and gold dragon. Jorge must have changed shape as well, because the video feed fell to the carpet. Magnus heard the battle begin. He willed the woman to pick up the video feed so he could track her, but he saw her boots as she ran past it.

He also saw that she carried the box.

Magnus heard the police sirens and cursed in seven languages.

The heist was falling apart. Magnus crushed the cell phone in his hand in frustration, then flung the pieces out the window into the night. "Go around the block. Now."

The big black sedan roared into action, separating itself from the shadows. Balthasar liked nothing better than to drive and he was good at it—Magnus would give him that.

"We're picking them up?" he asked.

"Don't be stupid. They can live with the consequences of their own screwup. I need to take the woman's scent. Go to the front entrance. I don't care who sees us."

"Yes, sir."

Magnus opened the power window with one fingertip as they drove. He sniffed, but caught only city and sewer, nameless human multitudes and their various stenches.

And *Pyr*. He inhaled again.

One *Pyr*.

And not just any *Pyr*. It was Erik Sorensson, leader of the *Pyr*. Magnus's mood turned even grimmer. The display hadn't been that good, but Erik was onyx and pewter.

Which meant that Magnus wasn't the only one who knew the location of the Dragon's Teeth, after all.

Eileen thought she was a goner when the thug who had shot Teresa came into the viewing room.

She knew she was a goner when he kicked the desk aside

and aimed his gun straight at her forehead. She refused to cower, just stared straight back at him.

She might not be able to stop him from shooting her, but she'd be damned if she would cringe.

Much less beg.

She saw his finger tighten and her heart leapt to her throat. He'd kill her as readily as he'd killed Teresa.

Then, against all expectation, Eileen got a second chance. There was a roar and a crash. Flames erupted in the main room. Her assailant glanced over his shoulder and Eileen seized the moment.

She ran.

As far as she knew, there was no such thing as a third chance.

Eileen hip-checked her attacker, then drove her shoulder into him. His shot went wild, hitting the ceiling. He swore in another language, and there was a flash of gold at her side.

Eileen didn't look.

She figured he'd shoot her in the back, but she ran anyway. She carried the box of teeth, because she'd been clutching it and didn't think she could let it go if she wanted to. She bolted into the main viewing room, where a massive black dragon was spewing fire and smoke.

Every rational thought left Eileen's brain at the sight.

He was enormous, large enough that his leathery black wings touched the high ceiling of the vault. He was dark and dangerous, his scales glittering and his eyes glowing. Fire spewed from his mouth and his claws were huge and sharp. His tail was a coil of power across the floor.

Eileen's breath hitched in her chest. She wasn't going to think about jumping from the frying pan into the fire. Maybe she'd collected one too many fantastic stories in her time. Maybe she was having delusions.

This dragon, though, looked real.

The fire was definitely real.

The dragon snatched at the other thief. That man changed

into a red and gold dragon in the dragon's grasp, right before Eileen's eyes. She blinked but he remained a dragon. He snarled and twined around the black one with fury.

His scales sparkled red, like a treasure hoard revealed to the sun. His chest even looked to be embellished with pearls. But these dragons weren't ornamental—they were all muscle and sinew.

And antagonism. The pair of dragons locked claws and breathed fire at each other, their tails knotting together as their claws tore. The fire they breathed, meanwhile, ignited the carpets and the spines of the sawed-down books. The room, which had been as cold as a mausoleum, became sizzling hot.

It was transformed into an inferno, smoke and flames on every side. The fire alarm began to drone.

Time to leave.

The black dragon smashed the red one into the far wall, making the whole building jump with the force of impact. The red dragon bled and spewed fire, but kept fighting. Eileen moved stealthily, coming closer to the fighting dragons. She hoped she could sneak past them without being noticed.

It was a long shot, by any accounting.

The black dragon ripped at the chest of the red dragon, his talons tearing long wounds in the red dragon's chest. The red dragon screamed in rage and pain. Black blood flowed onto the burning carpet, hissing on impact. Smoke rose from the stain and Eileen saw that the dark blood had burned right through the carpet to leave smoking holes in the concrete subfloor.

The black dragon flung the red one against the wall again and breathed fire at him. Eileen narrowed her eyes against the brilliance of the flames and crept along the opposite wall.

When the red dragon didn't move, the black dragon pivoted to survey the room. His gaze locked on Eileen.

Her mouth went dry in terror. He exhaled smoke as he

studied her and something about his intensity reminded her of someone.

The man in her dream?

No. That was crazy.

Even if the dragon's eyes were the same vivid green.

She felt warm but it was a different kind of heat than that sparked by the burning room. Desire was awakening deep within Eileen, and at a very inconvenient time. She thought of the old story that had lured her this far, then dismissed the idea.

The dragon took a step closer, setting the floor to vibrating. Eileen eased along the wall toward the exit, not turning back even though she was terrified. The smoke was getting thicker. His eyes flashed as he suddenly raised a talon and leapt toward her. Eileen yelped and jumped backward. He roared with fury.

A yellow claw abruptly closed around her waist.

Eileen screamed when she looked down at the massive talons, each gleaming nail as long as she was wide. Was it the other thief? She'd made a mistake in forgetting about him; that was for sure. She kicked and struck at her captor without success. The dragon tightened his grip on her and lifted her from the floor.

Chuckling.

Would he eat her, like a boa constrictor?

Or just crush her? There were things that Eileen didn't want to find out, and his intentions made the list.

Eileen raised the wooden chest with both hands and slammed it into her captor's knuckles. His grip loosened for just one beat but it was enough.

She squirmed free, jumped, and ran toward the stairs.

Toward the black dragon.

Eileen took her chances and kept running.

To her astonishment, the black dragon swept her past him with one leathery wing, then stepped into the space behind her. Did he intend to defend her, or save her for his own lunch? Eileen didn't much care about the details. She tucked the box under one arm and dove into the stairwell.

She heard the crash and roar of the dragons fighting behind her. She smelled the smoke and heard the crackle of flames, as well as the insistent ringing of the fire alarm. She heard one dragon get slammed into the wall and felt the building shudder to its foundation. The plaster on the ceiling was starting to fall in chunks. Each blow and bellow made her run faster.

She took the stairs three at a time, her leather satchel bumping against her hip, the wooden chest digging into her waist on the other side, her breath coming in anxious spurts. She skidded into the lobby, shouting at the guard for help, then froze.

The security guard wasn't going to help. He was sprawled across the floor in a pool of his own blood.

His sunglasses were smashed on the opposite wall, beneath a red spray of blood.

They'd blown his brains out.

Just like Teresa.

Eileen tried to not hyperventilate.

She had to get out. Immediately. She raced for the street exit, ignoring the blood, stepping around the security guard's body.

She hoped she could get out without a key card. Eileen kicked open the first security door, glad that it opened.

Her relief was short-lived. A large dark sedan was idling at the curb. It had tinted windows and an aura of invincibility.

Everything about that car said *organized crime* to Eileen. It must be the getaway car. Eileen slid to a graceless halt, only one locked glass security door between her and what her instincts told her was big trouble.

There had to be another way out of the building. There had to be a fire exit. She spun and snatched the inner security door before it closed. She nearly screamed when a man stepped out of the stairwell on the far side of the foyer.

It was the man from her dream. He was still dressed in black from head to toe, still intense, but his hair was mussed.

It was an action-man look that worked for Eileen in a big way.

He gave her that stare, the one that made her feel hot and bothered and gorgeous; then his eyes flashed.

Where had he come from?

"But how . . . who . . . when . . ." she stammered, unable to make sense of what was happening. It wasn't like her to be inarticulate, but she couldn't form a coherent sentence to save her life.

She hoped the price wouldn't be quite so high.

"This way, Eileen," he said crisply. He had a wonderful voice, deep and strong, and his British accent didn't hurt. With three words, he melted her bones and her reservations.

He spared a glance down the stairs, then offered his hand to her. Imperiously. Police sirens wailed in the distance, drawing closer.

His eyes flashed with impatience. "Hurry!"

For once in her life, Eileen did what she was told.

Erik's mate was holding up well, considering the circumstances. He doubted that happy situation would last. He avoided touching her when she came to the stairwell, simply ushering her past him.

The last thing he needed was the complication of having to explain the firestorm to her.

Its power was debilitating enough.

She sailed past him, leaping for the stairs, and he sizzled from head to toe. The cloud of her perfume—roses and lavender—nearly took him to his knees.

What was she doing wearing such an old-fashioned scent?

What was she doing choosing the same scent Louisa had worn?

She *was* Louisa.

And the Great Wyvern wouldn't let him forget it. Neither would his body. Erik bit back a curse, disliking the surge of desire that could lead to a miscalculation.

There was no margin for miscalculation, so he fought to concentrate.

He bolted up the stairs after his mate, glad that she was quick on her feet. He appreciated that she wore low heels and had an instinct for survival.

Erik heard the two *Slayers* stir in the basement vault and wondered whether they'd immediately give chase. Some *Slayers* preferred to stalk their prey over time, waiting for that moment of vulnerability. He didn't know enough about Jorge and his companion to guess their inclinations.

But Erik didn't imagine for a minute that this was over. Never mind that he had interrupted the *Slayers*' scheme, whatever it was, and they would retaliate for that. They would feel his firestorm and would be intent on stopping it. To his horror, they had the scent of his mate—Eileen had just become a target.

He couldn't risk leaving her alone.

She reached the top of the stairs and made a growl of frustration. Erik saw that there was no window and no exit.

A dead end.

She spun to face him, the swirl of her skirt giving him a distracting glimpse of her long and muscular legs. She held that wooden chest tightly. Her eyes were wide and her hair was working its way loose. She was breathing quickly and there was a sheen of perspiration on her upper lip. But even in her terror, she was seeking a solution.

Eileen Grosvenor didn't surrender.

That was different from Louisa.

Interesting.

"What now?" she demanded.

The *Slayers* roared and began to ascend the stairs. The police sirens became louder, the wail echoing through the building. Erik heard the police shoot out the security door. Glass shattered.

"Freeze!" two men shouted in unison, their command resonating in the concrete stairwell. Eileen's gaze flicked downward, then to Erik again.

"We're trapped," she whispered with obvious fear.

There was nothing for it. Erik had to do what he had to do.

"Not yet," he said, keeping his tone soothing. He really didn't want to shift in front of her, but there was no choice.

"But they won't believe me. . . ."

"Just close your eyes," he commanded.

"What? Why? Are you crazy?" Her blue eyes flashed with indignation and her cheeks flushed even more. "Ignoring the truth isn't going to solve anything—"

Gunfire erupted in the stairwell far below. "I warned you," Erik said, interrupting her tirade. He held up his hand before her face; then he shifted shape as quickly as he could.

Eileen must have seen something, because her mouth fell open. She started to speak, but Erik had no time for chatter. He swung his tail hard, taking out the wall on the far side of the stairs.

The concrete rumbled and cracked, but held.

"Holy shit," Eileen whispered. "It was you."

The police shouted. Erik swung his tail again, knowing there wouldn't be time for a third strike. The concrete broke, the chunks tumbling into the alley far below.

A twisted hole was opened to the night, its edges jagged with concrete and rebar. The police bellowed, but Erik didn't hesitate.

He snatched Eileen with one claw and winced at the shower of sparks between them. Eileen gasped and finally did close her eyes. Erik claimed her wooden box with his free claw and launched into the night, his astonished mate safely in his grasp.

Chapter 3

Maybe Eileen had been crazy to think that nothing else could go wrong on her trip.

She was shaking as the dragon carried her through the night, and as much as she would have liked to have found an alternative explanation for what was happening, she came up blank. Worse, she was so hot that she could have been burning up.

But this fever was sexual. There was no fire in her proximity anymore, just rain and clouds. Her mind had been washed straight into the gutter, conjuring sexual ideas with dizzying dexterity. Her skin was warm and flushed, she could feel her toes curling and that slow rumble of desire low in her belly.

Sex was the last thing that should have been on her mind.

Maybe going crazy would have been an improvement.

She couldn't help but admire the agile strength of the dragon as he flew, his muscled power, the gentle authority with which he held her. She liked that he had defended and saved her. His scales were warm; his decisiveness was masculine in a way she liked.

A lot.

There was major testosterone in her vicinity, and Eileen's body responded with enthusiasm.

But he was a dragon, at least some of the time.

The black dragon landed in Hyde Park, showing remarkable grace for his size and power. Once her feet were on the ground and she was a few steps away from him, Eileen extended her hand, silently demanding the return of the wooden chest. She noticed that her hand was trembling and hoped he didn't. She was pretty sure she didn't imagine his exasperation in handing over the wooden chest.

Was it weird that a dragon's emotions should be easy to read?

Not any weirder than having been saved by a dragon in the first place.

"Look away," he said, his voice exactly the same as it had been when he'd been the man from her dream.

Eileen pretended to do so, but watched out of the corner of her eye. The dragon shimmered with a strange blue light, shimmered so brightly that she had to close her eyes. When the light diminished, he was the man from her dream again.

Remarkably, he was as sexy as ever. Maybe more so. She was a sucker for a man with a secret and this was a big one.

Unlike Nigel, though, this guy's secret was already revealed.

He watched her, his gaze assessing, his arms folded across his chest. "Go ahead," he invited, his manner discouraging. "Ask."

There was something to be said for the fact that he wasn't going to pretend that what had happened hadn't happened. Eileen was a big fan of honesty. She felt short of breath and too warm, overdressed.

And a bit more aware of her single status than she felt was appropriate. She thought of how tightly he had held her, that he had saved her, that he looked skeptical and irritable and delicious as all get-out.

Maybe he'd had a lousy week, too.

Eileen found herself staring at the wry twist to his lips, the glitter of his eyes, the dusting of silver at his temples. He looked dark and dangerous and unpredictable.

And he pretty much was. Her mouth went dry as desire kicked it up a notch.

Eileen looked away, in case he could read her mind, too. Her gaze slipped across the deadened grass as she fought to gather her thoughts.

Everything seemed normal in the park. There was no snow, which she missed, and the grass was brown and muddy from the recent rain. It was dark here, darker than she would have expected in the middle of the city, and she could see stars overhead. The Serpentine shone like black glass to one side and she could hear the hum of traffic. She oriented herself, as much to take a few minutes as anything else, knowing that Kensington Gardens was in one direction and Buckingham Palace in the other.

He waited with surprising patience.

She exhaled and ran a hand over her hair, feeling that a thousand tendrils—more or less—had worked themselves loose. She probably looked as frazzled as she felt. Heat sizzled beneath her skin, as if she were coming down with something.

Who knew that insanity came in hot flashes?

Eileen eyed him again. "Did what I think happened really happen?" she asked.

"Yes." He spoke with authority and conviction, which might mean that they were both delusional.

Eileen cleared her throat. "I mean the dragons."

"Yes." The corner of his mouth lifted a little, the barest glimmer of a smile. The softening of his expression made her heart twist. "Trust me."

Eileen almost laughed at the lunacy of that. She looked across the park, then back at him, finding herself surprised that he was still there. He looked sane, his eyes bright with intelligence. She was so attracted to him that it frightened her—and she was no shy virgin. "Why should I?" she asked, surprised to hear flirtatiousness in her own tone.

"Why shouldn't you? Who else got you out of there alive?"

"I suppose I should thank you."

He shrugged, a twinkle appearing in his eyes. The sight did dangerous things to Eileen's equilibrium. "I suppose you should."

"Except I don't feel safe quite yet."

He laughed quickly, as if surprised by her, and the sight of his amusement sent a pang through Eileen. She wanted . . . well, it couldn't be healthy under the circumstances.

He bent to pick up the wooden chest but Eileen reached for it first. Their hands collided just above the leather handles and a spark flashed.

She blinked and the spark disappeared, although there was a golden glow between their hands. Fireflies would have emitted that kind of light, except there weren't any fireflies.

Good. Now she was seeing things.

Things besides dragons.

"Don't touch that," she said, hearing her anxiety.

He met her gaze steadily. "I was going to carry it for you."

"And I should trust you, right?"

His smile was crooked, intimate. "Yes."

They were angled together, each bent over the box, their hands almost touching and their faces just inches apart. Eileen could feel him studying her, could feel the languid rhythm of the blood coursing through her veins, could feel the slow melt of arousal unlocking her few inhibitions. She could smell his skin and a subtle cologne, one that made her knees shiver.

This was nuts.

She grabbed the handles and straightened. "I can carry it, thanks."

"Something precious in there?"

"Just a bunch of teeth." Eileen knew she didn't imagine the sudden gleam in his eyes. "Sentimental value."

"That explains a great deal." His lips tightened and he scanned the sky. She wondered what he was looking for.

She tried to think about what had happened and her brain refused to process it. She reviewed the sensible bits first. "You were outside the Fonthill-Fergusson Foundation when I arrived."

"Is that what it was?" he mused, his gaze dropping to the box. "Of course." His gaze flicked to hers. "Yes, I was."

"How did you get through the security door?"

"It was open."

Eileen remembered the thugs and nodded. It could have closed between his arrival and her attempt to depart. Maybe he'd even shut it. "But you were in my dream." Eileen heard that the question had left her tone. His conviction that all of this was normal was contagious.

He nodded once. "Yes. As you were in mine."

"Really?" Eileen held the leather straps with both hands. "Why? How?"

He averted his gaze then and shook his head. "It's a long story, too long for tonight." He frowned. "We need to get a cab back to the house. . . ."

Eileen froze. Did he know where she was staying, too? "What house?"

"My friend has a house in Hampstead Heath," he said, and Eileen was momentarily relieved. "We should go there tonight to ensure your safety."

"Excuse me?" She took a step backward. "You expect me to go with you?"

His eyes narrowed and he looked purposeful. He spoke softly. "It's for your own protection."

"Think again." Eileen turned and started to walk toward light and civilization. She had a feeling that the rational explanation would reveal itself once she wasn't standing in a dark park, alone with a sexy man who thought he could become a dragon.

Never mind a sexy man capable of convincing her that he was right about his abilities. It didn't help that she was so turned on and couldn't stop thinking about kissing him, just to see what it was like.

He followed her, staying half a dozen steps behind. His protectiveness irked Eileen. How was she going to get back to her sister's house without him knowing where she was staying?

She'd get in a cab and shut the door on him. He might follow in another cab, but with all the cabs looking the same, she should be able to convince her cabdriver to lose him. She'd go back to Lynne's and have a cup of herbal tea and figure out what had really happened.

What had happened was that Teresa had been shot in the head.

No. Eileen had to be safe herself before she could think about that.

Eileen pulled out her cell phone, shifting the straps of the wooden chest to one elbow, and started to punch in the number for the police.

"Calling the authorities?" the dragon dude asked mildly from behind her.

"Are you psychic, too?" Eileen glanced over her shoulder in time to see his wry smile.

"Not anymore, apparently." Then he sobered. "What exactly are you going to tell them?"

"That Teresa is dead, of course."

"They had already arrived when we left. No matter how competent or incompetent you think police forces are, I'm quite certain they have assessed the scene already and found the body."

The body. Eileen's fingers faltered and her mouth went dry. "I'll tell them that I saw the guy who shot her, then."

The man arched a brow. "The one who turned into a

dragon before your very eyes? Don't you think a story like that might affect your credibility as a witness?"

Eileen stared at him for a moment, then slapped her phone shut with impatience. "Then what should I do? Teresa is *dead!*"

His eyes glittered. "You should avenge her, of course."

Eileen stared at him and was pretty sure he had a plan for vengeance already mapped out. It would be tempting to step further into his world, but she knew better.

"No." Eileen pivoted and marched toward civilization, sanity, and the world she knew, which was devoid of dragons, sexy shape-shifting men, and big weird teeth.

Well, the teeth would go with her.

She reached the sidewalk on Park Lane and headed for the curb. A big black sedan slid to a halt right in front of her, as if she had summoned it.

But she hadn't.

The back door opened and an older man leaned out. He was well dressed, all in black, and looked both suave and European. "Need a ride?" he asked smoothly. "I would be delighted to be of service."

It was the car Eileen had seen at the foundation, the organized-crime mobile.

It—they—had followed her.

Uh-oh.

Eileen took a step back and collided with the man from her dream. There was a flash of bright orange light when they touched, like an electrical spark. She hadn't imagined the first one when their hands had touched. A languid heat spread over Eileen's skin, making her think inappropriately intimate thoughts about this stranger. She glanced at him in shock.

What was he doing to her?

How was he doing it?

And why?

He stepped around her, positioning himself protectively

between her and the car. "The lady doesn't need your help, Magnus."

The man in the car smiled. "All this and a firestorm," he purred. "How very special for you, Erik."

Erik. His name was Erik. It suited him.

Erik slammed the car door as Magnus laughed. The driver put the car into gear, but Magnus lowered his window. "Fear not. We shall meet again." He smiled at Eileen, his expression hungry. "Soon."

Eileen took a trio of backward steps, her gaze flicking between the two men. She could have given them the wooden chest, could have just put it down on the sidewalk and backed away, but Eileen didn't imagine for a minute that that would end anything.

She might need something to bargain with.

Magnus chuckled and murmured something to the driver. There were two others in the car—Eileen could see their silhouettes in the far side of the vehicle. She had a pretty good idea who they might be. The big car eased away from the curb.

Erik took a step toward Eileen, his hand extended.

She took one look and ran. The Benz driver would have to do a U-turn to follow her, which gave her precious time. Eileen sprinted as fast as she could, the wooden chest bumping against her knees. She heard Erik's footsteps, but didn't dare to look back. She just had to get back to the real world.

She just had to get to Wellington Arch and get a cab.

And then . . .

And then she'd think of something.

Erik had lived long enough to recognize when he was pushing his luck. He followed Eileen, letting her keep a bit ahead of him. He heard Magnus's car pull away from the curb and accelerate, but didn't care for the moment what his opponent would do.

He had to protect Eileen at any price.

A little distance gave his body the chance to regain its equilibrium. The firestorm was jangling his nerves and tangling his logic. It seemed to have become impossibly hot, and to have done so far more quickly than the last time. Maybe that was because—unlike the other *Pyr* who had never had a firestorm—Erik knew the fullness of its promise.

And how well it delivered.

The firestorm was disassembling his objections with frightening speed. He already admired Eileen's ability to think clearly under pressure. She was curvaceous and outspoken, purposeful and optimistic. He appreciated how resourceful she was, and that she hadn't been paralyzed by her fear at the foundation.

She was terrified and he didn't blame her. He didn't like that she had the Dragon's Teeth and he didn't like that Magnus and his bodyguards knew it. Worse, Magnus had Eileen's scent and would be able to track her anywhere, and Magnus had witnessed the spark of their firestorm.

The whole thing was a disaster. It was one thing for him to be the sacrifice, but Erik wouldn't let his mate share his fate.

The quandary was how to save her. He doubted he could persuade Eileen to willingly enter his protective custody. He didn't want to force her to go to Rafferty's home, but he feared for her safety if she didn't. Magnus would not let this go. Erik wasn't sure he could beguile Eileen and didn't want to try.

The best option might be following her and barricading her refuge with a dragonsmoke territory ring.

Assuming he could follow her.

Erik caught up to Eileen when she paused to hail a cab. He reached for the handles of the wooden chest.

"Don't touch that!" she said, and tugged it from his grip. "You can't have it." She backed away from him, holding the wooden chest in front of herself like a shield.

"I'll just carry it for you. It's heavy."

She gave him a scathing glance. "I wasn't born yesterday."

"But you'll only survive to see tomorrow because of me."

She hesitated and considered him. "You could be softening me up. It's a classic con strategy."

Erik couldn't hide that he was insulted. His integrity was his most precious possession. "I may be many things, but I am not a con artist."

She wasn't persuaded. "Isn't that exactly what a con artist would say?" She didn't wait for an answer, just stepped to the curb and waved. A cab came to a halt, but before she could reach for the door handle, Erik grasped it.

"I will see you to safety tonight," he insisted.

"I don't think so—" she started to argue, but he interrupted her.

"This cab will go up Park Lane, precisely in the direction of another car. Do you really want to head that way alone, without the only individual who has defended you tonight?" It was insulting that she had to think about it for a moment.

"I suppose you won't take no for an answer."

"You suppose correctly."

Her tone turned fierce. "You're not spending the night with me, so don't get any ideas."

Erik glared at his stubborn mate. "I assure you that any ideas I have, at this point in time, are purely concerned with your survival."

Eileen studied him, frowned, then got into the cab. She slid across the seat, and Erik got in beside her, leaving an arm's span between them.

"The Ritz, please," she said to the driver. He nodded, started the meter, and pulled into the light traffic.

Erik could have been reassured that she wasn't staying at some small cheap hotel. Little could stop a *Slayer* bent on destruction, but the greater obstacles presented by a larger hotel—one more concerned with guest security—could only be good.

The problem was that Eileen was lying about staying at the Ritz. He could sense it in her elevated pulse and discomfiture. As much as he admired that she thought on her feet, he didn't appreciate that she was lying to him.

He did not want to beguile her.

Erik drummed his fingers on his knee in exasperation. He hoped he was able to follow her. Would the firestorm remain as vehement, or would the Great Wyvern play another game with him? Erik would have welcomed a return of his psychic abilities in this moment.

His mate had no issues letting him pay the taxi fare, and Erik suspected it was a ploy to put distance between them again. She alighted with the assistance of the doorman at the Ritz as Erik paid. Eileen was nearly through the hotel doors before Erik caught up with her.

He touched her elbow, disguising the inevitable spark between their bodies. The bright lights over the entranceway ensured that the light didn't attract much attention. He was still jolted by the desire that shot through him at that small contact and was relieved to see Eileen flush with awareness of him.

"I told you—" she began.

"You have made yourself clear. I am not arguing with you."

"What, then?" She turned to face him, both hands locked on the handles of the chest.

"Will you give me the wooden chest for safekeeping?" Erik already knew the answer but had to ask.

Eileen smiled. "Be serious."

Erik exhaled and looked away. Magnus's scent teased at his senses, making him shiver with dread.

He sensed another *Slayer*, too, but he must be wrong about the *Slayer*'s identity. It couldn't be his old rival Boris Vassily. Boris was dead. Erik had killed Boris himself. There must simply be more *Slayers* in the vicinity.

It wasn't the most reassuring observation he could have made.

He realized that Eileen was studying him, and wondered what she saw. "I'll have one promise from you; then I'll leave you alone."

"Why should I make you a promise?"

"Because it's for your own welfare." Erik didn't linger on that, simply gestured to the chest. "You will promise me that you will take that to someone who knows what to do with it, that you won't keep it in your possession. You will part ways with it first thing in the morning."

Defiance flashed in her eyes. "Why?"

"Because you stole it, of course. Possession will link you to the crime we witnessed tonight."

She caught her breath and he could almost hear her thinking. He liked that she was logical. He hoped that his argument was persuasive. Since he couldn't claim the wooden chest, her passing it along in the morning was the best he could hope for.

"Okay," she said firmly. "I promise." She wasn't lying, to his relief, but meant what she said. She offered her right hand as if they were sealing a deal. "Good night then."

Erik looked at her hand and wanted more than a handshake.

It was his last chance to make an argument in his own favor.

Erik took her hand slowly, letting his fingers slide across her skin. His hand enveloped hers, securing the fragility of her fingers within his strong grasp. He felt her shiver as keenly as his own. Heat radiated from the point where their palms touched, a glow that awakened every vestige of lust within him. He wanted her and he didn't hide it, holding her gaze as she stared at him.

She swallowed.

She licked her lips quickly.

She flushed, her gaze dropping to his lips for a heartbeat.

He felt his pulse match hers, the two beating in rhythm at their palms, an insistent beat that demanded their surrender. He was stunned that that had happened so soon, then almost overwhelmed by his sense of union with her.

Eileen caught her breath and her cheeks were red. "He talked about the firestorm," she said, her words falling in a rush. "What does that mean?"

Erik couldn't resist the opportunity she offered. She was so close, so soft, so radiant with desire. He was burning and yearning for her touch, consumed with the firestorm's demand.

She was his mate.

"This is the firestorm," Erik murmured. He slipped his other hand into the hair at her nape, pulled her closer, and kissed her thoroughly.

Erik's was a kiss like no other.

Eileen had kissed a lot of men, but Erik's kiss was more than all of them put together. She couldn't figure out how it could be both sweet and hot, both gentle and demanding. She couldn't figure out how this man she knew so little about was able to curl her toes, much less how his touch made her want to peel off her clothes and do the deed right then and right there.

What she did know about Erik should have sent her running. Instead she sensed the strength in him, and admired how he held it in check. She appreciated his choice to be tender, yet knew he could be ferocious. She felt safe, cosseted, appreciated in his presence as she never had before.

That was sexy.

No wonder she was so enflamed.

His kiss wasn't a surprise. If anything, she'd been waiting for it. She'd seen the glint of intent in his eyes, and guessed what he might do. She was curious herself. The heat that leapt between them—this firestorm—had a way of awakening some primal yearnings.

She'd wanted to kiss him since he'd turned up in her dream.

If he hadn't initiated the kiss, she would have.

And it didn't disappoint. Eileen closed her eyes, savoring the strength of his fingers in her hair, the slow rhythm of his thumb against her earlobe. His skin was warm, his kiss was firm, and Eileen wanted a lot more contact between them. She was hot, burning with a desire beyond anything she'd ever felt.

She pulled away, more out of awareness that they were necking in a public place than any desire to end the kiss. His eyes were darker in color, his attention fixed upon her. He was so taut, so tightly controlled, that even the slightest quirk of his lips was a hint that she was reaching him. He could have been made of stone—but that kiss proved that there was passion beneath the surface.

She thought of volcanoes and wondered what it would take to make Erik lose control.

Then she wanted to find out.

She recalled her dream, her sense that he was injured and she could heal him. She thought of her sense of recognition in that dream, and wondered whether he was what she had come to England to find. Then she wondered what could have given him such firewalls.

Besides the fact that he had one whopper of a secret.

"Good night, Eileen," Erik said. He leaned closer, and although she half hoped for another kiss, he brushed his lips across her cheek. The slight touch sent a sizzle through her veins and an inferno over her skin. "I will protect you," he whispered against her ear, his breath making her gasp. "You may not trust me, but you can trust in that."

Eileen was ever·so tempted to take him home, but she knew better. She inhaled sharply and stepped away from him, pulling her hand from his. "He called you Erik," she said. "Is that really your name?"

"I am Erik Sorensson." He opened the door of the hotel

for her with a gallantry she was beginning to associate with him. "Leader of the *Pyr*."

"*Pyr*," Eileen echoed, recalling a long-ago language class. She paused on the threshold to study him. "That's Greek for *fire*."

Erik nodded curtly. "It's what I am."

She liked that he didn't pretend she hadn't seen what she had seen. All the same, it couldn't be healthy to get involved with dragons. Eileen wasn't much for playing with fire.

None of this could be real.

Given the evidence that surrounded her, her mind wasn't quite ready to accept that assertion, but Eileen struggled to make herself accept what had to be the truth.

She was certain that if she got back to Lynne's place, back to normalcy and routine, she'd think of a rational explanation for everything that had happened to her tonight. She was sure that in the company of regular people—even sleeping ones—everything would be fine.

Eileen ignored the voice in her thoughts that argued otherwise.

She had to get to Lynne's.

She forced a prim smile. "Thank you then, Erik, and good night."

He inclined his head and she spun, marching toward the elevators as if she really did have a room at the hotel. She felt Erik watching her, but by the time she had hit the button for the elevator, she was aware of his absence. She scanned the lobby, already knowing that he was gone.

She told herself not to be disappointed.

It was better this way.

Eileen was still trying to persuade herself of that when she grabbed a cab at the back exit from the hotel. No luck. She was freezing cold, maybe from the shocks she'd had. She tugged her purple sheepskin coat a little closer as the cab raced through quiet back streets. She felt vulnerable in Erik's absence, which she didn't like much.

At least she wasn't raging with desire anymore.

Or not quite as much. It was too easy to think about the way Erik smiled when he was surprised. It was as if a crack had been exposed in his armor. He looked less predatory then, but no less intense. Eileen swallowed as she wondered whether he would smile in bed.

She could make him smile.

Ha. She started to plan how before she caught herself.

But she probably wasn't ever going to see Erik Sorensson again. It was that simple and it was easier that way. Eileen dug the keys to Lynne's house out of her pocket.

She couldn't have seen dragons fighting at the Fonthill-Fergusson Foundation, could she?

Her gaze fell to the wooden chest of teeth, teeth big enough to be dragon teeth, and her conviction of what was and what was not possible wavered.

Had Teresa really been shot twice, shot dead, right before her eyes? Eileen closed her eyes and saw Teresa bleeding, the foundation's vault burning, the security guard's blood on the wall.

Eileen felt herself begin to shake. She was more than cold; she was chilled to her very marrow. In the middle of the night, alone in the back of a cab in a foreign city, was precisely the wrong time and place to review her adventure.

But she couldn't push the images from her mind. Her coat even smelled a bit like smoke, and that box nudged against her ankles.

Leaving Erik behind suddenly didn't seem like a very good choice.

Chapter 4

The cab finally pulled onto Lynne's street and Eileen shoved her notebook back into her satchel. She pointed out the house, paid her fare, and rummaged for her keys. On this particular night, she was glad that the cabdriver waited—it was very courteous of him—and waved to him once she had unlocked the door.

She tried to move quietly, since she assumed that everyone would be asleep. There was a light on at the top of the stairs, and Lynne called out, "That you, Eileen?"

"Me." She locked the door. "The dead bolt is locked."

"Thanks. There's a pot of herbal tea in the kitchen. It might still be hot."

"Thanks, Lynne. Good night."

The light snicked off, leaving the orange glow of the night-light at the top of the stairs. Didn't it figure that Lynne had waited up for her? Eileen smiled with affection, knowing that Lynne's two daughters would destroy her sister's sleep for years once they became teenagers.

The rhythm of Lynne's house was wonderfully normal. Eileen stood for a moment and savored it. The dragons under her nieces' beds and lurking in their closets were utterly fictional.

There was something to be said for that.

Eileen got a cup of tea—it was warm—and hauled her stuff up to the spare bedroom. That room faced the street. Eileen turned on the light by the bed, then reached to close the drapes.

A large black sedan was easing down the street. It paused directly in front of the house, its brake lights glowing red against the night.

Like embers in a fire.

Like dragon eyes in the night.

Eileen closed the drapes fast and leaned back against the wall. Her heart was pumping and her breath came quickly. That was Magnus's car. She knew it.

And he knew exactly where she was.

Eileen's gaze fell on the wooden chest. What would he do to get it? She saw Teresa's bleeding body in her mind's eye and began to tremble. Violence could happen again. She was in her sister's house, with her sister and her nieces and her brother-in-law sleeping just across the hall. She caught her breath at their vulnerability.

Erik had said she could trust him to protect her.

Did she dare?

Eileen peeked around the edge of the drapes, but the big sedan was gone. The street was empty, right to the end of the block in either direction.

She knew she hadn't imagined the car.

And she didn't imagine for a minute that Magnus was gone for good.

She needed a plan.

Erik followed Eileen's cab, lured by the heat of the firestorm. He settled on the roof of the small house in Notting Hill where she had taken refuge and settled to the task of breathing dragonsmoke. He had a niggling sense of Magnus's presence and didn't like it one bit.

Erik sent his smoke cascading over the shingles, down over the eaves, breathing an endless stream. He wove it around the house, ensnaring the building in a protective cocoon.

The dragonsmoke was a territory mark, one that could not be breached by another *Pyr* or *Slayer* without Erik's express permission. It was also invisible to humans. Erik breathed slowly and deeply, exhaling an unbroken ribbon to protect his mate for the night. He created a barrier of smoke, thicker and deeper than was strictly necessary, but he could not stop.

Erik was afraid.

He felt Magnus retreat, but knew the *Slayer* had not gone far. Magnus was simply awaiting his moment. Erik wanted to ensure that there never was such a moment. He sensed other *Slayers* as well, and knew there would be a long line of candidates anxious to prevent the successful completion of Erik's firestorm.

The easiest way to accomplish that was always to slaughter the prospective human mate. Erik hated that Magnus had Eileen's scent.

He hoped that Eileen would keep her promise, and that her relinquishing the Dragon's Teeth to anyone else would make her more safe.

With the firestorm burning hot, though, he didn't truly believe it. He wasn't convinced that Eileen would keep her promise, or that if she did, it would be in the way he expected. His mate in this incarnation was far less predictable than she had once been.

And even Louisa had surprised him.

Erik breathed dragonsmoke until it resonated with the crystalline ping of a secure territory mark. He closed his eyes and breathed some more, reinforcing what he had done well beyond what was reasonable or necessary.

"More is better?" a woman asked, amusement in her tone.

Erik gritted his teeth at the familiarity of that voice. A chat with the Wyvern, as infuriating as she could be, was the last way he would have chosen to end the evening's festivities.

Erik opened his eyes to find Sophie, the Wyvern, in her human form. She leaned against the chimney, her feet braced on the ridgepole, her blond hair flicking in the wind. She smiled.

"I have no problems with that philosophy," he said, knowing he sounded as irked as he was.

Sophie folded her arms across her chest and Erik had the sense that she knew something he didn't. "What if it's not enough?"

"I'll breathe more."

"What if dragonsmoke, regardless of quantity, isn't enough?" She tilted her head to study him. "You know the verse, don't you?"

"Sacrifice," Erik said. The very idea sent a chill through him, reminding him that there were no guarantees in a firestorm. He wouldn't jeopardize Eileen's safety, although he suspected he couldn't ensure her safety alone.

He swallowed his pride and admitted to his new, troubling weakness. "I can't see my own future; you must know that." Sophie inclined her head slightly in agreement. "Will you help me? If not for my sake, then for the *Pyr* and for Eileen?"

She studied him for so long that he thought she would decline, and when she spoke, her voice was soft. "Which comes first in your affections? You, the *Pyr*, or Eileen?"

It was a test, but not a very complicated one.

"The *Pyr*, of course! Leading them is my responsibility. . . ." Erik hadn't even finished his argument before Sophie shook her head. She sighed with what might have been regret and faded away as surely as if she had never been present.

Erik looked around but knew what he would find. She was gone.

"Wrong answer," she whispered in old-speak.

But how could Erik have answered any other way? He had told her the truth. Leading the *Pyr* to success was the most important thing to Erik. He was prepared to sacrifice himself to ensure the *Pyr*'s triumph. He would not sacrifice his mate, as that defeated the *Pyr*'s objective to breed. It would also be a betrayal of the bond between himself and Eileen, however tenuous it was as yet.

He'd betrayed Louisa once, after all, and didn't want to repeat that mistake.

But Sophie had expected a different answer from him. Which one? Erik sat down on the roof to think, despite his frustration.

He had some time to fill, after all.

The black sedan decided everything for Eileen.

Magnus was in that car, and Magnus wanted the wooden chest with the big teeth in it. The guys who had broken into the Fonthill-Fergusson Foundation were somehow associated with Magnus, and they'd killed Teresa without a moment's hesitation.

Never mind remorse. Eileen didn't dare risk her sister and her sister's family.

She had to leave Lynne's house. She chose to believe that her experience—or delusion—of this night was a sign. She had come to England seeking more details of a story known as the Dragon Lover of Madeley and now, against all expectation, she had seen dragons. She had been rescued—twice—by one particular dragon.

Although this was weird, Eileen was better disposed than most people to believe her own eyes. After all, she collected urban myths for a living. Sometimes the stories of things that went bump in the night could be attributed to some other reasonable cause. Sometimes they couldn't. Eileen had long ago made her peace with the possibility that there might be a whole lot more going on in the world than she and her fellow humans realized.

For the moment, she was less concerned with the fact that she was seeing dragons than with what she should do to evade them. Giving up the wooden chest was a possibility, but Eileen didn't think that would ensure her safety. She doubted that Magnus and his vicious pals would just let her walk away.

There was the principle, too. Teresa had died for those teeth. Eileen was going to figure out their value—even if it killed her.

That wasn't as funny as she'd hoped it would be.

The town of Ironbridge—in the old parish of Madeley—was as good a destination as any. Eileen's return ticket to Boston was Sunday. She'd planned to spend the weekend with Lynne, but Eileen could reorganize her schedule.

She *had* to reorganize her schedule.

It was also true that she'd just returned from Ironbridge, but she was pretty sure that she'd missed something there. This was as good a time as any to return and find out.

Eileen eyed the wooden chest and thought about its contents. She'd promised Erik that she'd talk to someone, and she would. She'd call this Rafferty Powell whom Teresa had mentioned.

She just wouldn't do it immediately.

Erik would never know the difference.

Eileen refused to feel disappointed that she was leaving him behind. The man was trouble. Never mind that he looked good enough to eat. Never mind that she literally sizzled in his presence. He invaded her dreams and clearly lived a dangerous life. She should be glad to be eliminating all prospect of crossing paths with him.

Except she wasn't quite.

Eileen checked her train schedule and found that the first train she could take departed at six ten the next morning. It seemed like an eternity away—four whole hours!—but it would have to do.

She removed the teeth from their distinctive wooden chest

and laid them across the top of the desk. The spare room also was Lynne's sewing room, where she made her gorgeous art quilts. Eileen quietly rummaged in the closet and appropriated some squares of fabric. She wrapped each tooth separately, then nestled them successively into her overnight bag. She closed the empty chest and put it by the door, her overnight bag beside it.

Then she packed for herself, putting her few toiletries and a change of clothing into her battered leather satchel. Her notebook was there, of course, as well as her identification. Eileen wasn't much for purses—a purse was just one more thing to carry—so her satchel did double duty.

She peeked out the window but the street was still empty. That didn't reassure her one bit.

Eileen found some stationery in the desk and addressed an envelope to Lynne at this very address. She thought for a moment of what to say, then knew.

> *Lynne—*
> *If I don't see you before my flight home, please take this to an antiquities dealer named Rafferty Powell. He should know what to do.*
> *Love, Eileen*

Eileen already had a roll of stamps. She put far too much postage on the envelope and left it unsealed. Then she addressed and stamped a bunch of postcards that she had yet to mail, hiding the envelope in their midst.

Three and a half hours to go. Eileen drummed her fingers and checked her watch several times in rapid succession. Going to a train station in the middle of the night was a worse idea than sitting here waiting.

All the same, she didn't want to awaken the household.

Eileen forced herself to think about her work instead. The Dragon Lover of Madeley was the story that had brought her to England in the first place. It was currently her favorite story, a kind of urban myth from before the days of big cities. People still had nightmares and fears of bogeymen, and it reassured her on this particular evening to be reminded that she wasn't the only one with dragons on the brain.

This story, though, had seized her imagination more than any other story she'd collected. It had haunted her. It might have been trying to tell her something—even if she wasn't having a lot of luck figuring out what it was.

In her rare whimsical moments, Eileen believed that the story held a clue to her niggling lost memory.

Either way, someone else's story might be the perfect distraction. She rummaged in her satchel and pulled out her notebook. She reviewed her notes again, seeking the clue she had missed, even though she already knew every word on every page. She needed a better plan in Ironbridge. Just hours ago, she'd been irritated with her own failure to add to the details she knew.

Funny how it no longer seemed like such a wasted trip.

His name was Erik Sorensson.

Eileen wondered whether she could Google him.

She booted up her laptop immediately, glad to have something else to do. The only Erik Sorensson she could find was a pyrotechnics designer in Chicago. He had a Web site and had won a number of awards for timing fireworks to music. There was even a video of one such display, but Eileen's laptop didn't have enough memory to download it quickly.

Wrong Erik Sorensson.

Eileen supposed that dragons weren't usually in the white pages. They probably didn't have driver's licenses, credit cards, or e-mail accounts. They probably didn't officially exist.

Maybe it would be better to consider Erik a figment of her imagination.

Disgruntled and impatient, Eileen lay on the bed in her clothes and stared at the ceiling, trying not to jump at every little sound.

* * *

Eileen must have slept, because she dreamed.

She dreamed of a child, a beautiful baby boy wrapped in a lace christening gown so fine and intricate that could have been from another age. She'd had this dream before, and as previously it made her smile. It lightened her heart and created a warm glow deep inside of her.

This was the sum of the dream: She held a new baby.

But it was so much more than that.

Eileen cradled the baby boy reverently, his chubby fingers locked around her index finger as he dozed in her arms. He blew small bubbles as he slept, and she watched them rise on the pink curve of his tiny lips. The fair hair on his head was as soft as down and as golden as sunlight.

He was beautiful.

He was perfect.

He was her own child. In her dream, Eileen knew it. She nestled him close and marveled at him. In her dream, she was exhausted but chose not to sleep.

She didn't want to close her eyes, in case her baby boy vanished while she slept. Her heart was bursting with love, her body sore from the delivery, her breasts aching with the burden of milk.

He slept and she watched, and the time slipped away.

The dream was precisely as it had been the thousand or so times she'd had it.

But this time, when Eileen awakened, her cheeks were wet with tears. The sweet love that had enveloped her clung to her heart, tempting her with what was not.

What would never be.

Eileen had no child and she was realistic enough to doubt that she ever would. She was thirty-seven. She was divorced. She had never been pregnant. She had a talent for picking men who quickly slid past their best-before date. She was a serial monogamist who had never had a relationship last more than two years.

Lately they'd been getting shorter. Maybe she just saw the signs earlier. Maybe she was just fed up with games. Maybe her expectations were too high.

Either way, she wasn't likely to be having any babies.

Relationships aside, Eileen had been the pillar of emotional support while her sister endured three years of fertility treatments. While she loved her nieces to pieces—as she often told them—Eileen knew she would never go that route herself.

She and Lynne had a lot of things in common and, given that she was the elder sister, Eileen would have bet on a reluctant uterus being another one.

She had made her peace with her reality a long time ago. Her life was good. She was happy.

Even if this recurring dream hadn't gotten the memo.

It was 5:15 and still dark. Eileen brushed away her tears with impatient fingertips and headed to the bathroom.

Eileen was making a pot of coffee when Lynne appeared in the kitchen doorway.

"What are you doing up so early?" As if to emphasize her point that sane people were still asleep, Lynne yawned and stretched with elegance Eileen couldn't emulate. Even sleepy and rumpled, Eileen's younger sister was gorgeous.

To be fair, Lynne couldn't help it. The red hair that ran in their family had found its best expression in Lynne's luxuriously wavy auburn tresses. Her deep blue eyes were almond shaped and tipped up exotically at the outer corners. Somehow she'd been given the gift of dark, thick lashes—unlike Eileen's reddish ones. Lynne was so tall and slender that even after she'd borne two children, it was easy to believe that she'd been a successful model.

That glamorous career had been before Roger and the girls, but Eileen knew Lynne's relocation to London for her work had led to her ultimate happiness. Theirs was an enviably good marriage, and being their guest always made

Eileen both happy for her sister and aware of her own solitude.

I'm happy, Eileen reminded herself, trying to dispel the lingering shards of her dream. She told herself that she just needed a coffee and some sleep. "I have a train to catch," she said with a smile.

That jolted Lynne awake. "But I was looking forward to our having some time together."

Eileen immediately felt guilty, but she knew she had to leave to ensure Lynne's safety. "I'll try to be back early Sunday, I promise. I just have to make one more quick trip."

Lynne looked skeptical. "Right. You'll come racing back in here with just enough time to get to Heathrow for your flight."

Eileen fidgeted, just a bit, at this slice of probability. She wouldn't come back at all unless she knew for sure that Magnus wasn't following her. "Well, I am here on a research sabbatical and I had an idea."

Lynne snorted. "What's his name?"

"I beg your pardon?"

"Don't pretend," Lynne scolded. "Your idea has a name."

Eileen blushed, even though there was no man. She was thinking of Erik and the way he made her tingle. "No, that's not it."

"Uh-huh." Lynne gave Eileen an assessing look, then opened the fridge to get cream.

Eileen knew her sister well enough to sense that Lynne was biting her tongue. "Go on. Say it."

"Say what?"

"Whatever you're pretending you're not going to say."

Lynne leaned against the fridge. "Don't take this the wrong way—"

"Oh, there's a bad opening."

"I know, but you asked."

"Spill it."

"Have you ever thought about this ability of yours to date

only men who can't or won't make a long-term commitment?"

"Unlucky in love, I guess," Eileen said lightly. "You're the one who used to joke about having to kiss too many frogs."

Lynne didn't smile. "No. I think you do it on purpose."

Eileen blinked. "What?"

"You're the most intuitive person I've ever known, Eileen. You follow hunches and find connections that no one else ever imagined existed." Lynne crossed the room, flinging out her hands for emphasis. "You're a brilliant scholar because of it, but you can't find a decent date to save your life. That doesn't make sense."

"Maybe I'm unlucky."

"Maybe it's the men you pick." Lynne met her gaze and spoke softly. "Maybe you pick the crummy ones on purpose."

Eileen grabbed the coffeepot, letting her sister see her annoyance. "That would be really stupid. Really, really stupid."

"And you're not stupid." Lynne looked wide-awake. "So, the rational conclusion is that you're avoiding intimacy on purpose."

"I get lots of intimacy, thanks."

"I'm not talking about sex. I'm talking about love."

Eileen poured two mugs of coffee, unsettled by her sister's comments. "I don't want to talk about this."

"I think we need to."

"You're forgetting Joe. Once burned, twice shy and all that." She pushed a mug of coffee across the counter to Lynne. "I wouldn't be the first one to be more cautious after a divorce."

"Except that I think your marriage was an expression of the same thing." Lynne stirred sugar into her coffee. "No one but you ever imagined that Joe was the marrying kind." She grimaced. "Mom said at the wedding that you weren't changing your name because you knew it, too."

Eileen sat down on a stool, surprised. "I didn't know that."

"Eileen, I don't think you were fooled. I think you knew that he would screw around. I think you knew it was only a matter of time. I think you thought you should get married, but you didn't want to get hurt, so you deliberately chose a man who wasn't worth trusting." Lynne arched a brow as she sipped her coffee. "Or maybe even loving."

Eileen drank her coffee, not really tasting it. "You make me sound so calculating."

"No. I think it's smart, in a way. Defensive. You didn't invest emotionally, so you didn't get hurt—but all along you were doing the so-called right thing. You just waited for the shoe to drop and when it did, you were gone." Lynne fixed Eileen with a look. "No tears."

"I cried!"

"Not much."

Eileen was insulted. She felt attacked first thing in the morning, even though she knew Lynne was trying to help.

Lynne put down her cup. "Look, Eileen, I just want you to be happy. . . ."

"Maybe I don't want what you have. I love my work. Marriage and babies aren't the answer for everyone, Lynne."

"No, they're not, but I don't think you want to be alone."

"I think you're wrong. What about Nigel? Don't I get a few months to mend my broken heart?"

Lynne snorted. "What about Nigel? Are you really telling me that my brilliant big sister had no clue that he was married?"

Eileen averted her gaze. She *had* had a suspicion that he was lying.

And she hadn't truly been surprised. Not right to her bones. In fact, she'd thought after leaving his apartment—and being greeted there by his wife—that she'd decided to surprise Nigel on purpose, following her instinct to "out" him and his lies.

Lynne caught her hand. "You have to see that if you never

take a chance, you never have a chance." She squeezed Eileen's fingers. "I want to see you happy, big sis, that's all."

Eileen forced a smile. "With a man and two-point-two babies, a house and a mortgage and a golden retriever?"

Lynne shook her head. "I don't care about the trappings. You're just way too interesting to be alone." She smiled.

Eileen forced a smile, recognizing that her sister was trying to make peace. "You're pretty profound this early in the morning."

"If it's the only chance I have to talk to you, I'll take it. I've been thinking about this for a long time."

Eileen poured the rest of her coffee down the drain and checked her watch. "Well, you can stop thinking about it. You're wrong."

"Really?" Lynne's eyes were cat-bright, a sure sign that she was convinced otherwise. "Don't you think collecting urban myths is a lot like living vicariously?"

Eileen bristled to find even her choice of specialty under attack. "What do you mean by that?"

"I mean you're writing down other people's stories instead of living your own."

Eileen stared at her sister in surprise, hearing a peal of truth in her words.

"Trust your instincts, Eileen. You do in every other facet of your life and they're good. Trust them with men, too."

Eileen heard Erik telling her to trust him in that velvety deep voice. There was a man who was trouble in spades. Her instinct had been to trust him, which showed how reliable it was as a guide.

Eileen pulled on her coat with impatience. "Well, sorry to disappoint, but this is really a research lead. I need to go back to Ironbridge once more before I go home."

"No man involved?"

"No."

"Well, keep your eyes open, big sis. The best ones lurk in unlikely places."

"Like frogs," Eileen joked.

Lynne grinned. "Princes in disguise."

Eileen gave Lynne a tight hug and wished one more time that they didn't live so far apart.

"No hurt feelings?" Lynne asked, pulling back to look at Eileen's eyes.

"No. I know you mean well." She grinned. "Even if you are completely wrong." She caught a glimpse of the wall clock. "Gotta go," she said, and hugged Lynne again. "You be good."

Lynne wagged a finger at her. "And you be careful."

"I thought I was supposed to follow my instincts," Eileen teased. She waited just long enough to see exasperation cross her sister's face before she laughed and left.

Eileen headed for the train station with the wooden chest in one hand and the overnight bag in the other, her satchel over her shoulder. Although it was still dark, she was relieved not to be walking in the rain for once. She had intended to take the tube, but decided it would have been awkward to carry luggage. She grabbed a cab instead, then found herself scanning the traffic for big black sedans.

None.

She wasn't reassured.

She tried not to think about Lynne's comments. The problem was that there was a core of truth in her sister's observation. It was true that she had rotten luck with men, that she always picked the one who would be unfaithful—like her ex, Joe—or the one who didn't want to make a commitment, the one who was bisexual, the one who was a chronic liar, the one who was married already . . . the list went on and on.

But Eileen was never surprised by the revelation. She could always see the pattern in hindsight, could always remember the conversations when she'd wondered. No matter how big the revelation, it was never a shock.

She cried over a lot of things—lost opportunities, friends

shot dead by thieves, babies who would never be born—but not men. She certainly hadn't cried over Nigel. She'd shed a couple of tears over Joe, but even at the time she'd thought he wasn't worth that much grief.

Could Lynne be right?

Eileen dated a lot and never had trouble finding a man who was interested in her. In a way, though, it was wearying to have every relationship be short-term. She could joke that variety was the spice of life, but she had to wonder.

Was it really that she was unlucky in love—or were her own choices shaping her luck?

At Euston Station, Eileen checked her overnight bag into a locker. She quickly rolled the locker key in another piece of fabric and pushed it into the envelope addressed to Lynne, the one with too many stamps and the note. She sealed the envelope, mixed it into the middle of the postcards, then went to a newsstand to mail them.

She handed them to the man who was selling papers and magazines, waiting while he checked that they all had stamps. She glanced over the shiny magazines and newspapers, the racks of gum and candy, then froze.

Bloody Heist Leaves Two Dead! screamed the headline on one newspaper. The accompanying picture was of sunglasses, broken and spattered with blood.

Eileen blinked. She knew those sunglasses. They were the security guard's sunglasses, at the Fonthill-Fergusson Foundation.

Eileen had to turn away before she was sick. The coffee churned in her stomach and her thoughts spun. It had really happened. Teresa was dead. The security guard had been shot. It was harder to pretend otherwise in the gray light of morning, with newspaper headlines announcing the truth.

"How tragic," said a man beside her. He had a French accent and his voice was uncommonly deep. The cadence of his words was melodic.

She gave him the barest glance, assuming that she was in

his way. "Excuse me," she said, gripping her belongings and meaning to step past him.

He stepped into her path again and she looked at his face. He was handsome, even though there was a harsh set to his lips. There was a bandage on his throat, one that rose above his shirt collar and looked starkly white against his tanned skin. His hair was a chestnut brown, his eyes as dark as chocolate.

And there were flames dancing in their depths.

"There's no reason to excuse yourself," he said smoothly. There was something odd about his voice. It was hypnotic, as if it dripped into her thoughts and turned them in other directions. "It's quite natural to be upset. What is the world coming to?"

"What is the world coming to," she found herself echoing.

What was going on? She sounded as if she were a thousand years old.

"Let me help you with that," he said, and reached for the handles of the wooden chest.

Eileen glanced down and reason seemed to reclaim her thoughts.

He had flames in his eyes. That wasn't normal.

Erik had said that the dragon men were called the *Pyr*.

That meant *fire*.

This guy had a chest wound.

Her intuition put two and two together. There had to be good *Pyr* and bad *Pyr*. Eileen knew exactly who Frenchie was and what he wanted. She also knew she wasn't going to give it to him.

Eileen shoved him aside, so hard that he stumbled, and ran.

When Frenchie followed, she broke into a gallop. She pushed her way through the crowd, using the wooden chest as a means of breaking trail, and didn't look back. She hoped Erik had injured Frenchie enough that he wouldn't be able to keep up.

Eileen's heart was thudding. People cursed as she pushed them aside. She heard Frenchie shout after her but didn't look back.

The clock at the end of the next platform said 6:04. A lot could happen in six minutes. Her train's platform was at the other side of the station and she halfway expected an interception. She couldn't see anyone moving toward her. Eileen glanced back.

There was no sign of Frenchie.

She knew better than to believe he'd given up. He might have help—like the gold dragon who had snatched her.

The one who had shot Teresa twice.

Or Magnus.

Eileen felt sick. She bobbed and weaved through the crowd, ducking and feinting. She took a tortuous path to her platform, leaving the train station by one exit and returning by another entrance. There was still no sign of Frenchie when she reached her platform.

Her train was idling on the tracks, and Eileen dared to feel a bit relieved.

It was 6:08.

If Frenchie didn't know what train she caught, he might not be able to follow her. Certainly Magnus couldn't follow the train easily in his car. She was almost in the clear.

She was feeling warm again, probably from anxiety and from running. She strode down the platform double-quick, ducking around people and luggage carts to disguise her presence. She'd open her coat once she was safely on the train.

Eileen darted toward a car with an open door. She tightened her grip on the handles of the wooden box, preparing to heft it high to climb the steps, and was shocked when someone lifted it out of her hand from behind.

"You promised," Erik hissed.

Chapter 5

Something wicked was in the air and, worse, it was new. Sophie couldn't pinpoint the force with any precision. She flew into the deepest tinge of the new stain in the air, hoping it didn't draw her to Magnus's dark academy. She hoped that he hadn't added some new horror to his arsenal.

The taint led her to Chicago.

A confused Sophie found herself near Erik's lair, the malice in the air growing with every beat of her wings. The stench of it was thick here, dark enough to singe her lungs.

But Erik was in London. She had just spoken with him on the roof of the house where his mate had taken refuge. Sophie didn't doubt that Erik had breathed a deep layer of protective smoke around his lair before he departed. It was entirely possible that one of the other *Pyr* had remained to guard it.

But Sophie couldn't sense any *Pyr*.

She smelled *Slayer*.

In choosing the shadow over the light, in denying the divine spark of the Great Wyvern within himself, a *Slayer's* blood turned from red to black. His scent changed as a result, taking on the scorched tinge of destruction, a smell that couldn't be mistaken for anything else.

Sophie approached Erik's lair with caution. It was quiet in the area filled with old warehouses, as many still stood empty and derelict. Sophie eased closer, taking in the *Slayer*'s scent in the hope of identifying him. Her hackles rose in sudden recognition.

Boris Vassily.

Sophie had no doubt. The leader of the *Slayer*s had captured and tortured Sophie just a year before. The cut below Sophie's wing still ached at the torment she had endured, the injury that Boris had ordered. She would never forget his scent. She had thought she might die then, a Wyvern in *Slayer* captivity, but she had survived with Sara's help.

There would always be another Wyvern born to the *Pyr*, although none could say when or where. Sophie, however, hadn't been quite ready to die.

That incident had tugged her from the aloof position traditionally held by the Wyvern right into the battle of *Pyr* against *Slayer*. She didn't want to sit back and observe— Sophie wanted to help the *Pyr* win.

No Wyvern had actively engaged so consistently in the past. At most, each Wyvern made one intervention in her lifetime. Sophie had a growing sense that she was courting her own destruction, but she couldn't stop and let the *Pyr* lose.

Boris's scent reminded her all too clearly of the price she might pay, the price she had nearly paid a year before.

But the whiff of his scent made no sense. Boris had been killed by Erik the previous summer. Erik had ensured that Boris's corpse was exposed to the four elements, so that the leader of the *Slayers* couldn't be revived or turned to a shadow dragon.

Sophie smelled Boris all the same. Her nose defied the truth she had been told. It was impossible.

Or was it? She feared again what Magnus might have done.

Or what lost lore he might remember.

Sophie saw Boris a heartbeat later. He was immediately outside Erik's lair. She shifted to become a small white salamander and hid in the cracks between the bricks of the building. Her body became the same color as the mortar, hiding her completely.

She was still afraid to be so close to Boris, but she watched.

Boris was pale and feral as ever in his human form. Sophie heard the clear, resonant ring of Erik's dragonsmoke and saw that it was woven high and deep. It was one of the best territory rings Sophie had ever seen, almost as good as the one Erik had just breathed in Notting Hill. She felt a certain satisfaction that Boris wouldn't be able to breach it.

Sophie hoped Boris tried. She would like to see him destroyed by dragonsmoke. She would like to watch the dragonsmoke singe him, suck the life out of him, and leave nothing but a charred shell behind. It wasn't like Sophie to be vindictive, but Boris had changed that.

She hated him.

Boris's manner was furtive. He looked to the left. He looked to the right. He sniffed, as if he sensed the presence of another of his kind, but even with his keen eyesight, he wouldn't be able to see Sophie at this distance.

She shuddered all the same.

Then Boris lifted a talon. He was in human form, but had a dragon talon on his right index finger. Sophie didn't believe her eyes. Boris was hovering between forms.

And he held the shift at only his right talon.

Neither *Pyr* nor *Slayer* hovered between forms: Once the shift began, it was impossible to stop, although a few *Pyr* learned to shift more slowly or to hesitate during the change.

Boris was frozen between the two forms.

To Sophie's further surprise, Boris used that talon to slice an opening in the dragonsmoke. Sophie gaped. Erik's dragonsmoke was breached, but it still rang true.

Sophie was shocked to her marrow. Neither *Pyr* nor *Slayer* could cross dragonsmoke without the express permission of the dragon who had breathed it—and live to tell about the deed. It was impossible for Boris to be doing what he was doing.

But he did it all the same.

Only the Wyvern could breach dragonsmoke unscathed.

Only the Wyvern could hover between forms, if she so chose.

Sophie's eyes widened as she thought of the other feats she could do.

How was Boris stealing her tricks?

Had he adopted them all?

Meanwhile, Boris severed the dragonsmoke to the ground. He let his nail shift back to human form.

Then he stepped through the breach in human form. Sophie gasped and sputtered. The dragonsmoke did not injure him. There was no mistaking the evidence of her eyes. Boris picked the lock on the door and entered Erik's lair, unscathed.

It was up to Sophie to stop him.

Somehow.

Sophie materialized in Erik's lair, her manner watchful.

Boris was in the room where Erik secured his hoard. How had he done that? It was less important to know how Boris had foiled Erik's defenses than that he had.

For the moment.

It certainly wasn't a time to be offended that some *Slayer* had usurped the abilities that should have belonged to the Wyvern alone.

Even if that made Sophie furious.

She eased closer to the hoard, seething at Boris's audacity. She heard him rummaging and wondered what he sought. Erik's hoard was very orderly—what reason was there to make so much noise?

She knew the answer a beat later.

She reached the door leading to Erik's hoard and glanced back at some minute sound; then Boris seized her by the throat.

"I thought that would tempt you closer," he said, bringing his face near to hers. "You're too curious for a Wyvern. Aren't you supposed to be above earthly concerns?"

Sophie caught her breath when his grip tightened. She could feel the sharp edge of his talon digging into her throat.

It couldn't be an accident that it was right over her carotid artery. Sophie didn't dare move.

She saw that Boris held the Dragon's Egg in his other hand, the obsidian sphere of stone freed from its velvet sack.

"What are you doing with the Dragon's Egg?" she asked in old-speak.

"Guess."

"You can't steal it."

"I could, but I'll do better than that." The hatred in his eyes made Sophie catch her breath. "I'll destroy it instead."

"No!"

"Yes." Boris leaned his cold smile close to Sophie's face. "The *Pyr* learn too much from this chunk of stone."

"You can't destroy the Dragon's Egg. It's forbidden—"

Boris interrupted her with a laugh. "Just as it's forbidden to destroy you?" Sophie felt her eyes widen, but Boris just smiled. "How accommodating of you to provide for one-stop shopping."

"I thought you were dead."

Boris chuckled. "I guess you were wrong." He stroked her skin with the edge of his nail, as if choosing a spot to slice.

"It is forbidden to injure the Wyvern."

Boris laughed. "I'm not going to start playing by the rules now." His grip tightened just a bit, as if he would remind her of who was in control. "In fact, I've decided that you are far too helpful to the *Pyr*. The Wyvern should be remote, unseen, uninvolved in the matters of the world. I can fix that."

Sophie flushed, because there was truth in his accusation. *"The Wyvern is obligated to aid the cause of righteousness,"* she said quickly. *"And these times demand more of me."*

"No," Boris said with finality. "Only one of us can challenge the rules, and that will be me." His talon dug deeper with sudden force and Sophie caught her breath at the pain. She gasped at the warm trickle of her own blood on her skin.

"Ready to die, Sophie?" Boris murmured in old-speak.

Sophie became aware of another presence in Erik's lair just before she saw him.

Nikolas.

The ancient *Pyr* raged toward Boris, shifting into an anthracite dragon en route. He bellowed and blew a fearsome stream of dragonfire.

Boris pivoted quickly, positioning Sophie between himself and Nikolas. Nikolas froze and stared, his breath coming in furious puffs of dragonsmoke. He was enormous and livid. When he remained still, he glittered coldly. His gaze was calculating.

"You have no scent," Boris accused. "How can this be?"

Nikolas's smile was predatory. "Perhaps you are not the only one who breaks rules." His tone turned deadly. "Release the Wyvern."

"It's not that simple," Boris said.

Sophie saw Nikolas's eyes narrow with the same suspicion she felt.

"You see," Boris said conversationally, "you'll have to choose."

Before Nikolas could reply, Boris hurled the Dragon's Egg toward the window. The glass bricks shattered beneath the impact of the large stone in the same moment that Boris's talon dug deeply into Sophie's neck.

Sophie screamed.

The Dragon's Egg plummeted toward the pavement six stories below.

Nikolas chose.

Chapter 6

Erik was livid. His mate seemed determined to put herself in the path of destruction. He knew she didn't understand fully about *Slayer*s or the danger of the Dragon's Teeth, but she had broken her promise to him.

He had come too close to seeing Jorge and Mallory claim her.

And he had no patience with people who didn't tell the truth.

Eileen had to hear his anger, but she wasn't afraid of him. She met his gaze and lifted her chin, her lips setting stubbornly as she reached for the handles of the wooden chest.

"Give that back to me." Her fingers closed on nothing as Erik held it out of her range.

"You promised me that you would talk to someone about this. You promised you would put it out of your possession."

She snatched for the handles again and he let her catch them. She tugged but Erik didn't let go. "I didn't say when. I have something to do first."

He leaned closer and saw her eyes wide with awareness.

At least he wasn't the only one snared in the heat of the firestorm.

"Look back down the platform," he murmured. "Do you see a short man with dark hair?"

Eileen didn't look. "Frenchie. He's wearing a green sweater." She wrinkled her nose. "Machine knit."

How did she know Mallory?

"He talked to me at the newsstand. He had flames in his eyes. And he has a bandage on his throat, probably from when you hurt him last night."

Erik swore.

Eileen tugged the leather handles out of his grip. "You should have injured him more. He's the red dragon, isn't he?"

"He's been following you since you left the house," Erik told her, glad that she looked worried. He arched a brow and met her gaze, feeling the need to remind her of another falsehood. "Or should I say, since you left the Ritz?"

Eileen flushed.

Erik had a beat to feel triumphant before her eyes flashed. "There's only one way you could know that," she retorted. "You followed me, too."

"Of course I did. You have no idea what—or who—you're up against."

"I think I'm getting an idea." Her lips tightened. "Here they come."

Erik glanced over his shoulder, guessing what he'd see. He was right—Jorge and Mallory were walking down the platform together.

"They looked like trouble about to happen," Eileen murmured.

"Get on the train now." Erik spoke with authority. He saw defiance in her eyes and knew she wasn't much for following orders. "Jorge, the blond, shot your friend."

Eileen inhaled sharply and stepped into the train. She began to move down the car, Erik close behind her. The firestorm sizzled between them, making Erik keenly aware of the sway of her hips, the luster of her hair, the haunting familiarity of her perfume. She caught at his senses more surely than Louisa had—as if her character had been distilled and fortified into the most compelling and enticing woman possible.

There were few other passengers in the car, most already settling into their seats. She chose a pair of seats together and made to put down her satchel.

"Keep going," Erik commanded. "Into the next car."

"This is fine—" Eileen started to argue with him just as the door opened behind them. She paled and Erik knew whom she saw.

"Go!" Although Erik kept his tone low, his urgency must have been clear.

Eileen went. The two *Slayers* came into the same car just as she swung open the door to the next one.

The whistle blew. There was a vibration beneath their feet as the train prepared to depart. Eileen trotted down the half-empty car, her satchel bumping against her hip and the wooden chest in her arms. Erik knew it was futile to offer to help her again.

"There's only one more!" she said to Erik after she swung through the next door. Erik hauled the door closed behind them and kept walking.

They'd done this dead-end trick before, but Erik wasn't going to change shape this time.

He had a different idea that just might work. Eileen kept glancing over her shoulder at him, her agitation clear.

Was she trusting him, or simply out of options?

Just as the train began to move, they reached the last door, the one at the front of the car. Erik heard Eileen catch her breath. He looked over his shoulder to find Jorge and Mallory unable to get past a couple with a lot of luggage.

"Off," Erik said, gesturing to the steps.

Eileen nodded. "There's another train in half an hour."

Erik thought they'd worry about that if they survived the

next half hour, but didn't say so. There was no point in frightening her.

Eileen jumped from the moving train and Erik landed right behind her. Jorge and Mallory leapt out of the adjacent car, only thirty feet away from them. The four of them were the only people on the platform beside the slowly moving train.

But Jorge and Mallory were between them and the station.

Jorge reached into his jacket and Erik guessed he had a gun.

"Oh, no," Eileen whispered, and seemed struck to stone in her fear.

"This way!" Erik seized her hand and tugged.

A spark leapt between them, sending a sizzle over his skin. Eileen caught her breath, but Erik urged her down the platform in the same direction as the departing train.

"I'm trusting that you have a plan," she muttered.

"Good."

Erik heard Eileen grind her teeth in irritation.

He also heard Jorge's and Mallory's footfalls on the platform.

The train picked up speed, running right alongside them. One car passed them, then another, the train moving faster. Erik was counting under his breath. The end of the platform was drawing closer and he hoped that Eileen would trust him.

He pushed himself faster and she matched his speed, her hand fast in his. The conductor was slow to shut all of the doors, to Erik's relief.

"Erik . . ." she began, but it was time.

"Now!" he said, then caught her around the waist with one arm. The last door on the last car drew alongside them in the same moment and he jumped.

He caught the railing inside the door with his free hand and swung them onto the steps. His back collided with the steel of the train car and he held his mate fast. If Jorge had chosen to fire, the train would have protected them.

He didn't.

Eileen's feet were hanging in the air as the end of the platform slid out of sight. The firestorm blazed through his veins, making Erik tighten his grip on her as his breath was stolen away.

Eileen's hair tickled his chin; her curves pressed against him; that damn perfume tempted him with possibilities. He could feel her heartbeat under his palm, and caught his breath as his own matched its erratic pace.

He peered back in time to see Jorge and Mallory skid to a halt at the end of the platform. Erik could almost hear them calculating the merit of shifting shape to give chase. The adjacent platforms were crowded and he knew the instant they decided against it.

There would be too much beguiling to do.

They'd wait for their moment.

Jorge spat onto the tracks after the train. *"This isn't done,"* he muttered in old-speak, the threat echoing in Erik's thoughts.

Erik didn't grace the comment with a response. He simply held Jorge's gaze, knowing his own stare was cold and relentless. He would protect what was his own.

And that included Eileen.

"They won't give up," Eileen murmured.

Erik thought she was beginning to appreciate the depth of Magnus's desire for the Dragon's Teeth.

"No. They won't," he agreed, his words tight. He lifted her into the train and reluctantly released her.

The conductor stood on the top step, his expression severe as he surveyed the two of them. "You might arrive a mite sooner in future, and avoid such unnecessary exertion," he advised. He reached past them and closed the door with more force than was strictly necessary.

Eileen smiled an apology.

Erik didn't bother. He took the wooden chest from Eileen's limp fingers and moved into the car, seeking a pair of seats. He had time to believe that they had won a moment's reprieve; then the world was split asunder.

"You're pale," Eileen said with a frown. Her concern melted barriers within Erik that the firestorm left untouched.

"I'm fine." But Erik wasn't. He was jangled to his core.

It was more than the firestorm's force.

Something terrible had happened. He sat down, feeling unsteady on his feet, and wiped the perspiration from his brow.

"I don't think so." Eileen's annoyance was clear. "You can do anything else, but don't lie to me."

"Okay. I'm not fine."

She forced a smile, but still seemed to be worried. "Thank you for that. Now, tell me what's wrong."

Erik chose not to comment or explain. He'd felt the destruction of something elemental and didn't have to close his eyes to feel the increasing shadow cast by Magnus's dark academy. Even without knowing precisely what had happened, Erik understood that the odds had risen against the *Pyr* again.

Significantly.

He had to consummate his firestorm and return to the greater business at hand. He needed to seduce Eileen and steal the Dragon's Teeth from her.

As soon as possible.

He knew his responsibility and the easiest solution, and yet the prospect annoyed him. It should have been easy to do what he had to do, yet he met Eileen's worried gaze and felt opportunistic.

Mercenary.

Erik had claimed two window seats that faced each other and Eileen sank into the seat opposite him. Why couldn't the firestorm ever be simple? He put the wooden chest under the window and offered to lift Eileen's satchel onto the overhead shelf. She shook her head, hugging it close. She kept her coat on but opened it as she watched him warily.

He let her look.

And he looked back.

The sheepskin was just as vivid a purple as he recalled, while the heavy scarf wound around her neck was purple and gold and blue. Otherwise, she wore black from head to toe. Her only jewelry was a single amber pendant on a silver chain and a silver ring on her right thumb that looked like a braid. Her red-gold hair was long and wavy, unsuccessfully bound at her nape. Her skin was fair and her eyes were a remarkable shade of blue. Erik wondered whether they seemed a brighter sapphire because of her obvious intelligence.

She stretched out her legs, crossing her shapely ankles and leaning her feet against the wooden chest.

Message received. It was hers.

And possessing it made her a target. The idea terrified him. Erik had to get the Dragon's Teeth from Eileen before she was hurt. He had a feeling that she wouldn't be easily persuaded to part with her treasure, but he had no choice.

Erik leaned forward, bracing his elbows on his knees. As he drew closer to Eileen, he felt that increasingly familiar tingle sweep across his skin, a brushfire that could easily be coaxed to a conflagration. He held her gaze and watched her catch her breath.

"Okay," he said softly. "Ask." He'd let her choose the questions, even though it went against everything in him not to take command of the situation. It was a concession, but a small one. It was, he sensed, a critical one.

He was curious as to what questions she'd ask.

"What just happened? What upset you?"

"I'm not sure."

She rolled her eyes at that.

"No. I truly am not. Nothing good, that's for certain."

Eileen studied him for a moment; then her lips set with a

determination Erik was starting to recognize. "So, the blond one was the one who grabbed me last night?"

Erik nodded once, liking that she was being careful with her choice of words. The car wasn't full but it wasn't empty either. "Jorge. I don't know the dark *Slayer*'s name." He studied her for a moment. "Have you truly come to terms with what happened?"

"No. But I decided a long time ago that there could be more going on in the world than most of us know." Eileen arched a brow and smiled, the unexpectedness of her attitude shaking Erik's assumptions. "This definitely counts."

Their gazes locked for a charged moment; then she frowned. "Maybe after this is over, I'll have time to work out an alternative explanation, but for the moment there are other, more important issues."

"Like?"

"Surviving."

Erik respected her ability to prioritize.

Eileen rummaged in her satchel and pulled out a pair of knitting needles and some yarn. The yarn was thick and glossy, composed of different threads of rich colors. "Don't think you've gotten off easily," she warned him. "I have questions, but I do my best prioritizing while I knit."

Erik looked out the window. They were passing through the city, behind yards and industrial spaces, past graffiti and dirty underpasses. He couldn't see any sign of pursuit, but knew better than to believe that there wasn't any.

He tried to appear more relaxed than he was. He knew that the drumming of his fingers on his knee gave him away. He watched Eileen knit instead and found the repetitive motion of her fingers soothing.

"You were explaining that you followed me," Eileen said.

"You were explaining to me about the Ritz's unfortunate loss of your reservation."

Her laughter was quick and sent an equally rapid stab of

desire through him. "Would you expect me to tell every stranger I met where I was staying? I'm not stupid."

"Clearly not."

She smiled. "But I didn't see you."

Erik watched her dancing fingers. "Maybe you didn't glance up."

She looked out the window and frowned, and he regretted having reminded her of his nature. Then she turned to face him again, her eyes bright with curiosity. "Did you watch the house all night, then?" The idea didn't appear to trouble her.

"I kept vigil, yes." Erik cleared his throat. "Ensuring your safety is my responsibility."

"Like in the train station?"

Erik nodded.

"Is that why Magnus's car left last night?"

He was startled. "You saw him?"

"The black sedan parked right across the street, just after I went into the house."

Erik nodded, not truly surprised but disliking the news. "I thought he was close. Either he saw me or the dragonsmoke. He chose to wait for a better opportunity."

Eileen frowned at her work. "What's dragonsmoke?"

"That's complicated."

To his astonishment, she leaned forward, her eyes snapping. She rapped one needle on his knee. "No. That's not good enough."

"Excuse me?"

"No half measures or partial explanations." She waved her needle with such gusto that Erik drew back. "It's my new policy. I only do complete disclosure. No shared truths or 'I'll tell you in the morning.' Lay it all out. I can take the honesty. In fact, I prefer it."

Erik was astonished. Her lecture could have fallen from his own lips. "Why does that sound like a warning?"

"Because it is." She made a cutting motion with one hand. "I have zero patience left for liars."

Who had lied to her? Erik was curious.

"So I've been warned?" he teased, and that smile curved her lips again. Her smile made her look younger and more playful, and reminded him of sunlight dancing on water.

He regretted that they would be spending so little time together, that he wouldn't be able to see her smile more often.

"Consider yourself lucky," she said, her tone ominous. "I don't always fire a warning shot."

"I do consider myself lucky," Erik said softly.

Her smile faded as their gazes locked. Erik let her see his admiration. He leaned forward, letting his knee touch hers as the train rocked slightly. The spark lit there, then settled into a golden glow. He felt heat emanate from that point, a heat that moved across his flesh, arousing him beyond expectation. Eileen caught her breath, but she didn't move her knee away.

In fact, she pressed her leg against his, redoubling the heat of the firestorm. Erik was thinking about the musculature of her leg, the soft strength of her calf against his own. He was thinking about sliding his hand under the hem of her skirt, about caressing her knee, about letting his fingers slide higher. Her thighs would be soft and warm, and the scent of her perfume would be stronger as he moved higher. . . .

He was thinking about changing seats to the opposite side, to the seat directly beside her, of sliding his hands into the silken mass of her hair. He was remembering the taste of her lips and knew Eileen was thinking the same thing.

He felt her heartbeat accelerate and his matched its pace; her eyes sparkled and her lips parted in invitation. They stared at each other, their legs touching, and the heat in the train grew more intense. Erik watched Eileen, sensed the tingle of her desire grow to a roar, was sure he could feel the shiver slide over her flesh. He imagined his fingers slipping over her, thought of the taste and the softness of her, inhaled deeply of her perfume.

And was interrupted.

"Tickets, please."

* * *

Eileen thought that if she looked up *lust* in the dictionary, there'd be a picture of herself.

Or a picture of her and Erik necking.

The conductor checked his watch while she rummaged for her ticket. "And you, sir? Do you have a ticket?" His expression turned even more dour when Erik admitted that he had to buy a ticket. "Where to, sir?"

Erik looked at Eileen and she made a quick decision.

She wasn't quite ready to be rid of Erik Sorensson. And it wasn't just because it was good for her health to have a *Pyr* on her side when other dragons were hunting her.

She was remembering that kiss and wanting another.

"Telford," she admitted.

She didn't think Erik recognized the name, judging by his expression. But then, just because he had a British accent didn't mean he had the entire country memorized. He paid the fare the conductor demanded, and his desire to be rid of the man as quickly as possible made her fight a smile.

"Advance planning would have saved you on this fare," the conductor noted, his tone arch. "But then, advance planning is rather a challenge for some of us, isn't it?"

"I'm sure it would have done," Erik agreed, not hiding his impatience. "Unfortunately I didn't know the lady's destination."

"Romance, is it then?" The conductor snorted and rolled his eyes at the very idea. "Change at Birmingham New Street," he droned as he handed Erik his ticket. He widened his eyes in mock alarm. "Only twenty-two minutes there to change trains. You'll want to allow for that."

"Yes, we will," Erik said. He clearly wished the conductor would move on quickly.

Eileen offered her ticket and the conductor approved it, then moved down the car. She felt as if she were burning up, and there was certainly an inferno raging in a more intimate vicinity. She wanted Erik more than she knew she should.

Eileen wondered what Erik would do next, but what he did surprised her.

He leaned toward her. The green of his eyes was so bright as to be electric, and his proximity made her pulse leap. Eileen was ready for another sizzling kiss—half a night was far too long to go without one.

But instead, Erik began to answer her question about dragonsmoke, his expression so solemn that she knew he was telling her the truth.

Even though the truth was beyond belief.

Chapter 7

Nikolas knew one thing above all else. It was a violation of everything *Pyr* to injure the Wyvern. Some rules could not be broken. In planning to kill the Wyvern, Boris had crossed into a land from which there was no return. Nikolas would shred him alive for his crime, with no regrets.

Boris had already made the Wyvern bleed.

The choice Boris offered was no choice at all: It would have been ideal to save the Dragon's Egg, but it was imperative to protect the Wyvern.

After all, she could not defend herself. It was the duty of the powerful to protect the vulnerable.

Nikolas lunged at Boris, seizing his head in both claws. Once released, Sophie shifted to a salamander and scuttled away. Boris roared and tried to stomp on her. He caught one of her legs under his heel and she screamed again.

The sound of her pain enraged Nikolas. He slammed Boris's head into the brick wall, not caring how much injury he caused. Dark blood ran over his knuckles as he drove Boris into the wall again.

Boris roared and changed shape in his grip. Nikolas didn't

let go. They grappled with each other, both fighting to kill. Boris bit and clawed and thrashed, but Nikolas gave as good as he got. Black and red blood mingled together on the hardwood floor, dragonfire and dragonsmoke filling the loft.

Then the Dragon's Egg shattered on the pavement outside the building. The crack of its rupture was far louder than it should have been. Nikolas felt a shock roll through him, an earthquake that rattled through his very bones. He was jangled and disoriented, shaken to his essence.

Worse, he lost his grip on Boris.

Boris leapt to the windowsill. He breathed a torrent of dragonfire behind himself to keep Nikolas at bay.

"What have you done?" Sophie whispered, her voice carrying from some hidden location.

"Evened the score," Boris snarled. He spun to break a larger hole in the window with his tail. He scanned the loft, but evidently couldn't see Sophie either.

Boris's old-speak echoed in Nikolas's thoughts, his venom unmistakable. *"You can hide for now, Wyvern, but I will find you and I will finish what I have begun. Prepare to die."*

With a final blast of dragonfire at Nikolas, Boris leapt through the broken glass and flew skyward. Aching to follow and destroy him, but reluctant to leave the Wyvern alone and unprotected, Nikolas stood with clenched fists and watched the villain go.

Boris could have allies who were yet unnamed. The prospect chilled Nikolas's blood. He had saved the Wyvern this time, but the threat against her was clear. He had to devote himself to her defense, at least until Boris—and whoever fought with him—was truly dead.

Nikolas scanned the loft, then saw a flash of white near the door to Erik's hoard.

The salamander turned into a woman before his eyes, a woman with fair hair and turquoise eyes. Nikolas couldn't keep himself from staring. Sophie was the most exquisitely beautiful woman he had ever seen.

Every time he was in her presence, he was awed. He had initially thought that his was the normal response of a *Pyr* in the presence of the closest representative of the divine, but his fellow *Pyr* didn't seem to feel the same sense of wonder.

The Wyvern was magical to him. As a boy, he'd been taught that only the blessed ever glimpsed the Wyvern. Now, in these days, she practically lived among the *Pyr*, gracing them frequently with her presence. He yearned for the rare sight of her smile. He ached to fix whatever vexed her. He wanted more than anything in the world to touch the silk of her hair. Nikolas couldn't deny his fascination with her, and frequent exposure didn't diminish it a bit.

He watched Sophie ease toward him, noting her curves and her grace. He saw the intelligence in her eyes, the burden of the secrets she held fast. He saw the weight of the knowledge she had inherited and had to wield with justice and temperance. Recognizing her responsibility and fallibility made her seem less divine to him, more mortal.

More like him.

That was the moment Nikolas knew that what he felt for Sophie was beyond reverence. He aspired far above his place, and he didn't imagine for a moment that his feelings might be reciprocated.

But he would defend Sophie with everything he had.

When the Dragon's Egg broke, Niall was on the prowl.

For weeks, Niall had sensed the presence of another *Pyr* near his home in New York City. The scent was weak and fleeting. It wasn't a *Pyr* he knew and he suspected that the *Pyr* in question wasn't in command of his powers. The elusive scent tormented him—strongest at night, it drew Niall out to search for the intruder.

Who was this *Pyr*? Why was he close? What were his alliances? Niall wanted to know all of this and more.

The trail invariably led to nightclubs, and Niall lost the scent in the mingling of cigarette smoke, pot haze, and perfume. The wind was no help to him, ignoring his queries.

Niall had too many questions to let the matter be.

On this night, the scent of *Pyr* had drawn Niall out again. He had followed it diligently and found himself in front of a bar. Niall wasn't much for the club scene, the noise and confusion and stimulants. The *Pyr* had keen senses, more sensitive than humans, and Niall found that some experiences favored by humans were overwhelming.

But he was sufficiently annoyed to ignore discomfort. He wanted to find this unknown *Pyr* and he wanted to find him immediately.

He went in.

The scents were as maddening as Niall had anticipated, muddying his impressions and clouding his judgment. He felt nauseated and disoriented, but he kept moving. The interior was crowded, dark, noisy. The lights pulsed through the darkness from the direction of the dance floor. The beat of the music was deep and loud, throbbing and insistent. He was sure he couldn't stand it much longer, but he kept going.

Then the world shattered.

The wind was knocked out of Niall and he had to grab the edge of the bar to keep on his feet. He felt as if someone had sliced him in half and stolen his guts.

It was such a strong sensation that he was shocked to look down and see that he wasn't wounded at all.

The people around him clearly felt nothing. The party went on; the music continued without interruption. As the pain faded, Niall had an urge to mourn, to weep, to rage at injustice.

The couple closest to him stared at him. "Bad stuff, dude?" the man asked, giving him a friendly nudge.

"I guess so," Niall said, accepting the excuse.

"Gotta watch where you buy," the woman agreed with a

sage nod. Niall moved away from them, thinking furiously. What had happened?

It wasn't good; that was for sure.

In that moment, Niall noticed a crowd gathering on the dance floor. He pushed his way through the throng and found a tall man collapsed on the floor, gasping for breath. His hands opened and closed, as if his fingers tried to clutch something that was irretrievably lost. He was writhing on the floor like a man caught in an electrical current, his expression pained.

Someone else had felt the jolt. But only another *Pyr* would have felt it. Niall knew then that he had found the one he sought.

The fallen man could have been a Viking warrior, with his long reddish blond hair and muscled build. He wore laced biker boots, tight jeans, and a tight blue T-shirt. The tendons on his neck stood out in his anguish and he had a number of tattoos.

Including a blue and black dragon on the back of his left hand.

"Do you know what you are?" Niall asked in old-speak.

The man on the floor started, leaving no doubt that he had heard Niall's words. No human could have discerned the old-speak. He scanned the crowd with fear, seeking the speaker.

Niall wondered whether he even knew how to use old-speak. He might not be able to reply in kind.

"I'm at your twelve o'clock."

Niall's conviction grew as the man looked directly at him. His terror was obvious, but so was his hope. He rose to his knees tentatively as he studied Niall, looking ready to fight.

"Because I do," Niall continued. *"You are not the only one."*

Niall didn't wait for the *Pyr* to rise all the way to his feet. He had more important issues to pursue. What had that shock been? He had to get to Erik and learn more. Niall left the bar, suspecting that the *Pyr* who had no mentor would follow.

He did.

"What the hell was that?" the man shouted after Niall once they were both on the empty street. "And how did you put words in my head? Who are you? How do you know what I am?"

His voice rose as Niall kept walking.

"What the fuck is going on?" he roared.

Niall turned into a darkened alley, waiting for the other *Pyr* to rage closer. That *Pyr* lunged around the corner almost immediately, his eyes lighting when he saw that Niall had waited for him.

"Can you shift on purpose?" Niall asked.

The *Pyr* scoffed. "Duh."

"Then come with me."

Niall's new companion was incredulous. "Now?"

"Now."

"Where?"

Niall took the scent of the wind, asking it Erik's location. The answer came to him swift and clear. "London."

"England?" The foundling *Pyr* was incredulous. "But how? Why? Are you out of your f—"

Niall shifted without answering, taking flight in one smooth gesture. The other *Pyr* swore with vigor behind him; then Niall heard the rustle of leathery wings.

The kid needed some practice.

A long, fast flight would be good for him.

In the moment that the Dragon's Egg shattered, Sara Keegan awakened abruptly. She sat bolt upright, her breath coming in anxious pants. Her heart was pounding, her thoughts filled with a conviction that something was deeply wrong.

But everything seemed normal. It was the middle of the night and the house was as quiet as the property outside the window.

Quinn was immediately awake. "Is it the baby?" He sat up beside her, his hand falling to her rounded belly. "Is it time?"

"No, no." Sara locked her hands over his, letting him entwine her fingers with his. She trembled. "I had a nightmare."

Quinn caught her close, wrapping his warmth around her. Sara closed her eyes and leaned against his strength, forcing herself to note how tranquil their home was. She loved Quinn's land, which was near Traverse City in Michigan, loved the serenity of the forest and the glimmer of the stars overhead. The house he had built for himself was solid and rooted like no other house she had ever occupied.

It was home.

It was haven.

"A nightmare or a vision?" he asked, his lips against her hair.

"Maybe both." Sara pulled back to look at him, letting him see her trepidation. Although she was the Seer of the *Pyr*, Quinn knew more about the symbols of his kind. She had missed the importance of her dreams before.

"I dreamed that the world had cracked in half," she said softly. "That there was a great fissure right to the center of the planet, one that released something vile from the depths."

His eyes narrowed. "Something?"

Sara shook her head. "I woke up before I saw." She had hoped that Quinn would reassure her, but instead he got out of bed. He stood and looked out the window, although she knew he wasn't looking at the snow covering the meadow.

"I felt it myself," he admitted quietly. "Something has gone wrong." He spared her a glance, his eyes gleaming blue. "Do you feel strong enough to travel? Erik will know what has happened and what we should do."

Sara got out of bed herself, feeling cold. She was seven months pregnant and would have preferred to have stayed home until the baby's arrival.

"I won't go without you, Sara," Quinn said with quiet force. "It's up to you."

"Is it?" She looked at him across the rumpled quilts on the bed. "Do you really think that I could choose to keep you from helping the *Pyr*? If you don't go and they fail, what kind of partnership would we have?"

He dropped his gaze and frowned.

Sara spoke softly. "I know that the *Pyr*'s mission is more important, but I'm afraid."

"I'll stay, if that's what you want." Quinn held her gaze, his own eyes bright, and she knew he would do what she wished.

She swallowed. "But you're the Smith and the *Pyr* need you."

"We could go to Chicago and wait for Erik. He will have breathed a smoke barrier, and it's a shorter journey, too." Quinn watched her, giving her the time she needed to decide. "Or I could breathe smoke here, if you wanted to stay home until I learned more."

Sara smiled a little. "But I'd rather be with you. We'll go."

Quinn crossed the room with the determination that still left Sara dizzy. He caught her close and she clung to his strength. "You know that I'll do anything to protect you," he murmured.

Sara felt her tears rise. "That's what frightens me."

He squeezed her more tightly and she heard the smile in his voice. "I'm not that easy to lose." Quinn lifted her chin with one hand when she didn't look at him or respond. One tear had spilled onto her cheek and he eased it away with his thumb. "Don't ever forget that you're my warrior queen," he whispered, then smiled the slow, hot smile that she couldn't live without.

Would she have to?

Sara held tightly to him as he bent and kissed her soundly. Was she just afraid of uncertainty, or had she seen more of their future than she recalled?

Sara wasn't sure she wanted to know.

*   *   *

On the other side of the world, Rafferty thought he was having a heart attack.

It was early in the morning when the pain shot through him, radiating from his heart to his extremities. He fell to the floor of his kitchen, one hand clutched to his chest. He closed his eyes against it, but when he might have called for help, the pain began to fade.

It wasn't in his body. His body was responding to an outside stimulus of some kind.

It was responding because he was *Pyr.*

That couldn't be good.

Erik hadn't returned the night before, but Rafferty didn't know why. It might have been because he had spoken his mind. It might have been because Erik was consummating his firestorm. Rafferty wouldn't be the first one to ask.

He was still annoyed with Erik for not appreciating his good fortune in having a second chance at his firestorm.

As the pain eased, Rafferty stumbled into his small garden. The ground was damp but he didn't care. He laid down on the patio stones, ignoring the frost on them, and put his cheek to the earth. He slowed his breathing and his pulse, spreading his palms flat on the soil. He strove to match his rhythms to those of the element he knew best.

He asked the Earth for tidings.

She didn't immediately reply, but then she never did. Rafferty kept his face against the soil, closed his eyes and waited.

He didn't care who saw him. His neighbors had long ago decided that he was odd.

Sloane was working late, pushing seeds into potting mixture one at a time. He had rows and rows of flats to plant to get the seedlings started for spring. Usually he liked working late in the quiet of the greenhouse at his nursery. He enjoyed seeing the stars through the glass roof and singing his soft song of encouragement to the seeds. His sharp *Pyr* sight allowed him to plant the seeds without artificial lighting, which Sloane believed the seeds preferred.

But he and Delaney had been arguing. There was an unhappy vibration in the greenhouse as they worked together but not in unison.

"You need to confront it," Sloane said for the hundredth time.

"Easy for you to say," Delaney replied yet again. He spared Sloane a glance of hostility, then kept poking seeds into soil.

Delaney had recovered a great deal in his months of working at Sloane's nursery—so much so that Sloane was convinced that the greatest impediment to Delaney's full recovery was his own conviction that he carried a scar that would not heal. Sloane was sure that Delaney had to face the truth of his experience in Magnus's dark academy in order to feel whole again. He thought there must be a way to convert a negative to a positive, but Delaney wouldn't even talk about it.

"I could hypnotize you," he suggested again. "You wouldn't even remember, unless I told you to. I could listen to you and decide."

Delaney shoved seeds deep into the dirt. "No one but no one is going to mess with my mind again." He glared at Sloane, looking a whole lot like Donovan in a temper.

Sloane would have argued again, but a jolt ripped through him, leaving him dizzy with pain.

His first thought was that the San Andreas fault had finally made its big move. That had been one of the hazards of locating his nursery in California—but the climate had been too big an asset to overlook.

Nothing was moving, though, and the earth wasn't shaking. He forced himself to take inventory. There was no damage to the greenhouse, which had been designed to neatly collapse in an earthquake.

The rupture had been within himself, but not an injury of his own. Sloane was puzzled.

Delaney was clutching the lip of the table in front of him. "What was that?"

"Nothing good." Sloane frowned as the pain diminished. "Maybe one of the other *Pyr* was injured."

"Do you usually feel that?" Delaney's skepticism was clear. "Because I never have. I think it was something else."

"Like what?"

Delaney's lips set and he put down the seeds. "Something we should find out about instead of playing with seeds."

"Maybe it was just a summons, some new trick Erik has learned."

"No," Delaney said flatly. "Erik didn't send that."

Sloane studied his patient, wondering what Delaney couldn't put into words. It wasn't like him to be so definite, but Sloane was prepared to trust Delaney's instincts.

Especially as they agreed with his own. "Let's go to Chicago, then," he suggested. "The others will be at Erik's lair."

"I can set up the computerized climate control." Delaney moved with purpose to prepare the greenhouses for their absence.

Sloane listened as the discord continued to fade. It had been the strangest sensation, and not a good one.

If Erik wasn't responsible, he would know what was.

Sophie had her arms folded across her chest when Nikolas returned to Erik's lair. She was cold, chilled right to the bone, as she never had been before. She felt sick and weak, as well. She saw that Nikolas cradled several things in his arms and didn't want to look at the damage.

But she did look as Nikolas laid the pieces of the ruptured Dragon's Egg on Erik's coffee table. The large orb had broken in half; then one hemisphere had shattered into three pieces.

The stone was cold and dead, just the way Sophie felt. She touched it to be sure, running her fingertips over the smooth stone, but knew its powers were gone.

Its icy emptiness touched her heart.

It was a portent of change, change for the worst.

For the *Pyr*? Or for her?

She shivered, aware that Nikolas was observing her reaction. "I can't fix it," she said, anticipating his question.

"The choice he offered was no choice." Nikolas's gaze searched hers. "I know that it is forbidden for the Wyvern to shed blood, even in her own defense. I could not let him kill you."

The intensity of his expression made Sophie's pulse leap and made her aware of him in a way that she knew was inappropriate. She studied the remains of the Dragon's Egg, but she was so attuned to Nikolas's presence that she couldn't see what was before her eyes.

Instead, she felt his heartbeat.

"I am sorry if you believe that I failed you," he said in a tone that wasn't apologetic at all.

Sophie made the mistake of glancing up, and the heat she found in his eyes stole her breath away.

"There are obligations that are sacred," he insisted. "Duties that are an honor to fulfill. Your defense in these times is a task I would welcome."

"The Wyvern should not have stronger bonds with any single *Pyr* or human—" Sophie began to argue, but Nikolas interrupted her.

"He will kill you." He shook a finger at her. "He will hunt you and he will kill you, although he will probably torture you first. You cannot ask me to stand aside and let that happen."

"I cannot ask you to prevent it." Sophie averted her gaze.

She jumped when Nikolas touched her throat with his warm fingertip. She glanced at him and found the glistening red of her own blood smeared across his finger. His dark eyes blazed.

"I will not permit him to do this again."

Sophie swallowed, distrusting how attractive she found the idea of having Nikolas as her champion. She was becoming too involved with the *Pyr*. She was losing her objectivity. She was no longer aloof.

But she didn't want to retreat.

"You have a destined role to fulfill," she argued. "My defense is not it. You must pursue your own destiny. . . ."

Nikolas scoffed. "Whether destiny exists or not is not mine to decide." He fixed Sophie with a hot look. "I believe in choice. I believe in principle and honor and beauty. I believe in dedicating my powers to a cause that matters."

He eased closer and Sophie's breath caught. Nikolas was all she could see, all she wanted to see, so she simply stared into his eyes.

His voice softened, falling low enough to make her shiver. "I believe that the Wyvern, our Wyvern, must be protected at all cost."

Sophie couldn't find the words to argue with him. She was too overwhelmed by his power, his determination, and the desire that both awakened within her. She studied the unruly wave of his hair, the resolve in the line of his lips, the sweep of his lashes. She met the glimmer in his dark eyes and her resistance melted.

What was happening to her? She was supposed to be above earthly desires, immune to their appeal.

But Nikolas undermined all of that with a single look.

She felt warm again.

Alive.

Nicholas abruptly dropped to one knee before her and bowed his head. The light made blue glimmers in the dark waves of his hair, touched his broad shoulders like a caress. Sophie yearned to slide her fingers into his hair, to caress his strength, but she knew better.

Intimacy was forbidden to the Wyvern.

But Sophie yearned all the same.

Nikolas glanced up at her. His eyes were deep brown, deeper than any brown she might have imagined, filled with devotion. "Accept my service in your defense."

"I don't understand," Sophie said, although she did.

Nikolas took her hand in his, swallowing. Surely he could not feel overwhelmed in her presence, as overwhelmed as she felt in his? His hands were warm, so warm that Sophie shivered again, but his touch was gentle. Reverent. "I pledge myself to your defense anytime, anyplace, at any cost."

"I cannot ask this of you."

His voice hardened. "I offer it of my own will."

Sophie shook her head and his eyes flashed. "You could die, just when the *Pyr* have need of every warrior."

"I know the risk, but the greater risk is in doing nothing. Sometimes, Sophie, a man must choose." Nikolas held her gaze, his intent expression making Sophie's heart leap. She pulled her hand from his, retreating until her back was against the wall.

"I understand the stakes," he said as he rose to his feet, his voice like silken velvet. "Perhaps even better than you."

"And if I decline you?"

"It changes nothing." He smiled then, a brief flash that made her mouth go dry. Sophie gripped the brick wall as he closed the distance between them. He towered over her, filling her view with his magnificence.

Would she be able to resist him if he were always present?

She had to. There was no choice.

"I will serve you until death, whether you command my service or not." Nikolas spoke with vehemence. "To take a sacred duty is right. It is noble. It is the essence of what it means to be *Pyr*." He caught her hand within his and she didn't have the will to pull her fingers from his tender grasp.

Then he lifted her fingertips to his mouth, smiled ever so slightly, and kissed her palm.

Sophie's knees went weak.

Nikolas's gaze filled with a desire beyond that of being champion. His intensity both thrilled and frightened her.

Sophie pulled her hand away and hastened to the other side of the room. There was nowhere to hide from Nikolas's conviction and devotion, though, and worse, he was right. She needed a champion, given Boris's plan.

Yet Nikolas was also wrong. Sophie knew that on some level he expected reward for his service and she knew what reward both of them would prefer. Sexual awareness crackled between them—it had all along—and it would only increase as they spent time together. If she surrendered to the promise he offered, she feared the price she might pay.

But if she declined Nikolas and dismissed him, she would likely be killed. She wouldn't be able to help the *Pyr*—that would be left to the next Wyvern, whenever she might be born or reveal herself. That might be too late.

Sophie eyed the warrior before her and knew what she had to do. If not for herself, then for the survival of the *Pyr*.

Whatever the ultimate price.

Sophie chose.

"I accept," she whispered. "But you must keep your distance." She saw the light of triumph in Nikolas's eyes; then he bowed again before her. Her throat tightened, and a pang of desire shot through her like a warning.

Or a portent of doom. Her gaze flicked to the broken Dragon's Egg and she feared the consequences of what she had done.

Yet she didn't possess a single regret.

Chapter 8

"Let's start with Magnus's departure," Erik began, liking how closely Eileen attended his explanation. He kept his voice low as he leaned toward her. "Dragonsmoke is a territory mark. I breathed a circle of dragonsmoke around the house you were in last night."

"To define the house as your territory?" Her needles clicked busily as she listened.

"In a way. We can't cross one another's territory marks, not without the express permission of the one who made the mark."

"I didn't see any smoke this morning."

"Dragonsmoke is undetectable to humans. You might have felt a bit of a chill as you stepped through it, if you're sensitive to such things. Otherwise, only we see it. And hear it."

"Hear it?"

"A closed ring has a resonance. It's a high tone, like the sound crystal makes when struck lightly."

"Why wouldn't I hear that?"

"Our senses are sharper than human senses."

The conductor strolled past them again, on his way to the next car. "Watford Junction next," he droned, then paused beside them. "If you'd care to have another romantic moment on the platform, I should warn you that it's quite a short stop. Pickup only."

Erik glared at the very annoying human. "I thank you for your courtesy."

The conductor moved on, whistling, as the train slowed.

Erik looked back at Eileen to find her biting back a smile. Her eyes sparkled. "Obviously those enhanced senses don't include your sense of humor," she teased.

"I have a perfectly good sense of humor, when no one is stalking my mate."

"I'm hardly your mate."

"Think again." Erik bumped his ankle against hers. A spark leapt between their boots, settling into a golden glow when he didn't move his foot away. He felt the heat increase between them, as if he had put his leg closer to a furnace.

He studied Eileen and noticed the thick spike of her lashes, the fullness of her bottom lip, the sparkle in her eyes, and the quickness of her breath. She licked her lips and he watched her gesture hungrily, wanting. It would have been easy to claim another kiss, to taste her again.

But they had issues to resolve.

He moved his leg away. "The firestorm is the mark of destiny."

"Destined love?" Eileen asked, her tone skeptical.

"Destined sex."

Eileen half laughed, then shook her head when Erik didn't laugh. She flicked a look at him, then returned to her knitting.

"What did I say?"

"Nothing."

Erik tapped her knee with a heavy fingertip. "We have a deal and it's reciprocal," he said softly. "Because I admire honesty, too. We have that in common."

She blushed then, blushed so crimson that her face could

have been aflame. But she did what he asked. She dropped her knitting into her lap and looked directly at him. "Okay, my sister gave me a bunch of advice this morning," she said, and he suspected that the truth was heavily edited. "She thinks I choose men who aren't worth the trouble."

Erik waited, letting her decide how much to tell him. Was he included in that company? He had to admit that becoming involved with him could have many repercussions for her.

Few of them good.

Having sex and parting ways would be simpler.

"Like this guy I was seeing," she said. "We met at a conference and had a long-distance thing going on. I thought when I came to England for this sabbatical that maybe it would get more serious." She flicked a look at Erik. "I thought I'd surprise him."

That sounded ominous.

"But?" Erik prompted.

"But I'm the one who got the surprise. His wife answered the door." She dropped her gaze, hiding her thoughts from him.

Erik winced. "Not very honest of him."

"No. I should have guessed something was odd when he had to always call me. Maybe on some level I did." She shrugged. It didn't appear to Erik that this man had broken her heart or even left a lasting wound.

"Maybe the trouble is that I'm a sucker for a British man," she said lightly, her eyes sparkling. "It's the accent."

"What a relief." Erik sat back, waiting for his moment.

"What do you mean?"

"I'm not British, so there's no issue between us."

"Of course you are!"

Erik shook his head. "Viking."

She shook a needle at him playfully. "We have a deal."

"We do," Erik agreed easily.

"There've been no Vikings for a thousand years. You can't

be Viking, Erik, so don't put me on. Those people are all dead."

Erik spoke with quiet heat. "But we're not *people*, Eileen."

She stopped knitting.

She stared at him as her lips parted.

She looked at the wooden chest, then back at him. There was a question in her eyes, one that she obviously thought was too crazy to say aloud.

"Yes," Erik said, knowing exactly what that question was.

Eileen swallowed and looked down for a moment. It was a shorter interval than Erik expected, and he admired her resilience.

She nudged the box with her foot. "Anyone you know?"

"Well before my time, I'm afraid."

"It would be easier that way."

"I think so."

She took a deep breath. "How many of you are there?"

"Too few, at least on the side of right."

"As opposed to those two thugs," she said. "And Magnus."

Erik nodded, watching her carefully. She was listening, making sense of what he told her with remarkable speed. Once again, he was impressed by his mate. "Those who choose darkness are called *Slayers*."

"Are you immortal?"

"No."

"Then how long do you live?"

Erik shrugged. "It depends. Anyone can die a violent death at any time."

"Just like us."

"Yes. My father always said that a *Pyr* aged more slowly until his firestorm; then he tasted his own mortality. I'm not entirely sure what he meant."

Eileen studied him, her gaze lingering on his temples. She seemed to be deciding what to ask next, but Erik didn't want to overwhelm her. He particularly didn't want to discuss the fact that satisfaction of the firestorm always led to a conception.

Yet.

So he changed the subject. "Why Telford, wherever that is?" He assumed it was a place so small and insignificant that it was unknown to him. Anywhere past Birmingham should be familiar to him, given all the time he had spent in Shropshire, but he'd never heard of Telford.

"Not Telford." Eileen winced. "It's a new town, established in the 1960s and not interesting at all." That explained Erik's ignorance of it—he'd left Britain right after Louisa's death. "But it's the closest train station to where I need to go. I'll rent a car to carry on. That's what I did last time."

"And where are we going?"

Even though Erik had a bad feeling when he asked, her answer shook him to his marrow.

"Ironbridge." Eileen started to knit again, oblivious to his dismay.

Ironbridge?

"Why?" he asked, his voice unnaturally strained.

Eileen must have mistaken his horror for surprise. She cast him an impish smile. "I know it's the founding city of the industrial revolution and all that gritty stuff. Not a typical haunt for a comparative mythologist, but I've been researching a local story. I decided to go back there one more time before I go home." Her words fell more quickly as her agitation increased. "I couldn't stay at Lynne's house with those *Slayer*s chasing me, not after I saw what they did to Teresa. . . ."

Erik grabbed her hand, stilling those busy fingers, and she fell silent. "What myth?" he demanded, fearing her response.

"It's known as the Dragon Lover of Madeley." She considered him, finally recognizing his agitation. "Do you know it?"

Erik caught his breath and dropped Eileen's hand. He

stared out the window without seeing the view. He felt exposed and vulnerable as he seldom did.

Did he know it?

He had lived it.

Eileen knew she had said something wrong.

She just didn't know what it was.

Did it bother Erik that she collected stories? Eileen couldn't imagine why. Even people who thought her work was useless were content to let her waste her own time.

Eileen, of course, didn't think her work was useless.

Erik was silent, more than silent. It was as if he had turned his attention away from her and only in its absence did Eileen realize how potent his interest was. If it hadn't been for the sizzle of heat that she already associated with his presence, she would have felt as if she sat across from a stranger.

She couldn't help thinking about Lynne's advice, especially in relation to Erik Sorensson. She shouldn't get involved with him. She shouldn't even talk to him. The man could turn into a dragon. He implied that he was hundreds of years old. If she hadn't seen him shape-shift, she would have assumed he was demented.

But he made sense. And he confessed his truths to her. And as strange as those truths were, Eileen believed him. Her gut said she should trust him, and trust this electricity between them. Was it some kind of bad luck that as soon as she decided to do so, she'd inadvertently annoyed him?

Erik got up abruptly as the train pulled into a station. He walked away without saying anything, his expression grim.

Was he going to leave? Had she made that big a faux pas?

Eileen craned her neck to watch him stride down the length of the car. She couldn't help but admire the fit of his jeans and the line of his shoulders beneath his leather jacket. He was wearing a great Aran sweater, knit in charcoal wool with twining cables that she desperately wanted to finger.

Maybe she wanted to finger what was inside the sweater

just as much. Who had made it for him? What was his own romantic experience? He hadn't even flinched when she mentioned Nigel being married, so couldn't believe that Erik was.

He wasn't lying to her.

She trusted him.

She liked the way he could look so focused when something caught his attention, as if there were nothing else important in the world.

She particularly liked when she had his attention.

Eileen could imagine that Erik would make love with his concentration on his partner and on her every gesture. She could imagine that it would take hours and hours to make love with Erik. The whole world would fall away, sacrificed to the pursuit of pleasure.

Sounded good to her.

She also sensed that lovemaking with Erik would only leave her hungry for more. He'd kissed her once and she wanted more. She couldn't put the kiss out of her thoughts. She could taste him on her lips, remember the pressure of his mouth against hers and the slow caress of his fingertips in her hair. Eileen sat alone in a slowing train and lusted.

Destined mates.

He'd said that with such vehemence. There was no wiggle room, no possibility of misinterpretation—he'd been talking about sex, about their having sex together.

Nothing more and nothing less.

And it sounded great. On the one hand, Erik was disconcertingly direct about what he wanted from her. On the other, hadn't she had enough of pretty stories and lies? He was honest, so honest that he startled her. She was fed up with men—like Nigel and even Joe—who promised happily ever after when they just wanted a little something physical in the short term. It was a relief to have a man be blunt. It was forthright and it was sexy.

Wasn't there a saying about being careful what you asked for, in case you got it?

Eileen watched Erik lean out of the car and scrutinize the platform. The conductor made some comment to him in passing, one that Erik didn't acknowledge. His expression was preoccupied, even concerned, as he scanned the sky. She watched him, noting the strength of his hands, the way he narrowed his eyes, the tightening of his lips. He looked taut, on guard and vigilant. He looked ready to fight.

He'd said it was his responsibility to protect her. That sounded good. She thought of Erik defending her the night before, sweeping her behind him before he took down the gold dragon. He was decisive and powerful.

If a dragon.

She couldn't have everything, apparently.

The whistle blew and the train lurched forward. Erik returned to his seat, looking for all the world like he'd rather be pacing. She felt warmth grow inside her with every step he took closer. By the time he came to sit down, she was ravenous for more than breakfast.

He avoided her gaze as he took his seat, which surprised Eileen. What had she said? It was common for her to stumble in where angels might fear to tread, to say too much and to offend people, but she still couldn't think of what the issue might be this time.

She waited to see if Mr. Direct would tell her.

The train began to move again, but still he didn't say anything. He drummed his fingers on his knee and looked grim. Eileen figured she'd minimize her misstep by keeping her mouth shut. She knit. The train began to rock as it reached speed and she adjusted the rhythm of her knitting to that of the train car.

And she watched Erik through her lashes. Eileen began to think about the little inn where she had stayed the month before, and how the sheer romance of it all had nearly killed her, right after Nigel's revelation.

Maybe she could erase that unhappy memory with a better one.

Tonight. A wild weekend might be the perfect end to a disaster of a research trip.

Assuming that they started speaking to each other again.

Eileen had a feeling that Erik could hold his silence longer than she could, and knew she would have to start the conversation again.

"You should wear colors," she said more abruptly than she intended.

"Why?" He didn't sound insulted, but intrigued.

"Because gray and black are boring." She looked up to find him watching her, amusement in his eyes. She smiled. "And you're not."

He seemed to fight a smile, then leaned forward to brace his elbows on his knees. His eyes were cat bright. "Any particular color?"

Eileen studied him, pretending to think about it. In truth, she already knew. "Red," she said in a tone that allowed no argument.

"Red," he echoed, then sat back, bemused. "I shall have to consider that advice."

Eileen blushed and looked down at her knitting, afraid that she had said too much.

It wouldn't have been the first time.

She felt the weight of Erik's gaze upon her. He might have been touching her, her awareness of his glance was so intense. She felt herself begin to blush—like the teenager she wasn't—and couldn't help licking her lips. Her mouth was dry, her nipples were tingling, and she felt as if she had the shivers.

Hot shivers.

"Why?" he asked abruptly. Eileen looked up from her knitting in confusion. "Why this story?"

Eileen blinked. The problem was the story she was chasing? How exactly could that be an issue?

Then she guessed and felt her mouth fall open. The story could be a problem only if Erik knew something about it.

The Dragon Lover of Madeley.

No. Her mind shied away from the obvious connection.

She stared at Erik and he stared back.

Eileen routinely taught that stories represented deeper social fears—that the "dragon" was the frightening changes brought by the industrial revolution, for example—but what if there really had been a dragon lover? Erik could have been someone's dragon lover—or he could have known the dragon lover involved.

Could the story have a bigger seed of truth in it than she'd thought?

There were those teeth, after all.

"I collect a lot of stories." Eileen thought that sounded more evasive than she meant to be. "I'm a comparative mythologist."

"So you said." He waited, eyes gleaming, seeming to know that it was only half an answer.

Eileen put down her knitting and launched into a shortened version of her introductory lecture for Comparative Mythology 101. "There are people who think that stories are silly, but I think they're important. Comparative mythology is a critical part of social history, because the stories people tell one another reveal a great deal about their expectations, living conditions, and view of the world."

Erik almost smiled, apparently recognizing her tone. "You teach, then."

Eileen felt herself blush one more time. "At the university in Boston."

Again Erik started and turned to look out the window. Eileen sensed that he was surprised by her answer. What was wrong with Boston? Was he thinking of a longer-term connection between them, one that would be complicated by the Atlantic Ocean between them? The prospect made her heart thump.

Eileen decided that she might as well put all of her cards on the table. "I have a term sabbatical this year, and this is the end of my eight weeks of research in England. I go home Sunday."

Erik faced her so abruptly that she jumped. "You focus on old stories, then?" She was surprised that he seemed to have missed her reference to her travel plans.

"No. I wrote my dissertation on recurring elements in urban myths at home. My interest in older stories is new, which was why I needed to come here and establish a grounding for myself."

Erik was watching her closely. "I'll guess there was a reason for this change in your focus. You don't seem to be whimsical."

"Thank you." Eileen nodded and picked up her needles again. Strangely, she felt more comfortable under his scrutiny, as if some balance had been restored between them. He'd made a decision; she understood that intuitively. She wondered what it was. "It was one particular story that changed everything. The Dragon Lover of Madeley. I don't know what it is about that story, but as soon as I heard it, I knew I had to find out more. It's driving me crazy, that story. I can't push it out of my head. I need to know why."

"And have you found out?"

"No." Eileen didn't hide her frustration. "I spent some time in Ironbridge last month, but learned nothing significant."

"Maybe you were looking in the wrong places," Erik said. His silky tone caught at her ear, but Eileen continued.

"I think the problem is that people have moved away from there, to newer places like Telford, and the story doesn't have a root anymore. There's no old gardener whose grandfather told him a story his grandfather had told him—or at least, I don't know where to find that gardener, if he exists."

She frowned at her knitting. "Oral history is such a big part of putting these stories together." She became aware that she was rambling and looked up, surprised to find Erik watching her with that same intensity. "Does that make sense to you?"

"It makes perfect sense." Erik spoke with resolve. He leaned forward, his elbows braced on his knees, and his eyes glittered. "What if I could tell you more about that story?"

Eileen's heart leapt, but she wasn't sure whether it was because of his proximity or his offer. "More, like what?"

"More, like the truth behind it."

Eileen saw the conviction in his eyes.

Erik *did* know. This was the lead she'd been waiting for.

He was the lead she'd been waiting for.

Careful what you wish for . . .

"You know the story." She tried to sound calm but heard her own excitement.

"You could say that," he acknowledged.

Eileen wasn't interested in half truths. She leaned forward, her knitting forgotten, and their knees bumped. That spark leapt and it singed her skin through her skirt, sending an urgent demand along her veins. "Did you know her? The woman?"

Erik eyed her steadily and she was disappointed that he didn't directly answer her. "What if we made a wager?"

"What kind of a wager?"

"I can take you to the places it happened. I can show you some of the root of the story."

"Will you tell me everything you know of it?"

He watched her so carefully that Eileen wondered what he wasn't telling her. "I will tell you as much as I think I should. It is not my story, and I need to respect that."

"No." Eileen grabbed her needles again, prepared to negotiate. "No. I want the whole story, no part measures. The truth."

Erik settled back and Eileen stole a glance at him. He looked both bemused and unpredictable. He caught her looking and arched a brow. "What if there's some of it that I don't need to tell you?"

"What's that supposed to mean?"

He smiled slowly, his expression so mysterious and sexy that her bones nearly melted. "Why don't we just wait and see? You'll have the whole story by the time this is done, I believe, but I also believe that you won't need me to tell you all of it."

He made no sense, yet she trusted him.

What kind of magic did this man—this *Pyr*—possess?

He had confidence in spades; that was for sure. He was utterly convinced of what he was saying and pretty sure that she'd take the deal. She thought of her dreams, of the dream with him in it, and wondered precisely what powers Erik had.

She shouldn't have been surprised by how much she wanted to know.

Eileen had a strange sense that she was making a contract with the devil himself. The idea was both alluring and a bit worrisome. Had Faust felt his heart skip when he agreed to the terms with Mephistopheles? What was the hidden cost to this agreement?

Her instinct was unshakably in favor of going for it.

Eileen put down her knitting. "Is this a transaction, then? Do you want something in exchange?"

"Everyone wants something in exchange, Eileen," Erik said softly, his gaze colliding with hers. The way he said her name made her shiver. His gaze was hot and she was steaming.

"Name your price so that we both know the terms." From his sultry expression, Eileen was sure that she knew what he would say.

Sex, sex, sex. She was ready to agree.

But Erik's gaze dropped to the wooden chest. "That."

Eileen looked at her knitting in an attempt to hide her disappointment. It was probably a failed effort, given how closely Erik was watching her. She felt a little flat that he hadn't demanded a night together as the price of his assistance.

But she'd asked for the truth, hadn't she?

Eileen wasn't about to tell him that the chest was empty, not unless he asked. His promise might be empty as well.

"Fine," she said, hearing irritation in her tone. "Deal." She offered her hand, prepared to shake on the deal, such as it was.

"No," Erik said, his voice dropping low. "We have to seal this agreement another way."

He moved to the seat beside her so quickly that she barely saw him move. She looked up, saw the anticipation in his eyes, felt the weight of his arm sliding across her shoulders. He was all heat and intensity, his touch sending waves of desire over her skin. If she'd been standing, her knees would have given out.

"Deal," Erik whispered, the deep timbre of his voice sending little earthquakes through her. He touched her chin with one hand, sending a cascade of sparks over her skin, and tipped her face toward his.

Eileen closed her eyes as his mouth captured hers. This kiss was more demanding, and sent a clear message—one that zinged right to Eileen's toes—that Erik wanted more from her, after all.

She slid her hand around his neck and pulled him closer. She slipped her tongue between his teeth, heard him catch his breath, and knew she'd surprised him again. It shouldn't have been so satisfying to surprise Erik, and she shouldn't have wanted to do so as badly as she did.

But she couldn't resist.

Chapter 9

Not far away, Magnus settled back in his car, dissatisfied. The large sedan slid through London like a dark serpent, roughly following the course of the train that carried the woman, Erik, and the Dragon's Teeth. Jorge had found out the destination of the train, but that wasn't nearly good enough.

Magnus glared at his two bodyguards, one seated opposite him and the other in the front seat beside Balthasar, not troubling to hide his mood. Jorge ignored him, turning to look out the window instead. Mallory fidgeted, his head bent as he sought the train schedule on his cell phone.

Balthasar drove, smoothly negotiating traffic, feigning obliviousness. He'd have to have been dead not to sense the toxic atmosphere emanating from the backseat of the big sedan.

He wasn't dead.

Yet.

Magnus had an inclination to slaughter all three of them, just to take the edge off his frustration. "Why would she take the Dragon's Teeth to Wolverhampton?" he asked of no one in particular.

"They could be getting off at an earlier stop," Mallory said.

"Such as?"

"Watford Junction, Milton Keynes Central, Coventry, Birmingham International, or Birmingham New Street." Mallory glanced back, undoubtedly proud of having read the scheduled stops.

Magnus didn't give points for literacy.

Magnus exhaled smoke at his minion, enjoying how Mallory twitched wherever it touched his skin. The dragon-smoke burned—Magnus knew it—but he didn't breathe enough to make a significant injury.

Mallory might still be useful.

"None of which make any more sense than Wolverhampton," Magnus said in a bored tone. He considered the pair of them, focusing on Jorge's profile. "How did Erik catch her when you two couldn't?"

Jorge shot a glance at Magnus. "It's the firestorm," he hissed, as if Magnus were so stupid as to have missed that salient point.

Magnus moved like quicksilver, his right hand closing around Jorge's throat. He partly changed shape and pinned Jorge against the headrest with one claw. He had the sharp edge of that talon on Jorge's windpipe and the younger *Slayer* didn't move.

His blue eyes glittered, though, glittered with a venom that Magnus respected.

Perhaps Magnus had shared his secret with the wrong apprentice.

Perhaps Jorge would have been a better choice than Boris.

For the moment, Magnus was more interested in discipline. He tightened his grip until Jorge's blood stained his claw. It ran over his talon, dripping black onto Jorge's shirt and jacket. Jorge eventually dropped his gaze, but it took longer than Magnus had expected.

He respected that, as well.

"You will remember whom you address," he hissed in old-speak.

"Or what?" Jorge retorted. "You'll kill me?" His lids rose lazily and he smiled slightly as he met Magnus's gaze again. He appeared to have forgotten the talon cutting into his flesh. Jorge spoke aloud, his scorn clear. "You'll just resurrect me as a shadow dragon. Who will be more invincible then?"

"You know nothing of invincibility!" Magnus scoffed. He laughed as he released the surprised *Slayer*, then sat back and brushed off his cuffs. "Shadow dragons are slaves." He spoke with a sneer, then flicked a glance at Jorge. "If that's your ambition, then I've underestimated you. You can go grovel at someone else's feet." Magnus lit himself a cigar, inhaling and rolling the smoke around his mouth.

Jorge's eyes flashed and he folded his arms across his chest. "You know more than you share."

"That's the privilege of age and experience." Magnus blew a smoke ring of perfect symmetry.

"Yeah? What happens if you die, Magnus? There'll be no one left to lead the *Slayers*." Jorge leaned closer, his eyes glittering as he slipped into old-speak. *"If you die, the* Pyr *will win."*

The prospect would have horrified Magnus more if he'd believed himself mortal.

As it was, he smiled. "I'm not going to die."

Jorge's eyes narrowed. "You *do* have the Dragon's Blood Elixir."

Magnus smoked with real pleasure.

"You should share!" Jorge said aloud.

"I wait only for a suitable acolyte to distinguish himself," he said, speaking with disdain.

"What about Boris?" Jorge sneered, and Magnus knew

that his decision to tutor the former leader of the *Slayers* hadn't gone unnoticed.

"What about Boris?" Magnus shrugged and brushed an invisible bit of lint from his trousers. "He might not be dead, but he's ineffective. I took the suzerainty of the *Slayers* from him without a whimper of protest." He shrugged. "Clearly I made a less than ideal choice of protégé."

Jorge leaned closer. "And what will distinguish your next protégé?"

"Effectiveness," Magnus spit. "I want my Dragon's Teeth back." He stared at Jorge and switched to old-speak. *"Yesterday."*

Jorge's expression hardened with a purpose that Magnus recognized. There would be no more mistakes, no matter what the cost. He knew ambition when he saw it and he recognized its merit.

But temperance had its place, too. Here, then, would be Jorge's first lesson.

And his reward.

Magnus put a cautionary hand on Jorge's sleeve, and the younger *Slayer* couldn't hide that he was startled by the touch. He didn't flinch, though, and he didn't pull back.

Another good sign.

"We'll give Erik some time and distance," Magnus advised. "Feed his confidence, let him do whatever it is he means to do."

Jorge smiled. "Let him screw up."

Magnus patted the *Slayer*'s sleeve, liking how well they understood each other. "You, meanwhile, will practice hovering between the forms. Shift only your right nail to a talon, if you can. Most have not the discipline and clarity of mind."

"And then?"

"Master the feat first. Then we'll talk." Magnus smiled to himself, feeling the intensity of Jorge's concentration. That would keep the younger *Slayer* busy.

And who knew—he might actually succeed.

*   *   *

The firestorm was even more enticing the second time than it had been the first. Or maybe Erik had forgotten its power. He liked that Eileen knew what he was and wasn't afraid of him.

Either she trusted him, or she hid her trepidation very well.

Once he had gotten over the shock of the story she sought, he realized he should have expected Eileen's fascination with Ironbridge and the Dragon Lover of Madeley. Why else would a soul be reincarnated other than to address the imbalances of the past? It made sense to Erik that Eileen was drawn to the same location, perhaps to make another effort at conquering those life lessons.

And he could help her. Opening Eileen's eyes to her own story was a small concession for him to make and it was one that made Erik feel slightly less mercenary.

He'd have to live with his remaining reservations.

Erik finally broke their kiss and Eileen smiled at him. Her lips were reddened and soft, inviting him to sample them again. He was enchanted by the sparkle in her eyes and the way she shyly dropped her gaze to her knitting again.

"Now, that was a kiss," she said with such satisfaction that he found himself chuckling.

"Indeed," he agreed, and she shot him a coy smile.

"I stayed at a wonderful inn the last time I was here," she said, that blush rising over her cheeks again. He loved that she could look so innocent and speak so boldly. She gave him a look through her lashes. "It was very romantic."

"We could use a refuge," he agreed carefully, understanding her implication. "One that I can protect with a smoke barrier."

She arched a brow. "One room or two?"

He liked how direct she was and answered in kind. "My choice is one, but I leave the decision to you."

"One," she said with conviction, and Erik caught her hand in his.

He held fast to her fingers, letting the firestorm build to an inferno between them. She stared up at him, an answering heat in her eyes. He brushed her fingertips across his lips, savoring the shower of sparks that erupted between them. He wanted to show her that her choice was a good one, but he was shocked at his rapid reaction to her skin pressed against his own.

He was hard and thick and ready. He could smell that teasing scent of her perfume and wanted to taste every increment of her skin. He wanted to peel away her black clothes and leave her in only her silver jewelry and her curtain of hair.

He moved his leg so that their thighs touched for their entire length and Eileen pressed her leg against his. His heart matched its pace to hers, making him feel part of an intimate union even though they only held hands. He felt their breathing synchronize and nearly lost himself in the assault of the firestorm.

Then he realized that he was oblivious to everything but Eileen, and *Slayers* were pursuing them. There would be a time to indulge in the firestorm but this wasn't it.

He still had tasks to complete before he died.

Erik pulled away and sat opposite Eileen again, putting an increment of distance between them. "You'll never finish your knitting," he said with a smile when she looked surprised.

She smiled. "Knitting waits. Not everything else does."

That was a telling reminder. Erik found his fingers drumming once more. What had broken this morning? What had happened? He sent a message in old-speak to Rafferty, who was the closest *Pyr*, and hoped that Rafferty would hear him.

He also hoped that Rafferty would answer him, after their dispute of the night before.

But there was only silence.

Erik had left Nikolas in charge of his lair, but Nikolas did not share the abilities of the more modern *Pyr*. Nikolas had yet to conquer the feat of sending old-speak at a distance, for example, which was inconvenient.

Erik cast his thoughts toward London, toward Chicago, toward the future, and found nothing at all. Not a ripple of a portent. Not an image or an impression.

The gift of foresight that Erik had relied upon for so long, the ability he had taken for granted, was extinguished.

He did his best to hide his trepidation from his observant mate. Would his foresight return when he consummated the firestorm? Was it lost forever in the firestorm's heat? Was his future irrelevant?

Or nonexistent?

"The Dragon's Egg is shattered beyond repair." Rafferty's old-speak slid into Erik's thoughts, the words startling him with both their abruptness and import.

"Are you certain?" Erik asked before he caught himself. Of course, Rafferty would have confirmed such a rumor before repeating it.

Rafferty didn't reply, an indication that he was still annoyed with Erik.

"Where is everyone?" Erik asked.

"Gathering at your lair in Chicago."

Erik refrained from checking his watch. It was still morning in England, so even earlier in Chicago. He calculated quickly, knowing what he could do.

What he had to do.

"I will be there as soon as possible."

"What of your mate?"

Erik didn't have to imagine Rafferty's disapproval. It dripped from every word. He decided to ignore it.

"The firestorm will be satisfied before I leave," he assured Rafferty. *"I will bring the Dragon's Teeth and we can proceed from there."*

Even in the silence that followed, Erik could feel his old

friend's disgust with his decision. Still he was shocked when Rafferty continued in old-speak.

"I will not be there."

It was the harshest condemnation possible from Rafferty and one that took Erik completely by surprise. He had never expected his oldest ally to break rank with him, especially in the midst of this conflict, but he knew that Rafferty wouldn't be easily swayed once he'd made up his mind.

Erik would just have to prove that his choice was the right one. *"The choice is yours, but I hope that you reconsider,"* he said, not surprised when there was no reply. Erik ignored his own misgivings and focused on Eileen.

Eileen glanced out the window and wrinkled her nose. "Listen to that thunder," she said, mistaking the old-speak for a natural force. "It figures that there couldn't be a single day of my time here that it didn't rain."

"I think rain is romantic," Erik said softly.

"I hate it," she said, and grimaced.

Her strong feelings about water were interesting. On some level, she must remember the past. "Maybe I can change your mind," he said in a low voice.

Eileen's gaze flew to his and he smiled slightly as he touched his ankle to hers. The firestorm's heat surged through him, turning all thoughts to cinders, coaxing desire to burn with new vigor. The slight contact was like gasoline tossed on a fire, sending a blaze though his body that made him catch his breath.

And want.

He watched his mate, seeing the firestorm's effects on her. Eileen blushed, her eyes sparkled and her lips curved; then she abruptly looked down. She shifted her ankle away from his and he knew that breaking the contact was the smarter choice.

Erik had no doubt that his firestorm would be consummated within hours. He should have been relieved by the relief that promised, but instead he found himself irritated with the need for haste. It might have been good to savor an event so rare.

But he had no time to languish over a seduction. He had to breed and return to his obligations as quickly as possible. His own inclinations were irrelevant.

For once, he resented the burden of his responsibility to the *Pyr*.

Eileen felt Erik's growing agitation. He checked the platform at the next station, then returned to his seat. He couldn't sit still, apparently, his toe tapping and his fingers drumming relentlessly on his knee.

Eileen was worried about Magnus and his thugs, too, but at least she had her knitting to soothe her nerves. Erik's vigilance reassured her as well—she understood that he knew more than she did and believed that he would protect her.

She would still have preferred to have been in a car or other vehicle under her own control, so she could make decisions or change direction. Traveling on public transit with a fixed schedule made her feel vulnerable.

It would be too easy to figure out where the train would be and when, too easy for Magnus to check whether she and Erik got off at any of the scheduled stops.

Eileen didn't doubt that that was what worried Erik, too.

He frowned and tried to hide his consternation, then suddenly looked directly at her. "Tell me what you know of this story," he invited.

Eileen understood that he needed the kind of distraction that her knitting provided for her. Maybe she could use it, too.

She rummaged in her satchel and pulled out her battered notebook. "A student of mine told it to me. She said her grandmother used to tell it, and she wondered what it really meant."

"And the grandmother?"

"Long dead, unfortunately. But she had come from

Shropshire when she was very young, and routinely said that her grandmother had told this story, so I came back here to look for details."

Erik sat back and studied the ceiling of the train car. Eileen could see him thinking and, from his haunted expression, she guessed that he was remembering something.

Something important.

Again, she wondered what she had said.

Then he looked at her again, smiled slightly, and invited her to continue. It wasn't the same kind of smile he'd offered her before, though. There was a shadow in his eyes.

"You were remembering something," she prompted.

"Nothing of relevance. Go on."

She closed the notebook. "That's not true. You looked upset for a minute, which means it wasn't irrelevant. Tell me, please."

"No."

They had a deal. Eileen picked up her knitting and ignored him.

She felt Erik glare at her but didn't look up. She heard him sigh with exasperation and almost smiled that he found her so infuriating. "If you must know," he said with obvious reluctance, "I was thinking of my son."

Eileen glanced up in surprise. "You have a son?" At Erik's terse nod, she sobered at the implication. "Do you have a wife, then?"

"I had a wife. She died, partly because of our son."

Eileen waited.

Erik took a quick breath and fired an annoyed glance her way. "He chose a reprehensible life. It broke her heart."

"And yours," Eileen guessed quietly.

Erik frowned. "I thought you were going to tell me a story."

Eileen should have left the subject alone, but she was curious. "How was your son's choice responsible for your wife's death?"

He glared at her.

Eileen held his gaze, waiting.

Erik grimaced, then sighed. "She committed suicide as a result of it. And I refuse to speak more of this right now."

"I'm sorry," Eileen said immediately. She saw the agitation that he couldn't hide and felt guilty for pushing him so much.

All the same, her heart softened toward him.

He had a rat of a son and his wife had committed suicide. Eileen understood that Erik would have emotional walls like nobody's business as a result of that experience.

She could respect that he had scars. Only a man who had cared deeply for his wife could look so stricken when talking about her death. He had married her. They had had a son. He was disappointed in his son's choices. This was all perfectly normal and very reassuring to Eileen.

It was good that he had some romantic history. Solitude was a warning sign, in her opinion.

At least those who were divorced had tried. People who tried marriage had believed in happily ever after, even if they had ultimately been proven wrong.

Eileen thought of Lynne's comments and opened her notes impatiently. "It's an occupational hazard, I guess," she said. "I sense a story and have to pursue it." She smiled and even though Erik didn't answer her, she saw his expression soften slightly.

"Some wounds don't close so easily," he said quietly.

Eileen understood that he had loved his wife deeply, perhaps so deeply that he continued to love her long after her death. The distinction between sex and love suddenly seemed very clear.

Fortunately Eileen knew which she wanted from Erik. Just sex would suit her fine. Eileen ignored the dissenting voice in her mind and began to read her clumsy version of the story.

Chapter 10

" 'Once upon a time, in the parish of Madeley, there was a young woman,' " Eileen said, noting that Erik closed his eyes. " 'She was beautiful, with dark hair and flashing eyes, and was avidly courted by every young man in the vicinity. She had a sister who was as fair as she was dark, and the people called them Sunshine and Shadow. Their natures were opposite to their coloring, for the raven-haired one was as merry as a beam of sunlight, while the fair one was so quiet that she was easily overlooked.

" 'Shadow was the eldest but had no desire to wed. She denied all of her suitors, declined every invitation and offer, much to the frustration of her father. Sunshine insisted she would wed only after Shadow did, which didn't please their father either.' "

Erik smiled ever so slightly but he didn't say anything and he didn't open his eyes. It was funny that his smile didn't make him look any less daunting. Even with his eyes closed, he seemed fully alert.

Dangerous.

Sexy.

There was a green glimmer between his lids, as if he were watching her. Eileen shivered with mingled dread and delight, then kept reading.

" 'The days passed and the sisters grew older, and fewer suitors came to call. The father argued with Shadow, but she refused to marry. Sunshine, in her turn, refused to wed first. Shadow had a tendency to go out into the fields and spend the day painting, and Sunshine often accompanied her. But Shadow took to disappearing before Sunshine was awake and returning late, after Sunshine was in bed.

" 'This annoyed their father still more and he became suspicious. He tried to follow his daughter and learn what she was doing. The first morning, he lost her in a sudden swell of fog. On the second morning, it rained, and he lost sight of her in the mist. Furious that even the elements were arrayed against him, he waited up for his errant daughter.

" 'They argued that night and Shadow admitted that she was with child. Her father's fury knew no bounds. He destroyed everything Shadow had ever contributed to the household, shredded her paintings and scattered her paints. He banished her from the house, sending her out into the night, and disavowed her in his anger.' "

Erik shifted in his seat. He opened his eyes and frowned, bracing his elbows on his knees. He watched Eileen, his eyes as bright as cut glass, and Eileen knew she'd reminded him of something.

"Go on," he urged when she hesitated.

" 'Sunshine was afraid for her sister, but she was more afraid to defy her father. At first light, Sunshine slipped from the house with food and a dry cloak, hoping to find her sister. She was relieved when she saw Shadow appear in the rain and the sisters embraced. Sunshine saw the shadow of a man, but he did not come close enough for her to see his face.

" 'Shadow had returned only to say farewell. She kissed her younger sister and bade her to be happy. As a farewell gift, Shadow gave Sunshine the only painting yet in her possession. Shadow bade her sister not to look at it until she was gone, to keep it safe forever as a talisman; then the sisters embraced one last time and the elder one departed.' "

"Forever," Erik interjected softly. "For the sisters never saw each other again."

Eileen was startled that he knew what she had written. She met the conviction in his gaze and the hair prickled on the back of her neck.

She was itching to ask him what he knew and how, but for the moment, she read on.

Eileen's story was close to the truth, but not entirely accurate. The differences gave Erik some distance from his own memories, some ability to review the facts with detachment.

Erik wondered who had been the grandmother of Eileen's student. It must have been a descendant of Adelaide. Shadow was Louisa—he had heard her called that in her day—and Sunshine, Louisa's sister, Adelaide. The sisters had been close and he regretted having severed that bond.

But he had had no choice, not then.

And when he had chosen otherwise, everything had gone awry. Erik moved restlessly, striving to focus on Eileen's voice.

" 'When Sunshine was finally alone, she looked at the painting for the first time. She was shocked by its beauty. It depicted a dragon, magnificent and powerful. He was dark and glittered like a jewel, and was shown with his tail coiled and his wings unfurled. Fire emanated from his mouth and smoke filled the air surrounding him.' "

Erik considered his boots. He'd wondered what had happened to that painting. Where was it now?

" 'She thought she should have been afraid, but every stroke of the brush was loving. Every dab of paint had been applied with affection. Sunshine knew that her sister's heart was full and that she loved the man she had chosen over her blood family.' "

Erik turned to look out the window and felt his eyes narrow. He'd thought his past banished from any power to influence him, but Eileen's whimsical retelling of the story caught at his heart.

" 'Sunshine understood that her sister didn't intend to reveal the identity of the man who had fathered the child she carried. She guessed that that man came from the great smelting factories of Coalbrookdale, which laid across the green of the land like a black dragon, spewing smoke and fire into the air.

" 'She also knew that Shadow chose not to be found. She hid the painting and kept her knowledge to herself, such as it was, and slowly their household returned to a routine, albeit one without Shadow's laughter. The new minister began to court Sunshine. By the time spring unfurled its first leaf, they married.

" 'And so it was that the following August, when the sun was setting over the hills, Sunshine straightened from tending her own small garden beside the manse. She was rounding with a child and tired easily. She heard the beat of leathery wings and stared as a dragon, a dragon precisely like the one in her sister's painting, spiraled out of the sky. She was too surprised to scream or run. She murmured a prayer and stood her ground.' "

Erik smiled despite himself. He remembered that meeting all too well, remembered the shock in Adelaide's eyes. He wasn't certain she could have run, she had been so terrified.

"What is it?" Eileen asked.

Erik arched a brow, choosing an easier truth than the one in his thoughts. "I like when the dragons are the good guys."

Eileen laughed, then sobered as she read on. " 'The dragon was as real as anything else surrounding Sunshine—she could hear the beat of his wings and feel the air they moved. He stretched out one claw toward her and she saw that something small and golden was on his nail. He waited in silence for her to take it, and so, finally, she did.

" 'It was hair. A golden lock of hair, hair so soft that Sunshine knew it was baby hair.

" 'And then she knew who he was and from whence he had come.

" ' "My son," said the dragon, his pride clear.

" ' "My sister?" Sunshine asked, fearing the worst.

" ' "Sends her best wishes," he said, much to Sunshine's relief. "She is tired but well."

" 'The notion warmed Sunshine's heart, as did the dragon's gallantry. She smiled and the dragon reared up, magnificent in his power. He inclined his head once to her, his eyes gleaming, then launched into the sky. His mission was complete.

" 'Sunshine watched the dragon until he disappeared into the darkening sky. When he was gone, she wondered whether her eyes had deceived her. She looked down at the little fair curl in her hand. It was as real as real could be. She knew then that she had not imagined him.

" 'She hid the lock of hair with the painting and kept her sister's secret safe. She never saw the dragon or her sister again, though each night she remembered both in her prayers. In time, the villagers said the the sisters had been named the right way after all, for Sunshine had the radiance of a happy woman, while Shadow had disappeared and was assumed to have met a dark fate.

" 'It was only on her own deathbed that Sunshine surrendered the painting and the lock of hair to her own daughter, the daughter she had named Louisa. This was the child she had been carrying when the dragon came to visit. Sunshine told her the story of her namesake and then she died.' "

Eileen closed her book and ran her fingertips across the cover with satisfaction.

Erik studied her. "You like this story," he murmured.

Eileen cleared her throat and nodded with enthusiasm. "Yes. I paraphrased it from my student's version, of course. What's interesting is that the story doesn't have the usual for-

mulaic ending of them living happily ever after—or the alternative, 'as far as I know they are happy still'—but I guess
there's too much ambiguity about Shadow's fate for that."

When he didn't say anything, she flicked him a bright
look. "Does it match the version of the story you know?"

"There is truth in it," he admitted. "But not all of the
truth."

She pursed her lips as she put her notebook away, then
began to knit. Erik wondered what question she was intent on
solving.

"I suspect the story is maybe a comment upon the changing role of women in the industrial society," Eileen said.
"How their movement to towns in search of jobs removed
them from the control of their fathers, maybe gave them different choices than marriage."

Suddenly Erik realized why he couldn't sense Magnus's
presence at all.

It was a trick.

Magnus was trying to lure Erik into complacency. Probably
Magnus was following the train at a sufficient distance that
Erik was unaware of his presence. Boris had learned to disguise his scent, after all—quite possibly Magnus had been
the one to teach Boris that feat.

Magnus would certainly know the train's destination, and
he might have discovered Eileen's destination. She'd bought
her ticket ahead of time, and Erik knew that Magnus had
more than one technical whiz in his employ. Any system
could be hacked.

It just took a bit of time.

If Magnus knew their destination, he could choose his
moment.

Unless Erik changed the itinerary.

Coventry would have to do. They'd rent a car and drive.
With any luck, they'd lose Magnus long enough for Erik to
find a temporary lair and protect its perimeter with dragonsmoke.

Then seduce Eileen and steal the Dragon's Teeth. It was unlikely that she would be of interest to the *Slayers* then.

It was not, however, out of the question.

Erik chose not to think about that problem for the moment.

"We have to go," he said as the train pulled into the station.

Eileen's expression turned to surprise.

He was on his feet, peering out the window as the train slowed. "We're getting off here."

"You're welcome to do so." Eileen settled into the depths of her coat and kept knitting. "I'm going to Birmingham New Street, which we won't reach for"—she looked at her watch—"another twenty-five minutes. I should be able to finish a couple more rows."

Erik knew how to change her mind quickly. He reached past Eileen and snatched the wooden chest. He paused to give her a steady look, as if he'd compel her to follow his command. "We're getting off here," he repeated.

He took the wooden chest and strode for the exit.

"Hey! Stop!" Eileen leapt to her feet, but Erik didn't even look back. He heard her swear with an earthiness that made him smile. That made him glance her way. He saw her jam her knitting back into her satchel. She shoved her arms into her coat sleeves and grabbed her satchel, then ran after him, furious but moving fast.

Perfect.

Eileen followed Erik, swearing under her breath. She wasn't going to surrender that wooden chest easily. When the train stopped, he got off and offered his hand to her with his usual gallantry. Given that he was making decisions for both of them, without consultation with her, Eileen wasn't charmed by the gesture. She jumped down by herself.

Once on the platform, she grabbed the handles of the trunk and was relieved when he released them.

If a bit surprised. The train began to move behind her.

" 'The course of true love never did run smooth.' " The conductor saluted them from the open door and there was no chance of jumping back onto the train.

When Eileen glanced at the conductor, Erik lifted her satchel from her shoulder instead. He marched toward the station with her knitting and her laptop and her notebook and her identification, compelling her to run after him as the train departed.

Eileen called him every name she knew.

Erik didn't slow down. He cast a glance over his shoulder and she was surprised that his eyes were twinkling. Maybe he just liked being in control of their options.

Actually, she felt better about this option, too, but she'd never tell him as much.

At least there was no black sedan in sight. Eileen looked.

Erik moved into the station with purpose, targeted the car-rental counter, and rented the best car available at a discounted price. They were driving out of town in record time.

"Why don't I ever have that kind of luck at the rental place?" Eileen complained. "Even when I have a reservation, they mess it up."

"Just my natural charm," Erik said tightly.

Eileen laughed. "Is that what it is?" He glanced at her, but she ribbed him. "Charm is one place you fall short, my friend. You may be effective and efficient, but charming?" She shook her head. "Nope. You missed the line when they were handing out charm."

"Yet here you are with me," Erik observed, his tone wry, "despite my lack of charm. I must have some appealing attribute."

He was teasing her. He seemed to have discovered some sense of humor, after all. Eileen decided to dish him a bit of truth, especially as she was relieved to be off the train. She might not like his methods, but the results were fine. "Just between you and me, I'm a sucker for men who are more than they appear to be. I like the unpredictable ones, who tell the truth."

Erik flicked her a glance, and she caught her breath at the sparkle in his eyes. "I shall keep that in mind."

"I bet you will."

"And I shall endeavor to remain both unpredictable and honest." He winked at her then, looking so unexpectedly mischievous that Eileen caught her breath.

She wondered just how much more there was to learn about Erik.

Then he negotiated the last roundabout heading out of town and put his foot to the floor. The car whizzed forward, going far too fast on the admittedly empty road.

"Whoa!" Eileen cried, gripping the seat. They rocked around a curve, Erik slowing only an increment; then he accelerated even more. Was he intending to kill them both? "Are you crazy?"

"Not yct."

"Then quit driving like a maniac."

"I'm in complete control," he said. He did appear to be. Erik drove with precision, his gaze fixed on the road. He was perfectly calm, despite their speed.

This kind of unpredictability Eileen could live without.

His next words were so low that they made her shiver. "I just want to see what this thing can do, before I need to know."

That sounded ominous. Eileen glanced over her shoulder and found only empty road behind them. She faced the windshield just in time to see a black sedan emerge from a side street, its front bumper easing into their path.

"Look out!" she shouted.

But Erik had already swerved around the obstacle of the car, his moves smooth and confident. He had to move into the lane for the oncoming traffic and Eileen saw a truck quickly approaching. Erik slipped back into his own lane in the nick of time, changed gears, accelerated again.

Eileen tightened her seat belt and caught her breath as he calmly checked the mirrors.

"Here he comes," he said softly.

Eileen turned to see that black sedan right behind them. Was it the same black sedan? "Is that Magnus?"

"Of course. He has your scent." Erik accelerated slightly. "He can find you anywhere."

Eileen stared at him. "That's not the most reassuring thing you could have said."

"But it's the truth, nonetheless. I thought you preferred the truth."

"Maybe I'm thinking I should be careful what I wish for."

Erik cast her a crooked smile. "Magnus doesn't want you. He wants this wooden box, and once he has it—or once you no longer have it—he will lose interest in you."

"Is that true of you, as well?"

"No." Erik negotiated a curve and spoke with force. "The firestorm means that I want you."

His possessive tone sent a shiver through Eileen. "You traded me the story for the teeth," she reminded him.

"It would have been vulgar to say otherwise."

"You just did."

"In privacy, anything goes." He flicked her a glittering glance, one that made her heart leap with anticipation. "In public, I prefer to be more reserved."

Eileen caught her breath at his intensity as he focused on his driving. Given the speed they were going, she wasn't going to interfere with that. She held fast to the box as they ripped past the hedgerows and wished she could remember a few good prayers.

A bunny hopped across the road, appearing suddenly from the undergrowth, and she almost screamed at what had to be inevitable.

Erik didn't hesitate. He geared down, changed into the other lane, avoided the bunny, missed an oncoming car, and raced onward.

Eileen caught her breath at how quickly that had happened.

She looked back to see the rabbit make the shoulder of the road, just before Magnus's car passed the car going in the other direction.

She took a steadying breath and figured the bunny was doing the same. She heard thunder again and peered out the window at the clouds. It didn't look ominous enough for a thunderstorm, but she was hardly an expert in local weather patterns.

Rain began to slant against the windshield. Erik turned on the wipers but didn't slow down. He was even more taut, which she wouldn't have believed possible just moments before. The road shone and looked slick in the rain. Eileen was sure they'd skid into a ditch, but didn't want to say anything or interfere with his concentration.

"It handles better than I expected," Erik said softly. "Not bad for a cheap car."

Eileen poked at the dash. "It probably doesn't have air bags, though."

"Not on the passenger side, I'm sure."

Eileen understood that he was teasing her. "Thank you for that upbeat note."

"Least I can do." He flicked a look her way. "Seeing as I have neither charm nor a sense of humor. Honesty and unpredictability will have to carry the day."

Eileen would have said something witty, if she could have thought of it in time. As it was, she was completely distracted by Erik's abrupt left turn. The road had been heading into a gentle left curve, but he took a sharp turn into a side lane. The back end of the car fishtailed as she hung on to the door handle.

The car rocketed down the lane Eileen hadn't even seen before they were in it. It was barely wider than the car, but that didn't slow Erik down.

Eileen looked back and the big sedan zipped right past the lane. "Think you lost him?"

"No." Erik's tone left no room for doubt. "I think he's playing with us, but that doesn't mean that he's in charge of all of the surprises."

Eileen wasn't sure she liked the sound of that. She shut up and hung on, trying to brace herself for the unexpected.

Brambles struck the car wetly and the rain settled to a steady drumming on the roof. The car bounced and jumped, splashing through puddles with manic speed. Eileen thought she saw a tiled roof and another chimney. She caught a glimpse of a wet garden and a stacked stone wall. The lane was probably a pretty walkway, taken at a slow enough speed to appreciate its charms.

Erik clearly wasn't in the mood for that.

Just as abruptly as the first time, he turned the car wheel to the right, hard. The car bounced out of the lane and onto a large paved road, one much like the one they had left moments before. The tires skidded, but Erik didn't hesitate. He floored the accelerator again, and the car skidded a bit before straightening its course.

"It could use ABS," he muttered.

"What do you usually drive?"

"A black Lamborghini. It handles rather better than this."

Eileen wasn't surprised to hear that.

Maybe Erik had taken racing lessons.

If so, she hoped he'd passed.

This road curved gently to the right, the hedgerows ensuring that not much of the pavement ahead was visible. Erik drove with relentless speed and it took Eileen a moment to realize what was wrong.

He was driving on the right side of the road.

In England.

That was a mistake she would make. He hugged the inside of the curve, racing toward whatever they couldn't see.

Uh-oh.

Chapter 11

"Aren't you on the wrong side of the road?" Eileen asked, trying not to startle Erik.

"Yes," he agreed without hesitation. Eileen was sure he accelerated even more.

Any question she had was stopped in her throat. A large black sedan appeared around the curve ahead, heading directly for them. It couldn't have been fifty feet ahead of them. Eileen made a little yelp of terror and clutched the wooden chest. She saw Erik's cold smile and heard thunder again.

Then the black Mercedes swerved hard, so hard that it rolled. It flipped onto its roof and slid into the hedgerows on Eileen's left, its wheels spinning.

Erik didn't slow down, but his smile became one of satisfaction.

"You did that on purpose," Eileen accused.

"Yes," he agreed, his manner more amiable than it had been.

"How did you know he would chicken out?"

"I didn't. But Magnus has a certain affection for his vehi-

cle. Pride of ownership, I guess. Either way, I assumed that
he would care more about his car than I do about this one."

"Big assumption," Eileen felt obliged to note.

"Yes. But smaller than you think."

"Because you're not driving the Lamborghini."

Erik smiled.

"You know him pretty well."

"Well enough." Erik winked at her. "Shame about the
paint job on the roof. I doubt his insurance will cover it."
Unrepentant, he geared down, took a corner, and negotiated
his way to the M6.

As they merged into the traffic, Eileen focused on steadying the wild pace of her heart.

"Give them to me, or I will take her."

Magnus's old-speak echoed in Erik's thoughts long after
he had first heard it, long after he'd left Magnus stranded in
his upside-down luxury car. The words were low and potent,
even for old-speak, and had an insistence that Erik didn't
like. The threat made him even more acutely aware of the
need to consummate his firestorm quickly.

And it gave him new doubt that Eileen would be safe
without him afterward. How could he take her with him?
How could he fulfill his duty to the *Pyr* without leaving her?
Would the other *Pyr* defend her—and his child—after Erik
was killed?

Magnus's words wound into Erik's own thoughts, min-
gling and mixing and infecting. Erik knew that a less resilient
Pyr might find himself confusing his own ideas with those of
Magnus.

He had to get the Dragon's Teeth away from Eileen. He
had to ensure her safety. He had to seduce her and get back
to his responsibilities.

But first he'd tell her more of the story.

He owed her that much. He'd promised. He was a man on
a mission and one with no time to loiter.

The scenery looked so similar to his memory in places that it brought a lump to his throat. It was cleaner and greener, though, less ravaged by the waste products of industry. The air was comparatively clear. It was amazing how the earth could heal, given the opportunity to do so.

Erik felt Eileen watching him as he stopped beside the iron bridge itself. Given the weather and the season, it wasn't surprising that no other tourists were visiting the historic attraction. He parked the car and turned off the engine. Rain drummed on the roof.

He glanced toward his mate. Her expression was wary.

Erik thought that was a healthy response to the events of the past day. He let her set the pace.

"So," she began, glancing pointedly out the window, "I assume there's a reason we're parked here."

"Did you visit the bridge when you were last here?"

She tried to repress a shudder and failed. "No." Her word was emphatic, more emphatic than the situation deserved.

"Why not?"

"I'm not interested in the usual tourist attractions. I'm interested in people, not things; in stories, not feats of engineering."

"I think you had another reason to avoid it." Erik opened his door before she could argue and got out. He went around the car and opened Eileen's door.

"I don't want to get out of the car."

"You'll have to if you want to hear what I'm going to tell you."

"You could tell me here."

Erik just shook his head.

Eileen wrinkled her nose. "Now? In the rain?"

"I don't think it's going to stop anytime soon."

Still, Eileen hesitated, her gaze darting between the wooden chest on her lap and the sky. She surveyed the bridge and he sensed her dislike of the place.

This wouldn't be easy for her, but he believed it had to be done.

"We'll lock the wooden chest in the trunk," Erik suggested, his tone more kindly. "We won't be long."

She studied him for a moment. "Why do I have such a bad feeling about this? You know, a 'Serial Killer Leaves Body of American Woman in Rural Shropshire' kind of a feeling? 'Charming Rogue Pushes Tourist Off Bridge.' That kind of thing."

It wasn't a coincidence that she'd raised the image of a deadly fall from this particular bridge.

"Remember that I have no charm, though."

He was relieved when her smile flashed, but she still didn't get out of the car.

"I won't injure you," Erik promised. "Something unpleasant happened here a long time ago. Maybe you're sensing that."

Eileen rolled her eyes, her practicality restored. "The last thing I am is some psychic flake. I just don't like the rain. I'm sick of it." She swung her legs out of the car. "I assume there's a point to our being here? A good reason to get soaked to the skin again?"

"You wanted your story. Part of it is here."

She met his gaze and held it for a moment, as if assessing him. "If you're lying to me . . ."

"Honesty is one of my few positive attributes, by your own accounting."

She smiled again. "Okay, let's get it over with."

Erik took the wooden chest from her and locked it into the trunk, along with her satchel. He locked the car doors, then, wanting to ease her uncertainty, gave her the keys.

She was so obviously surprised that he was irritated.

"This way," he said tersely, and turned away. He led the way onto the bridge, well aware that she didn't immediately follow. The tollhouse loomed large on the opposite shore, every surface slick with rainwater. The rain sliced coldly out of the sky, running into the collar of Erik's jacket.

At least they were alone.

The sky overhead was a flat gray, the rain and the cloud cover painting the scene in tones of silver. It was damp, the kind of dampness that went straight to the bone.

He heard Eileen's footsteps behind him.

"I don't understand. What does this place have to do with my story?"

"This is where you find another facet of the truth."

He stopped in the middle of the bridge and put his hands on the cold iron railing. Far below, the Severn rolled and churned, muddy and gray, swollen with rainwater. He shivered.

"Careful!" Eileen said, coming to a halt behind him. She shivered visibly. "It would be easy to slip."

Her concern was irrational, given that the bridge was enclosed with a high fence to prevent anyone from jumping.

"There's a fence," he noted quietly.

"Still." She looked down at the river with visible distaste. "I don't like it here. Let's go." She turned to leave but Erik caught at her sleeve. She glanced toward him, fear in the blue of her eyes, a fear that he understood.

He had to help her dispel it.

"Once upon a time," Erik began in a low voice, "there was a *Pyr*, a *Pyr* who felt his firestorm. And he came into the company of humans seeking his destined mate. He meant to find her and to breed, as he had been taught was his duty."

Eileen nodded and frowned, her gaze trailing to the river. Erik wasn't entirely sure that she was listening to him. This place had a strong association for her, one that she didn't yet understand.

He continued softly. "But his mate surprised the *Pyr*, who knew little of humans, and when he inadvertently revealed his true nature to her, she recoiled from his truth. She refused to share her body without his promise to deny his nature. Knowing the importance of the firestorm, he gave his pledge. They lay together, and she conceived his son."

Erik took a step closer to Eileen, well aware of the rain soaking his jacket. It beaded on his hands and ran through his hair, but his gaze never wavered from hers. She watched him steadily, apparently as oblivious to the rain as he, and the heat of the firestorm redoubled with every step he took. She was ensnared in the story, and he was relieved.

"This is the story of Shadow and Sunshine," she guessed.

"Only of Shadow," Erik agreed.

Eileen nodded, then spared a nervous glance at the river. He sensed that she focused on him and his story so that she could fight her own response to this place.

"For the sake of their child, the *Pyr* and his mate agreed to compromise: They would wed and raise their son in human society, at least until he came into his hereditary powers at puberty. She agreed to the *Pyr*'s condition that they make a new life for themselves, away from her family. He in turn pledged once more never to take dragon form again."

"Those are hefty promises," Eileen said softly, her gaze searching his. "Denying one's own nature in exchange for abandoning one's connections."

Erik was impressed that she understood the importance of what he was saying. "They did not know fully what they did."

She tilted her head to watch him, the rain beading off her curls and spilling into her scarf. "And did they keep their vows?"

"The lady kept her word, and they made a life far away from everyone she knew and loved. The *Pyr* kept his promise until their son came into his abilities. He kept his promise until that son turned to the darkness and left his mother weeping."

"What do you mean?"

"He turned *Slayer*." Erik heard the pain in his own tone.

Eileen's eyes narrowed. "What does that mean exactly? What's a *Slayer*?"

"Magnus is a *Slayer*, as are his minions. The *Pyr* are charged with protecting the treasures of the earth; the true *Pyr* believe that humans are among those treasures, while *Slayer*s believe that humans are the cause of Gaia's destruction. *Slayer*s would eliminate humans—and those who protect them—and preserve the earth and her elements for themselves alone. Their choice is a selfish one."

"It's a personal choice?"

"*Pyr* are born. *Slayer*s are made." Erik frowned down at the Severn, disliking that the direction of the conversation had changed. He'd intended to show Eileen her past, not review his own. "When they turn to darkness, they abandon the light of the Great Wyvern. Their blood turns black in the absence of the divine spark and they lose the ability to procreate."

"So they always need recruits," Eileen whispered. Her gaze flicked over Erik's features, searching every nuance of his response. "That *Pyr* must have been devastated by his son's choice, as devastated as his mate."

Erik nodded grimly. "The *Pyr* thought he could save his son, that he could bring back the child his wife loved beyond all else, that he could make matters right. He believed he had the power to turn events his own way." He stared down at the river, the sight of the swift water sending a pang through him.

He had broken a vow and Louisa had paid the price.

Erik's tone turned harsh, his heart becoming heavy with the reality of his own failure. "But the *Pyr* was wrong. He lost their son completely. And in breaking his word to his wife, he shattered her heart."

Donovan stood in Erik's lair and held the largest piece of the broken Dragon's Egg in his hands. He'd never held the orb before and was surprised that it seemed like nothing more than a chunk of rock.

To think that he'd dreaded its portents.

To think that he'd thought it animate.

Six of them had gathered instinctively at Erik's lair, and had found Nikolas pacing the perimeter like a caged wolf. The ancient *Pyr* wasn't talkative at the best of times, but on this day, he felt like a shadow of doom.

A silent one.

Delaney was quiet, as well, hovering close to Sloane, who was obviously concerned. Delaney looked leaner than Donovan recalled, more haunted, even though his color was better and he moved with more confidence than he had just months before.

Donovan examined the shattered edge that had been the inside of the orb, well aware of his partner, Alex, standing close beside him. He glanced at her as she ran a fingertip across the break.

"It's dead," Sara said, her arms folded tightly across her own chest. She shivered and Quinn put an arm around her shoulders. She was paler than Donovan recalled, instead of flushed with that rosy glow of pregnancy.

"What broke the Dragon's Egg?" Donovan asked.

"Boris," Nikolas hissed from the group's perimeter, his eyes flashing.

"Impossible," Sloane said. "Boris is dead."

"He didn't look dead when he broke the Dragon's Egg," Nikolas said. Donovan sensed that he wasn't the only one who doubted the word of this *Pyr* who had so recently joined their ranks.

"That makes no sense. How did he get it?" Quinn demanded. "Did you let him into Erik's lair?"

"No!"

"Then how did he get through Erik's barrier of dragonsmoke?" Sloane asked, his skepticism clear.

"Weren't you supposed to stay here and protect Erik's hoard?" Donovan asked before Nikolas could answer.

Nikolas's expression turned dark. "I was and I did," he insisted. "He entered anyway. It was Boris."

"That's impossible," Donovan said, and put down the piece of the Dragon's Egg. "None of us can cross the dragonsmoke of another."

Nikolas's voice dropped low. "Are you calling me a liar?"

The two *Pyr* stepped toward each other, the tension between them escalating. Alex murmured a warning, but Donovan wasn't going to put up with deceit within Erik's own lair.

"What you say is impossible," Donovan replied, meeting Nikolas's challenging stare with one of his own. It was outrageous that Erik had trusted the ancient *Pyr* with the protection of his lair, and that Nikolas had failed so spectacularly in just a week. "Boris is dead and no one can cross dragonsmoke. Why did you break the Dragon's Egg?"

"It is not impossible if it happened," Nikolas replied, his fists clenching. Donovan saw the glimmer around Nikolas's shoulders and felt himself shimmer on the cusp of change.

"We shouldn't fight among ourselves," Quinn said with heat.

"We shouldn't lie to each other," Donovan retorted. Nikolas's eyes brightened and he took a deep breath. Donovan was ready to shift along with him, and solve this dispute the traditional way.

"It's not impossible," a woman said softly.

They all jumped, although Donovan knew they shouldn't have been surprised that Sophie had appeared without an announcement. The Wyvern sat on one of the black sofas in Erik's lair, the darkness of the upholstery making her look small and frail.

She had all the substance of a mirage.

What had happened to her?

"At least Rafferty missed this surprise appearance," Sloane muttered, referring to the older *Pyr*'s distaste for Sophie's tendency to arrive unexpectedly.

Sophie didn't wave her fingertips as she usually did. Nikolas watched her, stepping closer. His manner was protective, but she ignored him. She rose from the leather sofa as if exhausted and stepped toward the others.

Away from Nikolas.

Sophie's eyes, to Donovan's relief, flashed as vividly as ever. "As Nikolas said, it happened, so it cannot be impossible."

"But how?" Sloane asked. "We cannot cross smoke—"

"Boris cut the smoke," Sophie said, and when the *Pyr* might have argued, she continued. "I saw him do it. He hovered between forms, only his right talon dragon while the rest was human, and he cut the smoke with his claw. Then he stepped through it and was unharmed."

"There was no sound?" Quinn demanded.

Sophie flicked a glance at him. "Only the resonant chime of an unbroken dragonsmoke ring."

"What happened to your neck?" Sloane asked suddenly. He lifted a fingertip to her scarf and pulled the sheer fabric away from her skin. There was a new wound there, one that still leaked blood.

The *Pyr* stared in horror. The Wyvern's blood had been shed.

Sophie swallowed and averted her gaze, her fingertips playing with the end of the scarf. "I was attacked," she admitted.

"She was assaulted by Boris Vassily, right here!" Nikolas interjected, his outrage more than clear. "He came to break the Dragon's Egg and lured her into Erik's lair. . . ."

Donovan swore and shoved a hand through his hair. The other *Pyr* were clearly just as upset. "But Erik killed Boris last summer."

Sophie met his gaze steadily. "How do you know?"

"Erik said so."

"Then Erik was wrong."

"But Erik said he exposed Boris to all four elements,"

Quinn insisted. "He said that he ensured that Boris was dead."

Sophie shook her head. "He did not know what Boris had done." She turned to Sloane. "There is one thing Boris could have done that explains all of this, only one substance he could have consumed before his battle with Erik."

Sloane took a step back, his horror clear.

"There is only one substance that could have pulled him back from the brink of death," Sophie insisted, following Sloane. "And you, Apothecary, you know its name."

"The Dragon's Blood Elixir," Sloane whispered as the color drained from his face.

Sophie nodded.

"Then it's real," Sloane continued. "And it does convey immortality."

"Of a kind," Sophie agreed.

Donovan's heart sank to his toes. He glanced at his fellow *Pyr* and saw his own dismay echoed in their expressions. He had always believed the Elixir was a myth, or at least a legend lost in the past.

But it was real.

The *Slayers* had it.

And they were drinking it.

Donovan felt a trickle of fear. Alex's hand slid into his and her fingers were cold.

Sloane swore and began to pace. "That ancient treatise talks about the powers of the Dragon's Blood Elixir and how it can be used to give immortality to anyone who survives the test of drinking it. I thought it was a metaphor. . . ."

Delaney sat down heavily and rubbed his temples with his fingertips. "Is that what they forced into us at Magnus's dark academy?" he asked, his words hoarse. "The potion that would either kill us, drive us insane, or make shadow dragons of us?"

Sophie dropped her gaze. "I fear as much."

Donovan frowned. "You mean that's what they gave to the

dead, to make them into shadow dragons? That's how they raised Keir and the others?" Sophie nodded, and Donovan shoved his hand through his hair. "What if you give it to the living?"

Delaney looked at him, his eyes filled with shadows that had not been there just a year before. "They either die or they become immortal. Like Magnus. Like Boris." He looked so pained that Donovan's heart clenched.

"What about you?"

Delaney grimaced. "Just call me one of the living dead."

"They couldn't turn Delaney *Slayer* because his heart was good and the spark of the Great Wyvern still burned within him," Sophie said. "You and Alex coaxed that spark to burn brighter, and pulled him back from the darkness."

"The shadow is still there," Delaney muttered.

"It's less impenetrable," the Wyvern insisted. Delaney didn't look convinced.

"Well, I sure hope I'm not immortal," Delaney said.

"You're not." Sophie's smile was fleeting and didn't seem to reassure him. "Those who become immortal are immune to the forces of nature." Her disgust was clear. "They become abominations and you, Delaney, are *not* in their company."

"Then whose company am I in?" Delaney demanded.

"Ours," Donovan said, but his brother looked away.

"They're like *Slayers*, then," Quinn said.

"Worse," Sophie corrected more sternly than Donovan had ever heard her speak. "Their immortality violates the entire impulse of life. Nature is cyclical. Life waxes and wanes, like the phases of the moon, like the roll of the seasons. Destruction is the partner of creation, death that of birth. The cycle constantly regenerates and renews, growing stronger and better over time, refining and rejuvenating. To be immortal is to step out of that cycle, to be fixed in the fluidity of the universe. It is not natural to be static. It is not right." She took a breath and squared her shoulders. "They must be destroyed."

The news just kept getting worse. Donovan shoved a hand through his hair and began to pace.

"But how do you kill an immortal?" Alex asked softly.

Silence filled Erik's lair.

Even though there were no answers forthcoming, Alex shook her head with her usual practicality. "Nothing is impossible," she said with the determination Donovan admired. "We need a plan. A good one. And for that, we need information. Sloane, please summarize everything you know about the Elixir. Delaney, you need to remember as much as possible about the dark academy." She put her hands on her hips and considered the broken Dragon's Egg. "And the rest of us have to figure out how to fix this thing."

"Fix it?" Sara asked, her doubt clear.

"Isn't stone formed under pressure and heat?" Alex asked, practical as always in finding solutions. "You *Pyr* do heat. Maybe you could fuse it back together again."

Quinn rubbed his forehead and uncertainty echoed in his tone. "We could take it back to my studio. I've never repaired stone, but we'd have the best chance of success with my forge."

"It can't hurt to try," Donovan said. "It's better than sitting around waiting for Erik."

"Except it won't work," Sophie said with conviction. "The Dragon's Egg was a gift from Gaia, a mark of favor extended from her to the guardians of the four elements. We cannot remake or repair it."

"Can we get another one?" Donovan asked, and Alex nodded approval of that notion. "I'll hunt it down if you point me in the right direction."

"The earth may not be so inclined to show us favor in these times. She may not have the will or the strength to make gifts when she is under assault."

"It couldn't hurt to ask," Alex said.

Sophie took a deep breath, looking frail again. "I will ask, although I cannot anticipate her reply. It may take time."

"Time is what we don't have," Quinn observed.

Sophie bowed her head and her hair fell over her face like a veil. Her next words were so soft that Donovan barely heard them. "Perhaps it is wiser for the Wyvern to remain beyond the concerns of the earth. Perhaps it is easier."

Before anyone could respond, Sophie's body began to sparkle. She could have been made of stars. Donovan knew that she was going to disappear again one beat before she started to fade.

"Sophie!" Nikolas roared, and leapt toward her. "You promised!"

Sophie reached out her hand; their fingers touched; then Nikolas's hand locked over hers. They disappeared in unison.

Both were gone, as surely as if they had never been present.

"She took him with her," Sara said as they all stared at the space the pair had occupied. Something sparkled on the floor, then faded to nothing. "I wonder why."

"I wonder where," Quinn said.

"It doesn't matter," Donovan said. "Alex is right. We need a plan against the Elixir. Let's compile everything we know, whether it seems useful or not. Erik left his laptop—maybe he already has some notes we can use."

Chapter 12

Something wicked had happened on this bridge.

Eileen was glad that she wasn't alone. In fact, she would never have come onto this bridge alone, and she certainly wouldn't have lingered. She had avoided it completely during her earlier visit here, despite many urgings from the locals to appreciate the view.

It was cold on the bridge, colder than iron in the rain. Instead of seeing the scene before her eyes, Eileen envisioned this valley blackened with industry, saw the sky dark and ominous.

She couldn't even look down at the churning river far below. She was chilled, colder than she could ever remember being.

The firestorm was a beacon in the darkness. Eileen stayed near Erik and tried to focus on his story. She ignored her own issues by attending closely to his own pain. She was soaked to the skin, but when he confessed the *Pyr*'s failure in such a harsh tone, she knew he was talking about himself.

Instinctively, she reached out and took his hand. Sparks leapt between them, making a golden glow in the cold light.

Erik caught his breath and Eileen felt a welcome heat roll through her.

It was a reassuring heat, one that drove both the chill from her body and the shadows from her thoughts. She met his gaze and saw the wonder there, felt sexy and beautiful all over again. She wanted Erik with such force that it was easy to heed only the summons of the firestorm.

As she held fast to his hand, the heat built. Eileen could feel perspiration on the back of her neck, under her scarf, and under her hair. She could feel the warmth between her thighs, desire making her tingle. She felt a line of fire in her veins, a simmering blaze that attuned her to Erik and Erik alone. She liked his firm grip on her hand, glanced down to admire his long fingers and his gentle strength.

She felt cocooned from the threat that surrounded them, safe in the golden glow of the firestorm.

Maybe it was because Erik was confiding in her. Eileen knew that didn't come easily to him. She would have bet her last dime that he was telling her the truth. She could sense his urgency and felt her own body rhythms respond. Her pulse picked up. Her breath came more quickly. She felt in tune with Erik in a way she'd never experienced before.

It was almost magical.

It certainly left her dizzy, and her desire compounded that. She reached out with the other hand and gripped the fence that rose above the railing, reassuring herself that she could not fall.

Erik stared down into the river's depths. Eileen swallowed and, holding fast to him and to the railing, she looked down.

The murky water rolled smoothly below them, slow moving but powerful. Inexorable. Eileen couldn't see anything in the water, between the darkness of the water and the patter of the rain on its surface. She knew that anything that fell into that water would be carried along, far beyond expectation. She knew that a person lost in that water would be tossed and tumbled, rolled with merciless power.

Until that person breathed no more. Eileen imagined how it would feel to take a mouthful of water, and felt ill. She really didn't like this place. Maybe it was the river. She'd never liked water, especially dark water, and had never learned to swim.

But this was a stronger response. Eileen thought suddenly of her dream, the one of Erik before she met him, and shivered. It was impossible to imagine herself enjoying the water, swimming through it with the grace and joy she'd felt in that dream.

Erik squeezed her fingers, holding her fast by his side. "This is difficult for you."

"I don't like water." Eileen heard her own nervousness.

"I know."

The rain fell harder, slanting out of the gray sky. It sizzled on impact with their entwined hands and made Eileen's coat heavy.

Eileen tried to recall his story, tried to think of something other than her gut response to this place. "You said the *Pyr* broke his promise to his mate."

"He did. But he never had a chance to explain himself to her." Erik flicked a sudden glance at Eileen. His eyes were so pale green that they might have been the same silver hue as the sky.

"What happened?"

"She returned here when she feared herself betrayed, because this was where their tale had begun. She came back to the home she had known. But she found only destruction and violence, not a haven. She witnessed the fullness of his deceit and ran. She knew then that she was utterly alone and always would be."

"But her sister—"

"The *Pyr* had never told her of that visit, had never told her of her sister's fate." Erik spoke harshly. "He was afraid that she would want to return, that she would break her vow, that she might betray his secret without intending to do so."

His lips twisted. "But in the end, he was the one who could not keep his promise."

"What happened?"

"She lost all hope," Erik said, his words low. He tightened his grip on her hand. "She responded with impulsive passion. The river was high and running fast. It was churning, just like this, filled beyond its banks and angry."

"No." Eileen whispered, taking a step back from the edge of the bridge. She had a sudden understanding of why there was a fence installed over the railings. "Not that."

"Yes, that," Erik said savagely. Eileen spun but he caught her other hand, holding her captive to hear the rest of his story. "She filled her skirts with river rocks before she jumped from this very bridge. It was newly constructed then." He frowned. "They found her two days later, miles and miles away. Dead, bruised, and battered almost beyond recognition."

He gave her a hard look. "Stems of water lilies were knotted in her hair."

Eileen fought her rising horror, telling herself that she was letting Erik compose himself. She refused to see the connection with her own dream, refused to admit that there could be one.

Why would Erik tell her this?

Because it was his story, and the root of his pain. She gave his fingers a minute squeeze. "You knew her," she guessed. "You knew Shadow."

He turned to face her again and his eyes were brighter. His expression was so avid that Eileen was reminded of a hawk—or another, much larger predator.

She knew what he would say before he did.

The dragon in Shadow's painting, after all, had been dark. *Black.*

"Her name was Louisa Guthrie," Erik said, his voice husky. "At least until she wed the *Pyr*."

Eileen waited. He never broke his gaze from hers, never so much as blinked. Eileen knew this was the truth.

"Her married surname was Sorensson."

Sorensson.

Eileen understood why Erik had been troubled that she had chosen this story, why it had startled him, why her recounting of it had made him so reticent. She understood that he was sharing his personal truth with her, that he was giving her what she wanted in exchange for the wooden chest that he wanted.

This was their barter made.

Erik was delivering, and at considerable cost to himself. She could see how hard it was for him to share the tragedy of his past and admit his own culpability.

She refused to consider that there was more to it than that.

His words were hoarse when he continued. "She took her last breath on this very spot."

Eileen understood that Erik blamed himself for his wife's suicide. But it couldn't really be his fault. She was sure there was more to the story than he had told her, because she already guessed that he was honest and principled.

Erik had loved. Erik had lost.

Eileen knew that he was wrong about his responsibility for his wife's death. So she did the only thing that a compassionate, impulsive woman could do under the circumstances.

She trusted her instincts.

Eileen reached through the silvery rain, framed Erik's wet face in her hands, and kissed him deeply.

Erik was shocked by Eileen's kiss.

Seared by it.

Of all the responses he might have expected, tenderness didn't even make the list. He had expected her to condemn him, the way he condemned himself, but she offered solace instead.

It wasn't just because of the surprise that her kiss struck a chord within him. It could have been a ray of sunlight sliding through a chink to light a room that had been dark too long. He felt the golden heat of the firestorm spread through him, launching from the insistence of Eileen's kiss.

She would forgive him for his crime.

She didn't know the whole story, didn't know the extent of his betrayal, but for the moment Erik didn't care. He was willing to take the pleasure she offered, to savor it, and not risk it with more truth than she asked from him.

She was too tempting to deny.

Her fingers slid over his face and she cupped his head in her hands, pulling him closer in silent demand. He felt her silver thumb ring against his ear, found his own hands in the endless softness of her hair. Her mouth was wet and hot and hungry; her tongue dove between his teeth and she nipped at his bottom lip. She might have eaten him alive with her demanding kiss.

And Erik had no desire to stop her. She pressed herself against him, the fullness of her breasts colliding with his chest and awakening a flurry of sparks between them. She was tall and strong, but feminine. He imagined again the softness of her skin—he was sure that naked she would look like an ivory sculpture.

Except her nipples. They would be as rosy as the blush on her cheeks. He wanted to unknot her hair and shove his hands through it. He wanted to lose himself in the sweetness and the scent of her. He wanted to push the firestorm to its limits and revel in the pleasure it offered. Erik was hard and ready, and a teasing waft of Eileen's perfume nearly drove him wild.

He couldn't evade Eileen or the brilliant light she shone on his shadows. He was seduced by her touch, by her impetuousness, by her caring. He had never known such kindness from a virtual stranger, and her ability to give warmed him in places the firestorm could never have reached. He had a feeling that she would never leave secrets buried, and a part of him yearned to have that kind of honesty with a partner. A part of him wanted to open the vault.

The other part of him knew better.

He reminded himself that the firestorm was about sex.

Erik could have taken Eileen right there, right on the bridge, but she deserved better. He wanted to give her the romance she yearned for, even if it wasn't for long.

He wanted to leave Eileen with a memory that would make her smile.

Besides, it wasn't safe to surrender to the firestorm without a protective barrier of dragonsmoke around them. Erik forced himself to think of realities. He had to remember Magnus and his animosity. The *Slayer* could be close by now, and Erik had to ensure Eileen's safety.

He broke their kiss with reluctance and smiled down at Eileen. He couldn't stop his fingertips from caressing the softness of her cheek. "Not here," he murmured, and brushed his mouth across hers once more. He found himself fascinated by the sparkle of her eyes and the flush on her cheeks.

"We need a hotel room," he said with heat. "So I can breathe a territory mark to protect you."

"One room," Eileen stipulated with a quick smile. "Not two."

"Lady's choice," he agreed, and they headed back to the car with purpose. Erik knew just the way to spend this rainy afternoon.

He could head back to Chicago by evening, with the Dragon's Teeth in his possession. It was a perfect solution.

But that wasn't the reason he strode so quickly to the car.

The little hotel was as elegant and romantic as Eileen remembered.

It was also virtually empty. They booked the largest room, the one Eileen had only glimpsed before. It was gorgeous, decorated in apple green and pale pink. The four-poster bed was mahogany and richly carved, the mattress laden with pillows and skirted with a deep ruffle. There was a step stool on one side, because of the height of the mattress, and the canopy overhead was made of lace.

There was a fireplace with an old mantel and a pair of armchairs in front of it. The owner lit a fire in the grate and turned on the lamps on either side of the bed. She checked the hot water in the bathroom and the number of towels there, chattering all the while about how rare it was to have customers at this time of the year. She embarked on a long story about needing to go to the store to get ingredients for a proper breakfast for them for the next morning, and Eileen didn't mention that she was starving.

She was, after all, hungry for a different kind of feast.

When the owner was gone, the room seemed both quieter and smaller. Eileen was aware of Erik's watchful presence. He seemed larger to her, more brooding and intense, and she tingled in anticipation of what they would do. It wasn't just the firestorm that made her body sing with excitement.

Eileen unwound her scarf and smiled at Erik. "I feel like I came to stay with a lonely auntie."

"As do I," he agreed with a rueful smile. "She won't be listening at the door if she's gone to the store, though."

"True. Do you care?"

He smiled, his features softening. When he smiled, she felt as if he let his guard down with her. She felt as if he trusted her. "No. Do you?"

Eileen smiled back at him. "No."

Their gazes clung for a hot moment; then Erik cleared his throat. "First things first," he said. "I have smoke to breathe."

"Duty before pleasure?"

"Something like that." He took off Eileen's wet coat and hung it over the back of a chair, close to the radiator. He took off his own jacket and did the same. She liked his gallantry, too. It would be like him to fulfill Shadow's wish to send word to her sister, and Eileen wasn't so sure that his wife hadn't realized what he'd done.

"Why not have a bath to warm up?" he suggested. He cast her a hot look, one that made her shiver in anticipation.

"How long does it take to breathe smoke?"

"It depends upon how impenetrable I want the barrier to be."

Eileen arched a brow.

"This will be a fortress when I'm done," he said, his tone fierce.

Eileen liked his protectiveness enough that she wished this weren't just going to be a fling. But she wasn't greedy— she knew what she was getting into, and she was sure it would be worth the price of admission. She took one glance into the large and luxurious bathroom, spied the claw-foot tub, and didn't have to be persuaded.

"Good idea," she said, and went to check the bath foam.

Rose scented. Perfect.

When she returned to the bedroom, Erik was standing by the window, his arms folded across his chest. He was taking deep breaths, breaths so long and steady that Eileen was amazed. She watched him surreptitiously as she tugged off her boots and wet skirt.

It couldn't be her imagination that he shimmered around the edges. His silhouette seemed to be traced in a sparkling light. It was hard to discern exactly where his body ended and where the air began.

What was the physiology of the *Pyr*? Erik seemed solid enough and real enough when he kissed her, but as she watched him now, he seemed ethereal. Not quite there.

Eileen couldn't look away, even as her thoughts raced. How old was Erik? She had a sense that the story she chased was several hundred years old, even though it had no firm date attached to it. Shadow's story had been told by her student's grandmother, who said she had heard it from her grandmother. Four generations at roughly twenty years apiece put the latest date for the story in the late nineteenth century.

It could have been older than that, which meant that Erik was at least a hundred and twenty years old.

And Louisa would be a century dead.

Eileen watched Erik and wondered about the parts of the story he hadn't told her. She didn't want to interrupt him to ask but she was curious. He seemed almost meditative, breathing deeply and regularly. He certainly was focused on his task. His eyes were partly closed, and were glittering in the slits. She had the sense that he was fully aware of what she did and where she was.

Self-awareness made her shiver, but not in a bad away. Could invisible dragonsmoke really protect her from Magnus and his thugs? It seemed to have worked at Lynne's house.

Eileen hung her skirt in the bathroom and tucked her boots under a radiator. She flung her stockings over the radiator in the bathroom. All the while, she kept circling back into the bedroom to study Erik, fascinated. When she was naked, she pulled on the thick white bathrobe left in the bathroom and shook out her hair. She drew the bath with the supplied bath foam, inhaling the scent of roses that wafted from the hot water.

Rain slanted against the window and she shut the curtains, welcoming the sense that she created a refuge from the storm. The room was warm and the light romantic. Maybe rain *was* romantic. She smiled, knowing that Erik would try to persuade her so. She could hear his steady exhalation, a reminder that she wasn't alone. That was romantic. She dug a handful of condoms out of her toiletries bag and cast them across the counter.

Erik was sufficiently perceptive to take the hint.

Eileen started to hum. She combed her hair, working out the tangles from their morning of adventure. The water rose high and hot in the tub, and the bathroom filled with steam. She turned off the water and ran her hands through the froth of scented bubbles.

Eileen pivoted at a slight sound and found Erik on the

threshold of the bathroom. He braced his hands on the frame and surveyed her, his expression hot.

Hungry.

His gaze danced over her bare feet, lingering on the electric blue nail polish, then slid up her legs. She could feel his perusal as keenly as a caress. He eyed the spot where the robe parted, where her cleavage was displayed, and visibly caught his breath. She saw him swallow, saw his fingers tighten on the frame, saw the line of his jeans change. She knew what he wanted.

Her.

"Lady's choice," he whispered, his words echoing in the small, tiled space. The rain pattered on the window as they stared at each other.

It made Eileen feel powerful that she could incite desire in this man who had such capabilities, who had lived so long and undoubtedly seen so many women. She was glad that he saw no need to change her, just accepted her as she was. Wanted her as she was. She liked that he was tough but vulnerable, and that he trusted her enough to let her glimpse his old wounds. She appreciated that he still gave her the choice, that he didn't just take what he wanted.

It meant that she would give him more.

Eileen lifted her chin and smiled at Erik. She unknotted the belt of the robe slowly, then shifted her shoulders so that the bathrobe tumbled to the floor.

Erik stared with such awe that she felt like a goddess.

Chapter 13

When Eileen dropped her robe, Erik's world stopped. His imagination hadn't begun to do her justice.

Her skin was as creamy as he'd expected, her nipples every bit as rosy. Her curves, though, were more dramatic than he could have guessed, her waist small and her breasts generous. She was slim through the hips, athletic and strong as he'd imagined, but more feminine than he could have believed.

Her hair was a magnificent shimmer of red-gold hanging down her back to her waist. There were freckles across her shoulders, a playful smattering that matched the glimmer in her eyes. She stood with confidence, comfortable in her own skin and with her body's allure.

He was reminded of his father's stories of the Valkyries come to collect a man's soul. Eileen was an irresistible siren, merciless in her demands and impossible to evade.

Erik didn't want to evade her. If she wanted his soul, he was hers. Her eyes shone blue, sparkling with a mischief that was vital and alluring. He was awed that she chose to be with him.

But there was no doubting her desire. She wasn't shy and she didn't pretend to want anything other than what she did. Eileen was an open book, and Erik liked her directness a lot.

They were both fans of honesty, but that wasn't the only thing they had in common.

She walked toward him, her movements elegant and rhythmic. He admired the sway of her hips, the slight bounce of her breasts, the dance of her hair. The mingled scents of rose from the bath and lavender from her own skin kicked his desire to a fever pitch.

He had breathed dragonsmoke high and deep, weaving it together with his usual fastidiousness. They were safe for the moment, cocooned behind his protective barrier, although Erik expected Magnus to challenge him within hours.

He would make the most of what time they had.

He waited for Eileen, knowing that his desire was evident but leaving the decision with her. It would have been easy to pounce on her and take what he wanted, but he suspected that she was a woman who preferred to make her own choices.

He was content to give her what she wanted.

As she came toward him, promise in her eyes and her smile, the firestorm raged through his body. Erik was aflame with desire for her, burning with the heat of a thousand infernos. This firestorm wasn't going to be overlooked, and here, within the security of the smoke he had breathed, he could give it all of his attention.

He could surrender.

He wasn't surprised by the ferocity of the spark when Eileen plucked at his sweater, but the lust that rocked through him nearly took him to his knees. She flattened her hand and slid it beneath his clothing and across his stomach, learning his shape with a bold caress. A flurry of sparks lit in the wake of her investigating fingers, heating Erik's blood to a boil.

"You're overdressed for this afternoon's activities," she had time to inform him before he bent his head and caught her mouth beneath his own.

Heat surged through him from their kiss, lighting bonfires across his skin. Eileen locked her arms around his neck and stretched to her toes, arching against him. He groaned and caught her close, deepening his kiss with demand. Her hands were in his hair again, pulling him closer, and she pulled back to nibble his bottom lip, teasing him with teeth and tongue.

Her skin was soft, so beguilingly soft that he wanted to run his hands over her entire body. His fingers moved against her of their own volition, sliding over the satin of her skin. He cupped her buttocks in his hands and lifted her against his erection, loving how she ground her hips against him.

"You need to get naked," she breathed against his mouth.

"So you've noted," he teased, and released her with reluctance. Her lips were reddened and swollen from his kiss, inviting him to kiss her again. She was so close, so warm, so fragrant that he didn't want to waste time with practicalities.

He peeled off his sweater and T-shirt, and Eileen's fingertips never left his skin. Her hands ran over his shoulders and back as he undressed. He knew she was reassuring herself as to his shape and he didn't mind.

In fact, he loved the sizzle that followed her questing fingertips. She awakened every increment of his flesh with her touch, igniting him and stirring him.

He pulled off his boots and socks, casting them aside. He dropped his jeans and discarded them, then kicked off his underwear. Eileen looked. There was no hiding his reaction when he turned to face her, and Erik feared that she might be alarmed by his size.

But Eileen wasn't shy. She considered him with a dawning smile, then reached for him.

To his shock, she locked her hand around his erection. They stared at each other for a potent moment as she caressed him. Erik's mouth went dry and he felt a tremble begin deep within himself.

Eileen smiled and he knew she had seen the effect of her

touch upon him. For once, he didn't mind having his secrets laid bare.

Erik let his hand rise to tangle in her hair. It was silky, the curls twining around his hand as if to ensnare him. He caught a fistful of it, loving the color and sheen of it, liking the sense of being entangled. He suddenly wanted to feel her hair against his skin, cast like a net across his body, holding him fast against her side. He wanted to wake up entwined with Eileen, and awaken her with a slow caress.

But he'd be gone within hours. And she would despise him.

Again.

The truth sent a pang through him, made him want to linger over the pleasure they could give each other.

Eileen must have seen something in his eyes, because her fingers stilled. She licked her lips and Erik watched the progress of the tip of her tongue, yearning.

"So, what's different about a *Pyr* in bed?" she asked softly.

Erik guessed her concern. "Nothing."

Her fingers tightened briefly on him and she arched a brow. "That's not nothing."

Erik swallowed as she slid her thumb across him, and he lost the thread of the conversation.

"I mean, do you change shape?" Eileen whispered, her busy fingers kindling his desire to a fever pitch.

"It's a fighting pose," Erik managed to say. "We shift only for defense."

A glimmer of humor lit her eyes. "So, if Magnus attacks us while we're, um, busy, it could get interesting. Otherwise you're just the way you are now."

"He can't attack us," Erik said with ferocity. "He can't cross my dragonsmoke. Don't imagine for a moment that you aren't safe with me."

She looked at him and he could see a dozen questions in

her eyes. He knew he couldn't make promises to her, but he had an irrational urge to do so.

She closed her eyes then, and bent to brush her lips across his bare chest. She caressed him with long, slow strokes and Erik gritted his teeth at the pleasure of her touch.

"I won't last," he protested, trying to lift her hands away.

"Of course you will," Eileen argued, but Erik didn't believe it. He caught her hands in his and had one glimpse of the sparkle of her eyes before she bent to take him in her mouth.

He fell back against the wall at the inferno that rolled through him. Eileen dropped to her knees in front of him. His hands found her hair again, his fingers locking into its silken abundance. Her tongue slid over him, stoking the firestorm.

Erik looked down at her and his heart clenched. Her toes curled into the thickness of the white fringed rug, looking luscious and delicate. Her hair cascaded over her shoulders, the light playing in its curls. The ripe curve of her rosy buttocks tempted him, as did the curve of her calf, the crescent of her arched foot, the indent of her waist. He closed his eyes and groaned when she slid her nails gently across his testicles.

He wouldn't last, if she kept that up.

She'd kill him, if she kept that up.

"Save that for the second round," he said, and she must have heard the tension in his voice. She cast a playful glance upward and he took advantage of the moment. He bent and claimed her mouth again, framing her face in his hands. She tipped her head back as he kissed her deeply.

When they paused to catch their breath, he bent and caught her up in his arms. He strode to the bath and set her gently into its warmth. She laughed as the bubbles slid around her curves. The foam eased over her skin, swallowing her, and her hair fanned across the surface. She looked up at him and crooked a finger in his direction. She could have been a mermaid, or a siren calling him to destruction.

That Valkyrie, perhaps, knowing as well as he did that he was doomed to die in the battle ahead.

Erik would answer her call either way.

When he stepped closer, Eileen pointed to the vanity. Erik saw the packages of condoms and understood. Would they impede the firestorm? Erik doubted it. He put one on beneath her watchful gaze and was rewarded by her smile.

He climbed into the bath, pulling Eileen into his arms as the water enveloped their bodies. The bath tub was long enough that he could stretch out with Eileen lying on his chest. She curled against him and steam rose from the bathwater as her curves pressed against him. He kissed her again, then slid his fingers through the water to her breast.

The bubbles made the water slick and slippery. Erik ran his hand over the fullness of her breast, savoring how the nipple tightened even more. He bent his head, blew aside the bubbles so that she shivered, then took her nipple in his mouth. He flicked his tongue against the peak. Eileen moaned and Erik liked the way her fingers tightened convulsively on his nape.

This was only the beginning.

He let his hand ease deeper into the water and slide to the top of her thighs. Her skin was smooth and soft, and he felt a jolt of desire when his fingers found the slick heat between her thighs.

Eileen gasped, then parted her legs.

Erik slipped his fingers through her pubic hair, excited that she invited his touch. She lifted one foot out of the water and braced it on the side of the tub, the bubbles dripping from her toes. He saw the arch of her wet foot, the way the foam glistened on her toes, the rosiness of her skin, the unlikely blue of her nail polish. She was a woman full of surprises and he was amazed by the power of his desire to discover them all.

He'd do the best he could in the time available.

Erik felt the heat gathering in Eileen, saw the steam rise

from the bath with greater intensity. He caressed her slowly,
still toying with that nipple. He heard her heart beat more
quickly and felt his own synchronize with her rhythms. The
water was hot and getting hotter. Her breath came faster. Her
blood pumped with vigor. The firestorm was coaxed higher
and brighter and Erik didn't want to surrender to it yet.

He didn't want it to end.

Eileen moaned and writhed as his fingers moved with purpose. She said something he couldn't understand, then
caught his chin in her hands. She pulled his mouth to hers
and he teased her, keeping their mouths apart while their
tongues danced in the steamy air.

The sparks leapt and played between them, painting
Eileen's features with a golden glow. She laughed and ran a
line of kisses along his jawline. He bent and kissed her ear,
blowing gently so that she shivered. She arched her back
again, sending her hair across the surface of the water, and he
kissed her neck. The sweet scent of her deluged him, and he
slid his fingers inside her with a decisive gesture.

Eileen gasped and trembled on the cusp of orgasm, but he
pulled his hand away.

"Tease," she accused, then straddled him in the bath. She
caught his wrists in her hands, keeping him from caressing
her. Her knees were locked around his chest, the width of the
bath keeping her from slipping. She knelt over him, her skin
rosy from the bathwater, the foam dripping from her breasts,
the wet tendrils of her hair sticking to her shoulders. Erik was
captivated by the sight of her.

Then she settled over him, and her tight heat stole his
breath away.

Eileen hovered over Erik, taking him inside her in slow in-
crements. She moved at a glacial pace, enjoying the obvious
signs of Erik's pleasure. She already knew that he wasn't one
to reveal his feelings very often and she enjoyed the sense of
power that came from tormenting him with sensation.

He was an open book to her in this moment. His eyes drifted closed and the line of his lips softened. He gasped when he moved and his hands tightened on her waist as if he couldn't control himself. Given Erik's power of self-control, that was saying something.

"Look at me," she whispered, leaning over him to kiss him. Her hair fell around them like a curtain and she moved with exquisite slowness. She liked that he hadn't argued about the condoms, liked that he was moving with deliberation himself.

His hand eased between them and he caressed her with gentle surety, making her gasp into their kiss. His eyes gleamed with sexual intent and Eileen moved to give him easier access. She watched a smile curve his lips as she writhed atop him.

"You just want to be in control," she teased.

"I just want to see you orgasm," he murmured, his voice low.

"Ditto." Eileen sat up and stretched her arms over her head, letting the bubbles drip from her breasts. She felt him watching her, sensed his hunger, and rolled her hips. He inhaled sharply, his finger and thumb caressing her more boldly. Eileen felt her hips begin to rock of their own accord. Her nipples were taut and she was simmering to the tips of her fingers.

"Show me," Erik whispered, his command firing Eileen's blood.

"Smile for me," Eileen retorted.

She knew immediately that she'd surprised him again. He smiled crookedly, his eyes shining like gems. She moved with greater force, setting the bathwater sloshing. They stared at each other as the heat rose, their bodies coming together in that ancient rhythm. The rain beat on the windows, seeming to drive them on to greater heights.

She abruptly dropped to his chest, writhing against him as she kissed him again. The water surged over the side of the tub but neither of them cared. Eileen rubbed her breasts against his chest, enjoying how his hair tickled her nipples. She kissed him deeply, demanding all he had to give, her tongue dueling with his and her fingers locked in his hair.

Erik more than met her halfway. He caught her close, his fingers moving mercilessly between her thighs. She bucked her hips against him, feeling him get harder and thicker, feeling him become as taut as a bowstring. The firestorm burned savagely through her veins, consuming her every inhibition and demanding that she surrender more. Steam rose from the bathwater even as their bodies raged.

Then Erik flicked his fingers, his quick gesture dispatching Eileen into the heart of the flames. Eileen cried out, clutching Erik's shoulders so tightly that she knew that her nails dug into his flesh.

He drove deeper inside her, filling her with his strength and power. To her surprise, he then pulled out of her. He bared his teeth and roared, his muscles flexing as he climaxed. Eileen collapsed against him, her breath coming quickly, and watched his throat work.

Then he opened his eyes and smiled at her, his features transformed with passion and pleasure. Eileen's heart skipped at the change in the look of him. He looked younger and more relaxed, confident and less wary.

"Again?" he whispered, and Eileen nodded agreement.

"Absolutely." She bent and nibbled on his earlobe. Maybe next time he'd trust the condom. "Once is never enough."

"Never," Erik agreed, and claimed her lips once more.

Sigmund Guthrie felt the growing heat of the firestorm.

He'd been waiting for it, his senses tuned to the heat that would signal the third major firestorm of the new age. He'd been charged by Boris to monitor this third firestorm, and he was going to fulfill his responsibilities.

He didn't care about Boris's objectives, just his own. Making Boris happy was Sigmund's only chance of getting a sip of the Dragon's Blood Elixir, and that was his only shot at immortality.

Sigmund's fascination wasn't purely academic, although he was curious to learn how the Elixir worked.

He was surprised when the firestorm drew him to an area he had known well. He was shocked as he focused on the central pulse of heat and found himself coming closer to his own past. Something softened within him as he found himself within familiar terrain. The curve of the hills, the smell of the land, the sound of the river all combined to make him nostalgic for the love he had lost.

Then he caught the scent of the *Pyr* involved and his lip curled with disdain. Erik still hadn't learned to disguise his scent from other *Pyr* and *Slayers*, a fact that gave Sigmund another reason to scorn his father.

On the other hand, there was something particularly satisfying about the idea of thwarting his father's firestorm. Sigmund shifted shape around the bend of the road and trudged toward the town with his collar up, looking for all the world like a poor scholar who had missed the bus. The rain soaked him to the skin quickly, but he didn't mind.

He was warmed by the promise of vengeance. Sigmund recalled the old prophecy about blood sacrifice. He wouldn't mind helping Erik to be that sacrifice. The old *Pyr* deserved no less for his betrayal of Louisa, Sigmund's mother. He deserved no less for killing Louisa's father, Sigmund's mentor and the only human who had ever truly understood him. Sigmund had taken his mother's maiden name as his own out of respect for his human grandfather.

Maybe Sigmund could ensure that Erik's sacrifice was a long and painful one. He had time to chuckle to himself before a black sedan came along the road behind him. Sigmund stepped aside to let the car pass, noting the nasty dent on the roof as he did so.

But the car paused beside him, the engine idling with a throaty purr. The tinted window on the back door descended

with a smooth hum and Sigmund was shocked to find
Magnus smiling at him.

"I warned you once to stay out of my business," Magnus
said in old-speak, his smile unwavering.

Sigmund refused to be intimidated. *"A prophesied
firestorm is every* Slayer's *business."*

"You are here on Boris's command, no doubt."

"I go where I want."

Magnus's eyes narrowed and he considered Sigmund as if
the younger *Slayer* might make a good meal. Then he spoke
aloud. "Lying to me, Sigmund, could have an adverse effect
upon your longevity."

Magnus emphasized the last word, his eyes glittering.
Sigmund wondered how much of his own ambitions the old
Slayer knew.

And he was afraid.

Someone in the car chuckled. Sigmund saw the silhouettes of three other men in the car: Balthasar, Mallory, and
Jorge, no doubt. He poised to shift and run, knowing he was
outnumbered and on the wrong side of Magnus's approval
rating.

It seemed suddenly to be a very bad thing to have a strong
association with Boris.

"You do have a personal connection in this instance, don't
you?" Magnus mused.

"The failure of this firestorm is of importance to all of us."

"But of particular importance to you and Boris, given
your various petty issues with Erik." Magnus made a dismissive gesture even as Sigmund bit back an argument in his
own favor. "My objectives are more sweeping and long-term.
More comprehensive, as befits a true leader."

Sigmund wondered what the old *Slayer* had in mind.

Despite himself, he was intrigued.

"I shall make you an offer, Sigmund Guthrie," Magnus
said before Sigmund could ask.

The *Slayer*'s tone was ominous, but Sigmund tried to hide his trepidation. "Yes?"

"You take the mate, if you so choose. The *Pyr* is all mine."

Sigmund felt cheated by the very idea. His argument was with his father. "Why should I agree to that?"

"Because I hold the cup of the Elixir," Magnus declared in old-speak, his words echoing in Sigmund's thoughts. *"Because I alone have the power to fulfill your deepest desire."* He stared at Sigmund, his eyes glittering.

"But Boris—"

"If Boris has told you otherwise, he is a liar. Do not imagine that the balance of power is anything other than what it is." He glared at Sigmund with such ferocity that Sigmund understood Magnus was demanding a change in his allegiance.

He also was being given a chance to get what he wanted.

Sigmund's thoughts flew. The fact was that Boris had nearly died from his sip of the Elixir. Then he had spent the better part of six months having reconstructive surgery after a battle with Erik that would have killed a *Slayer* who had not drunk of the Elixir.

Boris wouldn't take well to Sigmund's changing loyalty.

But Magnus held the Elixir; Magnus knew old secrets that everyone had forgotten; Magnus sought command of the *Slayers*.

If Sigmund had been a betting *Pyr*, he would have wagered his hoard on Magnus being triumphant.

Instead, he bet his life on it.

"Deal," he said aloud. He caught a fleeting glimpse of Magnus's smile; then the window rolled up, ending the conversation. The tinted glass might have been a black mirror—he saw only his own wet reflection staring back at him.

The car accelerated in that moment, its rear tires lunging through a puddle with such speed that the water splashed. Sigmund was soaked from the knees down as he watched the car move out of sight.

Still, he was relieved to have survived another encounter with Magnus. He was glad that Magnus hadn't offered him a ride—Sigmund had a feeling that he wouldn't have gotten out of that sedan alive.

It didn't really matter whether the mate died or the *Pyr* died—either way, the firestorm would be thwarted. Sigmund made his peace with his compromise as well as he could and continued his trudge toward town.

Chapter 14

For the first time in centuries, Erik Sorensson was indecisive.

He had showered and dressed, and stood with the wooden chest in his hand, poised to leave. He watched Eileen sleep, her hair strewn across the pillows and a small smile playing over her lips.

He hadn't been able to do it. He hadn't been able to come inside of Eileen.

The condoms had worked against the firestorm, because they had reminded him of what would happen. It wasn't fair to impregnate Eileen, not without telling her the whole story. It wasn't right to conceive a child without her agreement.

He didn't want to betray her.

He'd done enough damage in betraying Louisa. He had given Eileen a good chunk of the story she sought and he had pleasured her over and over again. Maybe that would start to balance the debt.

Maybe not.

There were similarities between them, certainly, but Ei-

leen was different from Louisa. She was bolder and more vibrant, more outspoken.

Infinitely more alluring. The spell Louisa had cast over
him had been nothing compared to what Eileen might do.

Erik knew that he should leave, while he could.

The firestorm boiled in his veins, taunting him with the
fact that it hadn't yet been sated. He burned with desire, even
standing a dozen feet away from Eileen, and he had watched
the sparks leap from his own fingers into her hair when he
had touched her one last time.

His task wasn't complete, yet he had to leave. He had obligations and responsibilities—he knew that the *Pyr* were
waiting at his lair in Chicago, waiting for his decision on how
best to move forward now that the Dragon's Egg was destroyed. He knew that he should step out the door.

But he couldn't quite bring himself to open the door. He
wanted to stay with Eileen. He wanted to slide under the
duvet beside her and awaken her slowly.

But it was more than sex that lured him. He wanted to tell
her the full story of the firestorm, and discuss with her how
best to proceed. He felt lighter for having shared even part of
his history with someone else, and the possibility of no
longer being alone was deeply appealing. He sensed that
Eileen, with her love of stories, might be able to see his direction more clearly than he could.

But he didn't dare jeopardize the *Pyr* with such a personal
choice. Erik knew what he had to do. In taking leadership of
his kind, he had known that his own desires had to be pushed
aside for the greater good.

He'd take the Dragon's Teeth to Rafferty, then come back.
Eileen would be safe within the barrier of his dragonsmoke.
He wouldn't be long. It was a compromise that pleased him
in concept, but Erik had his doubts as to its success. Could he
ever repair the damage of Eileen awakening alone? Could he
not take the Dragon's Teeth when he had the chance? Would
he survive the journey to Rafferty and back?

There were no good choices. That was getting a bit old.

Erik sighed and reached for the doorknob. He cheated himself of one last glance at Eileen, and hauled open the door with purpose.

Magnus was standing right outside the door.

Erik was shocked. How could Magnus be so close? Erik had had no warning, had detected no scent of another *Pyr* or *Slayer*.

How had Magnus broken through Erik's dragonsmoke without doing injury to himself or without Erik hearing the chime of the smoke break into discord?

Had he left a gap? Erik couldn't believe it.

Magnus smiled and took advantage of his surprise. *"A gift for me?"* he asked in old-speak. *"How thoughtful of you."*

Magnus snatched the leather handles of the wooden chest right out of Erik's grip. He pivoted and raced for the stairs, leaping down them as he shifted shape. He was out the door, his scales adorned with raindrops as he took flight.

Erik was right behind him, shifting in midair as he raced to retrieve the Dragon's Teeth.

Eileen dreamed of water.

She stirred in her sleep, struggling to free herself from the grip of the dream. The water was dark and cold. It closed around her like a trap, its murk ensuring that she couldn't even guess the direction of the surface.

She tried to cry out but took a gulp of dirty cold water into her mouth instead. She choked and sputtered as her fear grew.

The water churned, the current sending her spinning through the endless water. She glimpsed rocks, the bed of the river, reeds growing along the shore, but everything flashed past her so quickly. She couldn't grab anything, couldn't save herself, couldn't breathe.

Eileen panicked.

"You cannot fight the water and win," a woman advised in

a soft voice. Her tranquil tone was in direct opposition to Eileen's terror.

Eileen didn't dare open her mouth to answer.

"Water has its own will, its own power," the woman continued. "Surrender to it. Embrace its nature and it will permit you to move through it with ease."

Eileen didn't think so. She flailed and it made no difference. She kicked and struggled, but the river had her in its relentless grip. It would take her wherever it desired. It could destroy her. It could drown her or shatter her and there was nothing she could do.

Eileen wanted to weep at her impotence. She wanted to save herself. She wanted to be independent and in command of her own destiny.

But the water was too strong. It wore her out. In her exhaustion, she felt her body go limp and unresponsive.

She would die. She understood that she couldn't do anything about it, and surrendered her fate to the will of the river.

The current spun her, twisted her, pushed her, then abruptly surrendered her to a calm inlet. Eileen floated upward in the quieter waters, exhausted, her body drifting of its own accord.

She broke the surface and took a gasping breath, pushing the water from her face and shoving her wet hair back from her eyes. She stretched her feet down and realized that she could stand.

She straightened, shivering when the air caressed her wet skin. Her skirts dragged, their weight keeping her hips in the water and her legs bent. Eileen found stones in her pockets. She lifted them out, staring at them in her shaking hands.

She remembered Erik's story and understood with sudden clarity why the bridge had bothered her so much, why she had had dreams of drowning, why she had had such a powerful attraction to Erik. She knew why the story of the Dragon Lover of Madeley caught at her heart and awakened her memories, why she was drawn to Ironbridge, why Erik had invaded her dreams.

The truth was both shocking and simple: She had been Louisa.

She had been the woman Erik believed he had betrayed, the woman who had committed suicide over their son's turning *Slayer*.

How could she have made such a drastic choice?

How could she have ever distrusted Erik?

"You don't need those anymore," the woman said with confidence. "You never needed them."

Eileen glanced around and found a blond woman sitting on a rock on the shore. Her eyes were a vivid turquoise, and she was delicately built. She watched Eileen, and Eileen realized it had been her voice giving advice.

"Surrender to the water?" she echoed.

"Trust in goodness," the woman said. "You can be whole only if you love, if you feel, if you commit. Water teaches us about surrender, about commitment, about trust."

Eileen looked down at the stones she held. They seemed large and dark in her hands, heavy, restrictive. On impulse she threw them into the river and they sank. She took a deep breath and lowered herself into the water, her terror rising as she dipped her face below the surface. She moved underwater, swimming the width of the calm inlet, her confidence growing with every stroke.

It was like her dream, but not quite as good. She felt more powerful, more at one with the water, even though there was still room for improvement.

Even though her heart still pounded in fear.

When she broke the surface, Eileen turned to her companion. The woman's smile lit her entire face and Eileen felt triumphant.

Then the woman disappeared into thin air.

Eileen glanced around in panic, dismayed to find herself suddenly alone.

But she wasn't alone. A man's strong fingers appeared suddenly in her peripheral vision.

"Careful," Erik said. "It's slippery here."

Eileen looked into the steady green of his eyes and put her hand in his, trusting him not to let her slip. She had a moment to feel his grip close securely over her fingers, to feel his solid tug as she stepped out of the water; then the dream faded as abruptly as the woman had disappeared.

Eileen awakened in a lovely hotel room to the sound of rain pattering against the windows. What did her dream mean? She thought of recurring stories of reincarnation and past lives, myths that had always intrigued her, although she didn't believe in them.

Did she have some kind of connection to Erik's Louisa? It was a whimsical thought, the kind of idea Eileen could entertain only when she awakened from a powerful dream. It was the kind of idea, though, that she'd like to discuss with Erik.

He was a man who dealt with what seemed irrational or impossible, and did it all the time. She reached across the sheets for his heat, intending to awaken him slowly.

But the sheets were cold.

The bed was empty.

Erik was gone and Eileen was alone again.

This time solitude left her feeling lonely and incomplete.

Magnus shot into the overcast sky. The rain rolled over the jade of his scales, the muted light revealing the myriad swirling hues of pale green. The gold edges on his scales shone and his golden claws gleamed.

Erik flew right behind him, his gaze fixed on the prize of the wooden chest that Magnus had seized. He was impressed as always by the ancient *Slayer*'s vigor.

Where were Magnus's minions?

Erik felt a rush of air and realized that two of the younger *Slayers* had closed ranks on either side of him. Jorge was on Erik's right, a glow of topaz and gold. Mallory—Erik had to think of him as "Frenchie" after Eileen's comments—was on Erik's left, his scales a resplendent combination of garnet red and gold with pearls. He still had a scar on his chest from the slash Erik had given him the night before, and Erik found the sight of the wound reassuring.

"No turning back," Jorge said in old-speak.

Erik had no intention of leaving Magnus in possession of the trunk, regardless of how many *Slayers* were allied against him. The Dragon's Teeth were the key to the *Pyr*'s future, and if he had to die in retrieving them, so be it.

Erik thought he understood how the blood sacrifice would work.

He was glad that he hadn't tricked Eileen, even though it meant that he had left his firestorm unsatisfied. Maybe, just maybe, he had redressed the imbalance between the two of them by not betraying her this time.

Maybe that was why he had had a second chance.

Maybe Eileen's memories were the only place he'd survive.

Maybe that was good enough.

Magnus pivoted in midair and laughed. They were high over the hills, which still bore the scars of centuries of iron-work. "And so, the ancient prophecy will be fulfilled," he said with obvious glee. "Come on, Erik. Meet your destiny."

Magnus tossed the wooden trunk to Jorge, who lunged forward to seize it. The box swung heavily on its leather handles in Jorge's grip, and Erik imagined that the teeth jostled inside. Magnus raised his claws in the traditional fighting pose and Erik followed suit.

Then he dove for Jorge. The *Slayers* were so surprised by his move that Erik managed to land a solid strike on Jorge. His talons dug deeply into Jorge's shoulder as that *Slayer* turned, and his claws ripped beneath the scales. Black blood dripped from the gaping wound as Erik breathed fire to take the *Slayer* down. Jorge bellowed in pain and faltered.

In that same moment, Mallory dug his claws into Erik's

back. Jorge attacked Erik from the front, slashing across Erik's chest. Red blood flowed and the *Slayers* laughed, sure their prey was beaten. The pain was excruciating and Erik feared he had already lost.

Without claiming the Dragon's Teeth.

The possibility infuriated Erik. It invigorated him. He roared and twisted, turning to attack the *Slayers* with new vigor.

He was not quite ready to die.

He had goals to achieve.

More important, a taste of death had convinced Erik that he wasn't ready to abandon Eileen.

Eileen sat up in bed, considering the late-afternoon light. She dismissed the last shards of her dream from her thoughts and focused on the practical. She knew there was no chance that Erik was in the bathroom or that he had simply stepped out.

He was gone. There was no sense of another presence and, even more important, the firestorm's heat had died to that of embers. His clothes were gone, which meant he'd gone with them.

The wooden trunk was missing, too.

Eileen fell back against the pillows and stared at the canopy over the bed. She felt betrayed and irritated, and this despite a half dozen fabulous orgasms in rapid succession. It was illogical and undeniable.

She was hungry, too.

On the upside, Erik hadn't lied. He'd said what he wanted. They'd made a deal and he'd kept his end of the bargain.

Still . . .

Eileen scowled and rolled out of bed. He'd given her the real name of Shadow—Louisa Guthrie—which gave her another detail to search. He hadn't made any vows of the "together forever" variety, and had been clear that the firestorm was about sex. Eileen reminded herself that he'd been honest with her, but she wasn't any less annoyed.

She wanted more.

She wanted to be with Erik.

She wanted to talk to him. Right now.

But she was out of luck.

Eileen showered and dressed, attributing her irritability to hunger. Somehow, though, she doubted a sandwich was going to make everything better.

Lynne wasn't right about sex being a half measure, and she certainly hadn't been right about Eileen's needing to follow her intuition with men. And the woman in her dream had talked about water meaning trust. Eileen trusted lots of people—associates and acquaintances and family.

She had to admit that she'd never really trusted a man.

She'd worked with the assumption that each one would let her down, sooner or later. Did her assumption shape the results? Eileen had to wonder. She could have trusted Erik if he'd hung around—would that have changed their relationship? She liked that she had been learning to read him, and liked when she caught a glimpse of the passionate nature he kept so well hidden.

Of course, Erik had left.

Eileen snarled at her reflection. So much for the new plan. She needed food. Nothing more and nothing less.

On her way downstairs, Eileen met the owner of the inn. She asked for directions to a sandwich shop and the location of the town's archive. Hot food would have been better, but she wanted to get to the archive before it closed. She knew she was lucky that it was even open on Saturday. She tightened her scarf around her neck and headed out into the relentless gray of the rain.

It was cold in the absence of the firestorm.

In the absence of Erik's unexpected smile.

She was going to think about Shadow, not about Erik Sorensson. She was going to research a local myth, not recall the pain in a man's eyes when he talked about his wife's suicide. She was going to think about sustenance, not protective dragonsmoke she couldn't see or big teeth that dragon shape-shifters would do anything to possess.

The teeth were gone, the wooden trunk was gone, and apparently Erik Sorensson was gone, too.

But Eileen was going to blame her sour mood on the weather.

Too bad she knew a lie when she heard one.

When Erik turned to fight, Jorge breathed dragonfire at him.

Erik faltered as if fatally injured by Jorge's dragonfire. He took the bulk of the fire on his back, gritting his teeth and closing his eyes. Orange flames surrounded him on all sides, their heat searing his skin and burning his scales.

Through the pain, he forced himself to recall how Quinn had taught the *Pyr* to use dragonfire to build their own strength. The trick was to embrace the dragonfire's heat, to take it into himself, instead of flinching from it and fearing it. Erik didn't have the same mastery over the element of fire as the Smith, but he had to try.

He gritted his teeth as the flames leapt orange around him and willed the fire to be his ally instead of his foe. He welcomed its heat. Immediately, he felt a tingle of energy from the flame.

Erik followed his impulse, trusting the fire, embracing it, calling it on. It surged through him, heating his scales to become stronger and smoother. Erik felt himself grow larger and more powerful. He felt more in tune with the element of fire, emboldened and strengthened by it.

Jorge made a sound of astonishment in old-speak; then both *Slayers* breathed dragonfire upon Erik in unison. He twisted in the flames, reveling in their heat and power, drawing the *Slayers*' force into himself. Erik glanced down to find his onyx scales gleaming, hardened by the fire instead of charred by it.

"Well done," Magnus commented.

Jorge fell back in surprise, not sharing his leader's admiration. Erik seized the handles of the wooden trunk from Jorge. It was easy to rip the leather straps from the *Slayer*'s grip. Jorge pivoted to retreat and Erik struck a heavy blow on him from behind, strong enough that Jorge faltered in his flight.

Mallory fell on Erik in a flurry of talons and teeth, snatching at the wooden trunk. They locked claws and twined their tails around each other, tumbling end over end as they battled for the wooden chest. Mallory bit Erik's arm with savage force, hard enough to make Erik's blood run scarlet. The *Slayer* was young and virile, lithe and strong.

Erik was outnumbered. He saw that he would have to eliminate one of the *Slayer*s to give himself the chance to rest. Otherwise, they would gradually wear him down, even with the surge from the flames.

Erik remembered what he had learned from that last fight with Boris and knew where he would get the strength he needed.

When he and Mallory parted again, Erik exhaled dragonsmoke with power. He breathed it in one endless stream as he hovered, the dragonsmoke maintaining a conduit between Mallory and Erik. Mallory yelped and twitched as the smoke wound beneath his scales. It slipped into the wound on Mallory's chest, finding a way beneath the scabs to sting raw flesh. Mallory fought on despite the pain, but Erik kept breathing dragonsmoke.

The dragonsmoke stole vitality; that was its treacherous power. A *Slayer* or *Pyr* ensnared in smoke would be eroded to nothing but skin, his life force cheated away by the smoke. But by keeping the link and breathing one continuous stream of dragonsmoke, Boris had used the smoke as a conduit to steal Erik's strength for himself.

Erik had to be able to do the same thing. Just as it had with Boris, the dragonsmoke cheated Mallory of his power, feeding it directly to Erik. To his delight, Erik felt himself grow stronger even as Mallory was weakened. The *Slayer* fought valiantly, his eyes widening in terror as he felt his strength slipping away, but his was a losing battle.

"You will leave me an empty shell!" Mallory cried.

"Without remorse," Erik agreed, not breaking the stream of dragonsmoke. "The world would benefit from one less *Slayer*."

With a curse and a bellow, Mallory retreated, his flight pattern erratic as he struggled to outrun the smoke in his weakened state. Erik concentrated on maintaining the connection with his target, breathing more smoke to lengthen the link between them. It was heady to have this strength infuse him, to heal his wounds and increase his power.

It was exhilarating and liberating.

Then Jorge buried his claws into Erik's shoulders and Erik cried out in pain. His shout broke the line of dragonsmoke. Jorge dug his talons in deep, trying to rip the tendons to Erik's wings, but Mallory's strength had invigorated Erik.

Erik spun abruptly, loosing a torrent of dragonfire on the golden *Slayer*. Jorge flinched. He might have tried to turn the dragonfire to his own advantage as Erik had, but Erik hit him in the head with the wooden trunk. Jorge retreated, dazed; then Erik struck him out of the sky with his tail.

The topaz *Slayer* fell.

Erik spun in the air, his talons raised, ready. There was no sign of Mallory.

There was only Magnus, his cold smile, and the incessant rain. "You are a worthier opponent than I recall," the ancient *Slayer* murmured. He raised his claws. "But even with your new abilities, you cannot conquer me."

"Why don't we let the battle decide that?" Erik suggested, confident in his new strength.

Magnus's smile broadened. "But I have one trick more

than you, one that trumps all the others." Magnus dropped his voice to a hiss of old-speak. *"The Dragon's Blood Elixir."*

Erik recoiled. "That's a myth. The Elixir doesn't exist."

Magnus laughed. "Then what makes me immortal, Erik Sorensson, while you will be so very easy to kill?"

Magnus's eyes flashed with conviction. He wasn't lying. Erik struggled to accept that a fable had come to life; then the old *Slayer* attacked.

Chapter 15

Eileen drove the rental car into town, since Erik had left it behind and she had the keys in her satchel. It was a better choice than walking in the rain.

Was that why he had left it for her? It would have been the type of gentlemanly gesture she was beginning to associate with him. She thought of him offering her a hand in her dream, as solid and reliable as he'd seemed in real life, and sighed.

She had a hard time thinking of Erik as a mercenary opportunist, even though he had taken the wooden chest in exchange for great sex. That was especially true now that she had the rental car he'd paid for, never mind those half a dozen great orgasms.

Eileen wished she'd had a chance to thank him.

Maybe with more than just words.

She bought a sandwich and a cup of tea, neither of which filled the emptiness within her. She sat in the car and ate in the parking lot of the museum where the town archive was stored. She knew she should have been happy to see the rain turn to snow. She'd missed snow, but these flurries didn't lighten her heart.

They just made her feel more cold.

More solitary.

More lonely. Eileen locked the car, slung her satchel over her shoulder, and went to work. Maybe finding out about Louisa Guthrie would improve her mood.

Maybe not.

The archive was kept in a dusty overlooked corner in the back of the museum, the kind of space Eileen found reassuringly familiar. The furniture was old and the computer was a certifiable antique, but the woman working there was friendly.

When Eileen explained that she was seeking records of a woman from some era of the past, the archivist nodded with efficiency. She indicated a number of possibilities, pointed Eileen to some digitized photographs, and enthused about the record of social history that this museum had preserved.

She reluctantly left Eileen to search the files—or to do the dirty work, as they laughingly agreed—when she was summoned back to the museum proper.

Eileen quickly ran through the digitized twentieth-century records with no sign of a Louisa Guthrie. That would have been too easy a victory. She settled in to search the incomplete nineteenth-century records on the computer, making careful notes of the obvious omissions.

It could take every hour of every day she had left in England to find Louisa. These archives weren't all digitized or online, so Eileen focused on the local ones. If she had to go to the paper records and microfiche, she wanted to get to it as soon as possible. Eileen hunted and clicked, explored records and discarded them. Years of experience in this kind of research made her as efficient as was humanly possible.

She didn't know how long she'd been there when a man cleared his throat. Eileen jumped in surprise.

"Can I help you?" he asked.

Eileen found a sandy-haired man in the doorway. He was stocky, looked about thirty, and his trousers were soaked to the knees. He had the rumpled, sleeping-in-the-stacks look of the most committed graduate student. Eileen assumed that she was in his favorite space and that his offer was really an attempt to evict her.

"I'll only be a few minutes," she said, turning back to the computer. "But thanks."

"I'm sure I could help you," he said, his tone more insistent. "I know the history of Ironbridge like the back of my hand."

Eileen realized that his accent was American. She assumed that he was working for the museum on an exchange of some kind or had come to do in-depth research for his thesis.

She still wasn't moving.

"I don't think I need help, but thanks again for the offer." She eyed the screen, expecting him to go away.

He stepped into the room instead. "I'm a very good researcher."

"So am I," Eileen said with a less friendly smile. She glared at him, that smile still in place, and was surprised that he didn't avert his gaze.

There was an assessing glint in his eyes, one that was also familiar. Eileen knew she could die a happy woman without another grad student hitting on her in a deserted archive. She realized belatedly that it was getting dark outside and the museum had fallen quiet. It hadn't closed, but there weren't many people around.

This kid was younger than Eileen, though, shorter and softer. She could deck him if she had to. She looked him up and down, then returned to her database, certain that even the most socially backward man couldn't miss her implication.

Instead, she felt his presence at her elbow. He smelled of wet wool, of rain and wind.

Come to think of it, it was odd that an avid student had

stepped outside of his favorite research space for any reason. Most of them never left the library. Or their computers. Eileen had often wondered when the truly dedicated went to the washroom.

She felt a quiver of warning.

"What are you looking for?" He eased even closer.

Eileen bristled despite herself. "Why should I tell you?" She kept her tone light, not wanting to provoke him. She just wanted him to go away.

"Because I probably know where the answer is already," he said, with that cockiness that some bright students showed. "I could save you a lot of time."

Eileen was irritated, so she pushed him into declaring his intentions. "And why would you do that?" She swiveled on the chair to study him, practically daring him to make his play.

The glint in his eyes fed that doubt deep inside Eileen. There was something wrong with this kid. Something creepy about him. He reminded her of an animal on the hunt, a starving and desperate animal. Her intuition told her to run.

Immediately.

But that was crazy. He was just another grad student with poor social skills. And really, what kind of trouble could she get into in a sleepy little museum town like Ironbridge? Eileen stayed put. She needed to find Louisa. She turned back to the computer to continue her search.

He offered his hand abruptly, shoving it into her field of view. "Sigmund Guthrie, at your service."

Eileen was struck again by his awkwardness, then by his name. "Did you say Guthrie?"

"Yes."

Eileen knew countless students who chose their specialties to illuminate facets of their own family history. His family history could easily have drawn him to an area of research. She decided to take a chance, in case Sigmund could save her time. "I'm looking for a Guthrie, actually. Louisa Guthrie."

His eyes flashed and she knew he recognized the name. "Wrong century," he said sharply, his eyes narrowing as he read the screen. "She died in 1782, in March."

Eileen wasn't surprised that he knew the date. Avid students could remember an astonishing amount of detail on their preferred subjects.

Maybe he would be useful.

Even if every fiber of her being urged her to run.

"The Louisa Guthrie I'm looking for drowned in the Severn," Eileen said carefully.

"Yes, in March of 1782." Sigmund folded his hands behind himself and recounted from memory. "Survived by her sister, Adelaide, and her father, George. Their mother, Matilda, had died earlier, when the sisters were much younger."

Eileen couldn't completely quell her suspicion. She tapped into the database, finding the earlier century. She accessed some digitized archives from March 1782 and immediately found a newspaper article regarding the death of one Louisa Guthrie.

Who had jumped from the new iron bridge into the Severn.

With stones in her pockets.

Eileen shivered, even as she sent the article to the printer. "This is very familiar to you."

"Oh, I have large chunks of our family tree memorized." Sigmund smiled with a charm that could have been fed by confidence. "I told you that I could help." His tone sharpened. "You should have believed me."

"Yes, my mistake. Thank you." Eileen picked up the printed article and scanned it again. Louisa had been survived by a sister, Adelaide, who had moved to Birmingham with her husband, Reverend Jones. Louisa had also been survived by a son, who was taken in by his grandfather.

The son's name was Sigmund.

Eileen suddenly had a very bad feeling about the helpful student's real identity. She took a step away from him and picked up her satchel.

"Why Louisa?" Sigmund asked with open suspicion. "No one is ever interested in Louisa."

His accusatory tone caught Eileen's ear, giving her the sense that he was offended on Louisa's behalf. That made no sense, and she looked straight at him.

He stared back at her proudly, his stance reminding Eileen of something. Or someone. The way his eyes glittered, the coldness of his expression—the combination was not quite human. His body shimmered around the edges in a way that she had seen before.

When Erik was breathing smoke.

Erik's son Sigmund had turned *Slayer*.

Eileen grabbed her coat and tried to step past him.

"Something I said?" he asked mildly, as if he knew exactly what was troubling her.

"No." She looked into his eyes and chose not to be afraid.

"Then why the rush?" He planted himself right in her path and folded his arms across his chest. He looked larger and more dangerous, and his smile became meaner.

"You're Erik's son," Eileen guessed.

"Clever, clever," Sigmund said, his tone mocking. "For a human." His body began to glitter with savage brightness.

Eileen didn't stay to watch him change shape.

She shoved past him and ran.

Magnus and Erik fought with vicious force. They locked claws and rolled through the air, battling for supremacy over and over again. Each time one was struck, he rallied and returned to the fight.

The clouds darkened to the hue of slate, taking on a bluish tinge. The rain changed to snow, the white flakes falling more and more thickly. The light faded as the afternoon wore on.

And still the pair battled.

Erik could feel his body becoming more weary. Every blow that Magnus struck felt harder and heavier. Erik fought on, unwilling to cede the battle easily.

He had the strange sense that Magnus was toying with him. When once Erik had flagged, the ancient *Slayer* had breathed dragonfire on him, reinvigorating him, toying with Erik's newfound ability to use fire to his own advantage. It couldn't have been an accident.

Even now, Erik breathed a stream of smoke and stole energy from Magnus. The *Slayer* let him do it, laughing as the dragonsmoke bridged the gap between them.

"You prolong the battle," Erik accused.

Magnus chuckled. "An easy victory makes a poor tale." He swung the wooden chest, tossing it from one claw to the other. "And a prize such as this demands a worthy tale."

"This tale deserves an ending," Erik retorted, and lunged after Magnus.

Magnus waited until Erik was close, then shot upward suddenly. He streaked into the sky, evading Erik's assault. Erik followed close behind him, distrusting the low echo of Magnus's laughter.

"Let's raise the stakes," Magnus suggested, his eyes gleaming. "Who is faster? Who is more determined to gain the prize?" Before Erik could answer, Magnus tossed the trunk.

The wooden chest arched high, tumbling through the falling flakes of snow, then fell toward the earth like a rock.

Erik shot after it and snatched at the handles, Magnus close beside him. Erik felt the leather brush his talons; then Magnus kicked him aside. The ancient *Slayer* snatched for the trunk himself.

Erik fell upon him from behind, shredding his wings so that Magnus roared. The *Slayer* rolled backward, seizing

Erik's tail with his rear claws. The two thrashed each other as they fell, neither one prepared to surrender, making a fierce spiral of black and green. Erik ripped his tail free and walloped Magnus with it. Magnus rolled, then came up fighting. He slashed at Erik with his claws and the blow caught Erik across the forehead.

A single ebony scale lifted free of Erik's brow. It shone in the winter light, falling to the earth like a shard of obsidian. The two stared at it in shock; then Magnus began to laugh.

"Bad time for a new weakness, Erik," he said, and lunged for the leader of the *Pyr*.

The wooden trunk, meanwhile, was spiraling toward the earth.

"The trunk!" Erik reminded Magnus as the pair grappled, but Magnus didn't glance over his shoulder.

"The Dragon's Teeth belong in the soil," he said, striking Erik twice in rapid succession with his tail. "Let them find their way there sooner rather than later."

Magnus's eyes brightened as he began to chant. His song was deep and old, so resonant that it made Erik's marrow vibrate in unison with it. It was a dark, vile rhythm. Erik closed his ears to it, struggling to keep it from creating an echo within his own body.

He recognized it immediately. It was the same chant Magnus had used to make Delaney act against his will.

It had to be the same chant that Magnus used in the dark academy to make shadow dragons of the *Pyr* he had harvested from their own graves. It was a wicked summons and Erik knew why Magnus sang it now.

He was chanting to the Dragon's Teeth.

He was trying to persuade the enchanted warriors trapped in those teeth to take the *Slayer* side. He was appealing to them when they were weakened, when they couldn't so easily ignore his song.

Erik would not permit Magnus such an easy victory. He leapt at Magnus, his outrage fueling his strength, and fought with renewed vigor. As they rolled through the sky, biting and clawing, he saw the misshapen scale that marked Magnus's own vulnerability.

Magnus had lost a scale at some distant point in time, and though it had grown back, the weakness was there.

Erik targeted it. Magnus caught all Erik's claws, holding him away from the old wound. Erik breathed dragonfire at it. He directed dragonsmoke at it. He remembered Boris's feat and mingled smoke and fire together, dispatching them both at the damaged scale. He bit at it, but even his teeth couldn't find any grasp on the *Slayer*'s scales.

Nothing affected Magnus. His smile remained cold and confident. His chant continued at its slow, steady pace, even as Erik threw all of his might against his foe.

"Still skeptical that the Elixir exists?" Magnus asked.

Erik was horrified. The Dragon's Blood Elixir was real. The *Slayer*s were drinking it. There was an old story that the Elixir gave immortality to those who imbibed it—those who weren't killed by their first sip—and Erik had a moment to fear that the *Pyr* had lost the war before it started.

Magnus chuckled.

His laughter halted when the trunk shattered noisily against the rocky ground. The dry wood broke into a thousand shards. The trays that lined the box burst forth and broke against the earth.

The pair dove as one toward the Dragon's Teeth, Magnus increasing the volume of his chant. Erik hoped he could gather some of the teeth before Magnus did.

Except that there were no Dragon's Teeth on the ground.

Not one.

The trunk had been empty.

Eileen was in the car in a flash, turning the key in the ignition. She wished she had Erik's driving skill, but knew she didn't. She also wished she were better at driving on the wrong side of the road and shifting with the wrong hand. If her luck held, the roads would be quiet at this time of day.

The engine started. She glanced back and saw Sigmund closing fast. There wasn't time to worry about wishes and hopes.

Eileen put the car into gear and floored the accelerator. She didn't doubt that Sigmund would catch her, but she had to try to escape him.

Could she manage to find Erik?

Could she somehow send him a message?

Eileen didn't know, but she was going to try.

She shot out of the parking lot, taking the corner on two tires. The tires squealed on the pavement and the car skidded on the wet road. Several pedestrians stood back and shook their heads, but Eileen didn't care what they thought of American tourists.

She saw a big black Mercedes parked outside the hotel opposite, its roof badly dented. Her heart in her throat, Eileen spun the wheel and went the other way. She couldn't see Magnus, but that didn't mean he couldn't see her.

Erik had said Magnus could smell her, and find her anywhere.

In terror, Eileen glanced in the rearview mirror. She saw Sigmund running after her car. Could things get any worse?

She peered ahead, the heavy flurries obscuring her vision of the road. Where would she go? Where could she hide? She hadn't wandered far beyond the museum on her previous trip and didn't know the area well at all.

Then she heard a bellow, one that shook the windshield in the car. She looked up and through the veil of snow she could just discern two silhouettes.

Dragons.

Fighting.

One was black. They disappeared into the clouds and Eileen almost despaired. Then she felt a little thrum of heat

caress her skin, a familiar sizzle of desire, and understood intuitively how she could find Erik.

She'd follow the heat.

And whether he wanted to see her or not, he'd defend her.
She trusted him to do that.

Eileen chose a road that seemed to head toward Erik and
took the turn fast. She glanced in the rearview mirror in time
to see Sigmund follow, then change shape.

He breathed fire, his dragon form a gorgeous blend of
dark green and silver. He looked like a piece of jewelry, a
Mayan treasure maybe.

She'd assume that he got his dragon good looks from his
father.

The warmth on her skin was growing—if nothing else,
she was heading in the right direction. Eileen pushed the accelerator a little harder and hoped she reached Erik in time.

As if he'd heard that thought, Sigmund breathed fire at the
little car. All Eileen could see was a curtain of orange flames,
licking and flowing over the vehicle, heating the metal to a
sizzle. She yelped and put the gas pedal flat on the floor.

Nothing could be worse than being fried alive.

Pyr and *Slayer* surveyed the barren ground without com-
prehension; then Erik guessed what had happened.

Eileen had removed the teeth and hidden them elsewhere.

Eileen had put herself squarely in danger.

And the blood sacrifice foretold by the prophecy didn't
have to be his.

It could be Eileen's.

As if to emphasize that notion, the low hum of the
firestorm that he'd grown accustomed to feeling grew in intensity.

Eileen was coming closer.

Erik roared and seized Magnus before the *Slayer* could
react. He struck Magnus in the head and hauled him into the
sky as the *Slayer* sputtered in shock. He remembered a place

that would be perfect for Magnus, and provide an ideal solution.

If it was still there. Erik soared high, Magnus writhing in his grasp, and scanned the ground.

"What have you done with them?" Magnus roared, enraged that he had been cheated of his prize.

"I have them safe," Erik lied. "You're not the only one who plays games."

Erik spied the cemetery he'd been seeking. He managed to keep a grasp on Magnus, his fear for Eileen giving him new strength. The *Slayer* roared and twisted, but Erik plummeted toward the cemetery with Magnus fast in his grasp.

Magnus yelled, but it made no difference. Erik dove down toward the wrought-iron gates. He targeted one of the tall, ornate spires that stood on either side of the gate proper, and impaled Magnus on it with a single sure stroke.

The spear of iron punctured Magnus through the space left by his lost scale.

It was a perfect hit. The spire was an elaborately shaped piece of steel, teased and bent into a complicated tower, thick with points and curlicues. The top was shaped like a barb, which meant that it pierced Magnus more easily than it would be removed.

The *Slayer* bellowed in rage. He twisted and fought and swore but it made no difference to his predicament.

Magnus might not be dead, but he wouldn't be free anytime soon. Magnus struggled and squirmed, shifting rapidly between forms, but he was securely caught on the iron spire.

For the moment.

All Erik needed was time to reach Eileen.

"You cannot outrun me," Magnus bellowed as Erik streaked into the sky. "You cannot survive me."

Erik intended to try. He took flight, ignoring Magnus's cry.

"I will share the Elixir with you. . . ."

Erik didn't believe it for a minute. And he didn't want to

taste the Dragon's Blood Elixir. His father had been skeptical of it, suggesting that there must be a hidden price if such a drink existed. Immortality couldn't come for free.

Erik didn't want to know the details.

He was back at the hotel within moments. He shifted shape in the parking lot and raced into the inn, glad that the owner wasn't in sight. He took the stairs three at a time and burst into the room that he and Eileen had shared.

She was gone.

The scent of roses and lavender was already fading. Her satchel, her purple sheepskin coat, her boots, and her knitting were all gone.

She had passed through his dragonsmoke and gone into danger.

It was his own fault.

He had failed her again.

And now he had to make it right. He thought about the Wyvern's advice and understood that in choosing his responsibility to the *Pyr*, he had failed Eileen.

Just as he had failed Louisa.

Eileen wasn't the only one being given an opportunity to learn from mistakes and make matters right.

Erik just hoped he had another chance. He stilled himself and inhaled slowly. He caught the departing whiff of her perfume and felt the insistent throb of the firestorm. Now that he paid attention, he could feel her location more clearly.

To his relief, Eileen hadn't gone far.

To his despair, he could smell *Slayer*.

Sigmund.

And others, more than one, others who had learned to disguise their scents but hadn't been entirely efficient about it this time.

Who else had shared Magnus's Elixir and secrets?

Erik had to find Eileen first.

Chapter 16

Magnus seethed.

He was trapped on the spire of wrought iron, his own body betraying him with its bones and muscles and resistance. He struggled in both forms, to no avail. His position didn't allow him any way to use his arms or legs to free himself and he doubted that was a coincidence.

Erik, he admitted grudgingly, had struck well. The spire had run Magnus through only because of his own missing scale. That was one weakness the Elixir hadn't yet managed to repair.

The weakness had been lessened by the Elixir but was still there.

He breathed fire at the iron, hoping to break the spire so his weight would make him fall to the ground. The old steel was strong and didn't heat quickly. Magnus knew it would take too long to free himself that way. The ground was already dark with his blood.

Could he actually die?

Magnus had believed not, but the situation gave him

doubt. In the past, he'd drunk deeply of the Elixir when he'd sustained a serious wound.

What if he couldn't get to the Elixir?

What if his situation ensured that he never got the restorative sip that he needed?

He struggled with new desperation at that possibility and only managed to tear the wound wider.

"I'll bet that hurts," Jorge murmured in old-speak.

Magnus looked around wildly and found the most promising of his assistants staring up at him from the ground. Jorge was in human form, the wind lifting the fair blond of his hair. His gaze was steady and as cold as ice, his arms folded across his chest.

"Help me!" Magnus cried aloud.

Jorge smiled and didn't move. "Why should I?"

Magnus glared at the younger *Slayer*. He'd always appreciated that Jorge was a good negotiator but didn't like the view from the other side of the transaction as much. Jorge held all the proverbial cards, and Magnus wouldn't have to guess twice at what the younger *Slayer* wanted in exchange for his aid.

"It might kill you," he advised, knowing that Jorge wouldn't heed the warning any more than the others ever did.

Jorge's smile broadened. "I'll take my chances."

No surprise there.

Magnus found himself smiling at the perfection of the solution. If Jorge died in drinking the Elixir, then Magnus would be rid of Jorge's troublesome ambition. If he survived that sip, Magnus would have a faithful ally.

Jorge's alliance would be guaranteed, because he would need regular access to the Elixir, which Magnus controlled.

One sip was never enough.

One sip was simply the first sip.

Sooner or later, the survivors all realized that one sip made them beholden to Magnus forever. Magnus didn't see any reason to advertise that particular slice of reality.

"Hurry, then," Magnus advised. "Our task is yet unfinished."

Jorge's eyes flashed; then he changed shape with lightning speed. He broke the iron spire from its base with a single swing of his tail. He snatched up the length of it that skewered Magnus and breathed dragonfire to heat the metal. Magnus winced at the heat of the iron and the fire, but knew it wouldn't kill him.

He roared with pain when Jorge snapped the spire in half. It fell from Magnus's body, the rough edges tearing his body raw. Magnus fell to the ground, gasping.

It had been a long time since he had felt such agony.

Fortunately, he didn't have to endure it long.

He caught his breath, gritted his teeth, and moved. He took flight outside the gates of the cemetery, charting a course to the sanctuary, where the Elixir was secured.

He didn't glance back. He knew Jorge would follow.

Mallory and Balthasar could look after themselves for the moment. Magnus would find them later, once he was restored to health. He felt the lack of blood in his body and the weakness stealing over him, and didn't like it one bit.

He had to have a sip of that potent nectar, immediately.

Not only could Sigmund's dragonfire turn Eileen into toast, it made it impossible for her to feel the lure of the firestorm. She had no idea how to find Erik.

She heard Sigmund land heavily on the roof of the car and tried not to panic. There was a road on the right that looked like an overgrown lane—more important, tree boughs grew low over it. It must have looked like a good option because of the trick Erik had played on Magnus earlier.

Either way, Eileen was going for it. She rocked the car on its shocks when she turned hard. Snowy branches struck the windshield, and the spewing snow obscured Eileen's vision.

She drove under a dark, low bough and heard a *thwack*. There was a scratch and a shout and Eileen smiled, knowing that there wasn't a dragon on the car's roof anymore. A peek in the rearview mirror showed a large green and silver lump on the road. She turned on the wipers and didn't slow down, taking the curves of the lane with reckless speed.

She wondered where she was going. The lane looked as if it hadn't been used in a long time. There was bracken growing in the middle of it and brambles scratched along the car doors.

The rental company wouldn't be pleased, but then the scorched roof pretty much condemned Erik's deposit. The road twisted and wound, ascending constantly. Eileen knew she should have been concerned about its destination, but it felt almost familiar to her. She was sure she'd never been on this road before, but she had a strange sense of homecoming.

Her parents' house had been a tract home perched on a suburban street among its fellows, not a cottage at the end of a winding, vegetation-clogged lane. Eileen had time to wonder what tricks her mind was playing on her; then she emerged into a clearing.

It was a dead end.

There was no other road, no way out except the one she'd taken in. And Sigmund was back there, winded if not wounded. It was unlikely that he'd be friendly. The sky overhead was empty and Eileen felt no firestorm heat.

Her heart lodged in her throat and hammered. She turned the car around as quickly as she could, knowing that she had to go back as she had come and face Sigmund. There must have been a house in the clearing at some time, or several buildings, but only blackened foundation stones remained. There must have been a fire.

Eileen shivered, remembering Sigmund's blast at the car. She drove around the ruins, then headed back to the lane.

A man stood there, smiling coldly at her. It wasn't Sigmund. His arms were folded across his chest and his gaze was fixed upon her. He looked pale and purposeful and highly unfriendly.

The edges of his body were shimmering against the snow, and Eileen guessed that he was also a *Slayer*.

Eileen's suspicions were confirmed when a green and silver dragon alighted beside the man and immediately shifted shape. Sigmund wasn't surprised to see this man, so they were clearly allies.

That wasn't the best news Eileen had heard all day.

She decided to ram right through them and make a run for it. She gunned the car and headed straight for them, expecting them to leap out of the way.

Instead they shifted shape in unison.

And the big red dragon lunged directly at the windshield of the car, his eyes blazing. He raged fire directly at her, and all she could see were brilliant flames. Eileen screamed and closed her eyes, but didn't take her foot off the gas.

She hoped for the best.

No luck. The car hit a tree with force and the radiator began to hiss and steam. The air bag deployed and Eileen was utterly disoriented.

That only got worse when someone opened the door and seized her elbow.

"And so we meet," the fair man said with a faint Russian accent. He hauled Eileen out of the car with more strength than he should have had for his size. "Charmed, I'm sure."

"Excuse me." Eileen tried to push away from him. "I have to go."

"Oh, I don't think you have anywhere to go," he said smoothly. "After all, we have much to discuss, Erik's mate."

Eileen glanced up in surprise.

And then it was too late.

She made the mistake of looking into his eyes, which were so pale that they could have been made of water.

Or smoke.

Ice.

He smiled a reptilian smile and flames lit in the depths of

his eyes. Just like Frenchie at the train station. Eileen realized that the new arrival was trying to influence her thoughts.

Not surrendering the Dragon's Teeth immediately seemed like a much less clever strategy than it had just the day before.

Being without Erik when two *Slayer*s had her cornered was even less clever.

Eileen fought to look away from those dancing flames, but she couldn't even blink. Her intuition screamed but she was snared. There was nothing she could do to save herself.

Except panic. She had that option covered.

For once in all his days and nights, Boris wasn't irritated. He could even forgive Sigmund for almost losing track of Erik's mate, given that she had found her way to this site.

Boris loved when events came full circle. He'd intended to bring Erik's mate here, to lure Erik to this potent site for his own destruction, bringing a kind of poetic closure to their old antagonism.

Boris planned to kill Erik precisely where Erik's father had killed Boris's father. But Erik's mate had come here of her own volition.

It was just too perfect.

Boris regarded the agitated mate with a certain tenderness. She was making him look good.

Maybe he would kill her a little more quickly.

Maybe he would explain everything more clearly to her.

She deserved a reward of some kind, after all.

Boris decided what her present would be. He would remove the risks, eliminate her chances of escape, and loose her from the spell of his beguiling.

So Erik's mate could appreciate his brilliance before she died.

"Destroy the car," he commanded Sigmund in old-speak, not breaking his gaze upon Erik's mate.

"You said you'd leave this to me," Sigmund began to

argue, his tone petulant and his manner making Boris impatient.

"I lied," Boris conceded mildly. "Destroy the car."

"But—"

"Now!"

Sigmund muttered something uncomplimentary under his breath but Boris didn't care about his minion's attitude. Sigmund was proving to be not just annoying and incompetent but disposable. Boris would have to find another acolyte to train, but perhaps he would find a better one.

Immortality was somewhat tedious in terms of finding good help.

Meanwhile, Sigmund shifted shape and kicked the car over onto its roof. He blasted it with dragonfire and the upholstery started to burn. Boris led Erik's mate away, assuming that the gas tank would explode.

It did, sending a satisfying array of flames into the sky.

The snow fell thickly all around them, dusting the burned edges of the old foundation stones with white. "You remember this place," he said to Erik's mate.

"I remember this place," she echoed dutifully, and he knew his beguiling was working against him. He listened, but heard nothing. There was a distant scent of *Pyr*, which simply meant that Erik would arrive more or less on cue.

Boris let the flames die in his eyes and the woman quickly averted her gaze. She caught her breath and took a trio of steps backward, clutching her satchel as she stared around the clearing. Her gaze lingered on the burning wreck of the car, then flicked to Sigmund and back to Boris.

"Who are you?" she demanded.

"Boris Vassily, leader of the *Slayers*." He bowed slightly.

Her eyes narrowed. "I thought Magnus led the *Slayers*."

Boris inhaled sharply. "Magnus is an insurgent who will be put in his place."

"I see." She nodded, and he wondered what she was thinking. "So, Erik's son works for you, then, not for Magnus?"

Boris was startled that she knew Sigmund's identity, but smiled all the same. "We fight on the same side, as we have done for so long. In fact it was here, on this very site, that I first recruited Sigmund."

She surveyed the clearing, then met Boris's gaze with suspicion. "It's kind of austere."

"There was a regrettable accident, one that you must recall."

She shook her head. "I don't know anything about this place. In fact, I'm wondering what this has to do with me."

"Everything." Boris considered her, skeptical that she had forgotten the past. "You don't think it was a coincidence that you were drawn to take refuge here, in a location you knew so well?"

She glanced around again, a measure of doubt in her expression. "I've never been here before."

"Not in this life," Boris said softly, and her eyes flashed. Maybe she did remember.

"Hello, Shadow," he murmured, and she paled.

Erik's mate took a step backward, her eyes wide and her face pale. She held her satchel in front of herself like a shield, but she couldn't have anything in there to defend herself against Boris. "I don't know what you're talking about," she said, but there was a lack of conviction in her tone.

"Don't you remember how your father was obsessed with the secrets of alchemy, with the promise of turning dross into gold?"

She frowned and glanced to the most distant collection of foundation stones. They were the blackest and the most burned. "In the lab," she whispered. "In his workshop."

"Yes," Boris agreed. "I knew you could remember if you tried."

Her mouth worked in shock and dismay, so he gave her a minute to catch up. Humans could be so intellectually slow, and so physically feeble. He had the time to wait.

"What are you talking about?" Sigmund showed a regrettable tendency to fill a silence and shatter a mood. "This place has nothing to do with Erik's mate."

"You can call me Eileen instead of Erik's mate," she said tartly. "Or maybe Dr. Grosvenor would be better."

"Mate," Boris repeated, ignoring Eileen as he faced Sigmund. He bit out his words. "She is Erik's *mate*." Sigmund stared at him, uncomprehending, and Boris exhaled in exasperation. "And I thought you were bright."

"Just because Erik's last mate was my mother—" Sigmund began, and Boris couldn't stand his stupidity any longer.

"How do you imagine that Erik has had two firestorms?" he shouted, fed up once and for all with incompetence. "There is only one way! There is only one possibility!" He jabbed a finger through the air at Eileen. "She is the reincarnation of your mother, Louisa!" He spit at the ground and the spittle hissed through the snow. "You *moron*!"

Sigmund blanched.

Eileen ran.

Erik spiraled out of the sky like an ebony spear.

And Boris laughed, gleeful that his plan was coming together so very well.

Let the mate run: His battle was with Erik Sorensson.

The blood duel was yet unfinished between them.

Louisa!

Sigmund was appalled that he'd missed something so obvious. There was no other way for his father to have a second firestorm than for his mother, Louisa, to be reborn.

But if Eileen was the reincarnation of Louisa, he couldn't let Boris kill her. As much as Sigmund blamed his father for the sorry events of his life, his mother had loved him without qualification.

And he had loved her in return. There was proof: The only scale Sigmund had ever lost was the one he'd lost over his mother's death. Her suicide had devastated him, and he had hated his father even more for driving her to that decision. He ran after Eileen, closing the distance between them with long strides as she bolted into the woods.

He caught her satchel and she spun to face him. She backed into a tree, her eyes wide, and tugged her satchel back into her own grip. Her hair was loose and her face was pale. She looked small and vulnerable to him, fragile as only humans could look.

Then she lifted her chin and her eyes flashed. He watched her lips set and glimpsed a toughness that he didn't remember at all.

"Go ahead, then," Eileen said with quiet fury. "Fry me."

Sigmund couldn't do it.

There was hatred in her eyes, loathing and fear mingled together, and that look shredded his conviction. He halted and saw her flinch in anticipation of his assault. He heard Boris and Erik battling in the clearing behind them, knew logically that he should want to thwart Erik's firestorm, but couldn't confirm Eileen's assessment of him.

He let himself shift shape, taking human form once again.

She eyed him warily. "Changing your mind? Or do you just have a nastier plan?"

He shoved his hands into his pockets, remembering a hundred incidents that she had forgotten, all the times he'd come home as a boy with a confession to make, all the times she'd soothed his injuries, all the times that she had pushed the shadow away from his sun. His heart swelled with remembered affection, given and received, and the wound of that final break hurt all the more.

He hadn't made his choice in isolation.

"You have to remember."

She caught her breath and averted her gaze. "Reincarnation is flaky stuff."

"Does that mean it can't be true?" Sigmund asked quietly. She met his gaze, her own filled with questions. "Dragon shape shifters could be said to be flaky stuff, too."

She smiled a little and his heart clenched at the glimpse of Louisa in her smile. "If one myth comes to life, why can't the others do the same?" she asked, then nodded. He sensed that she was pulling thoughts and impressions together, making sense of them.

There was more she had to face than his reality.

"You blame me for turning *Slayer*," he said softly. "You don't approve of what I am, just the way you didn't approve of my visiting my grandfather without you."

"I'm at a disadvantage here," she said, taking a quick breath as she glanced toward the clearing. "I remember only bits and ends, and what I do remember is so vague that I'm not sure it really is my memory."

"But you came here today."

She bit her lip. "It felt right. And there weren't a lot of choices."

"No," Sigmund said flatly. "It's more than that. You remember and you know you remember." Her breath hitched and he watched her hand spread against the bark of the tree. It was as if she sought reassurance of what was real, what was tangible, what could be relied upon.

But Sigmund knew that his own memory was real.

"You saw the fire," he said, sparing a glance over his shoulder. "You saw that last fight, the explosion that destroyed the lab and the dragonfire that claimed the house. But I was here first. I saw my grandfathers die."

"Louisa's father?"

"And Erik's father, too. Both of them died here, both at Erik's own hand."

She inhaled sharply. "I have only your word on that."

"He'll probably tell you if you ask him." Sigmund shook his head. "He never had a problem admitting the truth, no matter how painful it was. Don't you remember?"

Her fingers clenched as she watched him.

"Don't you remember how he told you what I had become? I remember lying in my bed upstairs, listening to the two of you fight. You'd made him promise not to take dragon form. You were sure it was evil, the mark of Satan upon him. I was coming into my abilities, but you didn't want to know the truth. He made you hear the truth that I was *Pyr*, too. He made you listen." He took a breath, remembering that painful night. "He made me show you the truth."

She swallowed. "I don't remember," she whispered, but the glint in her eyes told him that she just might.

"And after he left, you said that all dragons are evil. You called me devil-spawn," he said, the heat of that old rejection filling his words. "You called me evil. You said you regretted bearing Erik's child and believing his promises. You cast me out and told me to repent of my sins—or never come back." Sigmund's throat tightened and he jabbed a finger at his own chest. "But I am what I am—I am a dragon shape shifter— and repentance changed nothing."

She was even more pale as she watched him and her eyes seemed more vibrantly blue. "You turned *Slayer* because I rejected you," she murmured, guessing his truth.

"I lost a scale for you!" Sigmund cried. "I loved you, but you refused to love me once you knew that I was like my father."

"I'm sorry," she said, and he heard a new compassion in her words. She swallowed and her eyes filled with tears. "I have this dream. I have it all the time. I dream that I'm holding a baby boy. And in that dream, my heart is so full of love for my son that I'm afraid it will burst."

She stretched out her hand toward Sigmund, seeking reconciliation, and he was tempted to meet her halfway. He held his ground, though, his mouth dry.

"I thought it was a dream for something that might never happen, but it's of you. It's a memory of your birth. And in that dream, my greatest fear is that my beloved son will be taken away from me."

Erik's mate shook her head. "I can't have meant to send

you away. I must have spoken in anger. I'm sorry. Sigmund, I am so sorry."

Sigmund felt that old wound ache again, but the pain was less sharp. Sunlight could have touched the ice that encased his heart, beginning the slow melt of spring. Her words lit a spark where there had been darkness for so long, and tempted him to forgive her. He stretched out a hand to Eileen, more than ready to meet her halfway. The sympathy she offered was all he wanted and more.

But their fingers never touched.

Boris Vassily was alive.

Erik couldn't believe it, but he would have recognized his old foe anywhere. He thought he'd ensured Boris's death the previous summer, but he'd been wrong.

He knew, too late, that he should have trusted his earlier sense that Boris was in his vicinity. His was a remarkable recovery from the burned remains that Erik had left on the dock, which could mean only one thing.

Boris must have drunk the Dragon's Blood Elixir, too.

And the blood duel to which Erik had challenged Boris all those months ago was still unresolved. It didn't matter that Erik had retrieved his challenge coin. It didn't matter that he had believed he had won. A blood duel was a fight to the death, a battle that left only one of the challengers breathing. So long as he and Boris were both alive, the blood duel was on.

Boris roared and locked claws with Erik, almost bowling Erik over with the force of his assault. Boris laughed, the tightness of his grip making Erik aware that Erik had already fought long and hard.

But he couldn't let Eileen down.

These *Slayer*s who had drunk the Elixir had to have a weakness, but Erik didn't know what it was. He wished, a bit late, that he'd paid more attention to old myths, even those he didn't believe.

Rafferty's accusation rang in his ears.

Erik refused to accept defeat. He couldn't win by brute force.

Which meant he had to trick Boris. He'd let Boris believe he was defeated, then have surprise on his side once more.

He deliberately didn't move out of the way of Boris's next strike quite quickly enough. Boris's tail caught Erik across the back and he let himself stumble. Boris laughed and came after him immediately.

Trickery wasn't the best plan Erik had ever had, but it was his only chance.

He just had to make it count.

Chapter 17

Eileen was reeling. Her dream of a baby was of Sigmund. Her infatuation with the story of the Dragon Lover of Madeley was a recognition of her own story and a need to address loose ends. Her attraction to Erik had occurred before, and it made sense to her that she still found him so attractive. Her fear of trusting men was rooted in her conviction that Erik had betrayed her.

But she had felt such despair that she had killed herself. Her fear of water made sense in that context, but the scope of her depression didn't. What had driven her to such desperation? Why had she been so willing to believe badly of Erik? How could she have condemned her only son, even in anger?

It was a story she wanted to know fully, one she'd unravel after surviving this ordeal.

Assuming that she did survive this ordeal.

Before Sigmund could take her hand, Boris set the trees aflame on every side of her, turning the forest into an army of burning torches. Eileen bolted. She ran through the woods, trying to put distance between them, but the flames followed close behind.

The snow fell ceaselessly all around her, eliminating her sense of direction. The forest appeared the same no matter which way she looked. Sigmund seemed to have disappeared. She wasn't going to stop and look for him.

She heard Erik and Boris battling for supremacy overhead, Erik attacking Boris to keep him from breathing fire. Boris seemed unstoppable, invincible, powerful, and tireless.

It seemed that each time Eileen dared to glance up, Erik took another blow. He was obviously tired and bruised, his blood running from a number of small wounds. There was a big cut on his forehead. He looked like a losing prizefighter just before he fell for the last time.

What would she do if Erik didn't get up?

Not much. She'd be lunch but quick. As she dodged fire, Eileen tried desperately to think of a way to help her defender.

Eileen leapt over a log and jumped for a gap in the trees ahead. She discovered that she had run full circle and come back to the clearing with the blackened foundation stones. Boris and Erik were locked in combat to one side, the rental car was burning, and Sigmund was nowhere to be seen. She stumbled, pivoted, and knew she'd find either destruction or salvation right in this space.

She had a vague sense of a past confrontation, of anger and recriminations, and felt her body respond with fear. She had to focus on the present, though, before she could explore her shattered memories of the past. She stared upward at the fighting dragons, red coiling around black.

Boris was choking the life out of Erik. In frustration, Eileen picked up a stone and threw it at the *Slayer*. It bounced off his back, making a metallic ding when it struck his scales. Meanwhile, Boris squeezed more tightly. Erik made a choking sound that Eileen didn't like one bit. She hurled another rock, then another and another, her vision blurred with tears.

But it was futile. Erik went limp and Boris held him easily in one brass claw.

Eileen felt sick.

Boris pivoted then, his eyes shining with malice. He flung Erik in the direction of the burning trees, then laughed as his opponent's body fell bonelessly into the forest. There was a crash as Erik tumbled to earth.

Eileen waited, but there was no sound of him moving again.

Boris raised his claws and dove toward Eileen, smoke and fire emanating from his mouth.

Eileen stood her ground and waited, her heart in her throat. She wasn't going to cringe. She felt the heat of Boris's approach and had time to hope that he slaughtered her quickly.

Then there was a flash of green in her peripheral vision. Sigmund leapt from the surrounding trees and lunged toward Boris. He shouted as he dug his claws deeply into the *Slayer*'s ruby red sides.

Boris, caught by surprise, spun in midair. He bellowed with pain and ripped at Sigmund, tearing open a long wound across Sigmund's chest. Sigmund breathed fire and Boris laughed as the flames had no effect upon his scales.

"Stupid coward," he hissed. "You should have been the shard of Erik's talon. You should have killed the leader of the *Pyr* and assumed ascendancy, just the way your father did before you."

Eileen was horrified by this accusation, but she knew it wasn't the truth. Erik couldn't have murdered his father for the sake of ambition. She knew him too well to believe it.

She was going to trust Erik until she knew the truth—and probably after that—just as the blond woman in her dream had suggested.

"Useless worm!" Boris roared, then exhaled a torrent of dragonfire upon Sigmund. The green *Slayer*'s scales blackened under the heat of the fire, but he kept on fighting. He tore at Boris's wings and struck him with his tail.

Boris smiled, untroubled. He drew himself up tall, wings beating steadily, an impressive vision of red and brass against the swirling snow. Eileen saw him exhale slowly, saw his eyes gleam, and guessed immediately that he was breathing smoke.

The way Sigmund jerked told her that she was right. Boris caught Sigmund's talons in his own and held fast as he breathed steadily, his eyes glittering. Sigmund writhed and twisted but couldn't break free of the *Slayer*'s grasp.

Strangely enough, as Eileen watched, Boris became larger and brighter. Sigmund faded, looking smaller and more crumpled with every passing moment. His struggles became weaker as Boris shone in increasing brilliance. The red *Slayer* smiled as his green opponent moaned, and his smile was blinding in its brilliance.

He was stealing Sigmund's life force. Eileen didn't know how he was doing it, but the evidence was clear. She threw another trio of rocks at the *Slayer*, but he didn't even seem to notice them bouncing off his back.

He was going to suck Sigmund dry.

And what would be left? Eileen didn't think much.

And what could she do about it? Even less.

Eileen's anger rose, but before she could lose hope, she spied a dark shadow separating itself from those of the forest. She didn't dare to look straight at the emerging figure, so fearful was she of drawing Boris's attention to him.

But she felt the heat of the firestorm kindle and knew who approached. Her heart sang that Erik had survived, and she knew she had to help him.

She threw another rock at Boris, a big one. It struck him in the temple and drew dark blood. She earned a glare from him for her deed, and was glad she had broken his concentration.

Boris turned that laser-bright gaze on her, his malice

enough to make her tremble. "Don't be impatient," he muttered. "You're next."

While his attention was diverted, Sigmund revived slightly and began to struggle again.

In that crucial moment, Erik came over the trees and attacked.

Eileen wanted to cheer.

Erik fell on Boris in a fury of talons and teeth, knowing that surprise was his only asset. He caught Boris across the back with dragonfire, searing his old foe. Boris flung Sigmund aside with a surprised cry and spun to lock claws with Erik.

He didn't get the chance. Erik kicked Boris out of the sky, following the *Slayer*'s descent.

Sigmund, meanwhile, hit the ground with a thud and a loud crack. He didn't move right away, but Erik was focused on his task. He was fighting for more than the unresolved blood duel, more than the debts of the past.

He was fighting for Eileen's life.

Boris struck a tree heavily and Erik breathed dragonfire as he flew closer. The tree ignited and Boris shouted as the flames touched his scales. He leapt out of the fire, but Erik struck him hard with his tail. Boris fell and Erik latched on to his wings. He tore at the leather, shredding it with new-found force.

Boris screamed and struggled, but his wings were rendered useless all the same. He snatched at Erik, catching one leg in his grip, and Erik flew high, dragging the *Slayer* with him. He spiraled as he flew, spinning ever upward.

The ground dropped away, trees and houses and even the valley of the Severn itself becoming small and distant. The pair punched through the cloud cover and Erik headed for the stars.

"You cannot kill me," Boris seethed. *"I have drunk the Elixir."*

Erik kept going, shooting into the sky like an arrow loosed from a bow. He flew higher and faster than he ever had before. The air grew thin but he continued, knowing that he had one chance.

He had to make it count.

Boris gasped and let go, taking his chances on the impact of the fall. Erik wasn't having any of that. He swooped through the air, looped around, and snatched the *Slayer* by the tail. He swung Boris's weight as he continued to ascend.

"You cannot destroy me," Boris insisted. *"I will heal from wounds that you would not survive."*

"Then I'll just have to hurt you badly." Erik kept flying.

"I have drunk the Elixir!" Boris raged.

When he couldn't breathe anymore, Erik spun like a dervish. He swung Boris's weight around. The *Slayer* struggled and fought, but centrifugal force kept his talons away from Erik.

"My father said that the Elixir was a trap," Erik said.

"It is a release from mortality's grasp!"

Was it? Or had his father been right? Erik wished he had listened more closely.

He wished he hadn't alienated Rafferty.

But first things first. He turned high in the sky, swinging Boris around so that he could see the twinkle of stars overhead.

"Guess what happens next?" he asked.

Boris shouted in rage and tried to snatch at Erik. *"You can't. You wouldn't. . . ."* His eyes shone. *"I can arrange for you to sip the Elixir. . . ."*

Erik wasn't interested. He interrupted Boris's attempt at negotiation. *"Let's just see how immortal you are."*

"No!" Boris roared aloud.

But Erik flung Boris across the sky and let him fall. He watched the *Slayer* spiral toward the earth, helpless against the pull of gravity but struggling to fly all the same. Boris screamed much of the way down.

Erik wondered where he would hit and what the locals would make of a broken dragon in their midst. He wondered whether Boris would feel up to beguiling all the humans who gathered, and the prospect made him smile.

No matter how strong the Elixir, it would take time for Boris to heal from the bruises he sustained in this fall. He'd be busy for the short term, just as Magnus was.

This was time Erik could use to ensure his mate's safety.

He dove toward Ironbridge again, hoping that Sigmund hadn't taken advantage of his absence.

Eileen couldn't understand why there was so much thunder during a snowstorm. It was the strangest thing.

But then, there were other, stranger things happening in her life recently.

Eileen winced as she surveyed Sigmund. When he'd fallen, something had cracked within him. He looked withered, more like a crumpled piece of wrapping paper than a dragon. A moment after hitting the ground, he had shuddered and changed back to human form again.

He didn't move and she didn't think he'd made the change on purpose. His eyes were closed and his breathing labored. He was even more pale than he had been before and there was a dark puddle spreading beneath him. The blood swirled on the ground, a curious mixture of red and black.

Red? Eileen went to kneel beside Sigmund. She wiped his forehead with the end of her scarf, not liking the sheen of perspiration on his skin. His eyelids flickered, their green hue glittering between the lids in a way that reminded her of Erik.

Then he opened his eyes fully and looked at her.

"Do I call nine-one-one for injured dragons?" she asked, forcing a smile.

Sigmund shook his head minutely. "No point." The words cost him dearly, she could see, and sweat broke out on his forehead.

"You can't be so sure. . . ."

He put his hand over hers for a moment, touching her tentatively. "Yes. I can." He spoke with conviction.

Their gazes held for a long moment; then he exhaled slowly again and shivered as his eyes closed. Just uttering those few words seemed to have exhausted him.

Eileen took off her coat and put it over Sigmund, not knowing what else she could do. He had defended her. He had saved her from Boris and paid the price himself. And she was not innocent—from what he had told her, she had had a role in his choice to turn *Slayer*. Her wholesale rejection of dragons was a choice that had devastated her in that past life and cost her the man she loved.

She could do better than that.

She could love better than that.

Sigmund moved beneath her coat, as if suddenly restless.

"Be still," she whispered as she sank to her knees beside Louisa's son. She picked up Sigmund's limp hand and held it between her own. His pulse was faint and irregular, as unsteady as his breathing.

"You didn't have to do that," she said, hearing a mother's scold in her tone. "You should have protected yourself."

Sigmund almost smiled, although his eyes didn't open. "I had to protect you."

Because he had forgiven her—or at least accepted her apology. "I'm sorry," she whispered again, holding his hand fast within her own. He nodded once and opened his eyes, his unflinching gaze reminding her of his father.

Eileen blinked back her tears as the pair stared at each other. So much pain, so much loss.

And so little time to make it right.

She kissed his knuckles, aching at the injury they had done to each other. The fullness of the truth would come to her in time, but for the moment she was glad they had made amends. Sigmund sighed with what might have been similar relief and his eyes closed again.

Eileen knew that he would die.

He knew it, too. She could see his resignation.

But she was content to sit with him. She wouldn't leave him or judge him or cast him out.

Not this time.

The snow fell around them steadily, burying the burned foundation stones in the clearing under a white blanket. The fire in the trees was extinguished and the world seemed a thousand miles away. There was only a light breeze, the falling snow, and Sigmund's soft breathing.

And thunder.

Eileen looked up at the overcast sky in confusion. "I never heard so much thunder in my life," she murmured, then glanced down to find Sigmund smiling.

"Not thunder," he whispered, and she had to lean closer to hear him. "Old-speak."

"Old-speak? What's that?"

"How we talk," he managed to say, then frowned and licked his lips. His grip tightened on her hand briefly and his eyelids flickered. "Save me," he whispered.

Eileen leaned closer. "How? What can I do?"

Sigmund shook his head slightly, that frown marring his forehead again. "Not you." He caught his breath and she ran a hand over his cheek, wanting to soothe his agitation. He turned his face toward her hand, seeming to welcome her touch. "Four elements."

Eileen didn't understand. She wanted to help him, though, and wished she could ease his concern. "Fire, earth, water, and air," she said, hoping to encourage him.

He nodded, the gesture so minute that she would have missed it if she hadn't been watching him so closely. "Erik," he said, and his eyes flew open as his voice rose. "Please."

Eileen didn't know what to say. She didn't understand fully what he was asking. As much as she wanted to help, she couldn't promise to do something without knowing what it was.

She heard the beat of leathery wings and glanced upward

in fear. Sigmund's grip tightened on her hand, but relief flooded through Eileen when she saw the ebony hue of the descending dragon. A glow settled around her heart, but it wasn't just from the firestorm.

Erik had come back.

And he had returned alone.

Erik landed in the clearing, shifting shape so quickly that Eileen couldn't even see the change. He strode toward her as grim as ever and filled with purpose.

"He wants to be saved, by you, with the four elements," Eileen said immediately, guessing that there wasn't much time. Sigmund's fingers fluttered within her grasp.

"I would wager that he does," Erik said, his expression impassive. He seemed more stern, more controlled, and Eileen guessed that he was hiding a tide of emotion. He hesitated only a moment before he crouched beside her.

Beside his son.

Beside their son.

"He intervened to save me, Erik," she said, her words hoarse.

"I know," Erik said, and shoved a hand through his hair. Eileen watched him, knowing that he was struggling with the legacy of the past as well.

"Can you give him what he wants?"

"I can," Erik acknowledged, but she heard his doubt of the wisdom of doing that.

Sigmund's eyes opened, his gaze fixing upon his father. "Please." He shook his head, but made no further sound.

Erik bowed his head and frowned, his consternation clear. Eileen knew that he wanted to help Sigmund but that something—some doubt—was holding him back.

"What does he mean?"

Erik sighed. "*Pyr* must be exposed to all four elements when they die, in order that their bodies return to the earth and their spark returns to the Great Wyvern. The *Slayers* have learned to harvest the bodies of those *Pyr* who have not been exposed to all four elements and turn them into shadow dragons. They become warriors for the *Slayers*, tireless warriors who do not bleed."

Sigmund's breathing became more shallow, his manner more agitated. "Please."

"And you can ensure that this doesn't happen to him?" Eileen asked. The choice was clear to her and she didn't understand why Erik hesitated at all. "Then you have to do it."

"Except that Sigmund was the one who rediscovered the process and helped to implement the plan."

Eileen understood.

She was horrified.

Sigmund shook his head slowly, tears falling in his fear.

"Did you find Magnus?" Erik asked. "Or did he find you?"

Sigmund closed his eyes and turned his face away.

"Did you awaken him?"

Sigmund winced. Erik sighed and pinched the bridge of his nose. "Where does it end?" he asked with impatience, as if not expecting anyone to answer him. "When does one have to face the wages of one's own choices?"

"That's not up to us. You have to do this," Eileen said, touched by Sigmund's terror. He knew the full horror of what he had done and feared having it done to him. "He tried to help me. He tried to make better choices. Isn't that the only thing we can do?"

Erik considered that for a long moment. He was so composed that Eileen couldn't guess what he was thinking. The fact that he wasn't saying anything meant that he was torn.

"Please," she said.

Erik cleared his throat and leaned closer to his son. "I shall make you a wager. Tell me how those who have drunk the Dragon's Blood Elixir can be killed. Give me a chance to save the world and I will do as you ask."

Sigmund swallowed and Eileen had the sense that he was

trying to gather his strength. He nodded, then licked his lips. He looked directly at Erik. "Only," he said, the word costing him dearly.

"Yes." Erik leaned closer.

"One."

"Yes."

"Way."

"Yes, I expect there is." Erik seized Sigmund's other hand, as if he would give him some of his own strength. Eileen knew that his attitude had changed. It was less the secret that he desired from Sigmund that had softened Erik's expression, and more the fact that Sigmund was trying to make amends.

"Destroy," Sigmund said, his head lolling as his eyes closed.

"Yes, yes, they must be destroyed," Erik whispered, his urgency clear. "But how? How?"

Sigmund made a choking sound. There was a gurgle deep within his chest and then his hand went limp within Eileen's grip.

She and Erik waited. Eileen knew she wasn't the only one holding her breath. Sigmund's chest fell and didn't rise again, and she couldn't feel the slow throb of his pulse anymore.

Erik bowed his head.

Sigmund was dead, and the secret of the Dragon's Blood Elixir was lost with him.

Erik sighed and frowned, then put Sigmund's hand back on his chest. He pushed to his feet and strode across the clearing, so obviously disappointed that Eileen ached for him.

And for Sigmund.

For all of them. Her tears fell as she stared at Sigmund's still features. She kissed his knuckles, regretting what had been done, past and present, and laid his other hand on his chest.

Maybe he was at peace.

She glanced toward Erik, who had bowed his head in grief. That one gesture revealed that he hadn't fully hardened his heart against his son.

Eileen rose slowly and went to Erik. She put one hand on his shoulder, and the spark that leapt beneath her fingers dispelled the chill that had taken hold of her heart.

"He tried," she whispered.

"Yes." Erik nodded. "He tried." He offered his hand to her, and she slid her fingers into his. They stood together in the snow, and the heat of the firestorm thrummed through Eileen's veins. She drew strength from its power and hoped Erik did, too.

"I guess children don't always bring joy," she said.

Erik cast her a sidelong smile. "There was joy, too. Do you remember?"

"No. Just bits and ends. Impressions."

"Maybe it's easier that way."

Eileen frowned at their interlocked hands and asked the question she needed to ask. "Did you come to me because I was Louisa?"

Erik raised her knuckles to his lips and, at his kiss, the spark between them settled into a vivid glow. "I came because of the firestorm. I was taught that the firestorm should never be denied."

"Destined sex," Eileen said, trying to keep her tone light.

Erik didn't smile. His grip tightened on her hand. "If there is a future for us, it's because you are not Louisa anymore."

The light painted his features with gold, making him look powerful and mysterious. Eileen's heart clenched as she stared into the conviction in his eyes. She liked the strength of his grip and the power of his convictions. She admired that he strove to make the right choices. And he explained things to her, even though it was obviously his nature to be reticent.

She felt lucky that he let her glimpse his hidden passion.

"If there's a future?" she asked, her words hoarse. "Don't you want there to be?"

Erik frowned. "I'm not sure the choice is mine to make," was all he said; then he kissed her knuckles once more. Before she could ask more, Erik retrieved her coat and put it around her shoulders. He looked tired, and there was a bleeding wound on his forehead.

Still he tried to smile for her.

Eileen decided to save her questions.

"Look away," he murmured. "You will not like to witness what must be done." Then he brushed his lips across her forehead, sending a frisson of heat to her toes.

Eileen turned away. She was aware that Erik changed shape. She felt his strength and his power close behind her but she respected his judgment.

She didn't look. Instead she counted elements. There was air everywhere, so that took care of one. Sigmund was lying on the earth, which provided the second element. She supposed that the falling snow, which was melting against her own skin, would provide the third element, water.

Which left only fire.

Erik would cremate his son, at Sigmund's own request. It wouldn't be an easy thing to do. Eileen shuddered.

She wrapped her arms around herself and walked to the perimeter of the clearing, her sorrow rising with such force that it nearly choked her. She looked up into the swirling dance of the falling snow. She heard dragonfire. She smelled flesh burning. She tightened her grip on her own elbows and prayed that Sigmund would find peace.

And when Erik caught her shoulders in his hands long moments later, Eileen reveled in his strength. She felt herself tremble and let him gather her into his embrace. She leaned against his chest and welcomed the heat of the firestorm as it sparked through her veins.

The firestorm reminded her that she was alive.

That she could make different choices.

That she could learn from the past.

That she could trust a man and create a future.

She tipped her head back, raising one hand to Erik's cheek. His face was wet, wet with tears, and she saw the pain in his eyes at what he had had to do.

But he had kept his promise. He had shown mercy to his son.

And she knew that was a change for him, too.

"Let's go home," he said, his voice husky.

Eileen nodded agreement. She didn't care where he called home, or what his destination might be. She wanted to be with Erik, and wherever he was was right where she wanted to be.

She was going to trust her instincts on that.

He nodded once, crisply, then caught her close. The next thing she knew, he had shifted shape and leapt into the sky. He flew high as the snow spiraled around them, leaving Ironbridge and their tangled past behind, holding her fast against his chest.

Eileen closed her eyes and laid her cheek against the silver splendor of his scaled chest. It was like armor, but warm. There was nothing demonic about what he was, what he could become, and Louisa had been wrong to deny Erik his truth.

When Eileen pressed her cheek against Erik's chest, she not only felt the glow of the firestorm, but she could hear the steady rhythm of his heart.

Strong.

Stalwart.

Exactly what she wanted to hear.

Chapter 18

B oris fell.

He tumbled through the sky, impotent, hating that his wings were useless. The ground came closer with astonishing speed, and he forced himself to think instead of panic.

Could he die if he fell from this height?

Could he be healed again?

It would be better to avoid the possibility. But how? He dropped helplessly through the clouds and saw individual figures on the ground below. One pointed at him, but he couldn't hear whatever was said.

It wasn't fair. It wasn't right. He had drunk the Elixir and survived. He could cut smoke and pass through it undamaged—just like the Wyvern.

Boris pondered that. What were the Wyvern's other skills? She could move through dragonsmoke, and he could do that. She could shift shape to a salamander, but if he could do that, it wouldn't help him much in this circumstance.

She could spontaneously manifest in any location.

Which meant that she could move between locations by force of will.

Could he do that?

Boris closed his eyes. He ignored the wind streaming past him. He ignored his sense of impending doom. He focused on where he'd rather be, knowing that a specific location would work best. The perfect answer came to him in a heartbeat.

Wherever Sophie was.

Yes! He'd kill the Wyvern, lull Erik into complacency by his absence, then return to finish the blood duel.

The wind rushed past him and he heard a human shout.

Boris filled his thoughts with Sophie. He recalled how she looked in both forms, how she smelled, how she moved, how her eyes shone.

He remembered the feel of her throat beneath his talon, of the vivid red of her blood sliding over his brass claw. He thought of her and only her and he turned his considerable force of will upon being in her presence.

Boris had a second to fear failure; then the rush of the wind stopped.

Sophie was lying in the desert as the sun rose in the east. Normally, she loved watching the rosy hues steal across the sand, loved feeling the grains heat beneath her cheek. She loved watching the flowers open beneath the caress of the sun and seeing the brilliance of the stars retreat.

There was no pleasure in this occasion, though. She had spread herself across the sand all night. She'd asked Gaia to reveal the location of another Dragon's Egg, another orb of stone with the power to reveal the future to the *Pyr*.

It felt rude to Sophie to ask for another gift, especially as the first had been destroyed, but she hoped that Gaia would make allowances.

Gaia, however, was caught in her own rumblings and mumblings. She stirred at deep levels, seething with her inability to achieve balance. She was uninterested in Sophie's low song.

Sophie had eventually stopped her chant and simply listened. All she heard was doom and portents of destruction, the cruel sound of mortality. Perhaps her attention would appease Gaia.

Her choice certainly didn't affect Nikolas, who hovered a dozen steps away. He was more motionless than the shadows, darker than the night sky, more intense than the midday sun. Sophie doubted she would ever become accustomed to his vigilance.

She knew she would never become accustomed to being so aware of herself, of her own femininity, in his presence. She knew she would never be able to completely ignore the unspoken offer in his eyes, or forget the fervor of his promise to defend her at any cost.

Nikolas stole her breath away just with his proximity. She'd banished him to a distance, but it made little difference. She could feel him watching her, could almost taste his admiration, and the power of firestorm was much easier for her to understand.

But she would never touch Nikolas.

It was forbidden.

Gaia moaned on a distant coast, hurling water from the ocean's depths to a rocky shore. Sophie stretched herself to intervene, to persuade Gaia to be more gentle, and forgot her surroundings.

In that moment, a dragon landed atop her.

Boris laughed with glee, even as his talons locked around Sophie's neck. Sophie was shocked.

"This time we finish what was begun," he said as he squeezed. His claws cut deeply.

Sophie struggled but he was on her back, holding her down, and his weight was considerable. She shifted shape, rotating rapidly between her three favored forms. Boris was ready for her, though, and held fast, squeezing more relentlessly when she became a white salamander.

Sophie heard a bone snap and knew it was one of her own.

She struggled for survival. But she was no fighter—it was not her destiny to fight—and despite her efforts, Sophie's world faded to black.

Nikolas was outraged.

If Sophie hadn't made him keep his distance, he would have been on top of her assailant more quickly. She had called him a distraction. He had trusted her judgment.

She had been wrong and he was terrified that she would pay the price. He moved as soon as he saw Boris, but it took precious seconds to reach her.

She was limp when he ripped Boris from her back.

If she survived, he'd never heed her command again.

"Too late," Boris murmured in old-speak, his eyes glinting with triumph. He released Sophie with a flick of his talons. She fell to the sand and didn't move again.

Boris laughed.

Nikolas bellowed with fury and slashed the *Slayer* across the face with all five talons. Boris stopped laughing as he fell back, then raised his claws to defend himself. Nikolas saw that the *Slayer*'s wings were damaged so badly that he couldn't fly. He had a heartbeat to conclude that the battle would be his; then Boris was gone.

Nikolas spun, seeking his opponent. He had disappeared without a trace.

Or shifted shape.

Nikolas spied movement across the sand and glimpsed a red salamander. He snatched up the salamander, knowing instinctively that it was Boris, and crushed him in one hand. Boris screamed and squirmed and shouted, but he could not get away. His bones crunched in a very satisfying way.

Nikolas opened his hand to find it empty; then Boris manifested in dragon form on Nikolas's back. Nikolas leapt backward into a cactus.

Boris shrieked, then disappeared again.

There was no movement on the ground, no whisper in the

air. The sun rose slowly. The wind stilled. The shadows were eliminated as the sun drew higher, but Nikolas knew that Boris wasn't gone.

He could smell *Slayer*.

He prowled the area, guessing that the *Slayer* was injured and close at hand. He had only to find him. Nikolas turned over rocks; he peered around cacti; he looked down holes made in the sand by other small creatures. Boris's scent was elusive, appearing and disappearing, as if the *Slayer* would have preferred to mask it but didn't have the strength to do so.

That worked for Nikolas.

He caught a waft of Boris's scent, pivoted, and pounced on a small rock. He turned it over and saw a flash of crimson streak across the sand. Boris wasn't fast enough to evade Nikolas.

Nikolas snatched him up, holding him between finger and thumb, piercing him from either side with a sharp talon. Boris struggled and spun. Nikolas lifted him high, then breathed a narrow stream of dragonfire. He roasted the *Slayer*, taking his time to maximize Boris's pain.

Boris had injured the Wyvern by choice and there was no punishment harsh enough for such a crime. While Boris begged for mercy in old-speak, Nikolas lifted the small creature above his head. He let Boris dangle there for a moment, then opened his mouth wide. He let Boris look down his gullet and anticipate his own fate.

Nikolas would eat Boris whole, crunch his bones, and spit out the remains. He'd ensure that there was nothing left of the *Slayer* who had so injured Sophie. He'd obliterate him and not have a single regret.

But before Nikolas could drop the twisting salamander into his open mouth, Boris changed shape back to a dragon again. His weight was too much for Nikolas to hold with two talons, his girth too big for Nikolas's grasp.

Boris fell on top of Nikolas with a bellow and the pair

wrestled in the hot sand. Boris fought with surprising power. The pair ripped at each other and blood mingled in the sand, red and black mixing and mingling under the hot sun.

Boris struck Nikolas with his tail and Nikolas caught the end of Boris's tail. He swung the *Slayer* around when he hit the ground himself, spinning so that Boris couldn't reach him.

Then Nikolas tossed Boris into a large clump of cactus, impaling the *Slayer* on a thousand sharp needles. Boris shouted in pain, and as he twisted, he only made his situation worse. Gravity drew him deeper into the nest of spikes and his wings were of no help to him. He struggled and flailed, caught by the cactus spines.

Nikolas hovered over the stricken *Slayer*, intent upon finishing him off. He breathed fire until Boris's ruby red scales roasted to black. He loosed dragonsmoke that made Boris flinch and twist and whine. He pulled back to strike Boris with his tail, but the *Slayer* abruptly disappeared again.

There was no salamander, red or black, anywhere to be seen.

There was no scent of *Slayer*.

Boris was gone.

And so was the Wyvern.

"Sophie!" Nikolas said. He turned in place, scanning the stillness of the desert. He saw nothing in any direction, no movement, no white salamander. Had Boris somehow captured her? How would he follow? How could he defend her?

"Sophie!" Nikolas roared, more frustrated than he had ever been in his life. He flew low over the area, his search circles gradually increasing in radius and his fear growing with every beat of his wings.

There was no sign of Sophie.

The sun crept higher, burning brighter and hotter. Nikolas landed and shifted back to human form finally, exhausted and terrified.

They were both gone, as surely as if they had never been there.

Was that what happened when the Wyvern died? She disappeared completely? Nikolas feared it was so. The world would be abandoned until another Wyvern took Sophie's place.

But Nikolas didn't want another Wyvern.

"Sophie!" he cried one last time.

Nikolas had failed the Wyvern after he had pledged himself to her defense.

He was guilty of the greatest crime of all.

Sophie was so terrified that she had a hard time manifesting at all. She was spooked by Boris and she had lost a lot of blood. She wanted to flee from all earthly concerns, to evade her responsibilities, to abandon the duties of living. She wanted to hide, as she and other Wyverns before her had hidden for centuries.

But she couldn't, not when she heard Nikolas's cry of anguish. His pain drew her back, back to the scene of Boris's assault, back to the obligations she had yet to fulfill. His conviction of his own defeat tore at her heart and awakened feelings she had never expected to feel. She heard him and wanted to ease his pain.

She had journeyed down a road that she should have avoided. She had become entangled in the immediate concerns of the *Pyr*, and in so doing, she had awakened yearnings of her own. She knew that desire was too worldly for the Wyvern. She understood, too late, why the path of involvement was forbidden. Once engaged, she could not retreat.

But she had taken the turn. She had made the choice and it had fostered change within her so that she could not return to her blissful detachment.

Sophie no longer cared what was forbidden to her, not when this *Pyr* who had volunteered to protect her had lost his conviction of his own power. It was not right that her fear of Boris and death could break his pride.

It was not her right to undermine his power so.

She could not hide. She could not abandon Nikolas to his own conviction that he had failed her. His anguish tore at her heart.

Sophie steeled herself and manifested as a white salamander in Nikolas's shirt pocket. She trembled like a leaf in the wind, but heard him catch his breath when he felt her presence.

"Sophie," he whispered, her name falling from his lips like a benediction. He cupped his hand over his pocket and sat down heavily in the desert sand in his relief.

His muscles were trembling from his fight with Boris, but his heart had skipped when he had felt her presence. He was pumped and ready to fight, agitated enough to destroy another, but he cradled her gently in his palm.

Caught between the thunder of his heart and the warmth of his palm, cocooned by his strength and surrounded by his scent, Sophie knew that her battle against temptation was lost.

She feared leaving him, but knew there were things she had to do first. There were places Nikolas could not follow her, but she would visit them only one last time.

She had to dispatch a dream or two.

Erik was exhausted, but relieved.

The firestorm rolled through him, filling him with new purpose and strength. He was glad to have Eileen safe, glad she had encountered some of her past without risking her sanity. He would have liked to have had the secret of eliminating those *Slayers* who had drunk the Elixir, but time had conspired against him.

The fact that Sigmund had tried to share it, though, meant that there was a way. Erik would simply have to seek it elsewhere.

He would have preferred that Sigmund had rejected his *Slayer* choice, but perhaps he had come back to the light as far as was possible. There had been some red blood mingled with the black. Perhaps the Great Wyvern would show their son mercy for protecting Eileen.

Either way, the matter was beyond Erik's influence.

It felt good to fly high, to stretch his wings and leave the past where it belonged. He was glad to be leaving Ironbridge again, glad to have no prospect of seeing snow on coal again. The despair he'd felt at Louisa's funeral and the sight of her grave would always linger with him.

But Eileen had lessened its potency. He held her a little tighter as he flew.

Erik doubted that Sigmund's death would fulfill the prophecy of sacrifice and dreaded the recovery of both Boris and Magnus. It wouldn't take them long, since they'd drunk the Elixir. Erik had only the barest moment of opportunity and needed to use it to make a difference.

There was one detail that had to be resolved immediately. Eileen nestled against his chest. He thought she might be dozing after her ordeal, but knew he had to awaken her.

"Eileen, where are the Dragon's Teeth?"

"In the wooden trunk," she suggested, her tone revealing that she knew otherwise. "Where is it?"

"Broken and empty." He met her clear gaze and knew that she had known as much all along. "Where are they?"

"I don't have them anymore." Her lips set.

"Whoever has possession of them is in danger," he said bluntly. "Magnus will do anything to possess them."

"Isn't he dead?"

Erik shook his head. "Injured but not dead. His injury would have killed another *Slayer*, but both he and Boris have drunk the Dragon's Blood Elixir. Apparently, it gives immortality."

"Is that new?" She sat up with interest.

"It's ancient, an old, old story. I always thought it was just a myth, but Magnus seems to have unearthed it."

Eileen snorted. "Even the most whimsical myths have their toes in a truth. Looks like I've got a few things to teach you."

Erik smiled despite himself, then sobered again. "Right at this moment, I need to know the location of the Dragon's Teeth so that I can ensure their defense. Who has them?"

Eileen exhaled. "No one." Before Erik could argue, she shook her head. "I put them in a luggage storage locker at the train station and mailed the key to my sister. I told her that if I didn't come back, she should take it to the antiquities dealer that Teresa mentioned."

"Who was that?"

"Some guy named Rafferty Powell." She kept talking as Erik grinned in his relief. "Teresa said he wanted the teeth, but she didn't know why. I figured he'd know what to do with them." Eileen watched him warily. "Why is that funny?"

"Because he will know exactly what to do with them," Erik said with satisfaction. "And if anyone can defend himself against Magnus Montmorency, it is Rafferty Powell."

"He's *Pyr*," Eileen whispered.

"Yes."

"So that's why he wanted the Dragon's Teeth. I should have figured it out."

Erik changed course, heading back toward London instead of over the Atlantic. He liked the idea of making amends with Rafferty by surprising the older *Pyr* with the one thing he sought. He'd let Eileen's sister take the Dragon's Teeth to Rafferty, but he'd ensure her protection while they were in her possession.

First, he'd lie to Magnus. He broadcast a message in oldspeak, hoping it found Magnus wherever the *Slayer* had fled. The good thing about the Dragon's Teeth was that, like Nikolas, they carried no distinctive scent. That made it comparatively easy to deceive Magnus about their location.

Erik let his tone fill with triumph, as if he were gloating. *"I have the Dragon's Teeth, Magnus,"* he said. *"Which means you have lost on every front."* Then he chuckled, guessing that his message would infuriate the *Slayer*.

Erik thought he heard a distant shout of rage.

Eileen, meanwhile, had noted his change of course. "Where are we going?"

"I need to guarantee your sister's safety for those moments that she possesses the Dragon's Teeth."

"Where should we meet?" Niall's murmur of old-speak came abruptly to Erik carried by the wind. At the sound of the other *Pyr's* old-speak, the weight of Erik's burdens was diminished again.

"London," he replied. *"I have a task for you."*

"A question to ask of the wind?"

"A human to guard."

"And I have a foundling for you. He can't even speak old-speak." Niall's disgust was clear.

"But he is Pyr?"

"Yes. His flying technique could use some work, as well."

Erik smiled at Niall's attitude, imagining that this young *Pyr* wouldn't take well to it. If he could hear the discussion but not participate or defend himself, that would irk him further.

It would be better for Niall to have a companion while he guarded the family of Eileen's sister. Erik believed that Magnus would take the bait and follow him, but the other *Slayers* were an unknown variable. Erik descended toward the city, sliding through the chill of the clouds and into the cold rain that fell below. Eileen shivered.

"So is that old-speak I'm hearing or thunder?" Eileen asked. She wrinkled her nose. "I'm thinking this wouldn't be the best place to be in a thunderstorm."

Erik smiled slightly. "What do you know of old-speak?"

"Not much. Sigmund just said it was how you communicated."

Erik scanned the suburbs of London below, orienting himself as he spoke. The rain slanted coldly down, painting the city in hues of silver and gray. He preferred the snow. "It's speech, but at a lower frequency, one that is difficult for humans to hear."

"Those enhanced senses again."

Erik nodded.

"So you hear it like we do?"

"But some of us can detect it from farther away, even dispatch it over distances to one another. It's an ability that comes with practice."

"And over the centuries, you've had the time to hone your skills."

"Indeed." Erik located Kensington Gardens and adjusted his course. He felt Niall behind him, and caught the scent of the *Pyr* he didn't know. Viking descent, he'd guess, a prospect that encouraged him mightily.

"Why are you suddenly so happy?" Eileen asked.

"My luck appears to be changing," Erik said. He had a fleeting thought that Eileen's presence was responsible for that.

She shivered elaborately in the rain, pulling her scarf more tightly around her neck. "How can you tell? Magnus and Boris aren't dead yet, and you still don't know how to kill them."

"But Niall is arriving with a foundling, just when we need assistance to protect your sister's family."

"Did you summon him?"

"No, so I feel the hand of the Great Wyvern, and this time she is working in our favor."

"Sounds good to me," Eileen said, then pointed at the house Erik was already targeting. "The dark roof, right there."

Rafferty paced the hall of his Highgate home.

He didn't miss the irony that he was pacing precisely as

Erik had paced, precisely as he had asked Erik not to pace, and that he was deepening the furrow that Erik had already worn in his own antique Persian runner.

He couldn't stop, not any more than Erik could have stopped.

He couldn't stop thinking of the stories in the newspaper about the murders at the Fonthill-Fergusson Foundation. He couldn't accept that Teresa MacCrae had been shot dead.

She had been attractive and clever, irritating and fascinating. He had enjoyed matching wits with her, and regretted having lost his composure on seeing the Dragon's Teeth.

She hadn't missed his response; he knew it. Teresa had been too observant for that. But what had she done about it? Had she acted upon his response?

Was it his fault that she had died, and died so violently?

As if his culpability weren't enough to worry about, there had been no mention in the media of the Dragon's Teeth. Were they still at the Fonthill-Fergusson Foundation, or had they been among the valuables stolen?

He'd spoken to the foundation's director, expressing his sympathy for Teresa's loss and asking about a revised date for the sale of the antiquities. They'd had a strained conversation, and the director had promised to get back to Rafferty. There hadn't been a word, and even though it had been only one business day, Rafferty was anxious.

Were the Dragon's Teeth lost, too?

He'd asked the earth for her news and she'd declined to answer—or at least to answer in the time that he could persuade himself to lie still and listen. Rafferty was restless as he seldom was. The old prophecy echoed in his thoughts and he feared for Erik.

What price would his old friend pay to aid the *Pyr*? Rafferty was afraid he knew. He feared that Erik would consummate his firestorm, then surrender himself as the blood sacrifice the prophecy foretold. He feared that Erik would care more for the future and for the good of the collective than for himself.

It would be perfectly in character. Once Rafferty had had that realization, it had been impossible for him to lie in the garden and listen patiently.

Instead, Rafferty had gone down to Holgate to visit the scene of the crime. The smell of *Slayer* had been inescapable, even from behind the police tape. He'd identified Magnus's scent and Jorge's as well as those of several other *Slayers* he didn't recognize. Not good. He'd even caught a whiff of Erik's presence. He sensed dragonsmoke and dragonfire and feared for Erik.

Had Erik captured the Dragon's Teeth?

Or had he been overconfident of the outcome?

What had happened to Erik's mate?

Had Rafferty erred in speaking to Erik in anger? Rafferty regretted the silence between them, realizing belatedly how much he relied upon his regular consultations with Erik.

He broadcast a message in old-speak, but Erik didn't reply. Had some wickedness befallen Erik, or was he still angry with Rafferty?

Rafferty didn't know the answers to any of these questions and didn't know what he could do about it. He felt impotent and old, used up and useless. He felt alone and abandoned, a sense all the more keen because he knew it was his own fault.

He regretted the death of Teresa, so young and vital, and disliked that he could have had a part in that. He resented his sense that hc was unimportant, that there was nothing good that he could do, and so he paced the day and then the night away.

Chapter 19

It wasn't every night that Eileen lounged on the roof of her sister's house with three dragon shape shifters in the pouring rain. Actually, she didn't lounge per se: She hung on to the chimney, trying not to slide on the wet and steeply pitched roof, and tried even harder to enjoy the novelty of it all.

The rain put a damper on that.

Erik had landed with his usual accuracy, and Eileen had been impressed by how securely his talons had locked onto the ridgepole. He handed her toward the chimney, ensuring with his usual gallantry that she had a grip before he changed shape. Once again, he shifted so quickly that she could barely see the transition.

"Why do you do it so quickly?" she asked. "I'd like to really see the change."

He spared her a wry look. "It is a sight known to drive humans to madness."

"I'd still like to see it."

"Forgive me if I don't indulge you." He sounded gruff, but

Eileen had seen the flash in his eyes. It wasn't all bad that he was protective of her.

But she still wanted to see. One of these days she'd change his mind.

One of these days. There she went, trusting in a future.

She couldn't deny that she liked the sound of it.

Erik turned his gaze skyward and Eileen followed his glance, watching as two dragons descended toward the roof. The first was a radiant purple. His scales could have been made of amethysts and edged in silver. He landed beside Erik, spared a glance at her, and shifted with the same speed Erik had. In human form, he was a muscular blond man. He stepped forward and shook hands with Erik, and Eileen heard that rumble of distant thunder again.

"More old-speak," she said, disliking that she wouldn't be able to hear or understand their consultation.

Erik nodded slightly, then began to smile. "You'd prefer that we spoke at a frequency you could hear."

"I'm a part of this. I want to hear what's going on."

The other *Pyr* might have argued, but Erik reached a hand toward Eileen. The spark that lit between their hands and made her sizzle to her toes presumably told the new arrival everything he needed to know. He bit his tongue, nodded once, then offered his hand to Eileen.

"Niall Talbot," he said, his American accent a welcome familiarity. His grip was warm and his gaze was steady, but he sent no shivers through her.

At least she wasn't just a potential mate or a general possibility of a mate.

She was *Erik's* mate.

Again.

Niall looked up and winced. His exasperation was almost comical. The third dragon was circling the house, and now that Eileen paid attention to him, she noticed that his flying style wasn't very graceful.

He was swearing with a creativity and enthusiasm that made her eyes widen.

He also glimmered with a silvery sheen in the rain. His scales were pale like rainwater and reminded Eileen of moonstones set in silver. He might have looked ethereal if he hadn't been so large and muscular, and so vocal in his discontent.

"I found him in New York," Niall said with disgust. "He's never met any of his own kind. He can't speak old-speak, although he can hear it. His flying and shifting skills need serious work. He felt the Dragon's Egg break, though, felt it so strongly that it knocked him on his ass."

"And he is *Pyr*, of ancient and noble lineage," Erik breathed. His eyes glittered like gems in the darkness as he watched the agitated dragon.

Niall blinked. "Do you know him?"

"Son of Thorvald, who was son of Thorkel," Erik cried instead of answering Niall. "Are you not *Pyr*? Are you not as fearless as your forebears? Has Thorkel's line diminished to cowardice?"

The wings of the dragon in the sky missed a beat and he dropped a dozen feet. "What? How do you know my father's name?" He looked insulted to Eileen.

"How far has the spark fallen from the blaze?" Erik demanded, ignoring the question. He pointed imperiously to the rooftop. "Here. Now."

"It's not cowardly to save your own skin. . . ."

"You are the spawn of warriors," Erik snapped. "We were the *drakkir*. We were invincible and fearsome. We were the mascots of the Viking raiders and they carved their ships in our likeness in homage to our power. We feared not man or beast, not elements foul or even death." He pointed again at the ridgepole. "Prove that you are worthy of your lineage, worm."

"Or what?"

Erik spit toward the garden. "Or return to whatever rock you have hidden beneath for all your days and nights."

"Hey, I didn't hide—"

Erik interrupted the silvery dragon. "I should have smelled you. I should have known of your presence. I should have heard your name in my dreams. I should have known that there was a living shard of Thorkel's talon."

"What, are you psychic or something?"

Erik straightened with pride. "I am Erik Sorensson, leader of the *Pyr*. I knew your grandfather. That I did not have any idea of your existence means that you denied your legacy." Eileen heard his disapproval. "You cowered, to your fore-bears' eternal shame."

"Maybe you just missed the memo."

"Maybe you should prove your worth while you have the chance," Niall muttered.

The airborne dragon exhaled in a low hiss of smoke and eyed the roof with obvious doubt. Erik didn't move, his stance sure. Eileen hung on to the chimney and thought about what she'd just overheard.

Erik had said before that he was Viking. If he'd been a mascot for the Viking raiding ships, she had a good idea how—and when—he'd come to England.

It made sense that he'd picked up a British accent in a thousand years or so.

The silvery dragon swore with new vigor, then stretched his talons toward the roof. "Here goes nothing," he muttered.

Niall took a step toward the opposite chimney, his trepidation clear. "This isn't going to be pretty," he warned softly.

It wasn't.

The silvery *Pyr* landed heavily. He failed to get a grip with his claws, swore thoroughly, and in his terror, shifted back to human form. He was tall and blond, built like a Viking raider, or a bouncer for a busy bar.

His eyes widened as he snatched at the roof without success and began to slide. He loosed a string of expletives as he scrabbled for a grip, slipping toward the gutters with alarming speed.

Erik shifted shape in the blink of an eye, snatched up the terrified man, and deposited him on the summit of the roof. He hovered over the man until he managed to grasp the chimney beside Eileen, then shifted back to human form.

Erik stood in the middle of the roof and eyed the new arrival, who was still breathing quickly in his fear. Niall, at the opposite end of the roof, rolled his eyes with dismay.

The new arrival locked his arms around the chimney and hung on. Eileen was amused by his terror. She also understood that Erik had placed the new arrival here only because he trusted him.

He might be trying to provoke the silver *Pyr* into embracing his powers, but he was certain that he wouldn't hurt Eileen. That was quite a vote of confidence.

"You couldn't just meet on the ground somewhere?" he asked. Eileen could see that he was shaking. He pushed a hand through his wet hair and spared her a glance, cursing under his breath as he eyed the distance to the ground.

"You are lucky that I was so fond of your grandfather," Erik said, subtly reminding the younger *Pyr* of his manners.

"Say, 'Thank you very much, Erik,'" Eileen whispered.

"Right. Thanks, dude. Don't mind if I don't shake hands. I'll just hold on to this chimney here."

"Do you have a name?" Erik asked.

"My friends call me T."

"T?" Erik couldn't disguise his distaste. "Your name is *T*?"

"As in teetotaler," Niall said, and chuckled.

The tall, tattooed man beside Eileen blushed scarlet. She could see the redness of his face even in the darkness. He even shuffled his feet a bit. "Well, no, not really, but my real name is weird."

Erik's expression was cold. His features could have been carved of stone.

"I'm thinking that your real name is the way to go in present company," Eileen murmured.

The new arrival flashed her a smile, showing a measure of charm now that he wasn't terrified. "No kidding." He cleared his throat. "How about Thorpe? That's pretty close and I can live with it. . . ."

"What name did your father bestow upon you?" Erik demanded.

The man beside Eileen swallowed. "Well, I—"

"What name?"

The new arrival looked down, then across the garden. He couldn't evade Erik's stare for long, though. "Thorolf," he finally admitted. He winced and nudged Eileen, evidently thinking she was an ally. "Weird, don't you think?"

"It's old, though," Eileen said. "Old names are strong."

"Thanks a lot."

"It's ancient," Erik interjected. "As is the word *weird*, and of similar origin. You were named Thor's Wolf, servant of the god who is foretold to slaughter Jormungand, the World Serpent, at Ragnorak. A weighty legacy, perhaps too weighty for one who chooses to be named *T*."

There was a silence then, one punctuated only by Niall's chuckle. Eileen wondered whether Erik would manage to awaken Thorolf to his own capabilities. The pair glared at each other; then Thorolf looked at the ground with obvious trepidation.

Erik immediately turned to Niall, ignoring the new *Pyr* completely. Eileen heard the rumble of thunder and she understood that he and Niall were conferring. She watched Thorolf's eyes widen as he overheard the conversation. He muttered something about things getting too bizarre and turned to her.

"Your sister's place, huh?" he asked, glancing down. "So, you're not *Pyr*?"

"It's a guy thing, from what I understand."

He nodded. "Then how'd you get into this?"

"The firestorm." Eileen smiled, finding it funny that she was instructing a *Pyr* on his own legacy. "I'm Erik's destined mate. And I had the Dragon's Teeth, too."

"Right." Thorolf clearly didn't follow all of that, which amused Eileen. She could see from his narrowed eyes that he was listening to the old-speak again.

She wished she knew what Erik and Niall were saying, but she could guess that Erik was bringing Niall up-to-date. She assumed that he was assigning the other *Pyr* to protect Lynne and her family. That would be something Erik would do.

His protectiveness was a trait she appreciated, especially given the powers of the *Slayers*.

She adjusted her stance and something jabbed into her side. There shouldn't be anything in her pockets, except maybe a tissue. Eileen reached down and discovered that there was something hard tucked into the inner pocket of her coat.

What had she left there? It was too big for a candy and too square to be a knitting needle.

It was a stone.

No, it was too flat for that. It could have been a Scrabble tile, but bigger and rounder. Its edges were roughly hewn, like it had been chiseled from stone. It was black and its two faces gleamed in the rain.

There was a carving on one side, an image that looked like a wheel. Eileen angled it, trying to catch the light from the streetlights so she could see it better. The wheel had eight spokes, and each terminated in what looked a lot like a fork. She turned it over but the other side was just smooth.

She'd never seen it before. Where had it come from?

"Whoa! Awesome!" Thorolf said with enthusiasm. Eileen glanced up to find him grinning at her. "Get it?"

"Get what?"

"That's the Helm of Awe. It's awesome." He laughed at his own joke, but Eileen frowned.

"What's the Helm of Awe?"

He stopped laughing. "You don't know? It's a symbol, made of runes. The old name is *Aegishjalmur*." He kept a tight grip on the chimney with his left arm, then used his right hand to shove up his sleeve. He had a tattoo on his left biceps of exactly the same image. "That's Elhaz," he said, pointing to the fork part. "A protective rune."

"So eight are even more protective," Eileen mused.

"The Vikings used to make little ones of lead and stick them on their foreheads when they went into battle." He shrugged. "I wanted to get the tattoo on my forehead, but Rox said it would look stupid."

Eileen remembered Sigmund moving beneath her coat and could make a guess where the runestone had come from. It sounded as if he might have been a person who had an interest in talismans.

She glanced up at Thorolf. "Who's Rox?"

He frowned and she guessed he'd twist the truth. "My, uh, sister. Yeah. Sister." He watched the *Pyr*. "Just a day ago I thought she was the biggest pain in the butt ever. Who knew?"

Eileen would have bet that Rox was his girlfriend, but it didn't matter. She could tell that Thorolf was listening to the old-speak again, because he swore beneath his breath.

"What?"

"These bad dudes can cut smoke?" he asked, incredulous. "I can't even make smoke yet and these *Slayers* move right through it?"

"That's what I hear."

"That's bad news." Thorolf shook his head, then tapped the runestone with a heavy finger. "You'd better keep that if you're going to hang out with Erik. There's shit coming down. I can smell it."

"What, are you psychic?" Eileen teased.

"No." Thorolf laughed. "I've just been taking care of my-self for a long time. If you want to survive, you've got to be able to guess which way the wind is turning." He fixed her with a bright look. "Keep that safe. It's important."

"Good plan." Eileen put the runestone back in her pocket. Even though she couldn't see the future herself, she was pretty sure that Thorolf's instincts were right on the money.

Erik was relieved. The battle was far from won and many challenges lay ahead. The sacrifice that fulfilled the prophecy had yet to be made and his ability to see the future was still MIA. He had a keen sense, though, that his luck had changed for the better, and with it the fortunes of all the *Pyr.*

Eileen had arranged for the Dragon's Teeth to be delivered to Rafferty. Niall had been en route to England when Erik needed someone to guard Eileen's sister and her family, to ensure both that the Dragon's Teeth were delivered and that the humans were kept safe during the transaction. Thorkel's line had not been extinguished after all, which was a wonderful revelation, one that gave Erik great hope for the future.

Erik felt lighter than he had in years, less burdened by bad choices of the past.

And he knew that the change was because of Eileen.

He dared to think about the future, his own future.

Erik wondered whether his old friend Thierry had been right, that a *Pyr* who committed to his mate during his firestorm could become stronger than he would have been otherwise.

The alternative was that Eileen truly was like a Valkyrie, but one dispatched by the Great Wyvern to collect the divine spark that was resident within him. She could be unconsciously aiding him to clean up the debts and imbalances of his life, before he was sacrificed for the greater good of the *Pyr.*

Perhaps it didn't matter whether he understood his fate or not, as the Great Wyvern held his destiny in her hand.

Once he had warned Niall sufficiently of the dangers ahead and ensured that the younger *Pyr* understood his task,

Erik strode across the roof to where Eileen stood with Thorolf. The young *Pyr* watched Erik warily while Eileen smiled.

Even her smile didn't hide that she was pale and shivering with the cold, though. Erik offered her his hand, watching the younger *Pyr* observe the crackle of fire between their hands. He caught her fingers tightly within his own and drew her close to his side. Thorolf's eyes widened at the brilliant glow of the firestorm, which burned brightest and hottest at their points of contact.

The heat surged through Erik's veins, warming him to his very core and lighting a blaze of desire. He caught Eileen around the waist and held her close, heard her quick intake of breath and felt the acceleration of her pulse. He smiled as his body matched its rhythms to hers, the pulse of two hearts in unison making him feel stronger.

"You will remain with Niall," Erik told the younger *Pyr*, speaking aloud for Eileen's benefit. "And protect the family of my mate. You will do as you are bidden and you will learn what you are taught."

"Hey, I don't have to do anything—"

"Of course you do," Eileen interjected. "Don't you want to know what you are and what you can do?"

Thorolf flushed and dropped his gaze.

"Don't you want to help kick the butt of those *Slayers* who cut smoke?" she asked in her teacher voice.

Thorolf lifted his head. "No one ever told me about these *Slayers*. How do I know which team is the good guys?"

His implication was as clear as his ignorance.

Erik exhaled. He felt the press of time, but knew he had to persuade the younger *Pyr* to join their ranks. How could Thorolf have learned of *Pyr* lore? His father had died centuries ago, after all. Had the boy been alone all this time? If he had been an infant at the time of his father's death, there would have been no one to instruct him.

Later, there would be time to learn his tale. In this moment, Erik had to return to Chicago while leaving Eileen's family protected.

Which meant gaining Thorolf's allegiance quickly.

"Fly with me," Erik invited, "and I shall tell you what you need to know to make your choice."

Thorolf grimaced and Erik was sure the younger *Pyr* was tired. But he changed shape and took flight all the same, which showed the depth of his desire for knowledge.

"Nothing like a story," Eileen said with a smile. Erik caught her close and leapt off the roof, shifting shape in midair. She gasped and hung on tightly to him, laughing as they moved through the wind. The rain beaded on her lashes and the wind made her eyes sparkle. She nestled against him with satisfaction, apparently enjoying the firestorm's heat as much as he did.

"I'm starting to get hooked on this stuff," she said, staring down as the city fell away beneath them. When Erik flew through the clouds with Thorolf at his side, Eileen laid her cheek against his chest with relief. "No more rain," she said with a sigh.

"Not for the moment anyway."

"You promised to tell me what was going on," Thorolf complained.

"And so I did." Erik cleared his throat as he flew. "In the beginning, there was the fire, and the fire burned hot because it was cradled by the earth. The fire burned bright because it was nurtured by the air. The fire burned lower only when it was quenched by the water. And these were the four elements of divine design, of which all would be built and with which all would be destroyed. And the elements were placed at the cornerstones of the material world and it was good."

Thorolf struggled to keep up with him, his wide eyes revealing that he'd never heard even this truth.

Erik paused. "But the elements were alone and undefended, incapable of communicating with one another, snared within the matter that was theirs to control."

"Okay," Thorolf said.

"I love a good creation story," Eileen murmured, though her eyes were closed. She curled against his chest, and Erik was relieved that she had stopped shivering. He liked the sense of returning to his lair with his mate, of carrying a treasure more precious to him than the richest of hoards.

He felt complete. He felt potent.

The situation felt right.

Erik continued his story. "And so, out of the endless void were created a race of guardians whose appointed task was to protect and defend the integrity of the four sacred elements. They were given powers, the better to fulfill their responsibilities; they were given strength and cunning and longevity to safeguard the treasures surrendered to their stewardship. To them alone would the elements respond. These guardians were—and are—the *Pyr*."

"Oh!" Eileen said, her eyes opening again. "That's why there are stories of dragons that are centuries old, even millennia old. Because there *were* dragons."

"Are," Erik corrected. "The tale of Cadmus is from ancient Greece. That of Perseus is perhaps an older tale of conflict between our kinds."

"But the bulk of stories about dragons are medieval," Eileen said. "Saints defeat dragons over and over again, but by the Renaissance, the whole dragon mania all dies out."

"Weren't you the one who said that stories reflect reality?"

Her lips parted as she stared at him. "The *Pyr* have been dying out," she whispered. "But why?"

"Yeah, why?" Thorolf echoed.

Erik understood that pride was at root, pride and divisiveness. "We were numerous, and like so many in positions of power, we took our ascendancy for granted. We believed that we could not be destroyed, especially by those we were charged to defend."

"Who were we charged to defend?" Thorolf asked. "The elements?"

"One of the treasures of the earth that we as *Pyr* are charged to defend is the human race. And so it was perhaps that responsibility that made us underestimate humans, much as a parent might underestimate the intent of his or her own child."

Eileen caressed his shoulder, a swift reminder that they had both been surprised by Sigmund. It was a reminder that they had endured much together, and it touched Erik as much as it surprised him.

Would he no longer fly alone? Maybe the sacrifice was his independence. It was an appealing notion.

"How so?" Eileen asked.

"Where once our rare appearances fostered fear and perhaps respect, familiarity made men bolder. They were no longer content to try to steal our hoards for their own—they wanted our abilities as well. Once Sigurd tasted dragon blood and then understood the talk of the birds as a result, the die was cast."

"Saints killed dragons," Eileen whispered, her face pale.

"Men still admired our power, but it was decided that healing cures could be made of our blood, our bones, our skins. They were no longer content to have us as mascots or to have us defend them. They wanted our substance to defend themselves. Bathing in our blood was said to give invincibility in battle. Ingesting an unguent made of our innards was reputed to dispel nightmares. Our blood broke kidney stones; our skin cured intemperate passion between lovers; our teeth gave grace to the bearer; our backbones granted luck in court. The fanciful list goes on and on in its distasteful detail."

"Ick," Eileen whispered.

"Major ick," Thorolf agreed.

Erik caught his breath, trying to hide his bitterness. "The

most troubling conviction, however, was based upon a lie. There was a tale that we carried a stone in our brow—some accounted it to be a ruby—that was an effective tonic for all poisons. The alchemists believed that this dragon stone had to be harvested from a live dragon. They were convinced that while dying, the dragon deliberately destroyed the efficacy of the stone. I will not trouble you with the vicious details of that process."

He fell silent then, his own memories choking his words.

"Medieval kings were concerned with poison," Eileen mused a few moments later. Erik didn't doubt that she had noticed that he was upset. He also didn't doubt that she'd demand the rest of the story later.

He'd have to think about whether he was going to share it with her.

"There are a lot of stories about food tasters and poison antidotes," Eileen said. "And heroes retrieving rare items like unicorn horns that reveal the presence of poison. Then they win the hand of the princess from her grateful father, the king."

"Stories," Thorolf scoffed.

"Reflections of popular culture and concern," Eileen corrected sternly.

Erik continued. "The demand for this fictional stone led to the hunting and slaughter of dragons, far beyond that of adventurers proving their audacity. And so it was that a schism developed within the *Pyr*. There were those of us who still chose to defend humans, but there was a growing contingent who believed that humans had sacrificed their right to be defended by us. With each death of a *Pyr*, the numbers of those in defiance of the Great Wyvern's initial mandate grew. Many dragons actively hunted humans, in animosity and often grief. . . ."

"Grief?" Thorolf asked.

"To be *Pyr* is genetic. We pass the power from father to son." He paused to consider whether he should tell Thorolf of his own legacy, and decided to not risk overwhelming the younger *Pyr*. "And so each slaughtered *Pyr* was a father or a son to another *Pyr*, and each slaughtered *Pyr* was grieved by those who remained."

"Humans kept making the split worse," Eileen concluded.

"It is difficult to explain the level of animosity within our ranks at that time," Erik said. "We have tempers, which made it worse, as did the fact that there had never been such a division among our kind. We fought one another over our alliances and the death toll rose yet higher. It rose so high that the Great Wyvern herself intervened."

"Your divinity revealed herself?" Eileen couldn't fully hide her skepticism, and Erik smiled.

"Not directly. Our metabolisms changed. We gradually realized that those who chose to defend humans remained as always we had been. But those who chose to fight against humans changed. Their blood ran black instead of red, and they were denied the joy of the firestorm."

"The destined-mating bit?" Thorolf asked with real interest, his gaze fixed on the radiant glow between Erik and Eileen.

Erik nodded. "We recently recovered a treatise that argued that those who turned their backs upon our initial mandate were denying the spark of the divine within themselves. They chose the darkness over the light, and that choice manifested in the hue of their blood and their fertility. They deny the Great Wyvern's command, and she, in turn, takes potency from them. It is said that *Pyr* are born, but *Slayers* are made."

"*Slayers* are the ones who fight humans?" Thorolf asked.

"And they fight the true *Pyr*, for they view us as erroneous in our choice. And so it was that we who had never been divided were divided, and that which had been one force split into two."

Erik pivoted and hovered in the air, confronting the younger *Pyr*. "And so it is that I ask you to choose your alliance. I will not lie to you. The *Slayers* have powerful assets.

They have recently roused *Pyr* from the dead and enslaved them to fight on the *Slayer* side. They can cut smoke. They say they have gained possession of the Dragon's Blood Elixir, which was long rumored to give immortality."

"You guys are losing big-time," Thorolf said.

"We have not lost yet. I do not believe that we will lose." Erik smiled. "But then, it is my duty to believe in our triumph, no matter how high the odds against us."

"You said you were leader of the *Pyr*," Thorolf said.

Erik nodded, then let his voice drop. "I knew your father and your grandfather. I will not tell you that they would have chosen the true path, because it would not be a fair comparison—their choices were not made in these times. I will tell you that I had nothing but respect for them both, and that I would be honored to have you, as shard of their talons and sparks from their blaze, fight in the ranks of the *Pyr*." He inclined his head. "And now, Thorolf—son of Thorvald, son of Thorkel—choose."

Erik thought the choice was obvious and was assured of his own success. He'd made a persuasive argument, after all, and he knew Thorolf's legacy.

But the younger *Pyr* shocked Erik completely with his suspicious question. "How do I know you're not a *Slayer* lying to me?"

A *Slayer*? How could Thorkel's spawn even suggest that Erik was one of those foul creatures?

Chapter 20

Erik was struck speechless but fortunately his mate was not.

Eileen laid her hand on Erik's shoulder, encouraging a shower of sparks. "The firestorm," she chided. "Weren't you listening?"

Thorolf dropped his gaze.

"And look," she said, gesturing to the scab on Erik's forehead. "He bleeds red."

"Right!"

"And they're teaching you about your abilities. Don't you think *Slayers* would want to keep you weak?"

Thorolf nodded thoughtfully. Erik was a bit annoyed that Eileen had to punctuate his lesson to get it through the younger *Pyr*'s head.

On the other hand, Thorolf was learning a great deal in short order. Erik tried not to judge the other *Pyr* so harshly.

"Count me in," Thorolf said then, his grin turning roguish. "I'm kind of fond of humans, and usually cheer for the underdogs."

Erik felt a profound sense of relief. "Then I ask you to return to Niall."

"I'm on it," Thorolf said, and his tone turned grim. "But this time I'm gonna nail that landing. You should watch."

"Sadly, I have not the time."

"You wanna know, though."

Erik grinned despite himself. "I do. You'll just have to nail all subsequent ones."

"Right." Thorolf cast a wink at Eileen. "See ya," he said, then descended toward the clouds.

Erik watched, seeing Thorvald and Thorkel in the silvery rhythm of the younger *Pyr*'s wings, and remembered a time long past. A lump rose in his throat and he was glad, glad to the tips of his talons, to be honored with the company of their descendant.

Erik would defend Thorolf. He would teach him everything he knew. And he would trust him with the truth of his legacy.

He glanced down to find Eileen watching him, speculation in her eyes. "You weren't sure what he'd do."

"No." It was surprisingly easy to share his doubts with her. "His father and grandfather could be impulsive and unpredictable. Loyal, though, and fierce."

"You're glad he's here."

"Very."

She yawned and snuggled into the collar of her coat. Her garments had already dried from the heat of the firestorm, which reassured Erik that she wouldn't catch a chill. Her battered satchel was tucked between them and he had her knees caught up with his other arm. "I feel like I'm in a big hammock," she said sleepily. "Just rocking gently in the wind."

"I like to think that I have somewhat more character," Erik said. "Or even charm."

She laughed. "More of a sense of humor, definitely."

Erik couldn't hide his smile. "I thank you for that."

She smiled back at him, an accord between them that was more than the raw desire of the firestorm. "Long ride ahead?"

He nodded in agreement, knowing she was watching him closely.

"Aren't you too tired?"

"Sometimes one's own state is not of import."

She touched his cheek with her fingertips, her gentle caress both surprising him and warming his heart. "Don't push yourself too hard, Erik," she counseled softly, and he savored how she said his name. "I'd like to talk more about that possibility of a shared future."

Erik didn't reply. By the time he had marshaled his argument into coherent order, Eileen had already fallen asleep. He held her closer and settled into a familiar rhythm, one that allowed him to cover long distances at a good speed. He was calculating their travel time when Erik felt the wind turn in their favor.

He smiled, because this wind would improve his speed.

His luck was, indeed, turning.

While Erik flew, Boris crawled, easing ever closer to the sanctuary where the Elixir was stored.

Anger gave him strength.

Because he knew that Magnus had lied.

Boris was exhausted, broken and bruised and blackened, but the revelation of Magnus's lie infuriated him. The evidence was clear. Boris's wounds were not healing. He did not have the power to recover that he had possessed just six months before.

Which meant that one sip of the Dragon's Blood Elixir did not make a *Slayer* immortal and omnipotent forever. It meant that the Elixir faded over time and needed to be restored within a *Slayer*'s body at intervals.

Boris understood why Magnus had been so coy about sharing his treasure, and solved the riddle of why Magnus had shared the Elixir at all.

The fateful sip wasn't the only sip. It was the *first* sip, the addictive sip, the sip that turned the *Slayer* who thought he was gaining immortality into Magnus's minion forever.

Because as long as Magnus controlled the source of the Elixir, Magnus determined who won those subsequent sips and who did not.

The name of the Elixir's custodian could change.

Boris finally reached the threshold of the hidden site and found it guarded only by Magnus's dragonsmoke. That was no barrier for Boris, although it cost him dearly in his current state to do what he had done easily just days before. He hovered between forms and cut the smoke with his talon, then crawled across it in human form.

He had only a hundred feet to go.

He followed the cavern that wound into the darkness and chill of rock, listening for any hint of another presence. There was none. Boris was alone, and that made him move more quickly despite his pain. Magnus was a fool to believe that dragonsmoke alone could protect his prize! Magnus was a moron who deserved to be replaced.

By a brilliant successor.

Boris had the perfect candidate in mind.

He emerged in the central cavern, catching his breath at the sight of the massive vial. It had been carved of rock crystal, not poured of glass, and contained facets and imperfections. The container, and the steps that wound around its perimeter to the summit, had been carved of the stone centuries before.

There was no sound in the cavern, nothing except the distant echo of dripping water. It could have been a sanctuary outside of time, a haven beyond time.

The cloudy red liquid swirled with its own currents and glowed faintly, illuminating the cavern with its vermilion light. The imperfections played tricks, making it look as if the Elixir were filled with mysterious shapes, half glimpsed before they faded from view. Watching it swirl was like watching clouds form and disperse in a summer sky.

But Boris knew that there was only one thing suspended in the solution in the massive vial. A dead dragon of cinnabar was preserved in the liquid—his body, in water, created the liquid; his rare color was the source of the prize and its powers.

It was a revolting notion, even for Boris, but knowing its abilities gave him the willpower to consume it.

Boris moved with haste, doubting that the vial would be left unguarded for long. Steam rose from its open top, filling the cave with vapor that gave him new energy with every breath.

He needed a second sip, and he would take it while Magnus was absent. There would be no terms or conditions this time.

Boris dragged himself up the spiral of stone steps that had been carved around the vial itself. He was panting by the time he had reached halfway, but he kept his eye on his goal. He shifted shapes as necessary, each change exhausting him.

Boris was crawling when he reached the top step. He dragged himself over it and slithered on his belly to the lip of the vial. He was breathing heavily, within a heartbeat of breathing his last, when he bent to dip his head toward the seething surface of the Elixir. He inhaled deeply, closed his eyes, and stretched out his tongue to lap the surface.

But before Boris could sip, something erupted from its depths.

Boris cried out in shock, thinking that the preserved cinnabar *Pyr* had returned to life.

But it was Magnus, massive and vital, who lunged from the cloudy depths of the Elixir and seized Boris by the throat.

"Tell me a story," Eileen whispered hours later. Erik had flown while she slept, and though he was aching with exhaustion, he knew he couldn't risk stopping.

They flew over the Atlantic, its darkness stretching in every direction and the darkness of the night sky high overhead. Eileen weighed nothing to him in dragon form—it was the weight of his own body that worked against him.

Erik had thought Eileen was still sleeping, but glanced down to find her eyes shining in the darkness.

"You should sleep," he advised, hearing his own exhaustion.

"Then tell me a story, please." She adjusted her pose and caressed his shoulder with an affection that touched his heart. "You must be dead tired."

"Not quite."

"Maybe telling a story would give you something else to think about."

That made a certain sense. "What kind of a story?"

"One in which the dragons are the good guys," she said, her tone mischievous. "Then you'll enjoy it, too."

Erik chuckled.

"Maybe one about Vikings and dragons," she added.

He sobered and concentrated on his flying. They'd been airborne for about a dozen hours. By his calculations, it should take about thirty-five hours to reach Chicago. It was a long flight, by any accounting, and one he would have preferred to have made without the pressure of time.

It would also have been preferable to have been fully rested.

Once again, Erik felt the burden of his obligations. The firestorm gave him unexpected strength, Eileen's presence sending a frisson of energy through him, as if he were hooked to an electrical current.

He'd take whatever he could get.

At least here, there was no one to beguile. He could simply fly and not worry about the effect of his presence upon unsuspecting humans and their preconceptions of how the world was.

It had been simpler, once upon a time.

He felt Eileen watching him and wondered what she saw. He wondered what she was thinking and wished he could have flown a route that didn't pass over so much dark water.

Surely that could only awaken upsetting memories.

"Maybe a story would be a good idea," he conceded, thinking only of distracting her.

Eileen nestled her cheek against his chest. "Tell me the one about the dragon who killed his father to assume leadership of the *Pyr*."

Erik felt a chill and nearly missed a beat in his shock. Eileen's eyes were bright with curiosity.

And devoid of condemnation.

"Boris told you that," he guessed.

Eileen nodded. "But you must have had a good reason." She spoke with a conviction that warmed Erik's heart. Her tone became more fierce. "You're too principled to murder for the sake of ambition. No, there's more to the story. Boris just picked that part to make you look bad. He would have murdered without a moment's hesitation, but not you."

"You sound quite sure of that."

"I'm a good judge of character," Eileen said with force. "Tell me, Erik. Tell me the myth; then tell me the truth that its toes are in." She spared a glance at the Atlantic far below them, its waves choppy and dark, and he saw her swallow. "I think we've got the time."

The very least he could do was distract her, especially when she had such faith in him.

And, really, it was past time that he shared his story.

Eileen sensed that Erik was choosing his words with care. She was content to give him whatever time he needed.

After all, he was going to tell her a story.

His story.

"I told you about the schism within the ranks of the *Pyr*, as men became determined to use dragons for their own purposes and treatments," he said.

"You did." Eileen closed her eyes. It was easier to concentrate on the richness of Erik's voice and be carried away by his story if she couldn't see the dark expanse of water beneath them. It was easier to forget the cold clutch of water, the inability to breathe, the terror of drowning, if she basked in the heat of the firestorm and savored the gentle strength of his grasp.

She knew he wouldn't let her fall.

She trusted him to protect and defend her.

It was a good feeling. For most of her life, Eileen had fought her own battles without any desire for a companion. But when the stakes were higher—when *Slayers* like Magnus were stalking her—she'd been forced to admit that she needed help.

And Erik's help and companionship were easy to rely upon. She liked that he treated her both as a lady and as an equal. Eileen didn't want to think about not being with him. She didn't want to wonder what had happened between him and Louisa, how she had ever distrusted him or cast him aside.

So she didn't.

"As the slaughter of our kind continued and we came closer to extinction, the battle heated. Each camp appointed themselves a leader."

"You said you were leader of the *Pyr.*"

"Now. Not then." Erik's voice softened with affection. "The first and greatest leader of the *Pyr* was my father, Soren. Among his innovations was the establishment of a high circle of seven *Pyr*. He chose to make decisions collectively, rather than be unilateral. He conferred with his fellows and together they determined the best course of action."

"The key to effective government," Eileen said.

Erik listed names with such reverence that Eileen guessed that many of these *Pyr* were no more. "Sigmund, Lothair, Gaspar, Thorkel, Rafferty, and my father were the oldest and wisest of our kind. Rafferty alone of that august group survives."

Eileen was confused. "Because Sigmund is dead now?"

Erik frowned. "No, it was my paternal uncle Sigmund who sat on my father's council. They were brothers, close in age and attitude." He spared her a glance. "I asked Louisa to name our son in that Sigmund's memory."

Eileen was beginning to understand how important family legacies and links were to the *Pyr*. She nodded, encouraging Erik to continue.

"So diminished were our numbers even in those times that I was permitted to fill the seventh seat."

"An honor."

She heard the smile in Erik's voice. "One that my father initially opposed. He was always convinced that there were more *Pyr* hidden somewhere, that we would find a gathering of *Pyr* who had abandoned the corner of the world we frequented. It was Thorkel who insisted upon my inclusion, and over time, as areas were explored and no *Pyr* were found, my father was forced to acknowledge that his dream would never be."

"You'd all been hunted."

"When Mikail Vassily became leader of the *Slayers*, my father knew he had to fill his council and fight for the *Pyr* mandate in earnest."

"Mikail was Boris's father?" Eileen guessed, recognizing the name.

"Yes. He was magnificent, like an ancient treasure come to life. He could command a room with his presence alone, but his oratory powers were also incredible. He was so persuasive. I think there were those who turned *Slayer* just because of the music of Mikail's speeches. My father was more vehement and blunt, but his passion was also persuasive to some."

Eileen was starting to see the patterns of family lines in

the *Pyr* and the *Slayers*, as well as to recognize names. "And this Thorkel who promoted you was Thorolf's father?"

"His grandfather. One of the *Pyr* who rode with the Vikings, as my father and I did, as my uncle Sigmund and so many others did. We were their mascots and their inspiration." Pride echoed in Erik's tone. "They carved their ships in our images. They honored us with tributes and feasts. They offered their most beautiful maidens to us. The world was ours to take and victory ours to claim. We feared nothing and no one." His voice dropped. "But we learned fear."

He fell silent and Eileen was content to give him the time he needed. It was soothing to feel the wind in her hair and the beat of his wings, to have the pulse of his heart beneath her cheek and the heat of the firestorm surrounding her. She fought to smother a yawn—she was tired from their adventures but wanted to hear the rest of his story.

"From whom?" she prompted silently.

"It was the alchemists who taught me fear."

Eileen remembered that Erik had mentioned them before. "Their quest was to turn dross into gold," she said. "Or to find the Philosopher's Stone that would enable them to do so."

He glanced down at her, his eyes glimmering, and she knew there was a connection she should be making.

"Which was supposed to have fallen from heaven with Lucifer," she continued, searching her mental inventory of stories and guessing.

"Or maybe was embedded in his forehead when he fell," Erik said quietly.

"You mentioned that fictional stone earlier," Eileen guessed, continuing when Erik nodded. "The beast of the Apocalypse was supposed to be a dragon, so Satan was a dragon, so the Philosopher's Stone should be the same as the stone in the forehead of a dragon that was an antidote to poison."

"And it made sense that the quest for immortality could

also be found in a species with greater longevity. We were associated mystically with the *prima materia* by many alchemists; some even called it 'the Dragon.' It was linked with quicksilver or mercury, which was said to be dragon semen."

"The alchemists were fascinated with you."

"But they liked us best dead or ensnared," Erik said bitterly. "And so it was that one alchemist brought all of the elements, so to speak, together. He managed to learn a song to which the elements responded, and when he chanted it under the right conditions, his power was immeasurable."

"What did he do?"

"Can you look into the water?" he asked. "Can you bear it?"

Eileen decided to trust Erik on this. "I'll try. Don't mind me if I hold on really tight."

He snorted, then began to fly in a low circle, dipping over the waves. He bent his head and blew on the surface of the water and the waves stilled. That left a clear, dark surface that was roughly circular, directly below them, one that reflected Erik and Eileen in his grasp.

A dark mirror.

Eileen shivered. "Just don't drop me," she said, and clutched at his arms.

"Never," Erik whispered with vehemence; then he began to chant.

Erik wasn't sure his ploy would work, but he had to try. He wanted Eileen to understand the stakes. He wanted her to see what had happened. He wanted his history to be more than just another story to her. He wasn't sure why it was so important to him that she believe him, but he chose to attribute that to her own demand for honesty.

If he showed her, she could have no doubt of his integrity.

He remembered the song Sophie had sung to the Dragon's Egg to use it as a scrying glass. He had practiced several times on the Dragon's Egg itself, back in the security of his hoard, and had managed to conjure images with greater dexterity.

But the Dragon's Egg was gone forever. Just as a seer could use any dark surface to conjure visions, it seemed reasonable to Erik that he could similarly improvise. The ocean's darkness might be the perfect choice. Eileen clung to him but she looked into the water, the power of her trust giving him greater strength.

He didn't think it was his imagination that the firestorm burned brighter between them. There was a sphere of golden light on the dark water below them, a beacon in the night.

He stared into the light and sang the low chant. Eileen didn't interrupt him, just watched. It was appealing that she was both skeptical and open to the notion that not everything adhered to the commonly accepted explanations.

He let his will radiate toward the water. He saw clouds swirl on the surface of the ocean and felt a stab of triumph. He glimpsed the change in her reflection in the clouded surface for only a heartbeat, his own image static behind her.

Her hair became dark, as Louisa's had been. Her features became finer and her expression less bold. She was smaller and more fragile, less in command of her life and her choices.

Eileen caught her breath at the difference in her own reflection, so Erik knew she had seen it.

She had learned so much since those times.

She might as well be a different woman, one better equipped to deal with the challenges of the past.

He wondered how to tell her that, how to express his admiration; then the clouds in the water cleared. Their reflection was lost in the image conjured there.

A room was shown in the dark mirror, a room that no longer existed. It was the very room that Erik wanted to show Eileen. His mouth went dry as he noted the familiar details: the apothecary jars on the shelves, the scales, the crucible, the crystal orbs. The bleached monkey skull that had always bothered him was there, as was the enormous glass bottle on the workbench before the fire.

There were two dragons sealed in it, one black and one red. Their scales were brilliantly hued and flashed as they spiraled around each other in frustration. They were miniature versions of the dragons he recognized them to be, bewitched to take a smaller size. They fought endlessly, knotting around each other in a silent, vicious ballet.

"Soren and Mikail," he said, his words husky.

The sight of their entrapment and desperation still sickened Erik.

As did the complacent satisfaction of the man who sat beside the fire and watched, as if the situation had nothing to do with him.

As if he were not responsible.

"They're trapped," Eileen murmured. "Why?"

"There is wickedness," Erik found himself saying, "and there is evil."

"Tell me the difference," Eileen whispered. Her fingers gripped him tightly but Erik barely felt them.

"To be wicked is not to care who is injured in one's single-minded pursuit of one's own goals. To be evil is to willfully destroy others in that same pursuit. It speaks of a selfishness and a disregard that the universe cannot support."

"A decision to turn away from the light and embrace the darkness," Eileen said, and Erik nodded. "Were they supposed to fight to the death?"

He nodded. "And the prize was to be release from captivity."

"I'll bet it was a lie," Eileen whispered, and Erik couldn't tell her that she was right.

He let her watch.

Soren reared back and struck a flurry of blows upon Mikail. The red *Slayer* fell heavily, and though he roused himself twice, after the third assault he did not rise again. The obviously exhausted black *Pyr* turned to the alchemist with expectation in every line of his body.

The alchemist smiled.

He roused himself and stirred the fire to greater enthusiasm. He lifted the sealed glass with some effort, then set it in a shallow metal pot filled with water that hung in the fireplace. He lowered the bath over the fire, so that the flames licked the outer metal pan. Steam rose from the water between vial and pot, and the black dragon moved with greater agitation, looking as if he danced in the flames.

The alchemist watched with a bemused smile.

"You promised release!"

Erik caught his breath as his father's voice echoed in his thoughts once again.

"I desire a greater prize first."

"Name your price."

"You can guess."

"I will give you my hoard." Erik heard the panic in his father's tone, heard his desperation and hated it even more in recollection. Perhaps knowing the ending made it worse. "I have gold from Samarqand and silver from Ireland. I have garnets and amethysts and—"

"I have no desire for gold and gems."

"What then? What do you desire?"

"There is only one thing I desire, and you must give it to me willingly."

"Secrets of the earth and her treasures, then."

"Perhaps."

"You could smelt iron here."

"They do."

"But they need to use coke instead of coal to make a better grade of iron. You can turn the iron in this valley into wealth by smelting properly. These are secrets known to me, and they are yours."

The alchemist made a note, then stirred the flames beneath the pot. "That's not enough."

"You will kill me and be left with nothing!" Soren raged. "What madness is this?"

"Give me the stone," the alchemist said. "Give me the Philosopher's Stone."

"I don't have it. I don't know what you mean."

The alchemist lowered the pot so that it was deeper in the flames.

Soren screamed.

"He'll kill him!" Eileen cried, her fingers digging deep.

"No." Erik said sadly. "No. He left that task to me."

Chapter 21

Eileen couldn't bear the view any longer. The desolation in Erik's tone told her all she needed to know. Eileen buried her face in Erik's chest and felt tears on her own cheeks. "Make it stop. I don't want to see more."

"You have to see this." Erik touched her cheek with one talon and she turned to look, fearful but trusting.

She saw another version of the ebony dragon appear suddenly in the alchemist's laboratory.

"So you came," the alchemist gloated.

The black dragon's eyes flashed fire as his gaze landed upon the fireplace and the contents of that bottle. He tipped benches, broke glass, and tore shelves from the walls in his fury to reach the hearth. She saw the alchemist back into a corner in fear as the new arrival snatched the bottle from the fire.

He shattered the glass with a mighty blow, and the smaller black dragon fell weakly to the floor. Something dropped from the alchemist's table, a small round stone that rolled across the room.

The large dragon started, obviously recognizing it.

Eileen recognized it, too. It was the rune stone she had found in her coat pocket.

The rune stone spun across the floor, coming to a halt at the feet of a young boy who halted in the doorway. He clutched a book and had sandy hair. He looked studious and vaguely familiar.

Sigmund.

Sigmund bent and picked up the rune stone, turning it in his hands with curiosity before he glanced into the room. Then his eyes widened in terror.

"Grandfather?" he asked, his voice rising.

The newly arrived dragon stared at the child in shock. "You took my son," the ebony dragon whispered, and the child retreated. The boy clutched the rune stone and stared at the dragon in mingled fascination and fear.

The ebony dragon moved to approach the boy, and the alchemist's mouth twisted with hatred.

"I raised a child of my own blood when his father abandoned him," he hissed, then his voice dropped low. "Then I summoned his father to a reckoning."

"I did not abandon my son!" the black dragon cried. "You stole him from me, after your daughter rejected him."

"Devil-spawn," the alchemist sneered. "Satan's vermin. How else could you be what you are? You cannot blame me for trying to save the soul of a child unfairly condemned by his father's foul seed."

"And how does teaching him sorcery save his soul?" the dragon demanded.

"It's not sorcery!" Sigmund cried, and the dragon turned to appeal to him.

"You must see the wickedness in this, in using others for one's own material gain," he began, but got no further.

While the dragon was distracted, the alchemist pounced, a knife in his hand. He buried the blade in the smaller black dragon's brow, digging furiously with the knife as the dragon struggled in his grip. Blood and brains and flesh spewed onto the floor; the small dragon roared in pain, but the alchemist kept digging. He grunted with the effort and the small dragon screamed in agony.

The larger dragon bellowed when he saw. He crossed the room in a single bound and snatched up the alchemist. The alchemist shrieked, but the ebony dragon roasted him with dragonfire as he held him high above the floor. The smaller dragon fell to the floor and twitched.

The alchemist struggled and fought; he spat and he crossed himself, but the dragon who was Erik showed him no mercy. He spewed dragonfire until there was nothing left of the alchemist but smoke and cinders.

Then Erik wept as he gently lifted the smaller black dragon in his hands. Eileen wondered at the strength of the alchemist's enchantment that the smaller dragon could not break free of it even after the alchemist's death.

She heard a rumble that might have been thunder, saw the younger dragon weep, then closed her eyes as Erik loosed the flames on his own father, incinerating the small dragon beyond recognition.

She thought she heard a sigh as he blew the ashes and scattered them. The laboratory was burning, being consumed by flames, and the ashes of the small dragon mingled with those of the structure itself.

"What did he say?" she asked.

Erik's voice was hoarse and she knew he hadn't had to hear the plea again to remember it. " 'I beg of you, spark of my blaze, do what must be done.' "

Eileen wept for what Erik had had to do and spared one last glass at the dark mirror of the past he had created.

Something moved in the conjured image, a motion in the shadows that startled the bereaved Erik. A woman stood in the doorway of the alchemist's lab, silhouetted in flames. The fire lit her face and showed her concern; it danced in the dark tresses of her hair.

It was the woman whose reflection had been on the water

instead of Eileen's just moments before. *Louisa*. Eileen's heart stopped at this vision of her past.

For a heartbeat, she could see the scene through Louisa's eyes. She felt a horror deep within herself, a revulsion and an anger, and she understood with sudden clarity why she had never been able in this life to trust a man fully.

But it was the alchemist who had betrayed Louisa by turning her against her beloved and turning their son against his own father.

Not Erik.

The dragon took a step toward her and changed shape. But the flames he had created on his arrival were spreading with savage fury—they made a barrier between him and the woman. She stared at him with accusation in her eyes, then turned and fled.

As he shouted after her, the alchemist's lab was consumed in the brilliant orange of flames.

The vision faded.

Eileen found herself looking into the dark depths of the sea.

"By his accounting, I had stolen the greatest treasure of his hoard," Erik said softly.

"He was Louisa's father," Eileen guessed.

Erik nodded. "He had always had an interest in alchemy, but once Louisa had left with me, his passion grew. He was determined to avenge himself upon me for her loss."

"Sigmund went to him?"

"Sigmund went to him, and ultimately her father took them both in. He made the boy his student, taught him many dark arts, and bequeathed his books to him. In return, Sigmund told him what he knew of the *Pyr*."

"Did he know that Sigmund was *Pyr*?"

"If so, he would have blamed me and my taint for that, as well."

"But you are what you are."

"For better and for worse." He sighed. "He schemed for years to destroy everything of importance to me."

Eileen reached up and kissed Erik's throat, knowing that it hadn't been easy for him to share this defeat with her.

"He didn't entirely succeed, did he?" she whispered.

"He came perilously close," Erik said, then held her tighter and soared into the night sky with new purpose.

"There," Niall muttered, his old-speak echoing in Thorolf's thoughts and jolting the younger *Pyr* to wakefulness.

Which was no small feat. Thorolf was exhausted. Since meeting Niall, he'd learned more than he'd learned in his entire lifetime. He'd made some rudimentary attempts to breathe dragonsmoke. He'd practiced his technique spewing dragonfire. He'd struggled to make some utterance in oldspeak, and he'd tried desperately to catch up with all of Niall's references. He'd learned to hide behind chimneys and in corners of roofs to avoid being seen by humans.

When he'd screwed up, he'd tried to copy Niall's ability to beguile humans into believing that they hadn't seen what they thought they'd seen.

Never mind that he'd flown farther than he'd even flown in his life without a rest.

He was bagged. This made working eighteen-hour days as a bike courier in Manhattan seem like a piece of cake.

It was in the wee hours of the night when Niall spoke, well past the time that even Thorolf would have been awake partying. The streets were quiet and dark, stillness permeating every corner. Even the alley cats had gone to bed.

All he wanted to do was sleep.

Niall was vigilant, though, charged with the responsibility of guarding these humans. Thorolf understood that they were important but wasn't entirely sure why. What he really wanted was to crash for a couple of days, then think about it.

No luck.

A dark-haired man was walking along the street toward the house. He sauntered, endeavoring to look innocent when his furtive manner revealed that he was clearly anything but.

"Take his scent," Niall advised so softly that his words were almost inaudible. Then he inhaled deeply.

Thorolf followed suit. He smelled darkness and rot, like a basement that saw no light or fresh air, like a place where condemned criminals were shackled and left to die. It was a foul scent, one that he couldn't have missed and never wanted to smell again.

"That's Slayer," Niall murmured in old-speak. *"You can smell their black blood."*

Thorolf watched the new arrival carefully, assessing his body language. He was looking around with greater care, as if he'd sensed their presence. Maybe he'd heard them.

Thorolf took another breath and caught a whiff of another dark smell. This one was distinctly different, more like ash and burned detritus than mold and dampness. It was no less nasty, no less desolate, and he guessed intuitively that the *Slayer* wasn't alone. He spun in time to see a garnet and gold dragon leaping over the chimney pots toward him, talons extended.

"Hey!" Thorolf shouted, pivoted, and shifted shape. He raged dragonfire at the *Slayer*, who flinched as their talons locked. Thorolf came on hot and hard, knowing he was too tired to last.

He'd have to thump this dude fast. He had size and strength on his side, at least. This *Slayer* was slender and much smaller than Thorolf. It was easy to hold him captive by his claws.

Thorolf breathed a stream of smoke, directing it at the *Slayer's* open mouth. The dragonsmoke wound into the *Slayer*, slipping between his teeth and down his gullet. The *Slayer* twisted and screamed, fighting against Thorolf's iron grip.

Bonus. He'd snagged one that hadn't learned to take dragonsmoke. Thorolf grinned and kept on breathing; then he beat the *Slayer* heavily with his tail.

He might have felt triumphant, but claws dug deeply into his wings from behind. He ripped himself free with an effort, and the *Slayers* laughed together. Thorolf glanced back to find Niall down and bleeding, and two *Slayers* in need of a lesson.

Thorolf knew just which one he'd teach them first.

If nothing else, Thorolf could fight. He'd been doing it all his life, and he wasn't afraid of being outnumbered.

He decked the garnet *Slayer*, surprising his opponent. Thorolf took advantage of the moment to study the *Slayer* and assess his weaknesses. He had a wound on his chest that would really hurt if it were reopened.

When the *Slayer* raged back toward Thorolf, Thorolf shifted forms, again using the element of surprise. The *Slayer* started but Thorolf jumped straight at him. The *Slayer* spewed dragonfire; Thorolf shifted shape right before his eyes, then ripped the scabs off those chest wounds.

The *Slayer* hollered with pain.

Black blood ran over his scales, staining the pearls that accented his splendor.

He lunged at Thorolf, who slipped out of his way at the last moment. The red *Slayer* collided with the gold and agate *Slayer*, who had been about to pounce on Thorolf from behind. The two fell toward the earth, breaking through the roof of a small greenhouse attached to a neighboring house.

They shot upward in unison before Thorolf could check on their fates. The blood that dripped from the red *Slayer* left burning holes in everything it touched, including roofs and sidewalks and automobiles. They both had shards of glass in their sides and bloodlust in their eyes.

They targeted Thorolf and he waited for them. Hard and fast was how he liked to fight. High stakes, no rules, fight to win. This worked for him in a big way.

He ducked their assault, pivoted, and grabbed the wings of the agate one from behind. He breathed dragonsmoke, knowing that this *Slayer* didn't much like it, and watched him twitch. Then he flung his victim at the red *Slayer*, sending a torrent of smoke after him. The pair writhed in unison, then came back for more.

The gold one latched onto Thorolf's tail, but Thorolf was bigger and stronger. He let the *Slayer* think he was in command, then flicked his tail hard, slamming the *Slayer* into the top of a parked car. The hood dented, the car alarm went off, but Thorolf did it again. The *Slayer* roused himself but Thorolf kicked him in the teeth, backhanded him, blew some fire, and left him on the roof of the crumpled vehicle.

The red *Slayer* shouted as he came after Thorolf, the mark of a real amateur. Thorolf kicked him square in the chops, using his kickboxing experience to advantage. It was even more fun in dragon form. After half a dozen solid high kicks, the red *Slayer* rolled through the air. Thorolf was right behind him. He grabbed the red *Slayer*'s tail and swung him around. He pivoted in time to strike the agate *Slayer* in the gut with his companion, knocking the wind out of him.

As a bonus, the red *Slayer* was breathing fire, and the flames caught his companion across the wings. They twitched and screamed in unison.

They both fell heavily on the roof of a neighboring house. The red *Slayer* broke the chimney, sending bricks tumbling through the hole he made in the roof. Smoke began to billow from the house and children wailed. The gold and agate *Slayer* slid down the roof tiles despite his efforts to get a grip and landed in the garden, breaking a stone fountain.

A woman screamed.

The *Slayers* snarled and took flight in unison, leaving Thorolf with a mess on his claws.

"Unconventional but effective, I guess," Niall observed, and Thorolf realized that the *Pyr* had roused himself. He looked a bit worse for wear and was rubbing a bump on the back of his head.

"That's me." Thorolf bristled, disliking that his efforts weren't appreciated. "I get shit done, but it isn't always pretty."

Niall snorted and surveyed the damage with obvious disapproval. Thorolf was about to tell Niall a thing or two about gratitude but never had the chance.

"At least you're good at something," Niall said with obvious approval. "A *Pyr*'s got to start somewhere."

His approval was short-lived, though. Niall grimaced as the sounds of a fire engine could be heard. Neighbors were peeking out of windows, more than one of them pointing at the dragons on the roof. The woman with the broken fountain was in her garden, her voice rising when she saw her shattered chimney.

Niall gave Thorolf a stern glance. "This is some kind of mess. We're not going to tell Erik about this, right?"

"Right," Thorolf agreed, then listened avidly as Niall instructed him further in the art of beguiling.

Eileen awoke alone in a king-sized bed. The sheets were smooth, so smooth that she repeatedly ran her hands across them in appreciation. If she was in a hotel, it was a more minimalist one, and unfamiliar.

Three walls were painted a silvery gray and the plain blind over the window was the same color. The other wall, the left wall, was exposed red brick and the heavy beams overhead were dark wood. The bed was black, like ebony, and simple. The floor was planked, old pine by the look of it, and sanded to a smooth finish. There was no rug.

Two lights with alabaster shades were mounted on the wall on either side of the headboard, and paired doors opposite her flanked a fireplace with a black wood mantel. She could see a dressing room through the open pair of doors on the left, the dark clothes there arranged with military precision. The tile floor looked like it could lead to an en suite bath and she heard running water.

The pair of doors to the right of the fireplace were securely closed. Presumably that led to the rest of the apartment.

Eileen had a pretty good idea whose bed she was in. The discipline of the space spoke loudly of Erik's usual demeanor. She thought that the revitalized warehouse space—because that was obviously what the building had been before—reflected his respect for the past and his tendency to view old things in new ways. The wide doors, generously proportioned rooms, and high ceilings left space for a dragon to maneuver.

It wasn't all bad waking up in Erik's bed. Eileen wondered whether she'd be doing it again. She was naked and hadn't undressed herself; that was promising. She wondered whether he'd joined her there, but there was no dent in the other pillow and the sheets on that side of the bed were smooth.

Her lips thinned with annoyance. He was *Pyr*, not Superman. She was going to have to talk to him about getting some rest.

She slid across the mattress to get out of bed and caught motion from the corner of her eye just as she got to her feet. A blond woman leaned against the brick wall, her arms folded across her chest. Her eyes were a brilliant turquoise and she looked strained. There was a scab on her neck and she seemed to be favoring one foot by keeping her weight on the other.

More important, she hadn't been there before.

She waved her fingertips at Eileen. "Surprise."

Eileen took a wary step backward. This was the woman who had been in her dream, the one who had counseled her about water meaning trust. Who was she? Why was she in Erik's bedroom? Or was Eileen hallucinating?

"The Wyvern," the woman said. "I'm here to give you a

message, and yes, you're in Erik's lair, and no, you're not seeing things." She spoke firmly, as if there were no doubt of her ability to read Eileen's thoughts.

Eileen took another step backward, then remembered that she was naked. She reached for the sheet, tugged it from the bed, and wrapped it around herself.

The Wyvern looked around the room and wrinkled her nose. "A bit Spartan, don't you think? Air and earth are accounted for, fire is a given, but where's the water?" She looked at Eileen and smiled, her eyes widening slightly. "Oh, there you are."

"Am I supposed to know what you're talking about?"

"If you don't now, you will." The Wyvern moved into the room, perching on the side of the mattress. She winced as she stretched out the leg she'd favored. She looked insubstantial, so fine and fair. She ran a hand over the sheets, smoothing them, and Eileen could almost see through her hand to the fabric below.

Was she really present?

"As present as I ever am," the Wyvern said, shooting Eileen a bright glance. "Dreams, you know, are my specialty. Maybe you're dreaming me. Or maybe I'm dreaming you. The distinction isn't that important."

"Isn't it?"

The Wyvern shook her head, considered her slowly moving hand, then impaled Eileen with a glance. "Was it important when you and Erik dreamed of each other?"

"Did you do that?"

The Wyvern nodded once, quickly, then frowned. "What's important now is your secret dream."

"I can't imagine that it's your business," Eileen said, taking another step back.

The Wyvern smiled. "I told you—dreams are my business. Go on, tell me your innermost dream. You can even think it. I'll hear you."

Eileen wrapped the sheet around her waist and tried to

look as regal as she was dismissive. "I don't think it's important . . ." she began, and headed for the bathroom.

The Wyvern stepped on the end of the sheet as Eileen passed her, compelling Eileen to stop. "I do." She spoke with authority.

Eileen thought about ditching the sheet and the Wyvern smiled. Instead Eileen gave it a hard tug and nearly fell backward when the Wyvern lifted her foot.

"Tell me."

"It's stupid. . . ."

The Wyvern gave her a hard look. "How strange. In my experience, the dream and the dreamer are always well matched."

"What's that supposed to mean?"

"That clever people have clever dreams, and foolish people have foolish dreams." The Wyvern's turquoise eyes shone with conviction. "So, are you less clever than I believe you to be? Or is your dream less foolish than you believe it to be?"

Eileen stared back at her, momentarily lost for words. "I don't think dreams are important."

"Ah!" The Wyvern raised a finger. "You're wrong, but that explains everything."

"No," Eileen said, stepping forward to argue. "No. Dreams are aspirations, goals to work toward. They motivate you and it's not that important that they're specifically achieved."

"Really?" The Wyvern was obviously unpersuaded.

"Really. They lead us on, to lessons and challenges we can't anticipate. They aren't necessarily fulfilled literally. . . ."

"So your desire for a child is going to be fulfilled how, exactly?"

Eileen caught her breath. "You already knew."

The Wyvern smiled. "It's a gift."

"Maybe I was dreaming of Sigmund. Remembering his birth, or remembering Louisa's memory of his birth."

"Maybe. But was he what you were yearning for?"

Eileen had nothing to say to that.

"If it was, we'd have nothing to talk about, because your dream would be fulfilled." The Wyvern gave Eileen a hard look.

Eileen kept her mouth shut. It was true that that little niggle of desire inside of her hadn't gone away.

The Wyvern nodded once, then rose to her feet, looking more imposing and stern than she had just moments ago. "We choose our dreams, and we choose them with an instinctive understanding of what we need to learn in our lives." She pointed at Eileen. "You trusted and you loved and you felt betrayed by ensuing results. But the issue wasn't that you trusted, nor was it that you loved."

Eileen was irritated by this woman's tendency to lecture, especially as lecturing was Eileen's department. "Well, I haven't had much better luck in this life, have I? I've trusted and I've loved and it's been a bomb so far."

"But if you don't commit yourself wholly, or if you choose to surrender your trust to those who are unworthy of it, what do you risk?"

Eileen folded her arms across her chest. "Do you know my sister?"

The Wyvern stepped closer and tapped her finger on Eileen's shoulder. "The consort who shares only her body is a plaything, not a partner. The distinction is not unimportant."

She looked into Eileen's eyes for a long moment, then disappeared as surely as if she hadn't been.

Eileen spun, knotting the sheet effectively around her ankles, but she was alone in Erik's bedroom again with the Wyvern's words echoing in her thoughts.

Come to think of it, it was strange that Louisa's past was more emotionally intense than Eileen's own past. She'd cried more reliving the tragedy of Louisa and Erik's shared past than she had over any incident in her own life.

Maybe Louisa had just lived a better story.

Maybe Lynne was right.

Someone was in the bathroom. Eileen had a pretty good idea who it was, and Erik was just the person she needed to talk to.

Maybe it was time Eileen did something about her own story.

Chapter 22

The firestorm was killing Erik.

He felt every change in Eileen's breathing as she slept in his bed. He knew the moment she awakened, because her heart changed its pace. He was haunted by the memory of the sight of her nudity, never mind what they had done together at the inn.

And it hadn't been enough.

Even if he had consummated the firestorm, it still wouldn't have been enough.

He was beginning to wonder whether he would ever get enough of Eileen Grosvenor, PhD. It was more than the heat of the firestorm, more than the persistent hum of lust—it was the light in her eyes just before she smiled, the utter conviction in her tone when she said she trusted him. It was her faith that Boris had been maligning Erik's character, and her certainty that his character was a noble one.

She trusted him. She believed in him.

Just as Louisa hadn't.

Just as his father had.

It had been a long time since Erik had told anyone so

much of his past, or surrendered so many of his secrets. Talking to Eileen was addictive. Would he lose interest in her when he ran out of stories to tell?

He doubted it.

Erik was both less and more in her presence, which both frustrated and thrilled him. His gift of foresight might be gone, but his sense of purpose was redoubled. He'd been able to use the ocean as a scrying glass, which was new.

Had his mentor and friend Thierry been right about a happy union being more than the sum of the parts?

Or was Erik simply getting everything right in the last moments before he was sacrificed for the sake of the *Pyr*? What had seemed inevitable and even right just days before was now a possibility he dreaded.

He wanted to spend more time with Eileen.

He stepped out of the shower, surrendering the battle against scrubbing her scent from his skin. He was thinking it was just seared into his memory and that he'd always smell her scent, no matter what happened between them or to him.

Erik halted in the midst of grabbing a towel when he saw Eileen in the doorway. She looked disheveled and determined, even wrapped in one of the sheets from his bed. Her arms were folded across her chest and that pose plus the sheet told him that she had reservations as well as questions.

About him?

Or about the firestorm?

Erik waited and he didn't have to wait long.

"So, did you want me or the Dragon's Teeth?" she asked. He liked how blunt she was and appreciated that he could reply with complete honesty.

"I came for the firestorm," he said, holding her gaze. "I left for the Dragon's Teeth and I returned for you."

She tipped her head to study him and he knew she wouldn't miss any nuance of his expression. "Me or Louisa?"

Erik crossed the bathroom to stand in front of Eileen. The

firestorm surged with a blinding heat and he left a step between them so that he could think. It was important that he express himself clearly—one false step now could condemn him forever.

"I loved Louisa, but Louisa—and the time I spent with her—is only a memory." Eileen's eyes narrowed, but Erik continued, intent on making her understand. "Although there is some of Louisa in you, there is probably just as much of her in me, because my time with her has shaped my choices ever since."

"How?"

Erik didn't want to review all of his mistakes in this moment. "I let Louisa run when she was heartbroken, when I should have pursued her. I like to think that I could have changed her mind about the choice she made. That mistake will never leave me."

"You talk about her as if she's not me."

"I don't think of you as the same person, even if you are the same soul. You're bolder, braver, stronger." He let his admiration show and saw her eyes brighten. "I don't have to protect you from my nature or my truth, and I like that." He held her gaze steadily. "I came back for Eileen Grosvenor."

She shook her head. "I would never kill myself. You don't have to stay with me to save me from myself."

"I know." Erik smiled. "It's just one of the thousand ways you're different from Louisa." He reached out and took her hand in his, savoring the flurry of sparks that erupted between their hands. "I'd like to stay with you to find out all of the others."

"You don't love her anymore."

He heard that there was no real question in Eileen's tone. He shook his head. "It's been a long time."

And that firestorm had never been this potent.

Eileen took a deep breath, turning her hand so that their fingers were entwined. "Is Sigmund the reason you don't want to have another child?"

Erik blinked at her abrupt change of topic. "How do you know that I don't?"

"You came in the tub, even using condoms." Eileen arched a brow. "That's the choice of a man who doesn't want a child."

Erik felt the press of time and the length of a full explanation. He knew the others were waiting in the living room for him, but also wanted to answer Eileen's questions. He felt he owed her as much, and for once, he decided the *Pyr* could wait.

He would choose his mate and her needs first.

"The firestorm marks a *Pyr* finding his destined mate," Erik said quietly. "It means that conception is possible, if not inevitable."

Eileen leaned in the doorway beside him, the relaxation of her pose revealing that her reservations were melting. Erik chose to be encouraged. He watched the bright glint of curiosity in her eyes and loved how analytically she listened to him.

"You can get me pregnant only during the firestorm?"

"Only the first time. Some *Pyr* have other sons subsequently, but the firestorm is about making more *Pyr*. See how it's getting hotter and burning brighter?" He lifted their entwined hands, putting their palms together. Eileen winced at the light, then nodded. "It becomes more and more demanding until it is sated."

"And when it's sated, that's because conception has occurred?"

Erik nodded. "It was not a choice I had the right to make for you."

"You don't want more children?" she asked again, watching him closely. The answer was important to her, although Erik wasn't certain which answer she most wanted to hear.

He'd have to trust in the truth.

But the words caught in his throat. Erik wanted more than

anything to have children with Eileen, to have a future with Eileen, to spend time with Eileen.

Unfortunately, the future was not his to promise.

"It's not a decision to make lightly," he said quietly. "I have said for years that every firestorm should be consummated because our numbers are so diminished." Erik frowned and fell silent, not certain how much to tell Eileen.

He should have expected that he had no real choice. She leaned toward him, her eyes flashing in the light of the firestorm. "Then why not with me? Because I'm not Louisa?"

"No, no."

"What aren't you telling me? Is it because Sigmund turned *Slayer*?"

Erik shook his head, knowing he'd have to share all that he knew. "Because there's a portent about my firestorm, about a blood sacrifice being necessary to ensure the *Pyr*'s survival. I'm not sure it's right to create a child who may not have a father."

Eileen paled. "You think you'll be the sacrifice."

Erik closed his eyes and nodded. He brushed his lips across her knuckles and stepped past her to dress. "I don't know. I do know that it wouldn't be fair to you to leave you alone with a *Pyr* child."

He felt her watching him. He could almost hear her thinking. But Erik couldn't talk about his lack of a future anymore, not yet.

He was too shocked to find himself desperately wanting a future, a future with Eileen, and he didn't want to burden her with what might not be his to offer. He was upset as he seldom was, shaken to his roots. He needed time to settle his thoughts.

He left before they argued about it.

Erik expected to die.

Eileen was deeply upset by the idea. It was unfair that she

should meet a man so interesting to her, so worthy of her trust and emotional investment, right before he died. She felt cheated already, although she supposed she wasn't the first woman to face tragedy in love.

There had been Louisa, after all.

But Erik had left before Eileen had summoned an articulate argument. She didn't think Erik wanted to die either, but he didn't think he had a choice. Why did he believe what he did? Was there any other option? What could she do to help?

Eileen emerged to find Erik holding court in his living room. She was rapidly introduced to the men—who were all *Pyr*—and the two women—who were mates. Not wanting to interrupt their conference, she put on a pot of coffee.

Erik's kitchen was spare but well organized, every tool that she would have wanted in place. He had fresh coffee beans and an electric bean grinder, the same model she had in her own apartment. Eileen instinctively liked his kitchen and saw his nature in its discipline. His home was almost monastic, a complete model of personal control.

That made it all the more exciting that he'd revealed his passion and his secrets to her. Eileen could also relate to the practice of presenting a defensive facade to the world at large, and protecting one's vulnerabilities from view.

She did the same thing all the time.

How much more did she and Erik have in common? She wanted the time to find out. She felt cheated by the very idea that he could be stolen from her right when they'd made this powerful connection. She ground the beans longer and finer than was strictly necessary, feeling that the world was unfair.

But there had to be another option.

Eileen just had to find it.

While the coffee brewed, Eileen sat on the end of one couch to knit. The coffee smelled wonderful, the warm scent wafting through the apartment.

The *Pyr* shared data, either Alex or Sara reminding them to speak aloud when they slipped into old-speak. Erik typed notes on his laptop. Donovan paced, his restless energy over-flowing. Quinn leaned against the wall, as still as Donovan was active, his eyes revealing how intently he listened.

Sloane perched on the other end of the sofa Eileen had chosen and spoke with soft intensity, tapping a finger on his knee to emphasize particular points. Delaney kept a distance between himself and the others, as if he feared infecting them with something vile, and alone of the *Pyr*, he seemed haunted.

Eileen felt a bit sorry for him, although she couldn't have said why. She was concerned about Erik, as he didn't look to have slept at all. He seemed haggard and driven, but she knew better than to ask him to take a break now.

He was serious about his responsibilities.

And apparently indifferent to the price he personally paid to fulfill them. He would never say that the price was too high, for example, or put his own desires above those of the *Pyr*. She had seen the longing in his eyes while he'd made his confession. Erik didn't think he had the right to ask for some-one else to be the blood sacrifice, however much he wished to be with her.

That touched her deeply.

It also reminded Eileen of an old story. She knit and thought about it a bit more before saying anything.

She was glad that the scarf was plain garter stitch. The wool was merino, both soft and smooth under her fingers, and the space-dyed colors were blending together in unantic-ipated but lovely ways. The result was vivid and full of life. She was free to think while her hands created something beautiful.

Which was good, because there was a lot to think about.

The two women were friendly, smart, and also visibly pregnant. Eileen recalled belatedly the *Slayers'* insistence on the use of the word *mate*, which had irritated her.

Now she understood and it irritated her for a different rea-son: She was supposed to be Erik's mate, but he didn't want to consummate the firestorm. While his objectives were noble, she knew she had to tell him that she'd figured out why he was wrong.

When the pot sputtered at the end of the coffeemaker's cycle, Eileen put her knitting aside. She asked who wanted a cup and wasn't surprised when Erik shot her a look and a quick nod.

He had to be exhausted. She'd save the Superman lecture for when they were alone, but he was definitely going to hear it. The others declined, but Eileen was ready to drink at least half the pot herself.

"Cream? Sugar?" she asked Erik on her way to the kitchen.

"Just black, please."

Austere. Minimalist. Of course. The man was nothing if not consistent. Eileen smiled to herself as she opened the cupboards in search of cups. She could get used to having that kind of consistency in her life.

Erik had white porcelain dinnerware, plain but elegant, and the mugs were directly above the coffeepot. Eileen took two down, poured the coffee, then ladled sugar into one. She added cream, well aware that she was no minimalist when it came to coffee, then carried the cups back into the living room.

She took Erik's to him, feeling the heat rise as she crossed the room toward him. She felt warmer with every step, and knew her cheeks were flushed. More than that, she felt an intimate heat growing. She caught her breath as desire kindled deep inside her and remembered all too well the afternoon they'd spent together.

It hadn't been enough.

She wanted nothing better than to consummate the firestorm, immediately and with enthusiasm. Eileen found Erik's gaze locked upon her, his eyes that glittering, intense green. Her mouth went dry and her face turned hot. She ran the tip of her tongue across her lip without meaning to do so and Erik caught his breath.

But they weren't alone.

The *Pyr* had gone silent. A pin could have dropped in the next apartment and no one would have missed the sound. Aware that they must also be aware of the firestorm—and its effects—Eileen felt self-conscious. She handed Erik the mug so quickly that she almost spilled the coffee onto his laptop. He caught the handle and their fingers collided.

A spark ignited, blazing brilliant orange from the point of contact. A tide of heat and lust rolled through Eileen, burned all the way to her toes, leaving her unsteady on her feet and yearning.

More.

She wanted more.

Even if more with Erik was never going to be enough.

He was right: It was burning hotter.

Erik swallowed visibly and dropped his gaze, his fingers cradling the mug.

"Wow," Donovan whispered, and Eileen was embarrassed that her desire was so raw and so public. She carried her coffee back to her seat and fixed her attention on her knitting to compose herself. When she glanced up, Erik was frowning at his laptop screen, Delaney had taken a step out of the corner, and the *Pyr* were still silent.

Looking between her and Erik.

Quinn cleared his throat. "Does anyone else find it ironic that Erik, of all *Pyr*, has been slow to consummate his firestorm?"

The back of Erik's neck turned red, but he scowled at his screen. "This is a personal matter."

Donovan grinned and Eileen recognized that these men knew one another well enough to tease each other. "Really? I thought it was the duty of each and every *Pyr* to breed."

"Your comment is inappropriate," Erik snapped.

Donovan and Quinn exchanged a smile. "I don't think so,"

Donovan said. He leaned a hip on the table Erik was using and folded his arms across his chest. He looked mischievous. "I mean, you were the one who told me about my duties with regards to Alex. In fact, you were the one who set me up, assigning me to protect Alex when you knew that she would be my destined mate."

Erik spoke tightly, without looking up. "It is my task to facilitate the scheme of the Great Wyvern."

"So, what's keeping you?" Donovan winked at Eileen. "I think your mate is cute, so it can't be that."

Erik rose to his feet abruptly, slamming his laptop closed. Sara winced but he spoke sharply. "We are gathered to decide upon a course of action with regards to the broken Dragon's Egg, not to discuss my personal affairs."

"Doesn't look like there is an affair," Donovan said wickedly. "Is there, Eileen? He's not so bad, you know. We could vouch for him."

Erik raised a finger, but before he could argue Quinn cleared his throat. "Aren't your personal affairs our affair?" he asked softly. "Isn't there a prophecy about the third firestorm after the moon changes nodes?" He glanced at Sara.

"Rafferty knew it," she agreed. "Something about King and Consort."

Consort. Eileen's cheeks heated. How strange to hear that uncommon word twice in rapid succession.

"Why isn't Rafferty here anyway?" Donovan asked. "It's not like him to miss anything."

Erik exhaled with obvious exasperation. "Because he and I argued, if you must know."

"About what?"

"About the firestorm." Erik shoved a hand through his hair. "I refuse to discuss this now, not when there are matters of import to be resolved." He turned back to his laptop with a frown.

He was obviously shaken, which Eileen found interesting.

It wasn't like Erik to let his feelings be so clear. She knew that already and she saw that the other *Pyr* also recognized as much.

Was it the possibility of sacrifice that had shaken him?

Or could it be her?

"But isn't this the big one?" Sloane asked. "Don't all three firestorms after the moon changes nodes have to be successfully concluded to give the *Pyr* a chance at defeating the *Slayers* forever?"

Erik looked discomfited, as Eileen imagined he seldom did. "Yes," he admitted tightly. "All the same, the progress of this firestorm is a matter between myself and Eileen."

The *Pyr* clearly didn't agree with Erik on this. Eileen had an idea that might resolve their conflicting viewpoints. "What's the prophecy?" she asked. "Does anyone know?"

Everyone looked around. It was clear that this Rafferty, who was absent, was the keeper of such stories. Erik drummed his fingers on the tabletop, scowled, then tossed back a mouthful of coffee. He glared at his companions, then heaved a sigh. He spoke in a low voice, but his words echoed through the loft.

> *"Third match of three demands sacrifice*
> *A blood cost of enormous price.*
> *Then King and Consort in union complete*
> *Choose trust over ancient deceit;*
> *Shed blood alone can give the power*
> *To aid the* Pyr *in their darkest hour."*

The room was silent as they each thought about it. King and Consort. The words recalled the Wyvern's comments all too clearly to Eileen. She thought about what she wanted more than anything, thought about Erik's needs, and knew what she had to do.

No matter what the consequences.

In fact, she was pretty sure that Erik had interpreted it wrong.

"Upbeat," Donovan said finally. "Gotta love prophecies. So who dies?"

"Nobody has to die," Eileen said, and put aside her knitting. "Blood is shed when a child is born, a lot of it. And there are other kinds of sacrifice, which just might be the point here."

No doubt about it, she had the *Pyr*'s undivided attention.

Chapter 23

"What do you mean?" Erik said, his voice breaking the silence that followed Eileen's statement.

Eileen smiled, her confidence in her own theory growing. "I was thinking of another motif, one that recurs in old stories of kings. There's a persistent idea that the health of the land is a reflection of the health of the king. That's why you have old fertility stories about the ritual slaughter of the king—in a warrior society, it was critical that the king be both virile and whole. A maimed king was no longer fit to rule, nor was an infertile king, a blind king, an old king, a crippled king—the list goes on and on, but the point is that the fertility and vigor of the land is a reflection of the king."

"So, you want a hottie for president," Alex said. Donovan rolled his eyes. "I'd vote for you," she said, and he grinned.

"Because having an injured king would have ramifications throughout the land," Sara said.

Eileen nodded and tried to choose her next words with care. "That's where the motif of the wasteland comes from. It's something you see in the Arthurian myths, like the story of the Fisher King. The king has turned inward because he has sustained a wound of some kind and, lacking his attention, the physical bounty of his kingdom withers away. It's a metaphor that's been used increasingly since the industrial revolution to refer to our own world—what is the root cause of the wasteland we're creating?"

Erik spoke abruptly and his tone was icy. "Are you suggesting that I am maimed?"

"No, but you haven't been balanced, not since Louisa's death." She continued before he could argue: "There are many kinds of injuries, just as there are many kinds of sacrifices. We could have consummated the firestorm the other day, but you chose not to do so. Why?"

"I told you that it wouldn't have been fair to you," Erik said. "You didn't know that you would conceive—"

"Maybe I did anyway."

He shook his head with finality. "No. The spark would have died. The firestorm fades when its demand is fulfilled."

Eileen gestured to Quinn and Sara, Donovan and Alex. "But you're still together."

"It's a choice," Quinn said. "One that my father advocated."

"The idea is that a team is more than the sum of the parts," Donovan said, and put his hand on Alex's shoulder. She smiled up at him. "That we're transformed by love and commitment."

"That the firestorm strengthens a *Pyr*, just as the forge tempers steel," Quinn added.

Erik had averted his gaze and Eileen understood that he had doubts about making such a commitment. "Let me guess," she said lightly. "There are others who think that it should be more like a Viking raid. Get what you came for and get out. If you leave little blond babies behind, that's life."

Donovan snorted. Erik flicked a hot glance at her and Eileen smiled. He watched her, his gaze slipping over her as if he would memorize the sight of her. She tingled as surely as if he had touched her.

"It's one perspective," he admitted.

Eileen rose to her feet and crossed the room, knowing what she had to do and perfectly willing to do it. "Then let me make you an offer. I have a good job and a comfortable life. I'll have your child, Erik Sorensson, under the assumption that you'll help me teach that child about the *Pyr* bits. You can have your freedom and do your duty, too."

Erik blinked. "You don't know what you're offering. . . ."

Eileen was dismissive of his objection. "I know exactly what I'm offering. My sister has had hellish pregnancies, but they don't last more than nine months. I've been there for her and I've seen it all. The fact is that I have good insurance, an employer plan for maternity leave, and no worries about my reputation suffering for my being a single mother."

"But—"

"But nothing," Eileen interrupted. "If you think I can't deal with the dragon stuff, you can think again."

"News update," Alex whispered, her conspiratorial tone loud enough for everyone to hear. "They don't come into their *Pyr* abilities until puberty."

Eileen flashed the other woman an appreciative smile. "Even better. I can hunt down one of you *Pyr* by then if necessary to help out."

The men exchanged glances as Sara folded her arms across her chest. "We'll make sure they're there to help." Alex nodded agreement, the two women looking formidable. Donovan smothered a grin with one hand while Quinn took a sudden and avid interest in the view outside.

"But . . ." Eric began to argue again.

"Don't protest on my account," Eileen interrupted crisply, "when the real issue is that you're afraid to have another son turn *Slayer*."

The *Pyr* inhaled as one behind her, because she had spoken the truth aloud. Erik glared at her.

Eileen wasn't going to back down, because she knew she was right. "But you're not the only one who wants to see slimeballs like Magnus lose everything. I'm on the *Pyr* team, too, no matter what happens between you and me. It's your duty as leader of the *Pyr* to make yourself whole, to balance your responsibilities to the world with those to yourself. Your main responsibility is to find balance, so that your equilibrium can be reflected in the world. That's how the story goes."

Erik might have argued again, but Eileen gave him no chance. "How can you expect to be healed unless you make the effort yourself? How will you know that you can do better unless you try again?"

It didn't sound that different from what Lynne had said to Eileen but she understood it now, understood it enough to advocate for that point of view.

She just hoped she could persuade Erik.

"You can't be worried about the prophecy," she insisted. "Fear of dying is a lousy justification for not doing anything, or not making a choice. We're all going to die sooner or later. Besides, if anything happens to you, the *Pyr* will help me raise your son."

Erik held her gaze for a long moment, then sighed and ran a hand over his forehead. He looked tired, more tired than should have been possible, and she wanted to help him.

She'd always been compassionate, but this was different. She had a feeling that she and Erik could make a good team, that they could balance each other's strengths and weaknesses, but the first step for her was trust.

The first step for Erik was putting balance back into his life.

She knew in her heart that this was the only way to do it. She didn't blame him for being stubborn after the events of the past, but she wasn't going to let him turn his back on opportunity that easily.

They had history.

She owed him a second chance.

She took his hand in hers, smiling at the crackle of sparks

that erupted. She lowered her voice, hoping that only Erik would be able to hear her but knowing that the *Pyr's* keen hearing probably precluded that.

"I'd like to have a child." Eileen met Erik's gaze, and saw in the surprise reflected there how long it had been since anyone had offered anything to him. She knew that as Louisa she had been in the company of those who took more than they gave. That realization made her more determined to give to him now.

Eileen smiled at Erik. "Given the choice, I'd really like to have the child of a man I respect." She lifted his hand to her mouth and pressed a kiss into his palm. "You win the nomination. I think, in fact, that the world needs a whole lot more Erik Sorensson than it's got right now. Let's secure the future of the Sorensson genetic string while we can." She felt him shudder and exhale, sensed that some barrier had tumbled.

Or maybe another crack had opened in his defenses.

"There is a lot that I should do," Erik said, looking down at her with a slow smile. "But maybe the world can wait an hour or so." The *Pyr* cheered behind them but Eileen didn't care about them.

She winked at Erik, letting her voice turn husky as the firestorm shimmered all around them. "Let's do it now."

Eileen offered a gift beyond his wildest dreams. Erik couldn't believe it, or his luck, but he saw the sincerity shining in her eyes. She meant every word of what she said, and her generosity humbled him.

If she could accept the lessons of the past and try again, he could do it as well. She gave him strength, or, more important, she gave him hope.

It was a precious commodity, one that had been scarce in his life. Was she right? Was he imbalanced? Erik had to admit that he had kept emotion at bay these past centuries, that he had focused on his duty to the collective rather than his personal objectives. He had made mistakes.

And maybe he did have it wrong.

Maybe Eileen's offer was one he couldn't refuse.

Either way, he found himself smiling down at her, urging her closer with a gentle tug. Her eyes shone with a thousand promises, and the firestorm heated to an insistent pulse. He cast a glance over the watchful *Pyr*, noting that each one averted his gaze. "Don't you all have things to do?" Erik asked, and they immediately moved.

"We should look at Erik's car while we're here," Donovan said, offering his hand to Alex. "Check out whether the engine can be converted easily."

"Good idea," she said, and got to her feet.

"I might be able to help," Quinn said, pushing away from the wall.

Delaney squared his shoulders and spoke to Sloane. "Better yet, I think it's time we tried your idea," he said with obvious reluctance. "Maybe you can hypnotize me so I can remember more details about the academy or the Elixir."

"You're willing to try?" Sloane asked.

Delaney cast a smile at Eileen. "She's right. You're right. I have to make the choice to be healed, even if it hurts first."

"Good plan," Sloane agreed with relief. He put a hand on Delaney's shoulder as if to reassure him. "Don't worry. Maybe Sara can help us, give me another set of impressions."

"You might be able to send me a vision of your experience," Sara said quickly, taking Delaney's other arm. Erik didn't imagine that it would be easy for Delaney, but he hoped it might yield results. "Especially if it's too painful for you to recall yourself."

"That's a great idea," Sloane agreed. The other *Pyr* closed ranks behind them, offering support to Delaney and making suggestions.

Then they were gone.

Within moments, Eileen and Erik were alone. Silence carried to Erik's ears, mingling with the scent of freshly roasted coffee and Eileen's perfume. She tilted her head back to look at him, her eyes dancing. "You ought to patent that," she teased. "Or at least teach me how to empty a room so easily."

He pulled her closer toward him. "You're sure about this?"

"I'm sure." She spoke with utter conviction.

"It's unconventional."

She gave him a haughty glance. "I paint my toenails blue. Is that the choice of a woman concerned with convention?"

Erik smiled despite himself.

"That's better," she said, touching her lips to his jaw. "You look less ferocious when you smile."

Erik wasn't sure what to make of that, so he let it be. "If you're sure, then I'll just have to make it worth your while," he murmured. He waited until her eyes lit with anticipation, then bent and caught her lips beneath his own.

Their kiss was hot and fervid, hungry and demanding. Eileen slid her tongue into Erik's mouth and caught the back of his head in her hands. She arched against him, nearly devouring him, and he met her touch for touch.

The firestorm blazed with new power as he lifted her against him and deepened his kiss. Erik had to close his eyes against the brilliant white light that emanated from Eileen's kiss.

His loft seemed darker, more filled with shadows and mystery, in contrast to the brilliance that they kindled together. He slid his hands through her hair, savoring the dance of the light through the red-gold curls.

This would be the last time he felt the firestorm. He knew there would never be another firestorm for him.

He knew there could never be another woman like Eileen.

He wanted to take it slowly, to enjoy every touch and watch every shower of sparks. He broke their kiss and framed her face in his hands, awed that she was so different from Louisa and yet similar. She was loyal. She was honorable. She would do anything for those she loved.

And she had learned to trust so that she could share more of her strength.

In so doing, she gave him more than Erik knew he deserved. He slid his thumbs across her cheeks, watching the radiance of the firestorm follow his gesture, noting how its light caressed her features. She was touched with gold, looking all the more precious beneath the flame's light.

Maybe this was the intent of the firestorm. Maybe it illuminated the greatest treasure a *Pyr* could possess.

Thierry had been right.

"What are you thinking?" Eileen whispered.

Erik shook his head slightly. "Just marveling," he said, feeling his own lips curve in an answering smile. "The sparks will extinguish once the firestorm is consummated."

Her eyes twinkled in a familiar way. "So you're suggesting that we take it slow?"

"It's a moment to remember."

Eileen shook her head. "I am never going to forget you, Erik Sorensson," she whispered with heat. "And I'm never going to forget this weekend. You can count on that."

Her words reminded him of how brief their acquaintance had been and how generous her offer truly was. He bent his head and kissed her sweetly, determined to give her more pleasure than she'd ever experienced before.

It was the least that he owed her.

And as her lips softened under his, as she pulled him closer and welcomed his touch, Erik wondered just how he would go about courting Eileen.

Since Thierry was right, Erik needed to think about the future.

He wanted a future with Eileen.

Then she slid her hands under his shirt, starting an army of bonfires with her touch, and he forgot everything except the splendor of the firestorm.

*   *   *

Eileen was raging. It seemed to her that a child conceived with this kind of passion had to have a good future.

Her child would have a good future.

She would make sure of it.

And she trusted Erik to do the same.

If nothing else, having his child would guarantee that she saw him again.

She tugged off his T-shirt, impatient to see him nude. He was buff and tanned, slimmer than the other *Pyr* but powerful all the same. She liked his sinewy strength, liked how long and lean he was, and wondered whether any *Slayer* was foolish enough to underestimate him.

What Erik lacked in bulk he more than compensated for with determination.

Eileen respected that. It was a trait she shared.

She looked at him this time, really looked, aware that this might be the last time they were ever so intimate. The dark hair in the middle of his chest was graced with a trio of silver hairs. Light radiated from her palms when she put her hands on his shoulders, sending the heat of desire through her veins. It weakened her knees, made her feel wanton and sexy. His eyes shone like gems and he was smiling. He looked both tender and possessive, both strong and vulnerable.

She wanted him.

Immediately.

Did mates ever manage to resist the firestorm? Eileen couldn't imagine that they did.

He reached for the clip in her hair and she shook it loose. Erik slid his hands into the thickness of her hair, spreading it over her shoulders like a veil. Sparks danced within it, limning the curls with radiance.

"Now you," Erik murmured. Eileen pulled off her sweater and dropped it, catching her breath when Erik's hands closed over her breasts. He opened the catch on her bra, then bent and flicked his tongue across the nipple.

A spark leapt between the tip of his tongue and her nipple, making Eileen sizzle. He caught her closer and took the sensitive peak in his mouth, the caress of his teeth across it driving Eileen wild. She knotted her hands in his hair and arched her back, closing her eyes as he teased her.

She could still see the red sparks of the firestorm through her lashes, still feel its heat coaxing her to burn hotter with desire. Erik bracketed her waist in his hands and bent, sliding his tongue down the length of her and making a sizzling line to her navel.

He rolled his tongue there, tickling Eileen even as she itched to feel him inside her, then unfastened her skirt and let it fall. Her pantyhose and boots and underwear had no chance against his determination—they were dispatched so quickly that they could have been incinerated.

Eileen didn't care. She was wet and hot and there was only one item of interest to her.

Erik.

He kicked off his own jeans and boots, then caught her in his arms. He might have headed for the bedroom but Eileen shook her head. "Here," she whispered with urgency. "Now."

Then she rolled her tongue in his ear to emphasize her need.

They tumbled together onto one of the black couches, a tangle of caresses and golden heat. His fingers were between her thighs, starting a conflagration that Eileen wanted to sate. He might have bent to taste her again, but she rolled him onto his back.

She wanted him fast this time.

Fast and furious and blazing hot.

She caught his hands in his and the light grew to a white radiance where they touched. Sparks flew from their interlocked hands, shooting into the room's darkness like sparklers on the Fourth of July. She pinned his hands to the couch, knowing that she could do so only because he let her.

Erik watched her with that dangerously sexy smile, his

eyes glowing as Eileen lowered herself over him. She took him inside her slowly but steadily, amazing herself at his size and watching his eyes widen. He caught his breath when he was buried deeply inside her, and his voice was strained.

"I won't last," he whispered.

"I don't care," she said as she bent to kiss him. She felt powerful and sexy, all because of the way he looked at her. "Let's finish the firestorm in a blaze of glory," she whispered against his ear, loving how her breath made him shiver.

Erik groaned and ripped his hands free of hers. He caught her buttocks in his hands and moved within her with purpose. Eileen sat up and arched her back, stretching her arms wide and high. She could see the sparks spilling off the ends of her fingertips, as if she had become a Roman candle herself.

She was burning and yearning, filled with Erik and wanting only more of him. She could hear the pounding of his heart and was amazed when it matched its pace with hers. The light emanating from them pulsed in the same rhythm, becoming hotter and brighter with every stroke.

The firestorm demanded and Erik delivered. His thumb slid between them, and he pinched her with a surety that made her gasp. Eileen clutched him tightly inside her and heard him groan. She reached for him, wanting his kiss when she climaxed, and he rolled her smoothly beneath him.

She welcomed his weight, his heat, his demanding fingers. She grasped his shoulders, felt her fingernails dig into his back, yet couldn't pull him close enough to satisfy. She wanted to merge them together, to fuse their bodies into one, to feel his heartbeat as surely as she felt her own.

The heat grew to brilliant intensity and she tasted the salt of perspiration on her lips—whether it was hers or Erik's didn't matter. She wasn't sure where she ended and he began—there was only the pulse of their union. She felt complete. She was afire.

She was right where she belonged.

She wrapped her legs tightly around Erik's hips, wanting

him and only him, wanting his truth and his secrets, wanting everything he had to give and more. The firestorm blazed, cauterizing old wounds, forging new strength.

He pulled back to look at her, marvel in his eyes. His fingertips were on her cheek, awe in his tone, when he whispered her name.

"Eileen," he said with reverence.

Not Louisa. That single word sent joy through Eileen, convinced her heart of what her mind already knew. She wasn't a substitute for another woman. She wasn't a return to the past. She wasn't a consolation prize. She was the woman Erik wanted.

And she wanted him. Nigel and Joe and all the other men in her life had contributed to make her what she was, but she didn't yearn for any of them anymore.

Her past had prepared her for this present, and for the future she and Erik might share. Erik had taken a different journey but one that had brought him to this place, as well.

And they were together, whole in their union. She smiled at him.

Then Erik moved his fingers.

Heat erupted within Eileen, stole her breath away, blinded her with its white fury. She closed her eyes and shouted with pure pleasure, her joy redoubled when Erik roared with his own release.

She felt him spill inside her and wondered whether the alchemists had been right about the power of dragon semen.

She felt transformed by it, invigorated and new.

Eileen lay there, holding Erik close, listening to their hearts beat in unison. His head was on her shoulder and his eyes were closed. She heard his breathing slow, heard him surrender to his exhaustion, and smiled in the darkness. His weight held her captive but there was nowhere else Eileen wanted to be.

Chapter 24

The Wyvern had done what she could.

And now she would do what she desired.

Sophie felt the familiar shimmer as her body worked its magic, felt a sense of new power as she became a woman. She returned to the desert in the blink of an eye, manifesting where she had left her loyal champion.

Nikolas was sitting against the rocks, his expression dissatisfied. He was chucking stones with impatience, obviously still annoyed with Sophie and her decision to leave his side.

She let herself manifest close beside him, watching him shield his eyes from the brilliant shimmer she could make when she chose to do so.

"I promised."

"It might not have been up to you," he scolded. "You shouldn't have gone alone."

"I'm back." She reached out and touched his shoulder quickly, her mouth going dry with just that caress. "Don't be angry."

And once they touched, there would be no turning back. She knew a corner had been turned and something had been set in motion, but Sophie did not know what it was. Worse, she didn't care.

Nikolas smiled crookedly and shook his head. "I was afraid for you," he said, his eyes dark and intent.

Sophie's heart skipped. "You couldn't follow me there."

"I will follow you anywhere."

"I know."

Nikolas stood and shoved a hand through his hair. He towered over Sophie, all masculine strength and determination. He looked at her with an admiration that buoyed her heart and made her feel full in a new and wonderful way.

They stared at each other for a long moment. His hair was dark with perspiration, his gaze stormy with desire. His features looked more sharp, his expression more hungry, and she could hear the beat of his heart as clearly as her own. Her breath came quickly, her breasts rising and falling as if she had been running.

Maybe she had been running, metaphorically.

Maybe she couldn't outrun the feelings Nikolas awakened in her.

Maybe she didn't want to try.

"Sophie." He whispered her name in old-speak and his voice resonated in her thoughts as if their thoughts had been one all along. As if she'd been waiting for him. As if the point to her entire existence had been this morning in the desert with Nikolas.

It was easy to believe.

This time, when Nikolas reached for her, Sophie didn't run.

She met him halfway.

Eventually Eileen became chilled.

She wiggled out from beneath Erik, being careful not to disturb him. The man was so exhausted that she wasn't sure anything could wake him, but didn't want to take any chances. She made a trip to the bathroom, then brought a towel to clean up. Erik barely stirred, so she got the duvet from the bedroom and put it over him. He slept on, untroubled.

He frowned even in his sleep, burdened by his responsibilities, and Eileen traced a gentle fingertip over his brow. She couldn't smooth out his concern, but she did see the scab on his forehead.

She remembered that he'd been bleeding after his fight with Magnus the day before. It was a strange place for a wound, and that made Eileen wonder if it was particularly significant. So much was significant with Erik and the *Pyr*.

These guys needed to offer a manual for mates.

Then she remembered Thorolf's comment about the Helm of Awe. Her coat was hanging in the front closet and she dug in its pockets until she found the rune stone that Sigmund must have given her.

She studied it in the darkness, running her thumb across the carved face. She was convinced that this had been the stone she had seen in the vision Erik had summoned, and that the boy must have been Sigmund in his youth. Had it been part of the charm that had been cast to lure Erik's father to his destruction?

Had it belonged to Erik's father?

Eileen didn't know, but she couldn't ignore Thorolf's comment. She took the rune stone and returned to Erik's side. He was sleeping on his back, the shadows under his eyes looking darker than they had when he was awake.

She bent, feeling slightly foolish, and placed the rune stone on his forehead, right over his injury. Maybe it would magically heal him. Eileen halfway thought Erik would move his head and it would roll down onto the couch. He didn't stir, except to take a deep breath, one that seemed to come right from his toes.

And his frown faded.

He didn't wake up.

Still feeling silly, Eileen headed for the shower. The *Pyr* would probably return at some point and she wanted to be ready for whatever came next.

Erik dreamed of the sea.

He dreamed of the waves stretching toward the horizon, the ocean so infinite and blue. He dreamed of promise and possibilities, that long-familiar sense of boundless opportunity that he had forgotten.

He stood in the prow of a ship as it leapt over the waves. He heard the great square sail snap in the wind behind him, cracking like a whip as the ship was pushed ever onward. He saw the carved head of a dragon arched high over his own head, the effigy snarling into the distance. It was thrilling to head into the unknown like this, to be a mascot on such a journey.

Erik glanced over the prow and recognized the figurehead, realized that he was dreaming of his very first journey. His hair was long and fair, knotted behind his neck. His jerkin was leather, his boots laced to his knees. His sword was long and sharp—he remembered its hilt like an old friend. He didn't let himself think about where they had gone and what they had found—he simply recalled that initial joy at setting out.

It flooded him, filling his mind and body with an optimism and vitality that he had thought lost with youth.

Tempered, maybe.

But that power was reawakened, kindled by his firestorm.

Eileen had forced him to reconsider what he believed to be true. Erik had tried, when he might have assumed he would fail. He had used the ocean as a looking glass and he knew he could do it again. He didn't need the Dragon's Egg to see the future.

He needed the faith that he could conjure a vision and nothing else.

Eileen had forced him to think about balance, about his own sacrifices that he had made to lead the *Pyr*. But his fellows had never asked that of him. They had never expected it. And in nursing his own wound, he suspected that he had not made the best choices in leading the *Pyr* to triumph.

He could fix that. He could learn from his mistakes and move forward with new confidence.

Erik felt a hand on his shoulder, knew his father had come to stand beside him. They had sailed together on that first journey, Soren watching over his only son. The memory made Erik smile, made him appreciate the connection that had been between them. It eroded the bitterness of what he had been compelled to do, flooding out the anger that had made it impossible to simply remember his father.

"We are Pyr," Soren said, his old-speak deep with authority. *"This world is both our treasure and our burden."*

Erik turned to see his father smile that secretive smile, the one that stole over his lips as if he had remembered a mysterious pleasure. His eyes glinted with confidence and pride; then he pushed something hard into Erik's hand.

Erik knew what it was, felt his fingers tighten on the rune stone. He knew it was his father's talisman and was surprised to be given it.

"Dream upon it," Soren advised. *"It will guide you true, give you the strength you need, provide direction when you are lost."*

Soren nodded once, narrowing his eyes to survey the endless stretch of the sea, and his joy in adventure was obvious. *"Who knows what we shall find? Who knows what we will learn?"* He turned that sparkling gaze upon Erik. *"But it is all ours to claim, to savor, to defend. Our gift and our responsibility."*

He squeezed Erik's shoulder once and his smile broadened. *"Remember to dream."*

Then Soren turned to scan the horizon once more with pleasure and anticipation. With optimism. He ducked his head and turned to hail one of his fellows, leaving Erik alone with the view and the echo of his father's old-speak.

And the rune stone. Erik opened his hand to find his father's prize cradled in his palm. It was marked with the Helm of Awe, the most powerful sigil of protection known to the Vikings.

That his father had given it to him stole Erik's breath away.

That Erik had given it to his own son and lost both brought a tear to his eye.

He didn't have to mourn that loss any longer.

He could choose to move forward with optimism.

Erik wakened suddenly and sat up, refreshed and filled with new purpose. Something fell to his lap, hitting the duvet with a thunk, and he was astounded that it was the very same rune stone.

It had come back to him.

He could guess who had brought it to him, although he didn't know how Eileen had gotten it. He turned it in his palm and let his gaze slide out of focus. Erik smiled as he saw the past and present mingled together on the smooth, dark surface of the stone, and a ribbon to the future.

His gift of prophecy was back.

Perhaps it had been lost in the firestorm. Maybe it had been overwhelmed. Either way, Erik chose to believe that it had been strengthened by his test and that his choice to trust Eileen had been the right one.

He looked into the future in the stone.

Erik saw the Dragon's Teeth, so close to Rafferty's grasp yet not quite within it, and knew he could help. He saw many dark challenges ahead, storms that would not be easily navigated. He saw light at the end of them, though, a company diminished but stalwart. He saw a sacrifice, but could not see clearly whose sacrifice it was.

He recognized that the Great Wyvern did not believe it fitting for him to know everything she knew.

He knew to accept what was offered and be glad of it.

Erik swallowed and kissed the rune stone, then rose to his feet with new determination.

There was work to be done.

Delaney had a bad feeling about this exercise.

He'd had the sense of dread ever since Sloane had suggested hypnosis. Although he respected Sloane's judgment, he had a niggling sense that the Apothecary of the *Pyr* didn't truly appreciate the extent of the wickedness involved.

Sloane hadn't felt his whole body respond to Magnus's whistle.

Sloane hadn't had that moment of terror when he knew his choices weren't his own.

Sloane didn't lie awake at night, fearing when the summons would sound again, dreading what his body might do against his will.

Delaney didn't trust Magnus. He really didn't like that the only way to find out what Magnus had planted in his subconscious was to trigger it. He didn't want to betray his fellow *Pyr*, or bring destruction upon them.

He wanted to be healed, though. He wanted to banish the last of the shadow implanted in him. And he couldn't continue to live like this. There had to be an answer, and Eileen's words to Erik made Delaney want to know the answer immediately.

All the same, he was afraid.

They stood on the roof of the building that housed Erik's lair. The city was just beginning to rouse itself for another workweek. The lake was choppy and dark, and there was a distant sound of automobiles and trains. The clouds in the sky hung low, their bottoms slate gray with the promise of snow. They stretched as far as the eye could see in any direction, blanketed the world in a way that seemed claustrophobic to Delaney.

He would have preferred to have been anywhere else.

"Try to send what you see to me," Sara said, slipping her

small hand into his. She smiled up at him with an optimism he didn't share. "Just because we haven't done it before doesn't mean it can't be done."

Delaney nodded, any words caught in his throat.

"Hey," Donovan said, bumping his other shoulder companionably. He winked at his younger brother. "You can do it. Let's get this fixed once and for all."

Delaney nodded and swallowed. He was up for that.

Sloane met his gaze, studying him with his usual intensity; then he began to hum. Delaney closed his eyes and felt Sara take a deep breath beside him. He was keenly aware of her as he never had been before.

Maybe that meant she was right.

Encouraged, Delaney bowed his head. He let Sloane's song wind into his mind. The song grew in intensity and volume, insistent and melodic. Delaney felt it open doors in his mind and heart, felt it spread through him like a healing balm.

Sara began to hum along, and Delaney heard her voice more strongly than Sloane's. Maybe because she was right beside him. Maybe because she was the Seer. If there was a connection between them, it might help. The other *Pyr* joined the song, tentatively at first, then gaining in confidence. It became demanding, pervasive, potent.

Sara's voice caught at Delaney's ear. The other voice he heard so sharply was Alex's.

Maybe it was because the women's voices were slightly higher.

Maybe it was because they were human, not *Pyr*.

Maybe it didn't matter.

Delaney felt the shadow stir deep within him, like a monster awakened in a hidden labyrinth, but trusted in his fellows. He let his thoughts meander, not truly surprised when memories of his time in the dark academy were summoned.

"It's deep in the earth," he murmured, surprised that the truth was so evident to him in this state. He felt Donovan give his hand an encouraging squeeze. "But under the water. A tunnel in the earth under the water."

"A mine shaft," Alex suggested, her words cutting directly into his thoughts.

Delaney shrugged and frowned. He didn't know.

"Can you smell ore?" Sara asked, and she too seemed to have a conduit directly to his heart. "Can you name it?"

He wanted to answer her. Sloane sang more stridently. Delaney let his memories take command, let them guide his thoughts into darkened and unknown territory. He heard the rhythm of Sara's breathing, felt her pulse through their interlocked hands.

Instead of visiting the academy in his memories, he found himself seeing Sara's child. He could feel the pulse of life in the baby she carried, could see the boy's fingers and toes, his lashes, his bones, his skin so sheer that it was almost transparent.

He could feel the force of the Smith in the boy's veins, could sense the legacy and the power of the child. The vision of Quinn's child was crystal clear to him and in close proximity. Sara's round belly was inches away from his hand.

So close.

So vulnerable.

So ripe for the taking.

Delaney was horrified. The monster in the labyrinth roared with fury and Delaney heard Magnus's imperious tones.

"Recruits!" Magnus hissed. Delaney didn't know whether it was in old-speak or in his thoughts.

He knew that he couldn't deny the command.

He shifted shape without any intention of doing so, rearing above his astonished fellows. His body moved of its own accord, flinging Sara away from the others while his claws stretched for her belly. He knew he was going to rip the child from her belly, steal it, and return to the academy, to offer it to Magnus.

He was horrified by his own move, but couldn't stop.

Sara screamed his name when he turned on her.

Quinn roared and shifted shape, breathing white-hot dragon fire at Delaney. He was large and livid, furious in the defense of his mate. Delaney took a blow from Quinn's massive sapphire and steel tail, and a trio of strikes.

Delaney fought for his own survival, but he couldn't match Quinn's determination to win. While he fought, Quinn breathed dragonfire, backing Delaney across the roof. Delaney saw his scales smoke, felt the pain of his injuries, and stumbled. He saw the rage in the Smith's eyes and a part of him wished that Quinn would kill him.

Another part of him was powerless to deny Magnus's command. He understood now what his mission was—Magnus wanted him to collect the children of the *Pyr*, to recruit them as *Slayers* from the cradle. Magnus had released him deliberately to fulfill this mission. Magnus had planted his command within Delaney and it was triggered when he relaxed in the presence of pregnant mates.

Delaney's gaze fell on Alex on the far side of the roof, less pregnant but still with child. To his horror, Magnus whispered a command deep in his own thoughts, one he could not deny. Delaney's body lunged to capture Donovan's mate.

He dove for Alex without wanting to do so, snatching at her as he made to take flight. She kicked him, although it was futile for her to defend herself against him, her anger as great as Quinn's. Donovan roared and latched on to Delaney's back, ferocious in his assault.

Again, Delaney wished the *Pyr* would destroy him, but Donovan beat him badly and cast him aside. Delaney fell from the roof, panting and bleeding.

"What's the matter with you?" Donovan shouted after him with disgust. "What the hell do you think you're doing?"

"Magnus," Sloane whispered in old-speak. Delaney was glad that someone knew what he endured.

He also heard the hopelessness in the Apothecary's tone.

He knew then that he'd exhausted Sloane's arsenal of healing potions.

He'd have to heal himself.

Somehow.

Delaney caught himself from hitting the pavement, and flew back toward the roof. As soon as the women were in view, that imperative sounded within him again. His body began to move in their direction and he felt viciousness stir within him.

Delaney wrenched his attention away from the women. He changed course with an effort and turned his back on his fellows.

There was only one answer. He had to banish himself from the *Pyr*. It wasn't safe for him to be around them. He wasn't going to injure their mates; he refused to capture their children.

He had to leave.

His life already wasn't worth living. He flew high over Chicago with no clear destination and decided that if death was inevitable, he'd make his death worthwhile.

Delaney would eliminate the Elixir that gave Magnus his power or die in the attempt.

"Where did you get it?"

Eileen was drying herself off when she heard Erik's voice. She knew exactly what he was talking about, even before she saw him tossing the rune stone into the air and catching it with one hand. He stood in the doorway to the bedroom, nude and confident.

Direct, as only he could be.

He cast her a crooked smile and she wanted him all over again.

"I thought you'd sleep longer."

"I seldom sleep much." He held up the rune stone, indicating that she hadn't answered his question.

"I'm not sure. It was in my coat pocket." She wrapped a

towel around her wet hair, feeling the appreciation in his gaze when she didn't cover up. It was cozy standing in his bathroom like this, and she felt comfortable in her skin in a way that she seldom did with a man. Where she might have found fault with this curve or that one, Erik seemed to like her just as she was. "I found it there when we were on Lynne's roof."

"Sigmund must have put it into your pocket when your coat was over him."

"I guess so. Thorolf recognized the symbol as Viking, so I assumed it must be yours." Eileen heard the question in her voice and saw Erik's quick nod of acknowledgment.

"It was my father's." He studied it as he turned it in his hand. "He gave it to me a long time ago."

"And you gave it to Sigmund."

Erik nodded slowly, turning the rune stone thoughtfully. He frowned slightly. "And he gave it to his other grandfather to use against my father."

Eileen remembered what she'd seen in the vision Erik had shown her and understood a bit more. "It was the core of the alchemist's spell?"

Erik nodded again. "He could never have done what he did without it. Another mistake on my part."

"You couldn't have known."

"I suppose not." Then he cast her a mischievous glance, his eyes dancing as she would have never imagined they could. He looked lighter and reinvigorated—his vitality stole her breath away. "But best of all, you've given it to me."

"So?"

"That means that the story has a better ending now."

"How so?"

"It can be the core of another ritual."

"What do you mean?"

Erik took her hand and put the rune stone into her palm, closing her fingers securely over it.

"Hey, there are no sparks." Eileen still felt aroused by Erik's touch.

"The firestorm is over."

Did that mean that their relationship was over? Eileen didn't believe it. Erik wouldn't abandon his child that easily—and she couldn't believe he'd abandon her either.

She knew she hadn't misplaced her trust this time and she chose to be confident in her choice.

"For someone who is answering questions, you're not answering them very well," she teased.

"I will. But first you need to call your sister," Erik said. "Immediately."

"You're right," Eileen said with a snap of her fingers. She looked into the bedroom for her satchel, knowing her cell phone would be in its depths. "I should have already called to say that I wouldn't be there before returning home. . . ."

Erik caught her hand and pulled her to a stop. "No. You need to persuade her to accept Rafferty's offer for the Dragon's Teeth."

Eileen paused to consider him. "You sound like you know something I don't."

"I do. And it's about time." He grinned when she eyed him with confusion, then stepped into the bathroom, as self-satisfied as Eileen had ever seen him.

Which was saying something.

Chapter 25

The woman phoned Rafferty's shop on Monday morning, hesitation in her tone. Rafferty agreed to meet with her immediately, as much to give himself a distraction from his worries as to offer any reassurance that he could. Lynne Williams was obviously concerned, and Rafferty liked the idea of being useful to someone.

When she arrived shortly thereafter, Rafferty acknowledged that Lynne Williams was also beautiful.

She arrived at his office with two little girls in tow, as well as a small suitcase in her hand. Rafferty was troubled by the sense that he had seen her before, even though he knew they'd never met. There was a gold wedding ring on her left hand, but his appreciation was simply an enjoyment of being in the presence of beauty.

He offered tea, which she declined, then settled the two young girls at a smaller table with a wooden Chinese puzzle. "They can't break it," he reassured their mother, then gestured to the chair opposite his desk. "How can I help you?"

"Well, this is very strange, even for my sister." She sat with the carry-on bag perched on her lap. "She was supposed to come back to visit before going home to the States, but I didn't really expect her to. She's always following stories and forgetting appointments—I mean, that's her job, so it's to be expected that she'd be fascinated by it—and when she headed back to Ironbridge after that Dragon Lover of Madeley story, I doubted I'd see her again on this trip. I figured she'd call me from Boston and apologize."

Rafferty settled into his own chair and folded his hands. He'd already heard enough to be intrigued. He let Lynne tell her story without interruption.

He'd made a lifelong habit of being patient, after all.

She heaved a sigh. "But I didn't expect to get a key in this morning's mail from her, with this note." She pushed a folded piece of paper across the desk to Rafferty. He flipped it open with a fingertip, read his own name, and understood why Lynne Williams had come to him.

His pulse quickened to see her sister's name.

Eileen.

Eileen Grosvenor?

"So, I went to the luggage locker at the station and picked this bag up. It's her bag—you see, it still has her luggage tag on it, so I'm not going crazy."

It was the bag of Eileen Grosvenor. Rafferty straightened.

His guest slid open the zipper. "But there are these things in it, and I'm hoping that you know what they are."

Rafferty's heart stopped cold when she lifted out the first bundle. A piece of fabric in brilliant chartreuse with orange and pink dots was wrapped around something the size of his guest's fist. He hardly dared to watch as she unfolded the cloth and put one of the Dragon's Teeth squarely in the middle of his blotter.

Rafferty caught his breath. He reached out and saw that his hand was shaking. He picked up the tooth with reverence and turned it in his grasp, confirming that it was what he believed it was. It was old, it whispered to him of the earth, and he was profoundly relieved to see it safe.

Where were the rest?

He glanced up to find his guest watching him closely. "You know what it is."

"Yes. I was afraid it had been stolen. Or destroyed." He set it down carefully. "This is a tremendous relief." Rafferty swallowed and eyed the carry-on bag. "Dare I hope that there are more?"

"How many should there be?"

"Ninety-nine. They were in a box when I saw them last, a wooden box that had been made for them."

She shook her head. "I don't have the box, just this bag." She reached into the bag and removed another bundle. She placed the next tooth beside the first one.

At his gesture, she put the bag on the desk. She and Rafferty worked together, unwrapping the Dragon's Teeth and aligning them in rows.

"Ninety-nine," she said, then wrinkled her nose. "Are they really teeth?"

"Yes. Ancient relics."

"Like dinosaur bones."

"Similar to that."

Her gaze flicked from the Dragon's Teeth to Rafferty. "Why do you think Eileen wanted me to bring these to you? Are you a dealer in bones as well as antiques?"

He understood that she already knew the answer to her question. He smiled. "Because she knew I wanted to buy them, and she knew I would pay you cash, no questions asked."

His guest raised a brow. "No questions asked."

Rafferty inclined his head in agreement.

She frowned and straightened. "Maybe I should take them back to whoever owns them."

"It looks like you own them now." Rafferty leaned across the desk, hoping he could persuade her to his view without beguiling her. "These relics were scheduled to be sold this very week, and I was, I believe, the only party interested in their purchase. I still am."

She reached for one tooth, frowning. "I think I'd better call the police."

"I would pay enough for both of your daughters to attend university."

She paused, her hand hovering over the tooth. "That's a lot of money. They might want to go to graduate school."

"Fine. At both the undergraduate and graduate level." Rafferty named a sum, then wrote it down so there could be no misunderstanding.

She looked from the number to her daughters and back to him.

"We'll put it in two trust funds," Rafferty said. "We can do the transfer from here, before you leave today." Rafferty pivoted and booted up his computer. He gestured to the phone. "Call your bank. Call your husband."

"You really want these teeth." She drummed her fingers on the bag, uncertain of what was the right choice. "I wish I could just talk to Eileen," she murmured. "There's no one at her apartment and I'm a bit worried. . . ."

A cell phone rang then. Rafferty watched his guest dig in her purse. She flashed him a smile of apology and he turned to his computer as she moved away for some privacy. He heard her exclamation of pleasure and wondered whether he could be so lucky that Eileen might call her sister in this critical moment.

If Eileen had been with Erik, and Erik had had his gift for prophecy back, Rafferty could have believed it. As matters stood, he was skeptical.

Lynne came back a moment later, her expression more relaxed. "Eileen said I should accept your offer, that that was why she sent me to you." Her smile broadened; then she pushed the piece of paper back across the desk to him. "But she said to insist on twenty thousand more, that Erik says you're good for it. Should I know what that means?"

Rafferty couldn't keep himself from grinning. He knew what it meant. Erik had consummated his firestorm and intended to stay with his mate—and his ability to foretell the future had returned, possibly as a result of that.

Rafferty had been right, and Erik knew it.

And they were allies again.

The relief that rolled through Rafferty weakened his knees, but he welcomed it. "It means that your daughters are going to university, that's all," he said with a smile.

His guest smiled back at him. "I have one request, though." Rafferty paused and glanced toward her, assuming she wanted the money deposited in a certain way. He was puzzled when she picked up one of the pieces of fabric that the Dragon's Teeth had been wrapped in.

"Can I have my fabric back?" she asked, her nose wrinkled in a way that made her look young and cute. "Some of this stuff is expensive and if you're not going to use it . . ."

"I'm not going to use it," Rafferty said with relief. "Take it and the bag, and welcome to it. Take the puzzle that your girls are enjoying, too."

"You're really pleased."

"You have brought me my heart's desire." Rafferty paused to amend that. "Or at least one of my heart's desires."

His firestorm, he chose to believe, would still come.

Sophie awakened in a beam of sunlight. Nikolas slept beside her, the sunlight touching the tanned strength of him. The sand was warm and golden beneath them, the sun just slipping over the horizon again. She smiled as she remembered what they had done, and ran her fingertips over Nikolas's shoulder.

She felt so good, so languid and satisfied, that it took her a moment to realize that something was deeply wrong.

Sophie couldn't hear the earth.

Once she realized as much, she couldn't think about anything else. She sat up and strained her senses.

Nothing.

She couldn't hear the anguish of the planet, couldn't sense the earth's frustration finding expression in the four elements. She couldn't see the wind's intention or feel the distant ocean or hear the earth moving deep beneath her. Sophie put her palms flat on the ground but felt only soil.

She eyed Nikolas and guessed what she had sacrificed. What would become of her? How could she aid the *Pyr* without her powers?

Sophie tried to cast her thoughts into the future and found nothing. She tried to hear the echo of prophecy, that little voice that always babbled in the corner of her thoughts, but found only silence.

Her breath came quickly as she tried to shift shape to a salamander, her favorite guise, and failed. She let her body do what it would and she became a dragon, just as the other *Pyr* could.

But she couldn't become a salamander.

She couldn't move through space, disappearing and manifesting at will. She doubted that she could move through smoke or dispatch dreams or hear thoughts.

She had lost what it was that made her the Wyvern.

The revelation sent terror through her. She shifted back to human form, relieved that she could still control that. How would the *Pyr* win their war against the *Slayers* without a Wyvern to help them? How badly had she betrayed those who relied upon her?

She understood the full price she had paid in breaking the old taboo against intimacy. She was no longer the Wyvern.

But maybe it hadn't been her choice that was responsible. The sense that Sophie had had for months of a deadline approaching could have meant that her time as Wyvern was ending. Perhaps her own choices had brought her more quickly to the transition. Perhaps she couldn't have chosen anything other than Nikolas.

The fact remained that it was for another Wyvern to aid the *Pyr*.

She watched Nikolas and wondered whether there was good in this change. She and Nikolas could have no future, both being *Pyr*, unless they chose to be outcasts. It was bad enough that she had allowed herself to be drawn into events and to become emotionally involved with the *Pyr*. But in mating with Nikolas, she had willingly sacrificed her abilities. She had no place among their fellows, not anymore. They would know that she had chosen her own desires over their needs, an outright violation of her obligation to them.

Plus *Pyr* did not have congress with other *Pyr*. It was so forbidden as to be unthinkable. Nikolas would be unwelcome among the *Pyr* warriors, tainted by his choice, his presence considered unlucky by the others no matter how much they sympathized with him. Homage to the Wyvern should not be tainted by base desire.

But Nikolas was a fighter to his core, and a life in seclusion with her, ignoring the needs of the *Pyr* in their time of conflict, would be worse than death to him.

It would destroy him to be compelled to stand aside.

She would not ask such a concession of him. If her time as Wyvern was ended, though, she and Nikolas might have another chance, much as Erik and Eileen had had.

The prospect made her dizzy.

Nikolas stirred, as if he sensed her agitation. He spared her a sleepy smile, one that made her heart somersault.

And she remembered her thought when she had first glimpsed him.

He was the one.

She thought again of his destiny, the strong sense she had had of his mission. Nikolas wouldn't go to the dark academy of his own volition, even to overthrow it. He wouldn't leave her defenseless. He wouldn't fulfill his destiny so long as she was with him.

Sophie didn't have a single regret, but now she understood

the Great Wyvern's desire. Nikolas patted the sand beside himself in invitation, but Sophie knew she couldn't go back.

Time was too precious.

She shook her head. "I love you," she said, and her voice was hoarse. "I think I have always loved you, or at least, I've always known that I would love you."

Nikolas's smile broadened and his voice was husky. "Then come back and do something about it."

"It is written that the *Pyr* should honor the Wyvern, worship the Wyvern, even pay tribute to the Wyvern, but never touch the Wyvern. Now I know why."

He sat up and pushed his hand through his hair, impatient with talk. "But I love you, Sophie. How is love not the greatest tribute of all?"

"Yes." She frowned as she looked across the hills, assessing the pace of the sun. What time was it? What day was it? How would she choose the best moment to act, now that her powers were gone? "I see that now," she said, and heard the wistfulness in her own voice. "But I am no longer the Wyvern."

"I don't care, Sophie. I still love you."

"I know."

Nikolas stood up then, his expression wary. "You're going to do something. What's going on?"

"You have a destiny. . . ."

"I don't believe in destiny." His eyes flashed. "I believe in choice and I believe in choosing to be with the one I love—"

"It doesn't matter what you believe!" Sophie shouted, both irritated and touched by his single-mindedness. Her tears broke free and he moved to comfort her. "There is something you must do, something you are fated to do, something that must be done to ensure the future of the *Pyr*."

His expression set and his eyes flashed with anger. "Don't start talking about that dark academy again. My obligation is to you and only to you. I choose to defend you, at any price, and I will do that so long as I draw breath."

"I understand," Sophie said, her words thick as she backed away from him. "But I don't think you do." She swallowed and shifted shape right before his eyes. "Yet."

Nikolas's consternation was clear. "Sophie? What are you doing? Where are you going?"

"Next time, Nikolas," she whispered in old-speak. *"Next time the Great Wyvern will smile upon us, even reward us."*

She saw the moment that Nikolas understood. She saw the flash of his eyes. She felt his anger swell as she took flight. She leapt into the sky with all her might and didn't look back.

She didn't dare risk changing her mind.

She knew what had to be done. She was going to die, and she would die for a good reason.

She would lead Nikolas to fulfill his destiny so they could be together in the future.

They would be the prophesied sacrifice.

"Sophie!" Nikolas roared from behind her, but Sophie flew faster than she had ever flown before. "No!"

Sophie heard Nikolas pursue her. Nikolas was larger, he was faster, but she was determined.

And maybe, just maybe, the Great Wyvern was on her side.

Sophie found a tendril of hate that wound out of the dark academy founded by Magnus and she latched on to it. She followed it like a fish on a lure, plummeting toward a heart of evil and her own destruction.

If Nikolas saved the *Pyr*, it would be worth it.

It might have been the strangest sight Eileen had ever seen.

She had a feeling that if she spent her future in the company of Erik Sorensson, she'd see stranger ones, but for the moment, this one took the prize.

She was on the roof of the building that housed his loft.

Eileen was glad of the thickness of her sheepskin coat. She'd slung her satchel over her shoulder before they came up to the roof, not wanting to lose her notebook or her knitting.

The old warehouse building was about six stories high, with a flat asphalt roof, and Erik's home took all of the top floor. It was a gray morning, clear, although the overcast skies threatened snow. The wind was damp enough off the lake to make Eileen shiver. Chicago was bustling with morning traffic.

None of this was strange.

That she was in the company of two other women wasn't particularly strange, either, even though the choice of location for a chat was unusual.

The dragons were definitely out of the ordinary.

The *Pyr* had emerged onto the flat roof as men, but had changed shape with remarkable speed. Quinn had become a dragon scaled in sapphire and steel. Donovan was brilliantly hued, scaled in lapis lazuli and gold. Sloane was like a rainbow in comparison to the others, his gold-edged scales shaded in all the various hues of tourmaline. From nostril to tail, his color slipped from gold through green to purple and back again.

The sound of thunder was something Eileen was getting used to. She folded her arms across her chest as the *Pyr* conferred, disliking that she didn't know everything that was going on.

"We've got to figure out how to listen to that," Alex muttered, and Eileen smiled that they were thinking the same way.

"It's usually stuff they don't want us to know," Sara agreed.

Alex tapped her toe. "We need something to modulate the frequency and move it into a range we can hear."

"Resident genius and scientist," Sara said to Eileen, indicating Alex. "She'll have it figured out in no time."

Alex rolled her eyes. "Not with any help from them, that's for sure."

"Maybe they like having a few secrets," Eileen suggested. "Although, I have to admit, they've got some big ones."

The women exchanged smiles; then Sara nudged Eileen. Quinn was off to one side, breathing dragonfire that burned white and hot. "This is your cue," Sara said.

"But I don't know what I'm supposed to do."

"Just come to me," Erik said.

Eileen realized that he hadn't changed shape yet. He stood watching her, the wind in his hair. She walked toward him and halted in front of him while the *Pyr* and their mates watched. "What are we doing?" she asked in an undertone.

His eyes glimmered, making her very aware of her femininity and teasing her with the recollection of all they had done. "Do you still want to see the change?"

Once again, she had the sense that she was making a wager without knowing all of the conditions. But she knew Erik better now, and she trusted him. She smiled. "Yes!"

"Tell me if it troubles you at all," he said, and she nodded her agreement.

He offered his hand and she put her hand on his. She watched as he began to shimmer. He was consumed in a flickering blue light, like that of static electricity, but it brightened and moved more quickly with every passing moment. She had a hard time discerning precisely where the man ended and the sky began; then the shimmer grew brighter.

And in the blink of an eye, he had changed from a man to a dragon. Her hand was still on his, except his hand had become a claw, his nail a long silver talon. His posture was the same, though, as was his gentleness and intensity.

As was the green gleam of his eyes.

Eileen looked. Erik seemed larger in the open air, even though it wasn't a small space. His black wings arched high and his tail covered a large section of the roof. His scales were black, as black as ebony, and they gleamed like jet.

They could have been edged in silver, made by a jeweler for all the precision of their shaping and color. His chest could have been made of rows of chain mail in hammered pewter. Eileen thought of her first glimpse of him, livid in the vault of the foundation, and much preferred his current mood.

She flattened her hand and slid it across his scales, surprised again to find them warm and dry. She kept expecting them to be cold, like armor, or slippery like a fish. They felt solid under her hand, but not repulsive. Powerful. Eileen surveyed Erik, sensing that there was something special she was supposed to notice.

The way the *Pyr* held their collective breath and waited was a big clue.

Then Eileen found it. Where Erik had the wound in human form, he also had one in dragon form. Of course. The red scab on his forehead was larger than it was in human form, and looked like a jewel. It shone like the ruby that the alchemists believed was buried in the dragon's forehead. Eileen shivered at the unwitting connection, then reached for it.

It was a bit funny that she felt protective of a man who could become a dragon at will, and that she kept feeling the urge to scold him for not taking better care of himself. She couldn't help it, though. She wanted him to be strong and healthy, not to push himself too far.

"Let me see that," Eileen said sternly, and Erik inclined his head, closing his eyes. She ran her fingertips over his brow, awed that he was both powerful and gentle with her. There was no infection, so far as she could tell, but the flesh was open beneath the scab.

"There's a scale missing," she said with sudden realization. "Will it grow back?"

"No." Erik spoke with resolve. He opened one eye to consider her. "When a *Pyr* loses a scale, it can be repaired only with the assistance of his mate, using a talisman given by her to him."

Eileen understood immediately. She held up the rune stone. "This."

"That," Erik agreed.

"I gave it to you already."

"Unwittingly. You volunteered it, which is critical element in its effectiveness."

Eileen smiled. "I thought the dragon was supposed to save the damsel in distress, not the other way around."

Erik snorted a puff of smoke and declined to comment on that. "It is the labor of the Smith to repair our armor," he said softly. "Will you aid Quinn in this task?"

There was no question in Eileen's mind. Erik had saved her a number of times, not expecting reciprocation. She wanted him to be fully armored, to improve the chances of their having a future together. "Of course. Just tell me what I have to do."

Sara stepped forward then, lifting the rune stone from Eileen's hand. She closed her hand over it and lifted it to her ear, as if listening to it, then nodded. "The proper union requires all four elements to be present and accounted for. The *Pyr* generally have fire covered and an affinity for one other element. The mate brings the other two to the equation."

"Eileen brings water," Erik said with conviction.

Eileen couldn't deny that she had a strong link to that element, for better or for worse.

"Compassion and understanding," he added, and she was sure he smiled at her with affection. "Sensitivity and intuition."

Eileen thought about the Wyvern's comments beside the pond. It seemed as if Eileen had gotten her water back this weekend.

"Erik must be air, as well," Sara mused. "He's the thinker

of the *Pyr*, the one most concerned with abstractions and ideas."

"And plans," Donovan interjected.

"Logic," Quinn added.

"Doesn't air govern the gift of foresight?" Sloane asked.

"Yes," Erik said. "And the ability to conjure visions."

Eileen stared at him and remembered how he brought the past to life in the ocean's dark mirror. "That leaves earth, then," she said. "What's its association?"

"Practicality, determination, resilience," Sara said.

"Gold," Alex said with a smile, touching the ends of Eileen's hair.

"Treasure," Erik said with approval. "Where no one has had the wits to seek it before."

"Dross into gold?" Eileen teased, and he laughed.

"No." His eyes shone as he regarded her, the intensity of his attention making her heart skip. "The extraordinary discerned where others have overlooked it."

They stared at each other, a new kind of heat kindling between them, and Eileen half wished the other *Pyr* would disappear.

Instead, Quinn took the rune stone from Sara in his talons, beat his wings, and reared high. He exhaled flames at the rune stone and it heated in his grasp until the stone turned white. The Helm of Awe was etched in black against the blinding white, the stone seeming to radiate strength and power.

Erik bowed his head before Eileen, and Quinn placed the hot stone over the missing scale. Erik winced and bared his teeth as the stone seared the raw skin. He caught Eileen close and beat his wings, creating a tempest around them.

It began to snow, the white flakes dancing out of the sky and swirling around them. Erik's wings turned the snow into a maelstrom, shielding the two of them from those whose surrounded them.

Eileen stared into Erik's eyes and recalled Sigmund's

death in the snow, Louisa's death in the swirling waters of the Severn, Erik's father's death in the smoke-filled haze of the alchemist's shop. She thought of how the past had shaped the future and hoped desperately that their current choices shaped a better future.

She hoped that Erik wouldn't be sacrificed, and hoped it with all her heart.

She looked at the bloodred wound of the embedded rune stone and believed that Erik's father's talisman, which had wound its way back to him against all expectation, would help him in the days and nights ahead. She wished he hadn't had to endure such pain, but she was honored to be in the company of the man he had become.

So she bent, touched her lips to the rune stone, and her falling tears sizzled as they eased the heat of his wound.

When she opened her eyes, Erik was back in human form. She was standing in the circle of his arms; he had a small mark on his forehead, and he was lowering his head to kiss her.

His possessive kiss was all she wanted and more.

Chapter 26

In Hampstead Heath, Rafferty Powell planted a strange crop in his garden. He had planted many mysterious seeds in his time, but these were the oddest of all.

He planted ninety-nine enormous teeth.

Niall and Thorolf had appeared after the departure of Lynne Williams, and Rafferty put them to work. The soil in his neglected garden wasn't easily worked, but the younger *Pyr* were strong and determined.

Rafferty focused on his low song, the same chant he had repeated when the tooth that had become Nikolas was planted. He sang to the teeth; he murmured to them of the challenges ahead of the *Pyr*; he beseeched them to fulfill their destinies. He sang until he was hoarse and then he sang some more. The three worked together, and by midafternoon the task was done.

"Now what?" Thorolf asked, wiping the soil from his hands.

Rafferty smiled. "Now I teach you about patience."

The new recruit looked exasperated. "Does that mean I can finally sleep?"

"For the moment," Rafferty said. "But do not sleep deeply."

Niall inhaled deeply and shimmered slightly around his perimeter. "No. There's change in the wind."

"More than change," Rafferty said. "Possibility." His gaze slid between the other two and he changed to old-speak. He recounted the old prophecy, watching the newly found *Pyr*'s eyes widen. "*Danger*," he concluded.

Niall nodded agreement and returned to the kitchen.

Thorolf shoved his hand through his hair. "Like there hasn't been enough of that going around lately," he complained.

Rafferty laid a hand on the young *Pyr*'s shoulder and guided him back into the house. He was in a mood to celebrate and unconcerned by the new recruit's frustration. "Once a burden becomes familiar, it seems lighter," he counseled.

Thorolf sighed and nodded. "I just need some Zs."

Rafferty smiled. "Then take them. There is a spare bedroom over the kitchen that you're welcome to use." He wasn't surprised that the young *Pyr* headed straight there, nor was he surprised to hear the sound of his slow and regular breathing fill the house shortly afterward.

"Amateur," Niall said with a shake of his head.

Rafferty smiled and opened a good bottle of wine. "But stronger than he guesses. You'll see." He poured two glasses and toasted Niall, then the Dragon's Teeth in the garden.

Rafferty Powell was relieved and didn't care who knew it.

"How convenient to find you all at home," Magnus said, his tone silky. He loitered at the top of the fire escape, one hand held casually behind his back. The snow fell more thickly, but it didn't obscure either Magnus or his malice.

Erik wasn't surprised to see the old *Slayer*. He had known it would be only a matter of time before Magnus tried to bargain for the Dragon's Teeth, especially after the others had told him about Delaney. All the same, he eased Eileen behind his back.

Magnus's smile broadened and he sauntered across the roof, heading straight for Erik. En route, he pulled his hand from behind his back, revealing a stoppered vial.

It was filled with opaque red liquid.

"What's that?" Erik asked, even though he knew.

"A present from me to you." Magnus offered the vial to Erik. "Or perhaps a last chance."

Sloane took a cautious step back. Quinn and Donovan held their ground, but slid their mates behind them. Erik knew that Magnus hadn't come alone, but he couldn't sense the presence of any other *Slayers*.

But then, Magnus knew how to disguise his scent. There could be an entire *Slayer* army lurking just out of sight. Erik braced himself for a surprise and knew that the *Pyr* took their cue from him. All of them shimmered slightly, on the cusp of change.

"That's no present," Sloane said.

"Isn't it?" Magnus asked, feigning surprise. "I would say it's the richest gift possible."

"Would you." Erik folded his arms across his chest.

Magnus considered the *Pyr*, each in turn. "You're not interested in the most potent substance of all time? You would spurn such a generous gift as immortal life?"

"You'll want something in exchange," Donovan said.

Magnus's smile faded. "I want the Dragon's Teeth. I want them all and I want them now."

"That's all?" Erik asked.

Magnus watched him warily. "You said you had them."

"Maybe I did." Erik shrugged. "Maybe I lied."

"No! You did not lie." Magnus scanned the company, his gaze locking on Eileen. "You had them and you hid them from me."

"Guilty as charged," Eileen said.

Magnus seemed to grit his teeth, then turned his attention

again upon Erik. "I come to negotiate with you. I offer this." He held up the vial. "And I would trade it for the Dragon's Teeth. Immortality in exchange for a few old bones." His eyes widened slightly and he took a step closer as he smiled. "You could be prepared for your mate to reincarnate, forever. You could have all of eternity together, one lifetime after another, in endless succession."

"And what's the alternative?" Donovan demanded.

"That I slaughter you all," Magnus said smoothly. "Eternal life or immediate death."

"Why offer a choice at all?" Sloane asked.

"We are always seeking new recruits." Magnus smiled coldly. "I will have the Dragon's Teeth one way or another. For the sake of old times, I'm offering you the chance to survive. It is incredibly generous of me, in case you aren't sure."

Erik kept his expression impassive, wanting Magnus to think that he found the idea appealing. He knew that there had to be a trick, but he chose to let Magnus think that he was considering the offer. "Eternal life," he mused, knowing that none of the *Pyr* would accept Magnus's proposition.

"But you'd never have sons," Donovan said.

"Your blood would turn black," Sloane added.

"You would be banishing the divine spark of the Great Wyvern," Quinn said flatly, his certainty of what Erik would do more than clear. "Turning from the light to the shadow."

"Erik would never do that," Donovan agreed.

"Wouldn't he?" Magnus moved closer, confidence in his every step. "Not even for an eternal love? Not even for the surety of finding his destined partner, time and time again?" He smiled at Eileen and she took a wary step back. "Think of the many futures you could have together. Think of how much more potent it would be to find each other over and over again."

Erik took the vial, cupping its bulb in his palm. It was warm, its contents having heated the glass in a way that was not pleasant to the touch. The liquid swirled inside the glass almost as if it concealed a dark secret in its depths. He intuitively disliked it, just as his father would have disliked it, and stifled his urge to shudder.

He wondered what the source of the Elixir was. He could feel its wickedness emanating into his palm. He thought of what had happened to Delaney, how Magnus had planted a charm deep in his thoughts, and wondered whether the Elixir had been part of the strategy.

He wondered how much Magnus would tell him.

"Ours could be a powerful union," Magnus whispered, perhaps believing that Erik was tempted. "An undeniable force for change. You could do anything, risk anything, confident in your own ability to survive. The world would be ours to command."

"Ours?"

"Ours." Magnus smiled. "The burden of leadership is great, as you know. We could rule together; we could be unrivaled."

Erik removed the stopper from the vial. It had a musty scent, earthy and yet repulsive. "And all I have to do is drink?" he asked, seeking more confessions from his opponent.

Magnus's eyes gleamed. "Yes!" He took a step closer and touched his fingertips to the bottom of the vial. "One sip will give you eternal life!"

Erik smiled as if his decision were made. He felt the *Pyr* watching him, and knew they had no doubt of his choice. There was no way he would ingest this vile substance and no way he would ever turn *Slayer*. Only Magnus, so ensnared in the grasp of his own greed and ambition, could imagine otherwise.

Erik took Eileen's hand in his. "I do this for us," he said softly. She watched him, her eyes filled with a conviction that he would make the right decision. She had no doubt in him. She had no need to give him advice.

She trusted him.

And he would prove that she was right to do so.

Rafferty awakened to a rumble in his garden in Hampstead Heath. It sounded like an earthquake, but one at close proximity.

"The teeth!" He leapt out of bed at the realization and took the stairs four at a time. He flung himself through his kitchen and hauled open the garden door.

Warriors were springing from the soil. They were muscled and determined, naked except for their tans. They looked virile and powerful. Before his very eyes, each one shifted to a dark dragon. They were indistinguishable from Nikolas in dragon form, all anthracite and ancient power.

An army of *Pyr*.

Ninety-nine soldiers.

One stood on the lip of Rafferty's patio, giving clearance to pairs of *Pyr* to take flight. At his crisp nod, each pair ascended into the dark sky with precision and purpose. Their wings even beat in unison, and their form was so perfect that they might have been mirror images of each other.

Rafferty understood. They were trained to work together, to follow a system, to be a greater force in sum than individually. Their discipline and order left Rafferty in awe as he watched the silhouettes of paired dragons form a straight line to the northwest.

He wondered their destination for only a moment before he guessed. They would respond like this only to a command they respected, to the summons of one whom they knew.

An earthy expletive alerted Rafferty to the fact that he wasn't alone. He turned to find Thorolf, half-naked and wide-eyed, standing behind him and staring into the garden. Niall was beside him in the shadowed kitchen.

"Where are they going?" Niall asked softly.

"I don't know," Rafferty guessed. "It's as if they've been summoned."

"We should go with them," Niall suggested, and Rafferty nodded.

"If they'll allow it."

"Am I supposed to understand all of this?" Thorolf demanded.

"No. But you can come anyway." Rafferty moved with authority. He locked up the house, shifted shape, and revealed his presence in his own garden.

Rafferty was coldly assessed by the *Pyr* who stood at the end of his patio. That soldier's gaze slid past Rafferty, moving up and down to study Niall and Thorolf. The survey took long enough that Rafferty feared they would be denied permission to accompany the force.

"I retrieved you," he explained in old-speak. *"I planted you and I awakened you."* Then he began to hum the tune he had sung to the earth while he planted them.

The ancient *Pyr* smiled ever so slightly. *"You are the one who saved us, but only our fellow can awaken us."*

Rafferty understood that Nikolas had made the summons, and he was more determined to go along.

To his relief, the sentinel inclined his head formally. *"We would be honored by your joining our company."*

At his crisp nod, the next ancient *Pyr* and the sentinel took flight simultaneously. They hovered for a beat above the roof of the house until Rafferty joined them, then closed on his flanks.

Like a ceremonial escort.

Niall and Thorolf took flight immediately after Rafferty, and two ancient *Pyr* flanked them as well. That foursome flew ahead of Rafferty and his two honor guards, ending the long line of warriors that ascended into the sky.

Why had Nikolas called them?

Something horrible must have happened.

Given that he didn't know their destination, much less what they would confront there, Rafferty was good with the escort.

*   *   *

Nikolas knew what Sophie would do and it terrified him. He couldn't catch her, though, even though he pushed himself to his full speed. She remained just ahead of him, elusive and beautiful, a glimpse of perfection that he'd briefly possessed.

Having tasted her sweetness, he wanted only to be with her.

They streaked through the sky, black after white, leaving a spiraling vortex in their wake. She crossed the country with alarming speed, tireless in her determination. She finally dove toward the ocean, targeting a barricaded opening to a half-forgotten tunnel. She speared through the wooden barricade, shattering it with the force of her impact, and plunged into the darkness beyond. Nikolas was right behind her, her long white feathers streaming just beyond his grasp. She flew deep and fast, guided unerringly by her sense of destiny.

The air chilled and he smelled dampness. He guessed that the tunnel had gone under the ocean, and spied water in side tunnels. He smelled coal and saw rotten timbers that had once braced the mine shaft. The rock had fallen in, but Sophie found spaces and gaps to slip through in her quest. He didn't like the place at all. He snatched at Sophie time and again, but caught only one silky white feather in his talons.

It became persistently darker within the tunnel, the smell of coal dust as omnipresent as that of men and machinery. Nikolas felt confined in the space, claustrophobic as he seldom was. He was painfully aware of the weight of water above them, pressing down. The earth had been torn open and ravaged, her wounds abandoned to heal themselves. Men had died in these tunnels, and he knew that if he slowed down, he would see their lost remains.

He gritted his teeth and followed Sophie as she flew ever deeper. He would have lost her in the darkness if she hadn't been so resplendently white, if she hadn't gleamed like a beacon beckoning him onward.

He feared that she was leading him to their mutual destruction.

The tunnel terminated in a long crack, one with jagged edges and a whiff of wickedness emanating from it. Sophie didn't hesitate, although Nikolas would have preferred to have turned back.

He wouldn't go without her, though. He leapt after her, his muscles screaming at the exertion. The path beyond was more tortuous, framed by so many broken rocks that Nikolas feared it led nowhere. He had time to panic before they rounded a corner and emerged abruptly in a cavern.

Nikolas saw the bolted doors ahead. Red light pulsed in the small space beneath the massive doors, reflecting in the water that was pooled on the floor of the cavern.

Sophie landed in front of the doors, raised a hand, and knocked. "Open to me!" she cried, and Nikolas was sure her quest had come to a failed end. If this was the dark academy of Magnus, the Wyvern would never be admitted. He was going to scoff at her demand, but the doors swung open.

Sophie cast him one last glance and he saw the magnificent turquoise of her eyes. She blew him a kiss, crossed the threshold, and the doors closed behind her.

Nikolas fell upon them; he shouted and he raged, but the doors didn't budge. They had locked against him, keeping Sophie captive inside. With closer proximity, he heard the wails of *Pyr* locked within the academy and the clatter of chains.

He heard Sophie scream and his rage redoubled. If they wouldn't admit him, he'd take the place apart.

He wasn't leaving without Sophie.

Erik lifted the vial toward his mouth. He saw Magnus's smile broaden, saw the *Slayer* shimmer around the edges of his body. Erik took a deep breath, easing toward the transition himself. He felt Eileen's pulse accelerate and saw the glimmer of his fellows in his peripheral vision. He lifted his hand, bringing the vial to his lips. Magnus seemed to hold his breath. Erik smelled new arrivals and knew who hovered just out of sight.

It was time.

In the last moment before the vial touched his lips, Erik spun. He flung the glass vial at the brick wall of the next building.

Magnus bellowed in outrage.

Erik shifted shape, and roared, "*Now!*" in old-speak.

The *Pyr* shifted with him and the roof was filled with dragons breathing fire. Magnus shouted and shifted shape as well. *Slayers* erupted from the fire escape to the street. Erik saw Jorge and the two other *Slayers* who had been with Magnus in London.

"Frenchie," Eileen muttered with disgust.

Shadow dragons leapt out the clouds, their stares empty and cold. They had no scent because they were not alive. Erik recognized two that hadn't been defeated before, Niall's twin and one of Quinn's brothers, before flames erupted on all sides.

The *Pyr* instinctively fought back-to-back to protect the three women sheltered behind them. Donovan began to sing the ancient chant of the Warrior, and the falling snow turned to missiles of ice, slanting out of the sky and spearing those it struck. Within moments, the roof had turned into a war zone.

Erik was determined to ensure Eileen's survival, no matter the cost. If he died in her defense—and that of his unborn child—he would count his life a victory.

He would much rather live.

He saw a flash of red and looked in time to see a red salamander leap from Jorge's grasp. The golden dragon had been darting across the roof, but swore and turned to seek the salamander.

The salamander was headed directly for the spilled Elixir with a determination that told Erik exactly who he was.

Erik smiled. The time to settle the blood duel, once and for all, had arrived.

Erik dove after Boris.

Rafferty was awed.

The Dragon's Teeth warriors streamed through the tunnel, so fixed on their destination that they were indifferent to the damage made en route. Rafferty saw that rocks were falling, that gaps were broadened, that timbers fell with their passage. He felt the surge of the ocean, sensed the chill of the water filling the spaces made available. The water was up to their knees when they burst into the cavern that housed the academy, swirling as it flooded the space.

It might have been a tide coming in. Rafferty was afraid they would be trapped beneath the ocean, prey to Gaia's whims when her mood was destructive; then he gaped at the dark academy.

This was the locus of Magnus's vile practice of turning dead *Pyr* into shadow dragons. This was the nexus of wickedness. He had never thought to see it himself, and he only hoped that he was witness to its destruction.

Was that what the Dragon's Teeth warriors would do?

A pair of dark doors stood in a wall of stone, their steel buttressed with iron bands. They arched high, filling a portal carved of stone. There was only this wall, the rest of the academy buried within the earth.

Rafferty didn't imagine that the threshold was easy to cross.

It was a soulless place, its evil so potent that his breath was stolen away. He stared at it in awe and terror, seeing red pulse beneath its doors. It was full to bursting, powerful and frightening. The sounds of fetters carried to his ears, along with the moans of those held captive there.

Thorolf swore softly behind him. Niall winced at the smell of death and destruction, of evil and despair.

Rafferty wondered who—or what—guarded the door.

"This is where shadow dragons are made," Rafferty told the new recruit, who stared in astonishment.

"We're gonna die here," Thorolf said, eying the water that rose around their knees. "We gotta get out."

"We are here for a reason," Rafferty insisted.

Nikolas was at the door of the academy, thrashing at it with his tail and breathing fire in his fury. He pivoted, eyes flashing, to confront his fellows, apparently not surprised by their arrival.

"The Wyvern is captive!" he roared in old-speak. His ancient fellows bellowed in consternation.

"It is forbidden to injure the Wyvern," declared the leader.

"It is our obligation to defend she who cannot defend herself," insisted another.

Then the Dragon's Teeth warriors joined Nikolas's labor. They ripped at the steel doors that secured the dark academy. They breathed fire in unison and pulled the reinforcing bands free. Many talons did indeed make light work of a massive task.

And still the level of the water rose.

The Dragon's Teeth warriors battered the barrier, using their tails in unison. Others, meanwhile, struck at the rock face, breaking away chunks of rock with sheer force.

The pulse of red beneath the academy's doors became brighter and more vehemently red with each passing moment. The water rose higher and higher, and Rafferty took flight to remain above its cold clutch. He could hear the earth rumbling in protest at this assault and wondered what would give first. He kept Thorolf close by his side, knowing that the untrained *Pyr* was his responsibility.

The screaming within the academy rose to a crescendo, but the Dragon's Teeth warriors didn't stop. They worked with the discipline of a well-trained force, persistent and powerful, under Nikolas's command.

Rafferty had time to admire their diligence and effectiveness before the battle changed. A crevasse broke open in the steel doors and a slice of darkness slipped into the ranks of the assaulting force.

"*Shadow dragons,*" Niall hissed in old-speak, recognizing them for what they were.

"*What foe is this?*" demanded the Dragon's Tooth warrior who had led the force. He turned his forceful gaze upon Rafferty, seeking an answer.

"Pyr, *harvested from their graves and compelled to drink the Dragon's Blood Elixir of immortality,*" Rafferty said, seeing the warrior's astonishment. "*They must be dismembered, incinerated, and their ashes scattered. They have no blood and fight relentlessly.*"

"*Vermin,*" the warrior said, his eyes narrowing as he lifted his claws.

Rafferty made no response. He saw the shadow dragon that had been his grandfather. He had feared that they would meet again, and the shadow dragon flew directly toward him, an unholy malice in his gaze.

Niall shouted when the shadow dragon that had been his twin brother assaulted him. Rafferty locked claws with the abomination that had been his beloved grandfather. The shadow dragon was fierce and powerful, bloodthirsty in a way that nearly overwhelmed Rafferty. A little too late, he thought about the blood sacrifice foretold by the prophecy.

Would Rafferty be it?

Erik snatched at the red salamander Boris had become, but missed. Boris scampered across the roof, limping slightly, but determined. He was heading for the spilled Elixir that dripped down the wall of the adjacent building.

Erik meant to ensure that the *Slayer* never reached it. He dove and snapped, but Boris slipped under an air-conditioning unit. He heard the patter of footsteps; then Eileen appeared below him. She reached under the unit, into a space he couldn't negotiate, and hauled out the salamander by its tail.

Boris shifted to dragon form before Erik could guess what he would do. He was blackened and burned, but his anger gave him strength. He snatched at Eileen and she turned to run.

Boris snagged the end of Eileen's scarf before Erik struck him with his tail. He held fast as he stumbled, coming precariously close to the edge of the roof. Eileen dove at his ankles, tripping him.

Boris fell.

But he grabbed Eileen first.

Boris's wings were torn, but he flapped them furiously all the same. He laughed when he saw Erik and dug his talons into Eileen. She struggled and squirmed, kicking him to no avail. Erik leapt off the roof in pursuit, spiraling down after the pair.

"You have to save me to save your mate." Boris chuckled. "But then, if I fall, I will live."

Erik snatched Boris out of the air and ascended rapidly. Eileen gasped and he could feel the panicked pace of her heart. He soared about the city and tossed Boris high, surrounding him with dragonsmoke. He kept a conduit open with the dragonsmoke, stealing energy away from Boris. He could feel the *Slayer* weakening.

Boris swore. He twitched. He writhed within the dragonsmoke that had no effect upon Eileen, but he held fast to Eileen. When the ground came too close, Erik caught Boris again.

The fiend breathed dragonfire at both Erik and Eileen. Erik shouted in frustration and lashed Boris with his tail. The sleeve of Eileen's coat was burning and she was pounding it on Boris to damp the flames. Erik grabbed the *Slayer* out of the air, spinning him with savage force.

Boris let go of Eileen.

Erik dropped Boris and dove after Eileen. He knew his priorities. He could fight Boris another day, but needed to save Eileen immediately.

To Erik's horror, Magnus caught Eileen first.

Chapter 27

Thorolf wasn't about to stand by and let his new companions get slaughtered. He was ready to kick some butt.

He wasn't ready to die either, and kicking butt was the best way to get out of this mess.

The battlefield had expanded beyond the doors themselves and things were getting ugly. Shadow dragons had cut down Dragon's Teeth warriors, and their blood stained the ever-rising water. Dragon's Teeth warriors, following their leader's instructions, were dismembering shadow dragons.

The ghouls fought on, oblivious to their missing limbs and wings.

Nikolas and a small company continued to batter on the doors of the academy, and the shouts of those imprisoned within got steadily louder.

The water was getting deeper.

The rock was shuddering.

Rafferty was getting thumped by the shadow dragon that had targeted him, while Niall was holding his own against the shadow dragon that so closely resembled him. Thorolf chose to help Rafferty first.

He latched on to the back of the shadow dragon, ripping one wing from his back with a savage blow. There was no blood, just as Rafferty had said.

They weren't real, in Thorolf's terms. They were zombies, or ghouls, the undead risen to torment the living. He could see the anguish in Rafferty's eyes and knew that the old *Pyr* had known this shadow dragon in life.

Maybe loved him.

So, the *Slayers* played dirty. That wasn't a surprise. Thorolf had no problems thumping the ghoul for Rafferty.

The shadow dragon spun and hissed dragonsmoke that smelled foul. It stung but Thorolf held on, cutting the other wing loose and letting it fall. He held the furious shadow dragon above the ground, letting him sputter and spew smoke and fire.

"Come on!" Thorolf shouted. "Let's finish him off."

Rafferty's expression was set when he attacked. The shadow dragon met him with a flurry of claws and teeth, but Thorolf successfully held him back. He was a slippery bugger and big, but Thorolf was stronger.

Maybe more determined.

He saw Rafferty weep as he sliced the legs from the captive shadow dragon. Thorolf breathed dragonfire, incinerating the falling limbs as best he could before they hit the water. The shadow dragon struggled with new force when he had no limbs left, and his old-speak echoed in Thorolf's thoughts.

"Remember when we sat by the fire," he said, and Rafferty retreated in horror. *"Remember the tales I told you. . . ."*

Rafferty choked in dismay.

"He's trying to trick you," Thorolf cried. "He's using your feelings against you. Just do it!"

Rafferty's gaze steeled. He raised his claws and dove at the shadow dragon, the force of his impact slamming Thorolf back into the rock wall of the cavern. The shadow dragon begged and cried; he shouted in some language Thorolf didn't know. Rafferty slashed and bit, he wept, but he did what had to be done.

The shadow dragon's head fell and Rafferty dove after it, exhaling a furious torrent of fire and smoke. He sought the other pieces and Thorolf helped him, the scorch marks helping them to identify the parts.

When the shadow dragon was no more, Rafferty took a shaking breath. "He was my grandfather," he said to Thorolf. "Or he had been my grandfather, lying peacefully in the earth, before Magnus turned him into this abomination."

Thorolf nodded, understanding why Niall bore such a resemblance to his opponent. He was fighting grimly on the other side of the cavern. His shadow dragon had lost an arm, but Niall was fading.

"Come on," Thorolf said. "Niall needs our help."

Magnus had to like how things were coming together. The shadow dragon he'd made of the Smith's brother was fighting Quinn, the Smith, keeping him fully occupied. It was charming how these *Pyr* had such difficulties bringing themselves to destroy the shadow dragons that resembled those they had loved.

It was so very predictable.

The other shadow dragons fought Sloane and Donovan. Even though Donovan had called upon the weapons he commanded as the Warrior, even though stone and hail fell down upon the battle, the shadow dragons were oblivious to that arsenal.

And Jorge was doing precisely what he was told to do. Magnus would be rid of Boris before this was over, and it looked as if both Erik and his mate would be slaughtered as well.

It would be a good day's work, all around.

He held Erik's mate close as he flew, putting distance between himself and Erik and making it look effortless. He discovered that he liked the scent of human female as much as he ever had. "So, was it worthwhile, ending your life with a firestorm?"

"My life's not over yet," she muttered with that human persistence he found so endearing.

If futile.

Magnus smiled. "Isn't it?" he asked, then opened his mouth to breathe the dragonfire that would draw Erik closer.

Erik ripped through the sky, right on cue, as bent on retrieving his mate as Magnus had expected. Jorge leapt out from behind the building to attack Erik from behind.

"There's another one!" the mate shouted, and Erik spun in the nick of time. He locked claws with Jorge, the two grappling for supremacy with savage force.

Erik, to Magnus's dismay, was no longer missing a scale. Some old talisman shone on his brow, a black stone that was etched with a symbol. The woman in his grip was responsible for that, no doubt.

Magnus held her at arm's length and loosed dragonfire again. He'd burn her to cinders, break Erik's spirit and then his body. Liking that idea, he took a good deep breath. He'd fry her in one long stream of dragonfire. It would be a poetic sign of his power.

Then something changed.

Magnus felt the break as surely as if something had shattered within him. His first thought was that the doors of his dark academy had been breached, but he knew that was impossible.

Was the stronghold of the Elixir in peril?

He choked on the very idea.

Impossible. *Impossible.*

And yet, something had changed. The change was deeply wrong.

In that same moment, the shadow dragon that had been Quinn's brother screamed, along with the other shadow dragons. They, too, sensed defeat at a distance. They abandoned the fight and retreated, disappearing like a flock of crows into the sky. Donovan gave chase, but they moved quickly and left him behind.

That was when Magnus was sure where the other battle raged.

His dark academy was no longer secure.

The shadow dragons responded to the cries of their fellows.

They should have listened to *him*.

"Where are you going?" Magnus roared. The other *Slayers* had deserted him, too—he couldn't even see that untrustworthy fool Boris. His entire plan was in tatters because someone had dared to breach the doors of the academy.

Magnus would find out who was responsible and make that individual pay.

Infuriated, he prepared to destroy Erik's mate before he pursued his disloyal minions.

To his astonishment, a flash of sapphire and steel drove between Magnus and his prey. Magnus's dragonfire never found its mark—the flames crackled orange in the air, leaving Magnus's talons singed but the woman unscathed.

She was falling.

The Smith took Magnus's dragonfire with a defiant roar, punching Magnus in the face as he did so. The sparkle of his scales grew to furious brilliance, as clear a mark of his lineage as anything.

The cursed *Pyr* fought together, much to Magnus's irritation. Once his opponent had fled, Quinn had fought to serve the greater good. He fought for the defense of Erik's mate.

Magnus disliked such noble impulses, especially in his foes.

He swore and turned to command Jorge. To his dismay, the gold *Slayer* had pursued the shadow dragons in an attempt to muster them.

Magnus was abandoned to the *Pyr*.

Erik caught his mate and held her in one possessive claw.

"He's missing a scale," the infernal woman said, pointing

at Magnus. She indicated a space on her own chest. "Right there."

The *Pyr* turned as one, targeting Magnus, their eyes gleaming. Magnus was furious. Despite all factors being in his favor just moments before, his victory had been snatched away by the *Pyr*.

He'd get even.

This wasn't done.

But he had to find out what had gone wrong.

As the *Pyr* closed ranks, Magnus decided that the time had come to leave. He wouldn't admit even to himself that he was leaving while he still had the chance. He was not retreating.

He was regrouping.

Rafferty was exhausted but the three *Pyr* were close to defeating the shadow dragon that had been created of Niall's twin brother. He thought one last blow from Niall would do it.

But before that blow was struck, the doors of the academy buckled completely under the assault of Nikolas and his crew. A foul stench emerged from the space within along with a scream of anguish. It sounded like an alarm, one that left the attacking troops surprised.

The shadow dragon attacking Niall took advantage of the *Pyr*'s surprise to flee. He flew for the tunnel entrance like a missile, followed by the other surviving shadow dragons. A dark cloud moved through the cavern, like bats stirred from a deep cave. Rafferty was shocked that so few of the shadow dragons had been killed. They streamed toward the academy, answering a summons to return to the place they had been created.

Maybe to defend it in this assault.

The Dragon's Teeth warriors didn't hesitate once the academy was opened. Nikolas leapt into the darkness revealed and they leapt after him. Rafferty followed suit, anxious to see what would happen.

The leader flew beside Rafferty, his suspicion clear. *"Who screams?"*

Rafferty guessed. *"Those who are being forced to become shadow dragons against their will."* He thought of Delaney. *"It is said to be a painful process, one that can drive a* Pyr *to madness."*

"Can they be saved?"

Rafferty shook his head. *"Not often."*

"We have no time to assess each one. I will not risk the escape of a single abomination." The leader divided his troops with decisive gestures, dispatching them down the corridors that snaked in every direction from the central chamber. Rafferty knew they would do what had to be done to put the captives out of their misery.

There was a central hall in the academy, housed in a natural cavern that arched high overhead. The marks of men and their explosives were less evident, as was the smell of ore.

A pulsing red light was cast over the confused expressions on the faces of the Dragon's Teeth warriors. The light came from everywhere and nowhere, making Rafferty's blood resonate with urgency.

In the midst of the chamber was a dervish, a blur of spiraling white. It was Sophie, caught in a wreath of dragonsmoke. She was spinning endlessly, fading visibly as she was powerless to stop. The smoke encircled her; then its extending tendrils slipped down the corridors that stretched in half a dozen directions.

As Rafferty watched, the dragonsmoke stole her vitality, feeding the pulse of red of the academy itself. It could have been the heart of the place. The light grew brighter and redder, more clearly the hue of blood. Sophie was withering, screaming, disappearing to nothing before their very eyes.

He leapt forward to help her, but Nikolas reached her first. The ancient *Pyr* lunged through the dragonsmoke—he bellowed with pain beneath its assault but he didn't halt. He caught Sophie, but instead of pulling her back to safety, he was snared within the dragonsmoke as well.

They spun together, a vortex of alternating black and white, one that grew smaller with every passing moment. The red pulsed brighter and hotter as the dragonsmoke sucked them dry. The beat increased pace and took on an urgency. It thudded through Rafferty insistently and filled him with dread.

Rafferty felt the first crack.

He sensed Gaia's first shudder.

He understood that the physical location of the academy couldn't consume the raw energy it gained from Nikolas. Nikolas and Sophie twisted together, a maelstrom of destruction that couldn't be stopped, that wouldn't be stopped until their life force was completely stolen. Anyone who intervened would only add his own life force to the strength of the academy.

Rafferty and the others could only watch helplessly.

And hope the end came quickly.

Sophie and Nikolas had each gripped the other's tail, the swirling black and white reminding Rafferty of a yin-yang symbol.

Or an ouroboros, snared in an even more ancient cycle of renewal.

The sight gave Rafferty hope for the future. It was true that Sophie and Nikolas would be destroyed, and there was nothing he could do to change that. He hoped, though, that they could take life again, as Eileen had. He hoped that they would find each other again, and have a second chance at happiness in that next incarnation.

The pair grew thinner and less substantial with each passing moment. As they became fainter, they spun faster so that their colors blurred. The force of the pulse grew, louder and more insistent. The academy couldn't cut itself off from the lifeline of the smoke. Still there was more energy in the conduit.

The floor began to vibrate.

The water that had flowed in behind the Dragon's Teeth warriors began to slosh around their hips.

The earth began to hum.

Rafferty realized that the sacrifice of Sophie and Nikolas could destroy the academy completely. It was the prophecy come true in an unexpected way.

Rafferty decided to help. He began to sing his ancient chant to the earth; he began to court her assistance in destroying this evil.

"It's going down," Thorolf cried.

"Sing!" Niall shouted at him, and they both did.

Rafferty sang with vigor. He would do what he could to make Sophie's and Nikolas's sacrifice count. He would ensure that they didn't die in vain, that the academy was destroyed forever.

Rafferty hummed and he chanted; he conjured every tune he knew and wove them together instinctively. To his delight, the Dragon's Teeth warriors took up his song, amplifying it to deafening intensity.

Sparks flew from Nikolas and Sophie, sparks that danced through the air of the cavern and lit the scene. The two of them were on fire, a radiant wreath of destruction and creation. Rafferty heard Sophie's voice join his song and he smiled, knowing that he had anticipated her desire.

The light blazed from the entangled pair, reaching a brilliance that nearly singed Rafferty to blindness.

Then all light was extinguished.

Silence reigned for a heartbeat; then the rock walls moaned and shuddered.

Rafferty looked up in time to see the ceiling crack overhead, opening in a long fissure. Chunks of rock fell, landing fatally upon some of the Dragon's Teeth warriors. Their leader shouted and they scrambled to organize themselves.

But the ocean already poured through the gap, cleansing the filth with its cold current and submerging the *Pyr*.

"I can't swim!" Thorolf shouted.

"It figures," Niall muttered, and that was the last thing Rafferty heard.

"The Wyvern is gone," Sara cried as Magnus disappeared into the distant clouds. She was pale and had her hands pressed to her mouth.

"What do you mean?" Quinn demanded, turning back in concern.

"She's gone." Sara looked bereft. "I can always feel her, but not anymore. Sophie's gone."

"She's dead!" Boris declared, then laughed. In his glee, he revealed his presence on the roof. He leaned on the air-conditioning unit in dragon form, burned and exuding confidence. "Where are the *Pyr* without their Wyvern?" he mocked. "My plan is succeeding, even without me. That must make it a divine plan."

Erik swore and dove toward the injured *Slayer*. Boris used the moment he had to aim dragonfire at the windows of Erik's lair. Erik heard the glass shatter. He heard the flames light inside and knew what would happen.

They had to be far away when it did.

"Fireworks," he reminded the other *Pyr* in old-speak.

"Will they go?" Sloane asked.

"Absolutely." Erik didn't have time to comment about a match being held to dry tinder. There would be a massive explosion when the dragonfire reached his storage room.

Quinn and Donovan immediately caught up their mates and flew into the distance. Sloane lingered a moment; then at Erik's command he dropped toward the lower floors. He manually triggered the fire alarms, and their ringing filled the air.

"What's going on?" Eileen asked.

"Sophie's dead." Boris chortled when Erik might have answered her. "I achieved two of my aims. No Dragon's Egg. No Wyvern. It's only a matter of time before you lose to the *Slayers*, Erik Sorensson."

Erik had heard enough. He caught Boris in one talon, pinning him down on the roof. Boris struggled, but he wasn't very strong in his current state. He shifted to a red salamander, but Erik wasn't startled by that feat anymore. Eileen stepped onto the roof, giving Erik the freedom to use both hands.

"You can't kill me!" Boris spat. "I have drunk the Elixir!"

Erik surveyed the wreck that Boris had become and noticed that his wounds hadn't healed.

Wasn't that the point of drinking the Elixir?

Did the fabled substance lose its potency over time?

"Odd how you haven't healed from our previous fight," Erik mused, and he saw a flash of uncertainty in Boris's eyes. "Look at your wings. Maybe the Elixir's power is overrated."

"Maybe Magnus lies," the *Slayer* hissed with fury.

Erik laughed. "Magnus? Dishonest? Surely not."

"He *lies*, that evil worm," Boris muttered. "It doesn't take one sip to confer immortality—it takes one sip to become addicted, one sip to make any *Slayer* beholden to Magnus forever."

Boris fell abruptly silent.

"Because Magnus controls the source," Eileen guessed.

"Because *Slayers* who sip of the Elixir need more at regular intervals to sustain their state," Erik added.

Boris snarled and struggled, which was all the confirmation they needed.

There was no doubt about it: Erik's luck *was* turning.

"Thank you, Boris," Erik said sweetly. "And now I think you've outlived your usefulness."

"You can't kill me!"

"Let's find out, shall we?"

Boris's last sound was a high scream.

Erik quickly drew his talon across the red salamander's

neck, severing his head from his body and silencing his laughter. He dismembered the small twisting creature, unable to hide his distaste for the task.

"Let me guess. You're doing what needs to be done," Eileen said.

"It's the only way to eliminate shadow dragons," Erik said grimly. "If they're all drinking the Elixir, it must work the same way for those who have drunk more."

The pieces that had been Boris twitched on the asphalt roof, as if he were still laughing at Sophie's fate. Alarmed that he might miss his chance, Erik reared back and loosed the hottest dragonfire he could conjure on Boris's remains. He burned him to cinders, then sent a torrent of dragonsmoke after the flames.

When he could feel no energy at all coming from the pile of ash, he halted, breathing heavily. The snow fell thickly, but the sight of white on black had no power for Erik now.

Eileen bent and swept the ash into a piece of paper that she ripped out of her notebook. She folded the paper and twisted the corners together, securing the ash tightly inside. She shook it like a rattle. "What now?"

"A *Pyr* must be exposed to all four elements to remain dead," Erik said.

"I count only three elements," she said with her usual practicality. "We need more water to be sure he's gone." And she pointed to the lake.

Erik lifted her with one claw and launched into flight, soaring high over the burning building that had been his home. He felt like a phoenix rising from the ashes of his old life, revitalized by the firestorm and given new purpose by the presence of his mate in his life.

He glanced down and checked that his few neighbors had left the building. They were gathered on the sidewalk, so busy watching the flames that they didn't appear to notice him. Even if they did, their stories of dragons would be dismissed as manifestations of trauma.

Reassured, Erik flew toward Lake Michigan without a backward glance. He watched Eileen with care as he swooped low over the water, fearful that her worries would return.

She surprised him once more with her resolve.

"Burn him again," she said.

As Erik loosed flames, she opened the paper, letting Boris's ashes scatter across the surface of the lake. They caught fire, burning like tiny embers before they fell on the dark water and sank.

Then Eileen let go of the paper and Erik burned it to cinders as well. He swooped high, holding her fast as the ash settled on the water, extinguished itself, and sank.

Rafferty broke the surface of the ocean and took a deep, gasping breath. Niall appeared beside him, sputtering, and between the two of them they hauled a struggling Thorolf to the surface. He choked and splashed, grasping desperately. He was big enough that he could have pulled both of them under in his fear.

"Just take flight already," Niall said with scorn, and the other *Pyr* looked surprised by the idea.

Thorolf did it, though, and once he was safely airborne, Niall and Rafferty followed suit. The sun shone brilliantly overhead, but there was flotsam and jetsam erupting from the depths on all sides. They were several miles from a quiet stretch of shoreline.

"How about we meet by that cliff?" Niall suggested. "I'll make sure the new kid gets his feet on the ground."

"Hey, you know, it's not a crime not to know how to swim. . . ."

Rafferty nodded and the pair left, still arguing. He was sure he could hear Thorolf muttering curses all the way to land.

But he was safe.

Rafferty wasn't sure the same could be said for the others.

He hovered, searching the surface for survivors. The Dragon's Teeth warriors seemed to have taken a lot of casualties. He wondered whether they, like Thorolf, had no ability to swim. He had seen a number struck down by the falling rocks. He wished desperately that Nikolas and Sophie would surface, but knew he would never see either of them again.

Not in their old guise, at least.

To his relief, the leader of the Dragon's Teeth emerged from the water's depths. He was gasping for breath, and Rafferty guessed that he had tried to save as many men as possible. Half a dozen soldiers accompanied him, their expressions grim. Rafferty went to him, offering assistance.

The warrior smiled very slightly, perhaps amused by the notion, then burst from the water into full flight. He turned a look on his men that might as well have been an audible command, and they followed suit, though none could echo his determination and strength.

He flew close to Rafferty. "We incinerated the shadows," he said gruffly.

"But you lost many men."

"It had to be done." His eyes narrowed. "We understand the importance of ensuring the greater good."

Rafferty looked down at the sea, which covered so many fallen *Pyr*, and wondered at the price. When he glanced up again, the leader of the Dragon's Teeth was offering him a token.

It was a ring. Half was black and half was white, although the hues twisted around each other to compose the whole. When he looked more closely, the white was more like spun glass. The ring was hard and cold, and Rafferty knew what had made it.

"This should be yours," the Dragon's Teeth warrior said.

"How do you know?"

He smiled and stretched his claw out farther. "I just do."

"Glass and anthracite," Rafferty said.

"Yes," the warrior agreed. "A talisman of power."

"How do you know it should be mine?"

The Dragon's Teeth warrior put the ring on his talon and it rolled around, so loose that it threatened to fall off. Then he offered it to Rafferty again.

Rafferty slid the ring over his talon and it fit perfectly. He had the sense that it adjusted its diameter to his, but that was madness. He glanced up to find the warrior smiling.

"It knows," the warrior said. "And that is good enough for me. Where do you lead us, singer of songs?"

Rafferty found himself surrounded by the dozen surviving Dragon's Teeth warriors, each watching him expectantly. "I'd like to introduce you to Erik Sorensson, leader of the *Pyr*," he said.

The warrior inclined his head in agreement. "Where you lead, we shall follow."

Erik landed in the park alongside Lake Michigan, shifting quickly so that Eileen was caught in his arms. She liked that. Snow fluttered down all around them, and the raging fire that consumed his loft was far behind. The other *Pyr* landed in the same park, turning to watch the display.

Erik led Eileen to a park bench, one that faced the blaze, and dusted it off for her to sit down. He was always the gentleman. Eileen smiled as he turned up the collar on his leather jacket and eyed the fire. She reached over and tugged up his zipper. "You need a scarf."

He smiled slightly. "I've no one to knit one for me."

"Is that right." Eileen settled back beside him, finding it reassuring how their shoulders bumped. They sat in companionable silence but she wasn't going to be the first to ask important questions.

"You're really going to watch your apartment burn?" Eileen asked in surprise, but Erik shook his head.

"Not just that. Watch."

No sooner had he spoken than the first fireworks exploded, filling the sky with red and yellow stars. They were followed by fireworks that looked like large blue and violet flowers, their petals arching wider and wider before the sparks died and fell. Eileen gasped at their beauty, then realized how he'd known what to expect.

"You *are* that Erik Sorensson who is a pyrotechnics wizard in Chicago," she accused.

He nodded once, then arched a brow, his gaze fixed on the display. "Albeit with a much diminished inventory now."

Eileen smiled. "Careful. Your sense of humor is showing again."

His lips quirked in a smile. "I'll have to be sure my charm stays well disguised."

"Too late."

He raised a finger, his eyes narrowed. "I was saving this one for a special occasion."

"Does this count?"

A twinkle lit his eyes. "I'd say so."

Red sparks shot up from the loft into the dark sky. The spray of lights expanded ever larger and became ever brighter. The fireworks curved and spiraled, looking for a heartbeat like a large red dragon poised against the night.

Eileen shivered. "Looks like Boris."

The sparks faded and died to nothing. Erik smiled. "Especially now." His satisfaction with that was obvious, and Eileen shared it.

There was a hiss as one rocket fired directly upward, leaving a trail of blue sparks following it. "These were supposed to look like birds-of-paradise," Erik mused. "I thought they might be spectacular."

As Eileen watched, the sparks arced through the air, changing color from blue to violet to brilliant orange. The crest was clear, as was the orange spear of the flower—a second took shape above it and to the right, then a third to the left.

"It looks like a flower arrangement," Eileen said. "Beautiful."

"I shall have to get more of those," Erik agreed.

It was both strange and comfortable sitting beside him as they watched his entire inventory of fireworks exhaust itself. He commented periodically on how the sequence could have been better, or how he would have preferred to have arranged the color scheme. Eileen listened and watched, impressed that he could dispassionately watch so much capital go up in flames.

He wasn't hiding his reaction either.

But then, given events of the weekend, she supposed his inventory wasn't much of a sacrifice.

"So where do we go from here?" she asked quietly as the display wound down.

Erik spared her a bright glance. His voice dropped low and silky, intent enough to make her shiver. "Lady's choice," he murmured.

Eileen looked away from him, from the intensity of his expression. She wanted to make the right decision. She didn't want to mess this up. She was deeply attracted to Erik. It would have been easy to take their relationship to a greater commitment immediately.

On the other hand, Eileen had a tendency to be impulsive and was trying to learn from her mistakes. She'd agreed to marry Joe after a week in Puerto Vallarta together and could do without repeating that fiasco.

It was true that she'd never had such a thrilling and dangerous few days in anyone's company, but that very danger could be affecting her perspective. Eileen knew that if she and Erik were meant to be together, a few weeks apart wouldn't make any difference to the bond between them.

It would, however, give her more confidence in her choice.

That sounded like advice her mother would have given. In fact, Eileen thought her mom had said something similar after the Puerto Vallarta fling–turned–instant marriage.

"It's been quite a weekend," she said.

"That it has."

"But I'd like a little time to think about what has happened, about what is happening."

"How long?"

"A month." Eileen glanced up, expecting to find disapproval in Erik's expression. He was simply studying her, no censure in his eyes.

"Solar or lunar?"

"A lunar month is shorter, right?" At his nod, Eileen nodded. "Lunar."

She was glad she was watching Erik. Otherwise, she would have missed both the fleeting smile that curved his lips and the gleam of satisfaction that lit his eyes.

It was a satisfaction that perfectly echoed her own, and something else that they had in common.

It was also a good portent for their future.

Chapter 28

Within two weeks, Eileen knew.

It was too early for a blood test, but she knew that she was pregnant. The rhythm of her body had changed, her breasts seemed heavy, and she had been sleeping more. She had strong aversions to certain foods, particularly dessert and her customary glass of wine before dinner.

She trusted her body and its message.

She was carrying the precious burden of Erik's child, and she was going to guarantee that she had a healthy pregnancy. She ate well, ensured that she got lots of sleep, and she exercised gently.

And she thought a lot about the future. She was positive that Erik would keep his word—he was predictable like that—so she considered what she would say to him. Increasingly, her weekend with him seemed less fantastical. Those couple of days became the most vivid parts of her life, the moments that were the most vehemently real.

She wanted more of that life.

The future was far from guaranteed, though. The one thing that Eileen could count on—assuming her pregnancy went well—was a child in her future. She thought a lot about Erik's legacy and how she could share that with a child. She needed the help of the *Pyr*.

She needed the help of one specific *Pyr*.

She waited for him, sure of her decision and content to be patient. Meanwhile, she tended to the details of life.

Eileen was trying to figure out an appropriate memorial for Teresa when she received a solicitation for their alumni association. There was a move to beautify the campus of their alma mater with landscaping and perennials. Eileen knew that was the perfect project to honor Teresa's memory and sent a healthy donation in the name of her former roommate.

She talked to her sister weekly and exchanged e-mails with her, enduring Lynne's tirade about her failure to return to the house for a visit. They agreed that Lynne would bring the girls to Boston during their summer break, and Eileen decided she'd tell her sister about the baby then.

Spring came reluctantly to Boston and, without classes to teach, Eileen walked a lot. She enjoyed the change of the seasons as she seldom had before, mostly because she previously hadn't taken time to witness it. She talked to her baby, sharing her joys and fears, feeling only incrementally less alone. She wrote course syllabi for the fall term and composed book lists; she consulted with her graduate students and continued her own research.

At night, she opened the window of her apartment, sat at the kitchen table, and wrote longhand. As much as she wanted to write up her notes on the Dragon Lover of Madeley and its deeper truth, Eileen couldn't do it. Not only would the truth damage her academic credibility, but it felt like a breach of trust to "out" the *Pyr* and their hidden world.

Eileen found herself instead writing a history of the *Pyr*. She liked the thought of compiling a book as a legacy for her child, and loved the idea of a reference manual for new mates.

In the beginning, there was the fire. . . .

Eileen had a good memory, particularly for stories, and she was sure after a week of nightly writing that she'd recorded every snippet of *Pyr* lore she'd heard and overheard. There were still holes in the story, though, and she yearned to fill the gaps.

She was missing the company of a certain forthright dragon in her life. The book wasn't the only reason she wanted to see Erik again, though.

Eileen talked to the baby about the challenge of compiling a history of the *Pyr*, of the real threat of losing her academic credibility if she published such a volume, of the paucity of sources, of her need to write it anyway.

The baby, not surprisingly, didn't reply.

But two days later, a package came by courier from Michigan. There was a book inside, a receipt for postage paid on its return, and a note from Sara Keegan.

Quinn's mate.

Eileen—
    I dreamed that you needed this.
    If I'm wrong—or when you're done—please send it back to us. We can't afford to lose this volume.
    All my best,
    Sara

The package was rolled in bubble wrap, then sealed in plastic. After Eileen opened that protective layer, the book was carefully wrapped in tissue paper. She smiled, remembering that Sara was a bookseller, liking that Sara found books as precious as Eileen did.

This volume was old, its leather cover stamped with gilt letters and embossed. The title made Eileen sit down hard.

The Habits and Habitats of Dragons: a Compleat Guide for Slayers.

The author's name made her eyes widen. It had been written by Sigmund Guthrie.

Eileen looked out the window and ran her hand across the cover, marveling that Sara had sent her precisely what she needed. But then, Sara was supposed to be the Seer.

Then Eileen opened the book and began to read.

At the end of that lunar month, Eileen was teaching a guest lecture on research. She had her back to the auditorium and was writing a couple of references on the board to conclude her lecture when she felt the atmosphere of the hall change.

She knew why.

Even without the firestorm, even after a month's separation, even with her back turned, she knew that Erik had arrived.

She was sure she could pinpoint the seat he had taken.

She tingled from head to toe, a wild joy taking hold of her and making her heart pound. It wasn't the firestorm, but in a way it was more powerful. His presence made her smile.

She wrote the last of her references on the board and completed her lecture with her usual flourish—she pivoted, tossed the chalk into the air, and caught it.

"Any questions?" she asked. She saw Erik immediately, exactly where she guessed he was, and her smile broadened.

He had slipped into the back of the hall and probably had hoped to be incongruous. The man couldn't have been incongruous to save his soul—or his spark. He was older than most of the students and carried himself with more confidence than the others in the hall. Students in his vicinity were casting sidelong glances his way, and she could hear the whispers beginning.

But Erik's gaze was fixed on her.

And he was wearing a red T-shirt.

It would go perfectly with the scarf she'd knit for him.

Even from the podium, Eileen was sure she could see the glitter of his eyes and the question in their depths.

Her heart skipped. He'd come right on time, right when he had said he would.

A promise from Erik Sorensson was a promise kept.

Eileen liked that.

There were several questions from the students, which she answered easily; then the professor who had invited her to speak to his class thanked her. There was a smattering of applause and Eileen exchanged a few private words with her fellow professor. Then she gathered her notes, pushed them into her satchel, and headed for the man waiting at the back of the hall.

"You missed the best part," Eileen said with a smile.

"I heard it all," Erik replied. "I didn't want to risk being a distraction."

"As if. I'm an old pro." Eileen laughed at his skeptical expression, then slipped her hand into the crook of his elbow as they left together. "You're right, of course. I might have lost my place if I'd seen you sooner. I was afraid you might not come."

"You changed my mind about fleeting connections," he said with a resolve that sent a thrill through her. He cast her a glance, and his eyes gleamed a vivid green. "And I think we make a good team."

"I decided exactly the same thing," Eileen agreed, and smiled at him. She was rewarded by Erik's smile, one that made his lips curve in a sexy way and put a sparkle in his eyes.

"Is question period over?" he asked in a low voice. "Because I didn't ask my question."

"Why not?"

"I thought it might be inappropriate for the lecture hall."

"You wouldn't ask me in front of everyone whether the story of the Dragon Lover of Madeley was true or not, would you?"

Erik laughed, a wonderful sound. "No. My question was whether you'd have dinner with me tonight."

Eileen tightened her grip on his arm, liking the solid strength of him. She'd been thinking about more than talking with Erik. "Dinner would be great, but I have to insist on dessert, too."

Erik squeezed her fingertips and Eileen knew he understood exactly what she meant. "Not breakfast, as well?" he teased, his words too low to be overheard by anyone else.

Eileen felt her cheeks heat. "No. There's no chance of breakfast." She enjoyed the sight of his surprise, then smiled. "I have a swimming lesson first thing in the morning."

"You?" He was visibly startled.

Eileen squared her shoulders. "I'm getting used to the water and becoming a better swimmer. It's less frightening each time." She cast him a mischievous glance. "Besides, it's supposed to be great exercise during pregnancy."

His grin was all the reward she needed.

Eileen tugged him into her small office and closed the door, leaning her back against it. She liked that he spared the room the barest glance before meeting her gaze again. She also liked that he could probably name several dozen of the books she had on the shelves even after such a quick survey. He was so observant.

"So, you've had it confirmed." Erik was cautious, and Eileen knew he was watching her response. "Are you pleased?"

She dropped her satchel on the desk and pivoted to face him. Her office was sufficiently small—and sufficiently full of books—that they were only a step apart. The intensity of his gaze made her feel warm and sexy, as if she were the axis of his world.

It was an intoxicating feeling, one that she'd missed, one that she doubted would ever change. She could count on him—her instincts told her as much—and Eileen had learned to trust her instincts.

"I think we can do better this time," she said softly. "Especially if we do it together."

"I agree," Erik said with such conviction that Eileen smiled. She reached up and touched the silver hair at his temples, letting her fingers linger against his skin. "Is there more of it now?"

He nodded once.

"I thought at first that you *Pyr* were all immortal."

"No. Long-lived, at least until our firestorms; then the aging process speeds up for us. A *Pyr* often gets his first gray hair after his firestorm."

"But you could live long beyond your mates," Eileen whispered, feeling that this was incredibly sad.

Erik shook his head slightly. "My old friend Thierry believed that commitment to one's mate made those years more precious, that love made a *Pyr* more than he could be otherwise." He smiled crookedly. "He was the Smith before Quinn. He said that the firestorm made a *Pyr* stronger, just as the forge tempers steel."

"That's not an effortless process."

"Is a love worth having easily won?" Erik didn't wait for an answer, but lifted Eileen's hand in his own. "Thierry believed that a *Pyr* would choose to die, either consciously or unconsciously, after the loss of his mate. He believed that the days and nights would no longer have any point to that *Pyr* after years of companionship."

"That happens to people, too, after they've been together for a long time."

Erik bent and kissed her palm gently.

Eileen caught her breath. "Why didn't you die after Louisa did, then?"

He looked up at her, his expression intent, and Eileen's heart clenched. His words were soft and low, and his gaze searched hers. "I guess we had unfinished business, you and I."

"You waited."

"Not consciously, but I think on some level it was a choice."

"And now I'm back."

"No. You're here, and well worth the wait." He smiled and she found herself smiling back at him. "The choice is yours as to what we do about it."

Eileen cleared her throat, feeling a little bit nervous about her recent decisions. She and Erik had a deal about honesty, though, and she wasn't going to lie to him. "You should know that I sent my c.v. to a couple of schools in Chicago."

"Really?" His eyes shone with a delight that he couldn't hide.

"I've already had one request that I come out for an interview in the next few weeks."

"You'd move?"

"There's only one place I want to be." Eileen echoed his own gesture, pressing her lips against his palm in turn. "With you."

"And they'd be lucky to have you," he said with a smile.

"I think so," Eileen agreed.

"Not as lucky as me, though."

Eileen grinned at him as her heart thumped.

"I'll assume that you're agreeable to dinner, then," he teased, and she had time to laugh before he kissed her soundly.

Erik lay beside Eileen hours later, his body tired and his heart full. She nestled against him, sleeping sweetly, and he caressed her shoulder with his fingertips. The window was open and he could smell the sea, feel the wind.

Spring had arrived. He'd seen green leaves pushing from the ground on his walk through the campus today; they'd discovered some yellow primroses in bloom in a garden they strolled past this evening. The earth was redolent with the fresh promise of rebirth.

Erik didn't miss the fact that it coincided with his own

change. He felt lighter. He felt complete. He felt aware of the possibilities and excited by them—a new optimism had seized him.

Or maybe an old optimism had been reawakened.

Something inside him, a wound he had never known he had, had healed. And like the king in Eileen's story, he could feel the land responding to his own state of health. There were still challenges before him and the *Pyr*, but Erik was confident that he would face them better with Eileen at his side.

Thierry had been right.

Erik hoped that his old friend knew that he had been persuaded.

He smiled in the darkness, knowing that Thierry would appreciate that Erik's destined mate had been the one to change his mind.

His mate.

His partner.

His love. Her hair was cast across his chest, a tangle of red-gold curls. It could have been a Valkyrie's net for gathering her plunder of souls. But this Valkyrie had given Erik back the part of his soul that he had lost.

He would do anything for her.

Maybe his necessary sacrifice had been surrendering his independence, or the idea that he could be complete alone, or the conviction that duty came before everything else.

Erik's firestorm had been aptly named. It had swept into his life, incinerating his objections and preconceptions. He might as well have been tossed into a crucible, heated and purified beyond all expectation. His defenses had been dissolved. His protests had been eliminated.

And when the air had cleared, when the balance had been restruck and the past had been addressed, he had risen from the ashes of his own history like a phoenix. He felt new and strong, powerful and capable. Erik didn't have to choose between the *Pyr* and himself—he could be whole if he held the right balance between the personal and the collective.

Eileen had taught him that.

Eileen had helped him to heal.

Erik dozed beside Eileen, content as he had seldom been, lulled by the soft sound of her breathing. He thought of their child taking shape inside her, savored the way his body matched its rhythms to hers. He was not quite asleep, so he was surprised when he dreamed.

"There is only one way," Sigmund murmured in oldspeak.

Erik's eyes flew open at the familiar sound of his son's voice, but he couldn't see him in Eileen's apartment or sense his presence.

Perhaps Sigmund was only in his dreams.

"How?" Erik replied in kind.

"You must destroy the source, the source of the Dragon's Blood Elixir."

"But where is it? What is it?"

"Close your eyes. Open your thoughts to me."

Erik did as he was bidden, trusting his son in death as he seldom had in life. An image formed in his mind's eye, and he smiled at the sight of Sigmund in human form. He was in Erik's old lair, on one knee beside the coffee table.

Where the broken Dragon's Egg still rested in majesty.

Sigmund picked up one half of the obsidian orb and blew upon it. The surface came alive as it had not done for Erik, as it had once beneath Sophie's song. Erik leaned closer, as he had once before, and peered into the stone.

He saw a cavern, a massive cavern with a smooth tower in its center. He leaned closer and the tower appeared in greater detail, as if he walked toward it. It was made of glass or crystal and it shone in the light.

It wasn't a tower—it was a massive vial, carved from rock crystal. There were stairs carved into its surface, a spiral of stairs that wound to the summit.

But there was no light in the cavern. The light emanated from the massive cylinder.

No, it radiated from its contents. They swirled like ruddy fog, opaque and mysterious, cloudy and red. Erik realized that the cylinder was filled with liquid just as its contents began to pulse.

The Elixir!

The clouds of its contents shifted and moved, and Erik had the horrible sense that something was trapped inside the massive vial. Then he saw a talon hanging limply from a claw scaled in red.

"Cinnabar," Sigmund said as Erik recoiled.

Someone had preserved a dead *Pyr*. Erik understood why the Dragon's Blood Elixir was red, why it possessed the name that it did, and was revolted by the thought of anyone drinking such a liquid.

Sigmund straightened, then looked steadily at Erik. He looked as he had when he was younger, not burned and broken, not bitter. He was less substantial, though, perhaps ghostlike. *"I didn't let you down this time."*

"No."

"You kept your promise to me. Did you know I would return to keep mine?"

"No." Erik smiled. *"I only hoped. It was time for one of us to trust."*

Sigmund inclined his head once at the truth of that. *"Thank you."*

"Thank you."

And in the dream, Erik's son offered his father his hand. Erik wished it weren't a dream, as he would have liked to have felt that last handshake with his own son.

"How did you do this? How did you come to me?" Erik asked, wondering what other secrets Sigmund had unearthed.

"The Wyvern."

"But there is no Wyvern," Erik argued. Before he could

explain that Sophie had died after Sigmund's death, his son smiled mysteriously.

"Isn't there?" Sigmund asked quietly. He smiled, waved, then turned away. Before his back had fully turned, he faded to nothing.

Erik blinked and stared at the ceiling, his throat tight that he had had one last precious exchange with Sigmund. His heart leapt that Sigmund had given him the piece of the puzzle he needed to eliminate Magnus, the *Slayers* he made immortal, and the shadow dragons. And he wept that he had not made peace with his son sooner.

Eileen stirred in the darkness and pressed a kiss to his shoulder. "What's wrong?" she asked sleepily. "You were gone."

"No, just dreaming."

She braced herself on her shoulder and looked down at him sleepily, then touched her fingertips to his cheek. "And what kind of dream makes the leader of the *Pyr* weep?"

"I dreamed of our son," Erik admitted, his words thick.

Eileen shook her head and yawned, nestling down beside him. "Don't be silly; we aren't having another son."

"But the *Pyr* . . ."

"Yes, I know, but your big myth is going to be proven wrong. We're having a daughter. I know it as well as I know my own name."

"How?" Erik whispered.

"I dreamed of her." Eileen opened one eye to give him a look. "Definitely a girl." Then she smiled at his shock and settled back to sleep again. "You'll see in seven or eight months," she threatened, her words already slowing.

Erik couldn't sleep then because his heart was pounding. The stories of the *Pyr* weren't being proven wrong at all. There could only be one female *Pyr*, a prophetess who returned to flesh time and again to aid the *Pyr* in their quest.

Another Wyvern was coming into the world.

She would be their daughter.

Erik was honored and awed by the responsibility, and he marveled that this Wyvern was already dispatching dreams. The luck of the *Pyr* was turning, and it was because of Eileen.

He pressed a kiss into her hair, overwhelmed by the abundance of his blessings.

The future was theirs to command.

Read on for a preview of the next book in the Dragonfire series from Deborah Cooke. . . .

Delaney had realized that he was on a suicide mission.

He drove his rental car aimlessly through the southern Ohio countryside as he came to terms with that truth. He'd vowed to destroy the source of the Dragon's Blood Elixir, and he hadn't imagined for a moment that it would be easy. But now he'd found the refuge and spent a week observing Magnus's security measures, and he knew the truth.

He could destroy the Elixir, but he wouldn't survive.

In fact he knew that he would die in his attempt. The trick would lie in ensuring that he actually did destroy the source of the Elixir once and for all *before* he died.

He didn't mind dying—his life had become a living hell since Magnus had force-fed him the Elixir—he just wanted to make a difference. He wanted to do something for his fellow *Pyr*, other than being unpredictable and a burden. He hated how the shadow Magnus had planted in his heart refused to be banished, hated how he had been unable to stop himself from attacking Donovan's pregnant mate, Alex. It was disgusting and reprehensible. If dying eliminated that threat to the *Pyr* he loved, Delaney was okay with it.

But he wanted more. He wanted to ensure that none of them ever had to endure what he had suffered. He wanted to give them a better chance to defeat Magnus and the *Slayers*.

Which meant that he had to destroy the Elixir, before he died in the attempt.

He could smell Magnus's presence, as well as that of Magnus's current favorite, Jorge. The *Slayers* seemed to be gathering, maybe to fortify themselves with the Elixir.

Delaney had to act.

He had already decided to attack the next day, early, so as a result there was no question of his sleeping on this night. He drove on endless country roads, past fallow fields, past snow under moonlight and forests of bare branches. Just when he tired of his own company, he saw lights.

Delaney pulled into the parking lot of the roadhouse on instinct, and realized he was craving the company of the humans that he and the *Pyr* were charged to protect. He didn't give himself time to think twice.

He strode into the noisy bar, savoring the sounds of laughter and music, the sight of people dancing and celebrating, and knew there was a point to his sacrifice. They would all be oblivious to what he did, just as humans were always oblivious to the efforts of the *Pyr*, but their optimism and energy would carry on.

That made it worthwhile.

He had ordered a beer and a tequila shooter before a woman rapped him on the elbow. "Hey, this is a private party," she began, falling silent when a spark leapt between her fingertip and Delaney's elbow.

He felt his own eyes widen as an unfamiliar heat spread through him like wildfire. Even though he'd never felt it before, Delaney knew exactly what it was.

His firestorm.

His last chance to do something right.

His blood seemed to sizzle and he became keenly aware of everyone around him. He felt a desire so sharp and hot that it nearly took his breath away, and he knew then the role of this woman in his life.

It didn't hurt that the petite redhead at his side was the cutest woman he'd ever seen. She was as small and delicate as a fairy, but more curvy than any fairy could have been. Her hair was a mass of golden red curls and her eyes were blue and bright with curiosity. She looked on the verge of laughter, reminding him of a beam of sunlight dancing on the sea.

She wore a black sparkly camisole that highlighted the curve of her breasts and a flirty black skirt that danced around her hips. Her dangly earrings were set with amber, one of his favorite stones, and they swung against her cheeks as she talked. She was wearing very high-heeled, strappy black sandals, but even with them, she stood only as high as the middle of his chest.

She was also a bit unsteady on them, as if she wasn't used to wearing such high heels.

She pursed her lips, flicked him a look, and touched her fingertip to his elbow once again.

The spark of the firestorm flared right on cue, lighting her features with its golden splendor. She stepped backward in astonishment, caught her balance by grabbing the edge of the bar, but didn't run away.

Instead she whistled in admiration, licked her fingertip and made a hissing sound. Then she laughed.

It was the most enchanting sound Delaney had ever heard.

She wasn't afraid of him or the firestorm, which had to be a good sign. Delaney held her gaze and knew with utter clarity how he'd be spending his last night. He'd make one more play for the team. He'd consummate his firestorm and give Erik another *Pyr* for the ranks of his warriors.

It would be the right thing to do.

"You're a real firecracker," he teased, and she smiled. Her smile lit her face, and Donovan sensed that she smiled often.

He liked that.

"You stole my joke," she said, not looking offended in the least. "I was going to toss you out, but maybe there's more to you than meets the eye." She gave him an appreciative survey, her eyes shining with mischief. "Maybe I should say that you're hot stuff."

"Maybe we should find out just how much sparks fly."

She laughed again and Delaney felt less burdened. "Or whether those who play with fire have to get burned."

"Now you stole my joke," he complained, unable to keep himself from grinning.

"Turnabout is fair play." She laughed again, then put out her hand. "Ginger Sinclair. Eternal bridesmaid, go-to party organizer—"

"And the light of the night," Delaney said, wanting only to make her laugh again. She did, and he felt triumphant.

"Delaney," he said, taking her hand. When his fingers closed over hers, the firestorm's heat surged through his body from the point of contact, leaving him shimmering in its wake.

Leaving him unable to think of anything except peeling Ginger out of that camisole and skirt. There were freckles in her cleavage, a smattering of them that would extend across her breasts and over her shoulders. He wanted to find them all, caress them all, kiss them all.

Meanwhile, Ginger's eyes widened and she caught her breath, a flush launching over her cheeks as she stared up at him. She swallowed visibly. "Delaney what?"

"Just Delaney."

Her eyes sparkled again. "All this and mystery, too. That could be too much for a little country girl like me."

"I think you can handle anything I've got."

Her smile turned coy and she let her gaze slide over him again. "Maybe."

"Everything I've got."

Her smile broadened. "Maybe."

"Maybe a little chemistry is all we need."

"Maybe." She nodded, and her gaze flicked to their interlocked hands. Donovan let his thumb slide across her skin, savoring the silky smoothness of it. A trail of embers followed the wake of his slow caress.

Ginger stared at it, then licked her lips. "I think I've had too much to drink," she said, and fanned herself. "Do you find it hot in here?"

"It's only going to get hotter," Delaney said. The bartender brought his beer and shooter, but Delaney wasn't interested in drowning his sorrows anymore.

He was interested in seducing tiny, perfect Ginger.

ASAP.

The DJ put on a slow song and Delaney knew his luck had turned. He paid for the drink and spun Ginger toward the dance floor. "Come on, they're playing my tune."

She spared a glance over her shoulder at him, tilting her head to meet his gaze. "My momma told me not to slow dance with strangers." She was smiling, so he knew she was teasing him.

Flirting, maybe.

It felt good.

Delaney grinned. "I only slow dance. Are you turning me down?" He let his fingers slide up her bare arm and Ginger shivered with what he knew was desire.

"My momma also said that you only live once," she said firmly, and took his hand in hers. She pivoted on the edge of the dance floor to face him, anticipation in her eyes. The floor was old, with lights pulsing up from it, and the pink and blue light made intriguing shadows as her skirt flared out. "Show me your best moves, Delaney No-surname," she challenged, and Delaney didn't need a second invitation.

He knew they'd be doing more than one slow dance together before the night was through.

When he pulled Ginger into his arms and the firestorm

shimmered between his chest and her breasts, she caught her breath and looked up at him in awe.

That was when he knew that she knew it, too.

"Only if you show me yours," he teased.

The mischief in her smile made his heart skip. "You've got a deal, hotshot."

About the Author

Deborah Cooke has always been fascinated by dragons, although she has never understood why they have to be the bad guys. She has an honors degree in history, with a focus on medieval studies, and is an avid reader of medieval vernacular literature, fairy tales, and fantasy novels. Since 1992, Deborah has written more than thirty romance novels under the names Claire Cross and Claire Delacroix.

Deborah makes her home in Canada with her husband. When she isn't writing, she can be found knitting, sewing, or hunting for vintage patterns. To learn more about the Dragonfire series and Deborah, please visit her Web site at www.deborahcooke.com and her blog, Alive & Knitting, at www.delacroix.net/blog.

Also Available

THE FIRST NOVEL IN THE DRAGONFIRE SERIES

KISS OF FIRE
A Dragonfire Novel

by DEBORAH COOKE

For millennia, the shape-shifting dragon warriors known as the Pyr have commanded the four elements and guarded the earth's treasures. But now the final reckoning between the Pyr, who count humans among the earth's treasures, and the Slayers, who would eradicate both humans and the Pyr who protect them, is about to begin...

When Sara Keegan decides to settle down and run her quirky aunt's New Age bookstore, she's not looking for adventure. She doesn't believe in fate or the magic of the tarot—but when she's saved from a vicious attack by a man who has the ability to turn into a fire-breathing dragon, she questions whether she's losing her mind— or about to lose her heart...

Available wherever books are sold or at penguin.com

Also Available

THE SECOND NOVEL IN THE DRAGONFIRE SERIES

KISS OF FURY
A Dragonfire Novel

by DEBORAH COOKE

Scientist Alexandra Madison was on the verge of releasing her invention which could save the world—until her partner was murdered, their lab burned and their prototype destroyed. When Alex learns that her recurring nightmares of dragons have led to a transfer to a psychiatric hospital, she knows she has to escape to rebuild her prototype in time. The problem is that she has to return to the wreckage of the lab for one last thing...

Handsome, daring, impulsive Donovan Shea knows the Madison project is of dire importance to the ongoing Pyr/Slayer war, but resents being assigned to surveillance of the lab. He's surprised by the arrival of a beautiful woman there in the middle of the night—not that she's being followed by a Slayer, not that she won't admit her name, but that she's his destined mate. As the sparks of the firestorm ignite and the Slayers close in on their prey, Donovan knows he'll surrender his life to protect Alex—even risk his heart, if that's what it takes...

Available wherever books are sold or at penguin.com

Penguin Group (USA) Online

What will you be reading tomorrow?

Tom Clancy, Patricia Cornwell, W.E.B. Griffin,
Nora Roberts, William Gibson, Robin Cook,
Brian Jacques, Catherine Coulter, Stephen King,
Dean Koontz, Ken Follett, Clive Cussler,
Eric Jerome Dickey, John Sandford,
Terry McMillan, Sue Monk Kidd, Amy Tan,
John Berendt...

You'll find them all at
penguin.com

*Read excerpts and newsletters,
find tour schedules and reading group guides,
and enter contests.*

Subscribe to Penguin Group (USA) newsletters
and get an exclusive inside look
at exciting new titles and the authors you love
long before everyone else does.

PENGUIN GROUP (USA)
us.penguingroup.com